DEADLY MEDICINE

Visit us at www.boldstrokesbooks.com

By the Author

Agnes

The Common Thread

Bouncing

Deadly Medicine

DEADLY MEDICINE

by

Jaime Maddox

2015

DEADLY MEDICINE
© 2015 By Jaime Maddox. All Rights Reserved.

ISBN 13: 978-1-62639-424-7

This Trade Paperback Original Is Published By
Bold Strokes Books, Inc.
P.O. Box 249
Valley Falls, NY 12185

First Edition: September 2015

Credits
Editor: Shelley Thrasher
Production Design: Susan Ramundo
Cover Design By Sheri (graphicartist2020@hotmail.com)

Acknowledgments

The ladies at Bold Strokes Books make my job as an author an easy one. Thank you to Rad, Sandy Lowe, Cindy Cresap, and Stacia Seaman for their hard work. Sheri created another great cover and I'm in awe of her talents. A special thanks to Toni Whitaker for ensuring that I receive my monthly sampling of new works from the many talented BSB authors. Finally, to my editor, Shelley Thrasher, who continues to teach me how to write with each edit we do.

My background in medicine helped with this book, but if it wasn't for Carolyn's cousin Bobby, I would know very little about fishing, whether on ice or on land. Thanks, BC, for all the fun times. Thanks also to my alpha readers, Margaret Pauling and Nancy McLain, for their feedback. I also must thank Nancy for her help in creating the character of Frieda. Nancy lived much of Frieda's very exciting life, and I'm grateful to her for taking me back in time with her.

As always, everything I do is with the love and support of the three people who are helping to raise me: my beautiful partner, Carolyn, and our sons, Jamison and Max. Love you lots.

Dedication

To Shelley Thrasher
If I hit a home run, it's because
you helped me with my swing.
Thank you.

CHAPTER ONE
DISCHARGED

Edward Hawk sat perfectly erect in his chair, ignoring the pile of magazines on the table beside him and the woman at the desk before him. He reviewed the reasons he found himself in this waiting room, appropriately named, as he awaited his fate. His termination had obviously been decided, but the question that plagued him now was why. *Why?*

Details, details. The devil lived there.

Why was he here? He asked himself again, then realized he could add a few other questions. Who? Where? When? What?

The question "Who?" could have seventeen answers. Seventeen names. Seventeen dead bodies—but which one had caused the bright light of suspicion to be cast onto his darkest secrets? Likely it was someone he'd recently encountered, but humans tended to trivialize details and rationalize unpleasantries, and it really could have been any one of them. Fuck! He had to find out. He needed to know what he'd done wrong, so he wouldn't make the same mistake again. A person could change jobs only so many times before prospective new employers began to ask questions of their own.

Shifting his position, Edward stretched his legs out in front of him, admiring his Cole Haan loafers. He noted a smudge that required buffing. He refused to be seen looking anything less than perfect. His fastidious nature was just one reason bullies had targeted him at school. Not now, though. Now, he chose the targets.

Glancing casually at his Rolex, he noted that he'd been kept waiting for fifteen minutes. He had nowhere to go but that didn't matter. His time was important, and his superior should show more respect.

Edward was worried, irritated, and annoyed at the wait, at the imperfection on his shoe, at the mistake he'd obviously made to land him in his boss's office. He was trapped here, awaiting the inevitable. But was more than termination in store for him? He felt a flicker in his chest as his pulse pounded, and he willed his heart and his breathing to slow. In a minute, he felt better.

No one could prove anything, he told himself. They might suspect what he'd been doing, but not a shred of evidence existed that he'd done anything wrong. If there was, he'd be waiting to talk to the police instead of his boss. Edward knew—he'd been in this seat before.

Hospitals were too concerned with lawsuits to do anything more than quietly dismiss employees like him. If the hospital actively investigated the deaths of any of the patients who'd died under his care, a surviving family member might get wind of their concern and file a lawsuit. If the hospital harassed him in any way, he'd file one. Hospitals hate lawsuits—even ones they win—because they cost money and raise questions about competence and ethics and all other sorts of messy subjects. So, the people in charge would discreetly ask for his resignation and send him on his way, pretending nothing unusual had happened during his tenure.

That he might do something questionable somewhere else didn't concern the people in power. They just wanted him gone.

Finding another job didn't bother him; his personal assistant would handle it. Hospitals were always hiring, and he never had a bad recommendation, despite being asked to leave half a dozen places over a ten-year period.

The secretary's voice was muted as she addressed him, as if she was in on the conspiracy to keep his dismissal quiet. "Dr. Fowler is ready for you." Edward buttoned his cashmere blazer as he stood, then carefully swiped away nonexistent wrinkles in his pants as he walked toward the door to the ER director's office and entered.

"Have a seat," Sam Fowler said in a booming voice, and Edward did as instructed. The inner office contained no more color or character than the waiting area. Drab colors, institutional furniture, canned artwork. Blah, blah, blah. Only the Christmas cards, tacked with pins onto a cork message board, brought color to the room. Nothing like he'd decorate if his name were written on one of the most important doors in the building. Yet it suited the man, who wasn't gifted with good looks or the ability to assemble a fashionable wardrobe. He was all business in the ER and took that same approach with Edward now.

"I'm sure you're wondering why I asked you here. I'll get straight to the point." He barely lifted his eyes from the blotter on the desk before him. "We're letting you go. Effective immediately. I've typed a letter of resignation for you. That way your dismissal won't appear as a blemish on your resume. Your salary will be paid through the end of the schedule, which carries you to New Year's Eve. I'll take your ID badge. Do you have anything in your locker you need to remove?"

Edward wasn't shocked that he was being terminated, but that Fowler offered no reason surprised him. That was typically the main focus of the parting speech, concerns about incidents and people talking and advice to watch himself. It was upsetting. He wanted— no, he needed to know what Sam Fowler knew—so he wouldn't repeat his mistake. Was it the forty-year-old man having the heart attack or the teenage girl with diabetes? Or the little boy who'd been hit by a car? Had his method betrayed him, or had one particular coworker noticed something odd? Or, perhaps, had this just been too long a run? Maybe it wasn't a single incident, but perhaps the accumulation of dead patients connected only by their association with him?

"May I ask why?" Edward made a game of it, meeting Sam's gaze as if he had nothing to hide. He enjoyed games, and right now watching the director squirm amused him.

Fowler reached for a pen and began doodling on his desk pad, but from his angle Edward couldn't determine the product of his efforts. His eyes remained down.

"We no longer need your services," he said, then finally looked up.

Sighing dramatically, Edward shrugged. "As you can imagine, I'm quite surprised. Does something about my performance concern you?" Come on, he thought. Tell me where I screwed up!

"No, nothing," Fowler said, but again he diverted his gaze.

Fuck! Edward thought. He's afraid of a lawsuit. He pursed his lips, shook his head, and ran his hand across a closely shaved face. "I can't think of anything, either," he said honestly. Since his summons earlier that morning, Edward had gone back two years in his brain, reviewing all the particulars of the deaths of his patients. Nothing stood out. "And I'm sorry to leave. I've enjoyed my work here." He had. It had been a wonderful place to work, with little oversight and tremendous opportunity to kill people. He paused, but Fowler didn't speak. "I'd like to ask you for a letter, if I may. Saying something like 'we parted on good terms.' You know how things are, Sam. You could be fired tomorrow, and then when I'm looking for a job, no one will be around to explain why I resigned."

Sam met his gaze and studied him for a moment, and Edward allowed his face to betray his emotions. He was upset, damn it, and he wasn't trying to hide his feelings. Sam wasn't very good at hiding his either. Doubt seemed to cloud his eyes, paving the corners with wrinkles. Good, Edward thought. Let him wonder.

"Sure," Sam said after a moment, and then he stood, announcing the end of their meeting. He held out his hand and offered a weak handshake. "I'll have Deb type it up. Just give her a minute."

It took fifteen minutes, but it was worth the wait. The letter was so perfect, he might have written it himself. Sam made it sound like he was sorry to see him leave. Edward would have no trouble finding work. And he needed to work. He'd been killing people for many years, and murder was his addiction, a hunger greater than his need for food or water or any drug he'd ever used. He might last a month or two, but then he'd start to grow anxious and his need would drive him to do something stupid, something that might put him in danger of discovery. And he could never, ever be discovered. The bullies in prison would make the teenage boys he'd dealt with seem meek. No, he needed another job, in a hospital, where people die every day and no one suspects a thing. He'd put his assistant to work immediately.

He folded the letter, carefully placed it in the inside pocket of his jacket, and smiled sincerely at Deb. "You've been very kind," he said. "Thank you for your help."

Her hesitant smile slowly became full and warm. She'd known him for two years, after all, and he'd just been tossed into the frigid North Jersey cold at Christmas time. The least she could do was offer him a smile.

"Good luck, Doctor," she said as he left the office.

It's not about luck, Edward thought as he closed the door behind him.

Chapter Two

Frostbite

Four inches of fresh snow, frozen by single-digit temperatures the night before, crunched beneath Ward Thrasher's new boots as she walked out into the bright January morning. She'd found the boots in a catalog and had circled their picture, written her size in the margin, and discreetly left it in Jess's briefcase. Lately Jess had been so out of sorts she needed such hints, and Ward was trying her best to be supportive. It worked. On Christmas morning, she'd found the boots beneath the tree, with a note from Santa, thanking her for the suggestion. Looking at them made her smile, one of the few things that could turn up the corners of her mouth on this blustery New Year's Day.

Somewhere above the canopy of snow-covered trees sheltering the cabin, the sun was shining. Scattered rays filtered through and reflected off the ice, blinding her. She pulled her sunglasses from the pocket of her ski jacket, and they helped ease the pain of the light hitting her eyes. When she could finally see, she smiled again, at a picture so perfect it resembled a Currier & Ives.

Pristine snow covered every tree on the mountainside, shimmering where light hit the uneven angles created by the odd shapes of each branch. Gently sloping hills that led to the lake below also wore a clean coat of white, and the only colors were the perpetual greens of resistant pine needles and the cloudless, impossibly blue sky. She saw no sign that man existed, and the serenity filled her with a sense of peace she'd come to associate with her time in the mountains.

It was almost enough to make up for the fact that she was here with Zeke Benson, and not his daughter Jessica. Almost.

"Can you give me a hand with this?" Zeke asked.

Despite her slim build, Ward was strong and easily lifted the back end of the toboggan, using both hands to steady the old wooden frame and prevent the contents from spilling. It was packed with wood for a fire, folding chairs, tip-ups, a power auger—all the necessities for a day on the ice, and some extras, too. Zeke lifted his end and together they transferred it to the bed of his truck, then climbed up front for the quarter-mile ride down to the lake. It would have pleased Ward more to jump on the toboggan and take the short route, but she was there for Zeke, not her own amusement. Maybe, though, on their next day off, she and Jess might come out and play. And then go back to the cabin and find creative ways to warm up.

They'd only gone a hundred feet when Zeke interrupted her daydream. She blushed at where her mind had been, but Zeke didn't notice as he pointed at a spot in the woods. "That's the original road to the cabin," he explained. "Before they built the highway, we had to come up over the mountain."

Ward followed his gaze and could barely discern a path leading into the mature forest. Or was it her imagination? Covered with snow, it looked to be a treacherous venture, nearly straight up the mountainside. "When was that?" Ward asked, showing more respect for her father-in-law than interest in his response.

"Sixty-one."

"Well, I guess you don't use it at all now. It's really grown in."

"No need. Besides, they built that damn palace on the other side of the mountain, and those city slickers don't want anyone near their land. They closed off the access road to keep us out. Can you imagine? They bought land next to a hunting club and call to complain about the gunfire!"

"Good thing you're the sheriff, Zeke."

"I don't understand people."

She could certainly relate. It was why she kept to herself, listened instead of speaking, and tried to mind her own business. She had many acquaintances but few true friends. Zeke's daughter was the best of them, and her lover of six years. Jess was working today, and so Ward had volunteered to babysit Zeke.

If only they could stay in the truck, or even the cabin, instead of venturing out into the cold. The dashboard thermostat read twenty-two degrees Fahrenheit. Brrrr. In the warmth, she'd listen to Zeke babble all day long, and then she'd take him out for dinner and they'd stop off at the hospital and feed Jess. It sounded delightful. Well, maybe not, but at least it would be warm.

"How long have you been coming up here?" she asked as he coasted down the hill from the cabin.

"All my life, seventy years. My father and his friends bought the place before I was born and incorporated the club. Towering Pines Sportsman Association. Sounds impressive, doesn't it? Farms were startin' to get divided up, even then, and they figured if they bought this spot they'd always have somewhere to hunt and fish. The land can't be sold for profit. If it ever came to that, where we couldn't pay the taxes or no one's left who uses it, the land will be donated to the Boy Scouts. And it may come to that. Not many of us left that use it. So many of our children left home. Like Jess." There was regret in his voice, and perhaps sadness, too.

Ward's partner, Dr. Jessica Benson, had left home at eighteen and hadn't been back. Not until recently, anyway. After four years at Pocono Mountains University for her undergrad degree, she spent another four at medical school in Philly. Ward had met her there, when they were both emergency-medicine residents. They'd been together for six years now, worked in downtown Philadelphia and owned a house nearby. Their jobs and their travel agenda left few chances to come back to Jess's hometown of Garden in the mountains of Northeastern Pennsylvania.

The hills melted into the lake and Zeke coasted into a small clearing. He parked the truck, and once again she helped him with the toboggan. This was his show; she was just along for the ride. She'd never even fished before coming home with Jess. She left all her gear—gifts from the Bensons—here at the cabin for their visits. Now, as she felt the frigid air, she was happy her in-laws had insisted on the warm coat and gloves, and that Jess had given her the new boots. It was going to be a long day.

Her face was the only exposed flesh on her body, and with each of her steps on the unyielding surface of the ice, her cheeks grew numb. Avoiding holes in the ice slowed them down. When she dared to look up, she saw the same view as the one behind and to either side: blurry mountains became snow-covered trees that blended into hills of ice that bled into this frozen lake below her. For a second she feared getting lost out here in the wilderness, where everything truly looked the same. She might never find her way back. Zeke would, though. This was his home.

The air was still, and quiet, and the only sounds disturbing the peace were the hissing breaths escaping their lungs and the swish of the toboggan Zeke pulled behind him. A complaint about the cold came to mind, but she kept quiet as she tried to keep pace with the man nearly twice her age. Instead, Ward thought back a few months to a blissful Saturday afternoon when she and Jess had spent the day kayaking on this lake. They'd just moved to Garden, returning to help her mother die peacefully. The chemotherapy was killing Pat Benson more quickly than the cancer, and she'd decided to stop treatments and just enjoy her remaining days.

Jess had seen the crisis coming, and they'd planned the sabbatical from their jobs in Philly months before they actually changed their address. Garden was the largest city in the county, with a population of five thousand, and home of the only hospital in a wide and rugged radius. Luckily, the hospital needed ER doctors, and after a decade of practice in the inner city, both she and Jess were well qualified. They never worked together now, but they were on duty only three or four days each week, so they still had some quality time as a couple.

In the beginning, they had spent much of that time at Pat's bedside, but since she passed away at the beginning of December, their mission had been to fill Zeke's hours. He'd lost his partner of forty years, and although his job as the local sheriff kept him busy, he was still hurting. Jess had the day shift in the ER, and so Ward found herself on this frozen lake on the first day of the year, with only memories of that other day and the woman she loved keeping her warm.

They walked on silently, carefully, until suddenly, Zeke stopped. "Here," he said, and turned to the toboggan. "You set up the tent and the fire. I'll get the auger."

Ward knelt on the ice and felt the cold in her knees, even through three layers, but she'd be warm soon enough. She knew what to do. Zeke had taught her.

Ward had grown up just outside Trenton, New Jersey, and never held a fishing pole until Zeke put one in her hands on her first trip home with Jess. She never could have imagined how much she would come to love fishing. It wasn't the fish—she usually threw them back. It wasn't a desire to outsmart the little guys— they usually won that battle. She suspected it was the solitude she enjoyed, alone with the towering pines and a plethora of thoughts. At home in Philly she sought other solitary activities to occupy her time—visits to museums, hikes through parks—past times that nourished her body and her mind. Fishing seemed to refresh her spirit.

Ward placed the worn, aluminum sledding disk on the ice and set a few small logs in the center, atop a mound of kindling and paper. She threw a match into the pile, and a minute later she was warming her hands above the blazing fire. The tent practically set up itself, and within a few minutes, Zeke was seated next to her at its entrance, their feet stretched out toward the flames as they watched the ten flags over the holes in the ice. When a fish nibbled on the bait, it would tip up the flag, indicating they might have a catch. Or maybe just an empty hook, but it didn't matter to her. She wasn't here to catch anything but peace.

"Ice is a foot thick. Strong enough to hold a car's weight."

"Good thing you have that power auger." It had been a gift from her and Jess a few Christmases back.

"You're not kidding. Used to take a half hour just to open the ice with the hand auger."

"See, Zeke, everything modern isn't bad." She knew how he felt about electronic gadgets.

In response, he cleared his throat. "I guess you're wonderin' why I brought you all the way out here," he said as he handed her a steaming cup of coffee he'd poured from the thermos.

Ward unwrapped her peanut-butter sandwich and studied him. "Actually, Zeke, I thought you brought me out here to ice fish." Something told her she'd been terribly naive in her assumption.

"Hmmfp, ha," he said, and Ward knew from experience he was laughing. "You're such a kidder, Ward. You always know how to get a chuckle out of me. We're pals. And that's exactly why I need your help."

"With what?" she asked. Taking a bite of her sandwich, she studied him cautiously. Something strange was going on.

"With Jess. I know you two are more than just friends. We've known about Jess's lesbian phase since college."

His pronunciation of lesbian required only two syllables and sounded like something that might be served in an upscale restaurant. *Thin slices of roasted duck on a fresh baguette, served with a side of lez beans.*

"But I think it's time she settles down and finds a husband, before her baby clock stops tickin'. Emory Paldrane's still around. Divorced with a couple of kids, but he's a nice boy and was always fond of Jess. And he's willing to overlook her past. I just don't think she's gonna date him with you in the picture." He dipped his chin and turned his head slightly, but his eyes never wavered, holding hers, allowing his words to sink in.

Ward leaned against the sturdy frame of the chair and sipped her coffee. It scalded her tongue, but she barely noticed it as she studied the only relative Jess had left in the world. He'd always been kind to her, accepting her as his daughter's partner. Ward had spent holidays and vacations with him and his wife, and they'd visited the home she shared with Jess. And on all of those occasions, she and Jess openly shared a bed. They'd done nothing to conceal the nature of their relationship, and Jess had come out to them a dozen years earlier, while she was in college.

So Zeke knew the truth and was obviously hoping to change things anyway. As Ward ran her blistered tongue across her teeth in an effort to dislodge persistent peanut butter, she considered her possible responses. After all, she was in an unusual situation—in the middle of nowhere, on a frigid cold mountain, ice fishing with the local sheriff who was wearing a gun and wanted her to stop sleeping with his daughter. Refusing him could have life-altering consequences.

Yet she couldn't very well agree with him, either.

"It's up to Jess to decide who she wants to date, Zeke. And I think she'd prefer me over Emory, or any man, for that matter. Have you discussed this with her?"

"Eh, Ward, you know Jessica. She's as loyal as a puppy. As long as you're around, she's not going to look at anyone else."

"I'm not forcing her to be with me, Zeke. Jess and I love each other. Just as you and Pat did. We don't have a piece of paper that proves it—except a mortgage, but it's just as binding." She chuckled at her joke, but the strained look didn't leave his face.

"I think she's too polite to say if she wants you to go. We raised her better than that."

Suddenly, Ward felt a chill that had nothing to do with the weather. Did Zeke know something she didn't? Ward had to admit her relationship with Jess was far from perfect, and Jess hadn't been happy in some time. But that had nothing to do with Ward. Watching her mother die, giving up her staff position, moving home—all that stress had taken its toll. Wouldn't those burdens melt, like the winter snow, as her sorrow softened with the passage of time? Ward thought they would and hoped they would. She'd never questioned that they wouldn't. She'd never had a reason to, until this moment.

She tried to shake her doubts. Even if Jess told her their relationship was over tomorrow, Jess wouldn't be looking for a man to help her rebound. She'd look for another woman. Jess was a lesbian! Hell, Jess had seduced her, way back when. And a dozen other women, too, before Ward.

She looked across the frozen lake and pictured Jess on that day not so long ago—her red hair pulled back in a ponytail, blue eyes flecked with green squinting in the sun, her strong shoulders and arms effortlessly pulling her kayak across the water. She was beautiful, and she looked so much like Ward they could have been sisters. Ward's hair was brown, not red, and she wore hers short, but their eyes were the same, their faces both oval and their skin fair. Jess was decidedly more feminine, but they both tended to dress down, doubling the size of their wardrobes because they wore exactly the same size in everything. Bras. Shirts. Pants. Shoes. Jess fit Ward perfectly. Didn't she?

Ward imagined Jess's face, the blue eyes meeting hers, smiling. The passion in those eyes as she made love to her, and the gentle way Jess's hands slid across her body. All that was magical, and they would get it back. Ward had no worries about her and Jess.

The sheriff's gun was another story.

Chapter Three
Surgical Abdomen

A bby Rosen pulled her goggles down over her helmet and her scarf up. It was fucking freezing, and as she gazed down the trail she asked herself once again why she was doing this. Was anything worth this torture?

Abby had grown up twenty miles from this mountain and had spent the winters of her childhood following her dad down the hills and trails. They'd skied from November to March, weather permitting, thousands and thousands of runs every winter. Whenever her father had a few hours off and the conditions were favorable, they threw their equipment into the back of his truck and headed for the slopes. So many times that it lost its appeal on days like today. There was so much else she could be doing.

Glancing to her left, she saw Cassandra readying for their run and imagined her as she'd looked a few hours before, naked on the hotel room bed. And on the floor by the fire. And on the couch. It didn't require much debate to formulate her conclusion. Yes, it was worth it.

Cass lived in Philadelphia, where there were no ski slopes, so when she came to the mountains, she wanted to ski. As long as she wanted to fuck, too, Abby could weather the weather.

They pushed off and glided across the glistening surface of the trail, taking the circuitous route down the mountain. Low temperatures and a biting wind had created icy conditions, and Abby didn't want to risk an injury. Cass was an expert in bed, but her skiing skills weren't quite at that level. In a soft powder, the diamond trails challenged her. Today, they bordered on dangerous.

Looking up, she took a moment to enjoy the view. In spite of the cold it was a brilliant day, with a bright-blue sky backing up the shimmering mountain peaks. Few others had come out to celebrate the new year on the slopes, and the quiet was blissful.

It lasted for about three seconds.

"Fuck," she murmured as her phone began vibrating in her breast pocket.

In spite of her helmet, Cass heard her. "What's wrong?" she asked in the sweet way Abby adored.

"My phone is ringing," she said.

"Do you need to get it?"

"I can't do anything before I reach the bottom, so we might as well enjoy the run."

Suspecting this would be the last, Abby concentrated on the world around her, the feeling of her skis beneath her, the tension in her calves and her thighs and hips, and the vibration that rattled all the way up when she cut a corner too sharply. The wind hit the exposed flesh of her face like a razor; she'd need some extra makeup in the morning to cover the burn. Still, she was sorry when she reached the bottom of the hill and checked her phone.

Cass's eyes were waiting for hers when she raised them a second later. "It's the hospital."

"Maybe it's nothing."

Abby snorted. "It's always something, Cass," she said as she dialed the number.

"Abby Rosen," she said when the ER answered.

"Hi, Ms. Rosen. Let me get Frankie for you," the clerk said.

A moment later she heard the always-cheerful voice of the ER's head nurse. "Happy New Year, Abby," he said.

In spite of the intrusion of the call, Abby returned the greeting. Frankie was a third-generation hospital employee and as loyal as they came. Like so many from this area, he was the first to attend college and chose to use his nursing and leadership skills to help his friends and neighbors in his hometown. Abby had the pleasure of working closely with him on various committees, and because of her nature and his, he was never afraid to call her when problems arose.

"So, what's up?" she said after a moment.

"I thought you'd want to know. They just brought Dr. Rave in. He's pretty sick."

"Shit," Abby said. Dick Rave was the ER director, a dedicated doctor who'd been the head of the ER since she first started rounding with her parents as a toddler. He'd indulged her then, with lollipops and soda, showed her X-rays and amputated fingers, hoping to lure her down the same path her parents had chosen. She'd gone the other way, though, into administration, and when she was offered the job as CEO of the hospital a few years earlier, he was one of her biggest supporters. Like Frankie, Abby worked closely and well with Dick and was very fond of him. Her worry was more personal than professionally motivated.

"Is it serious?"

"He's on his way to the OR. It looks like a ruptured diverticula."

Although the words sounded vaguely familiar to Abby, she had no clue what they meant. "Speak English, Franklin," she commanded him.

"Diverticulitis. Little potholes in the colon. One of them got infected and ruptured, so now he has poop floating around his belly. If the surgeon doesn't fix the hole and clear up the infection, he'll die."

"Oh, wow. I guess I asked for that. Is he really that critical?"

"He's stable now, but this is a big surgery."

"When does he work next?"

Frankie laughed, bitterly. "Seven o'clock tonight."

Abby whistled softly. "I'll be there in an hour."

When she looked up, Cass was still watching.

"That doesn't give us much time," she said.

Abby glanced at her. She'd also removed her helmet, and her blond hair was cascading down her back. The form-fitting ski suit showed off her curves, and once again Abby remembered Cass naked. It would be so easy to invite her over.

Abby's house was less than half an hour away, and she had to stop there anyway before heading to the hospital. She had no keys, and she wouldn't even think of going in dressed in jeans and a sweatshirt, as she was for her day on the slopes. She'd change into something more professional, go help solve this crisis, and be back home in a few hours. How much nicer to be back home with someone to snuggle up with beside the big fireplace in the living room. How nice to make love and fall asleep beside a warm body.

But Cass had never been to Abby's place before, and it scared her to set that precedent. They were good friends, great playmates, and phenomenal lovers. But they would never be more than that, and Abby feared the invitation to her home would send Cass the message that more was a possibility.

They gathered their gear and hugged good-bye. "I'm really sorry," Abby said as they kissed in the parking lot.

"Are you sure you can't come back?" Cass asked.

"I'm sure this is going to take up the rest of the evening, and then I don't think I'll be much company."

One of Cass's best features was her sense of decorum. She didn't push it. "I'll call you soon," she said before walking away.

An hour later Abby found Jan Rave and her son Rich in the surgical waiting room at Endless Mountains Medical Center. It was far away from her office in the administrative suite, but she'd been in this position many times before and didn't hesitate to walk right in and offer support. After they exchanged hugs, Abby sat beside Jan and held her hand. "What happened?" she asked.

Jan shook her head in frustration. "He's had pain for a few days. He knew it was diverticulitis, but he thought he could treat himself with antibiotics. This morning he developed a fever and his pain got worse. Then he started vomiting, so I called the ambulance. Dave Simpson said he wouldn't have lived through the night."

Dave Simpson was a very capable surgeon, and Abby trusted his opinion. When he emerged from the operating room two hours later, the grave look on his face alarmed her. She had difficulty swallowing as she waited to hear his report.

"He's in recovery, and he's stable. But it was bad in there. I had to remove an entire section of infected bowel and create a colostomy," he explained.

Jan's hand flew to her mouth and she burst into tears.

"But he'll live?" Abby asked.

"Yes, I think so."

"When can we see him?" Rich asked.

"Half an hour. They'll come let you know."

Abby motioned for the surgeon to step aside and speak to her privately. It was time to be the CEO. "Tell me what I'm looking at, Dave. A month? Two?"

He ran a hand across a stubbly chin. "Months, Abby. Three, at least, just to recover from the surgery. Then, there's the infection, the weight loss, the weakness. And at some point, I'm sure he'll want that colostomy reversed. That's another three months. Honestly, at his age, this might be the beginning of his retirement."

A thousand curse words came to mind, but they stayed put. "Happy New Year," she said as he turned and walked away.

"Now what the fuck do I do?" she asked the snow that had begun to fall outside the window. Not surprisingly, the snow didn't answer.

CHAPTER FOUR
ANXIETY ATTACK

"Jess, it's time for us to go home."

Ward had been waiting for her, on the couch of the old Victorian they'd rented, an opened, unread book in her lap. She had spent her afternoon defrosting in front of the fire after Zeke abruptly ended their day. Contemplating his demands had consumed her thoughts and left little time for relaxing. He definitely wanted Ward out of the picture, freeing Jess to pursue a relationship with a man. They couldn't stay in Garden under such circumstances.

To say that she was surprised about Zeke was an understatement. After all their time together in the six years of her relationship with Jess, and in spite of all she'd done for Zeke and his late wife in the months leading up to her death, he still didn't accept her as Jess's spouse. He wanted a heterosexual daughter and saw Ward as the obstacle preventing that. If the moments they'd shared in the years leading up to this day hadn't convinced him of her place in Jess's life, Ward was sure nothing could.

At the sound of the garage door opening, she bounced up and met Jess at the door, taking her briefcase from her as she spoke.

"What? Why?"

"It's time, honey. We've been here almost five months. It's time to go home. We have a life, we have a house, we have friends. Let's go back to Philly."

Jess ran fingers through her shoulder-length red hair and shook her head, shrugging at the same time. "I thought you liked it here!"

Ward couldn't argue that point. She did like it in Garden. The people were real, and kind, and had manners, from the cashier at the grocery store to the waitress at the diner. Everyone knew each other, and everyone cared for their neighbor, even the ones they didn't like. Over the years she and Jess had been visiting, she'd come to enjoy the country and the land, kayaking on the lake and hiking in the hills, breaking up the monotony with an occasional round of golf. Living here had caused her to fall in love with the place, and until this day, she could have envisioned growing old here.

Even the medicine was more challenging than she could ever have imagined. After spending a decade with instant access to specialists and imaging studies, she was now forced to be better—to be the best. Because, most often, she was *it*. She had no consultant to call when a patient was crashing. The scalpels and the tubes were in her hands, and it was a new and exhilarating feeling.

Truthfully, before her trip to the lake with Zeke, if Jess had asked her to sell their Philly home and make this their residence, she would have agreed. The Victorian was for sale, and they could buy it for a song, fully furnished, because the son of the late owner wasn't the least bit interested in anything once owned by his mother.

That was yesterday. Today, she knew the truth about Zeke, about how he really felt, and she would spend the rest of her days—or his—looking over her shoulder, wondering what he would do to undermine their relationship. Wondering where his gun was pointing. And that was no way to live.

"It's not that I don't like it, Jess. Garden's a nice place. It's just…your dad wants me to leave, so you can marry Emory Paldrane. He wants you to put an end to your *lez bean* phase and settle down and have some babies."

Ward saw the pulse beating in Jess's neck, saw her swallow. "Ward, stop! He's just worried about me."

"Stop? Stop what? He told me to leave, so you can be free. He thinks I'm holding you down. I don't feel comfortable with that, Jess. I don't want to stay here anymore!"

"Well, I do! This is my home, and I like it here. Why should I leave just because you want to? Why do you get to decide where we live?"

"Jess, we live in Philly. I didn't decide that. We did. We worked there, we met there, we bought a house there. We live there. And it's time to go home."

"I don't want to go back, Ward. I want to stay in Garden."

Ward suddenly felt as if the room was spinning, and she walked into the kitchen. "I need a drink," she said, and poured herself a Ketel and tonic while Jess stood silently watching. Ward carried it back into the living room and sat on the couch, her drink in her right hand as she ran her left through her hair. She'd taken a bubble bath—mostly to warm up after her day out of doors—but the troubling memories of her conversation with Zeke hadn't allowed her to relax. The conversation with Jess wasn't helping to improve her state of mind.

Sipping her drink, she studied Jess. When she'd talked to Zeke that morning, she'd had no question about Jess or her loyalties. Doubts were beginning to creep in now, though, and she gulped the crisp drink and swallowed. Ward met Jess's eyes, forcing down the bitter question forming on the tip of her tongue. Could Jess be straight? Did she want to date men? The thought was so at odds with everything she knew about her, but Zeke's words, and Jess's actions, forced Ward to ask. "Jess, do you want to date Emory?"

Jess shrugged in response instead of answering the question, and Ward's hand began to shake so badly she could hardly bring the glass back to her mouth.

Focusing on the drink in Ward's hand, instead of their issue, Jess went on the attack. It was a typical strategy for her lately. Attack instead of defend. Argue instead of debate. "Oh, that'll solve everything, Ward. Why don't you have another drink?"

"Jess, tell me the truth. Do you want me to leave? Do you want to be with Emory?" Ward could hardly believe she was asking such a ludicrous question. Yet Jess's body language, and each passing second, lent it more credence.

After endless moments of silence, Jess sighed. "I don't know, Ward. I don't know what I want."

Ward poured another drink.

CHAPTER FIVE
ADVERSE REACTION

In the typical fashion, patients began to pile into the ER as the change of shift approached. Ward glanced at the clock and then at the stack of charts of patients waiting for her services. Only half an hour left on her shift, and five patients to see. Oh, well. Jess was relieving her, and Ward would gladly stay late to help her clear out the mess. Jess was why she was here. Why go home to an empty house when she could stay and sneak an occasional peek at the woman she loved? Even if that woman was acting a bit strange, Ward still loved her.

They hadn't said much else the night before, and when Ward had reached for Jess, for the comfort of her arms, Jess chastely kissed her and rolled away. Ward's night had been sleepless, but in the morning, things had seemed brighter. Jess could have slept in but instead rolled from their bed and made coffee before Ward left for her shift, even packed some snacks to help her make it through twelve hours in the ER. It was the kiss good-bye, though, that had gotten her through the day, and the smile she knew she'd soon see that pushed her to see the next patient.

Taking the top chart from the rack, Ward headed into exam room five to evaluate the man who'd come in for wrist pain.

"Hi, there," she said. "I'm Dr. Thrasher. Are you Mr. Billings?"

"Well, if you insist that I call you doctor, I insist you call me Tom."

Ward chuckled. "You got it. What's going on with your wrist, Tom?"

Tom looked to be in his fifties, and a glance at his chart confirmed that he was, but his mop of unruly hair and the twinkle in his eyes made him seem much younger. He grinned. "I kinda rolled my quad," he confessed.

"What?" Ward asked, instantly alarmed. Six-hundred-pound ATVs on top of two-hundred-pound men often proved to be hazardous, causing a variety of life-threatening injuries. He seemed to understand her alarm and made an effort to reassure her.

"I jumped clear of it, Doc. Just landed on my wrist when I fell."

"Well, that's a good thing. I've seen quads cause too many injuries to count." In just a few months in the country, Ward had witnessed two fatalities, one irreversible spinal-cord injury, and a host of broken bones. They were dangerous machines, and she wished there weren't so many of them roaming the woods around Garden.

"Something's gonna kill me eventually, Doc. If it's not a beautiful woman, or her husband, it might as well be a powerful machine."

Ward couldn't help but laugh again. "Can I check you out, anyway? Just for my own peace of mind?"

Reluctantly, he agreed, and Ward went over him from head to toe. He seemed fortunate to have escaped a near-catastrophe with just a wrist injury. It was badly deformed and Ward suspected a fracture. "Did they x-ray it yet?" she asked.

When he nodded, Ward pulled it up on the computer screen on the exam room's wall and showed him the crushed bone fragments in his wrist. They continued to chat as she numbed his wrist, tugged on it to realign the bone, and applied a splint to hold the pieces in place. While she worked, he kept her laughing with stories and jokes.

"Where do you ride?" she asked.

"It's getting harder to find places. Mostly, my buddies and I just keep to Towering Pines. Didn't I see you up there last fall?"

Of course, in this small town in the center of this small county where she was dating the sheriff's daughter, everyone knew who she was and where she'd been. His question was a formality.

"Oh, was that you the day Jess and I were kayaking?"

"Yep, that was the day. Must have been a weekend. A bunch of us go out every weekend."

As Ward recalled, it was quite a large group, and they'd been an impressive sight as they came out of the woods, one after another, spreading out as they reached the flat lands near the lake, then disappearing into the woods on the other side. Ward told him her thoughts.

"Let me give you my number," he offered. "In case you ever wanna go out ridin'."

He must have sensed her hesitancy. "Your reputation's safe with me, Doc. Marla and I have been happily married for almost forty years."

"All right, then," Ward agreed, just to keep the peace. She entered his number into her smart phone and saved it as Quad Tom Billings. One day, when she was scrolling through her contacts, she could laugh as she recalled her encounter with this funny man.

After escorting him to the discharge area, Ward walked back to the nurses' station and smiled with delight as she saw Jess putting orders into the computer. "Hello, gorgeous," she said, and she thought that, perhaps, the corners of Jess's mouth turned up in a smile.

"How was your shift?" Jess asked. "Busy, huh?"

It wasn't a particularly busy day, but a few time-consuming patients had slowed her down. One needed a spinal tap, and she'd had to sedate another to reduce a dislocated shoulder. The most harrowing part of her day hadn't been playing the part of doctor but that of daughter-in-law. Zeke had stopped in to visit her and inquired about her discussion with Jess. He was none too pleased to learn she hadn't yet started packing.

Ward needed to sit down with Jess and talk about this, really talk, because she feared it would only get worse. Maybe Zeke was suffering some kind of psychosis induced by his wife's death. Or perhaps it was early dementia. Whatever the diagnosis, something had to be done. Ward didn't feel comfortable with the sudden pressure he was putting on her, and for whatever reason, Jess didn't seem the slightest bit concerned. She'd said she didn't know what she wanted! What did that even mean?

Yes, they needed to talk. About Zeke. About their future. Ward was on the schedule for the next two days, and Jess was on her first of three consecutive nights, and then they'd have a few days off. Together. "Why don't we go to Philly when we're off?" she suggested.

Jess didn't even bother to look up. "I can't. I have meetings, and then I have a GYN appointment."

"What?" Ward asked, confused. Why would Jess schedule her appointment here, instead of with her doctor in Philly?

"It's just easier to do it here," she said.

"Oh. Okay. So any chance you can reschedule that, and we can do something together?"

Now Jess did look up, and Ward wished she saw something in her eyes to give her reassurance. A little laughter, or warmth, or love. All she saw was irritation and impatience, as if the answer was obvious, or she'd explained it a hundred times already and wasn't in the mood to do it again. "No, Ward. I can't."

"Do you want to tell me what the problem is? Or should I just start guessing?"

Jess looked around to assure herself that no one was listening. "Now isn't the time."

Grabbing the chart on the desk, Jess picked it up and walked away. Ward followed with her eyes, wondering what the hell was going on, because, until the day before, she hadn't even suspected there was a problem.

A few patients later, Ward said good-bye to the staff and left for the night. Jess didn't seem to care that she was leaving, and her attitude truly bewildered Ward. They'd never had a problem in their relationship—nothing major, anyway. They were happy. They liked the same food and movies, enjoyed their friends, and were good company for each other. Yeah, their sex life wasn't what it once was, but Ward figured that was because of Jess's stress level. The year of her mom's illness had been a bad one for her. They'd get it back though, as soon as Jess felt better.

It was just after eight, and instead of pointing her SUV toward home, she drove to the local pub. They grilled a great burger, and it was often a stop-off for her on the way home from work when Jess was at the hospital. It was a small place, with a friendly bartender and a cozy fire blazing in the corner fireplace.

"You're late," George, the bartender, said as she hung her coat on the stool at the bar.

"What?" she asked, puzzled.

"You usually get her by seven thirty or so. It's after eight. I didn't think you were coming."

"What made you think I was coming at all?"

"Well, you usually eat here when Jess's working the night shift, don't you?"

She pursed her lips. "If you know so much, smarty, I don't have to tell you what I want."

George smiled as he pulled a clean glass from the dishwasher tray. "Your burger's already on the grill." He handed her a beer, and as she took a sip, a man screamed from the doorway.

"Call an ambulance!" he said.

Ward was on her feet instantly, running toward the door and whoever needed her.

Emory Paldrane wasted no time. He still wasn't entirely sure if he liked this idea, and he was absolutely sure it was illegal, but the sheriff wouldn't allow him to get into trouble. After all, it was Zeke's idea.

As soon as Ward and George headed for the front door, where his brothers Elliot and Edmund were causing a racket, he bolted from the bathroom and headed toward the bar. He might have had misgivings, but they weren't going to slow him down enough to get caught in the act.

He was able to calm himself with the knowledge that he was doing the right thing. It was a good deed, even if the way he went about it wasn't. Jess was unhappy with Ward Thrasher, and he could make her happy. Emory remembered the way she'd looked on the night of their junior prom, so beautiful in a blue dress that matched her eyes, carrying the roses he'd bought for her with his grass-cutting money. She'd been happy back then, on that one and only date they shared. She'd told her parents she was a lesbian, and she'd been living with Ward down in Philadelphia, but didn't the fact that she was back here in Garden say something about that? She was unhappy, and he was going to help Zeke make her happy again.

Emory had been successful in his landscaping business, so he'd be able to provide for Jess. She'd want to give up her career once they began having children. His home was almost paid for, and he owned both a pickup truck and a car, all paid for with the profits of the company. Two crews worked for him, cutting grass and landscaping in the summers and plowing snow in the winter, and he was so respected in the county that he was on the commissioners' advisory board.

With the thought of Jess's smiling face in the back of his mind, he poured the powdery substance into Ward's drink and then followed her out the door.

Ward shook her head in disbelief as she sat back down at the bar. A man had passed out in the snow and after regaining consciousness refused to go to the hospital. The episode might have meant nothing, but it could also have been a harbinger of something ominous. Without further testing, she couldn't tell what was happening, but she had been unsuccessful in her attempts to persuade him.

"I'll check on that burger," George said, and as he headed through the swinging doors leading to the kitchen, Ward tilted her glass back and swallowed a mouthful of beer.

A minute later he returned and, glancing at her near-empty glass, offered her a refill as he placed her plate of food before her.

"Just some water, George. I have to drive home." She didn't say anything to him, but she suddenly didn't feel well. Her peripheral vision was becoming blurry, and she had difficulty focusing as she squeezed ketchup onto her burger and fries. Perhaps the food would fix her problem. She was plagued by the occasional migraine, and skipping dinner could certainly trigger one. Not to mention the stress she was under with Jess. The weird things happening with her eyes certainly seemed like a migraine, and the sooner she ate and went home to bed, the better off she'd be.

"Sure thing," he said, then looked down the bar where a man was seated, quietly nursing a drink. "Another one for you, Emory?"

Although the man wasn't very noticeable, with average looks and size, his name was certainly distinct. Ward turned and studied him a little more closely as she popped a fry into her mouth. "Are you the Emory who took Jess Benson to the prom and tried to grope her in your pickup?" Ward asked.

George chuckled, but Ward wasn't amused. It was a serious question and deserved an answer. Suddenly, it was more important than the food before her or her impending headache. The answer to her question was more important than anything. Emory was trying to take Jess from her. Her partner. Her lover. Her heart. Ward had never hit another human being in her life, yet she was suddenly filled with rage, with the desire to beat thoughts of Jess from his mind. "Hey! Emory! I'm talking to you!"

Ward stood, and although she was dizzy and her vision had blurred even more, she registered the fear in Emory's eyes, and it made her happy. "Are you after my partner?" she demanded, so close to him she could smell his sickening cologne. Ward barely registered George's presence as she grabbed Emory by the neck and slammed his face into the wooden surface of the bar. Clutching a handful of his hair, she raised his head and saw blood pouring from his swollen nose, then slammed his head into the bar again. She pushed George aside as he tried to restrain her and managed to get in a few kicks to the belly and the groin as she pulled Emory to the floor, before someone much larger finally pulled her away.

She felt cold metal handcuffs close around her wrists and heard Zeke's voice then, behind her. His words echoed and she had difficulty focusing, but she concentrated and turned her head to face him. She tried to speak but couldn't manage to form an answer as he asked her, "Ward, what have you done?"

Looking around, she saw George sitting on the floor, bleeding from the head, and another man at her feet, bleeding and not moving. Then she slumped back against Zeke and passed out.

CHAPTER SIX

COMA

Zeke watched as the stretcher carrying Ward was loaded into the ambulance. Since she was still unconscious, the paramedics decided she was the most seriously injured of the three patients at the bar and should travel on the stretcher. George was riding in the front of the ambulance, looking like a combat victim with gauze wrapped around his head, blood soaking through from the gash he'd sustained when his head hit the floor. And Emory was riding in the police vehicle, getting blood all over the SUV Zeke so meticulously maintained.

"What the fuck happened, Emory?" Zeke demanded as he closed the door behind him and started the engine. "You were supposed to slip the stuff into her drink and then get her into her car, not start World War III!"

"She broke my fuckin' nose, Zeke! And I didn't do nothin'. I slipped it in her drink, just like you told me, and sat at the end of the bar waiting for it to work. The next thing I knew, she was pounding on me. If you hadn't showed up when you did, she probably would've killed me. That's one violent dyke. Forget about this idea of me with Jess. If I have to put up with this shit, it's not worth it. I want Ward Thrasher in jail, too, and I'm willing to press charges."

"Shut up! You're not doing anything of the kind, you fool. What if they run a drug screen on her and find out you put something in her drink? You wanna go to jail?"

Zeke drove in silence, following closely behind the ambulance, thinking about how he might turn these surprising events in his favor. He'd been the sheriff for forty-five years, and he'd done it hundreds of times—hiding a little evidence here or there so someone didn't have to get arrested. The favors always came back to him in spades, but this was the greatest reward ever—the chance to get Jess out from under the spell of Ward Thrasher.

"This is what you're gonna do, Emory," he said, and began to speak.

As the ambulance reached the hospital, Zeke parked in the emergency spot beside it, and rather than helping escort the patients, he raced inside, anxious to find his daughter and give her the correct spin on things. "Jess," he yelled when he saw her standing at the counter. "Come quick. It's Ward!"

Jess ran to his side, and they hurried down the hall. "What happened, Dad?"

"Ward got drunk and beat up Emory. She's passed out cold."

The stretcher bearing Ward's limp body appeared in the hall, and Jess raced to her side. "Stop!" she ordered the medics.

Pulling a penlight from her pocket, she pulled up Ward's eyelid and shined it on her pupil. It was normal in size and reacted briskly to the light, as did the other. No signs of head injury or drugs. "Ward!" she screamed as she shook her lover's body. "Ward! Open your eyes!"

In response to the command, Ward's eyelids fluttered but didn't manage to open. "Put her in the trauma room, guys. Dad, tell me what happened!"

Before he could respond, an ambulance attendant appeared, escorting George Stiles and Emory Paldrane, one on each arm. Both men were bleeding and moving slowly. "Good God," Jess said as she moved to assist.

"Good God won't be enough to help that bitch!" Emory responded. "Sheriff, I want her arrested immediately! I know people, and I'll have her thrown out of this hospital and she'll never work again. She's a disgrace to her profession!"

Jess took a deep breath as she guided Emory toward a treatment room. "Take it easy, Em. Just tell me what happened." Her eyes met the medic's and she gave him instructions. "Put George in room one, hook him up to the monitor, and I'll be over there as soon as I can."

Jess guided Emory to the stretcher in room eight and peeked up to see the nurses hooking Ward up to the monitor. She only had a few seconds for Emory. Ward was the more critical patient. "I was just having a beer, Jess, and she attacked me. Blind-sided me and smashed my face into the bar." As he spoke, Jess felt his neck, checked his pupils, looked into his nose and ears, and then felt his chest and belly. He seemed fine, other than the nose. "Did you get knocked out?" she asked.

When he denied loss of consciousness, Jess reassured him he'd be okay, ordered an X-ray of his nose, and then went to check on Ward. A glance at the monitor told her all the vital signs were in the normal range, although her blood pressure was in the lower end. "Ward, open your eyes!" she demanded, and this time, Ward responded. "You're in the ER. Do you remember what happened?"

Ward's response was an incoherent grumble. Jess went over her from head to toe, looking for signs of trauma—blood, scrapes, swelling, bruising. Nothing but some scrapes on her hands. Then she used her tools and searched the back of Ward's eyes for swelling and her ears for blood. Everything appeared normal, except for Ward.

"Let's get a stat CT of the head," Jess instructed the nurse.

"Tox panel?" the woman asked.

Jess shook her head. "Not yet. Let's see what the CT shows." If she ordered the toxicology panel and it was positive, Ward was screwed. Jess had never known Ward to use drugs—other than alcohol—but something funny was going on. Had Ward given in to the pressures of the past few months, of the strain of leaving home and caring for a dying woman, all the while watching her drift further and further away? A flash of guilt caused her to step back, but she quickly squashed it. She wasn't responsible for this. Maybe she'd caused Ward's distress, but she certainly hadn't put the bottle in her hand. And from the first day they'd met, Jess had suspected alcohol could be a demon that would bring Ward down.

She closed her eyes and focused, finding her objectivity. She'd treat Ward like any other patient—identify the problem and fix it, hopefully without having Ward lose her license to practice medicine. Jess would run all the other tests, and if she found nothing, no other explanation for Ward's condition, then she knew the answer. Ward was drunk.

Her father wrapped a loving arm around her shoulder. He was a rock, and Jess was so proud of how he'd handled her mother's final months, making her laugh and seeing that she was comfortable. Jess only wished she had half of his strength. The stress of her mother's illness had crippled Jess, and she still felt like she couldn't cope with it. Coming home to be with her had been a great decision, and life here was so much easier than in Philly. There was little crime, and friendly faces greeted her everyplace she went. The only problem was Ward.

Jess knew Ward wasn't really happy in Garden, and Jess wasn't happy with Ward. Emory Paldrane wasn't the answer, but maybe another man—someone a bit more sophisticated—might make her happy. She'd never been in a relationship with a man, but did that mean she couldn't be? Her mother's illness had brought a sense of finality that was eating at her, and it had awakened a need she'd never known before. Suddenly the idea of children wasn't so scary. Instead, it seemed like a wonderful way to honor her parents, to give them life for generations to come. Settling down with a man might help ground her, and having a family might give her the sense of purpose that always eluded her.

She and Ward had never discussed having children. Ward's flippant comments about other people's kids had killed any desire to speak of it, and Ward wouldn't be a good parent. She was too busy. When they'd lived in Philly, Ward had memberships at every museum and spent her free days studying art and science. She volunteered for countless hospital committees and mentored students. Since they'd moved to Garden, she'd taken on new hobbies. She played golf in nice weather, kayaked and hiked on her days off. In the winter she skied—cross-country, no less. Traveling was a passion for Ward, and Jess had a hard time imagining dragging a child up the Spanish Steps or through the Louvre. Ward drank too much, too. Hell, look at her now! She was pathetic. How in the hell would she handle a child?

Looking to her father for strength, she focused on him instead of the sadness that coursed through her. They had been heading this way for a while, but now they'd reached the end, and Jess didn't like the feeling coming over her. She was sad, and there was no time for that. She still had three patients to care for. "Dad, what can you tell me about tonight?" Jess asked him.

"I guess she just drank too much. It's a good thing I saw her car there and stopped in, though. She might have killed him. And I feel bad, Jess, because I told her Emory had a thing for you. I think that's why she did it."

Jess's jaw dropped. Ward had told her about her conversation with her father, and Jess knew Ward was upset, but she'd never known her to be violent. Apparently people were capable of reaching new lows under stress. *You know all about that, don't you?* she thought.

Jealous. Ward was jealous. That explained it all, although it certainly didn't justify it. She tried to reassure him with a hand placed on his. "Dad, it's not your fault. She did it, not you."

"Has she ever done anything like this before?" he asked, studying the still form beneath the white sheet, the only signs of life coming from the electronic gadgets monitoring Ward's vital signs. "Has she ever…"

Jess jumped to Ward's defense. She was having problems with Ward, but she knew it wasn't all Ward's fault. And no matter what she did to drive Jess crazy—badger her to travel or hike, blow off things that irritated Jess, kill her with kindness—Ward had never been violent. Not to her. Not to anyone. She was a kind and gentle woman, perhaps too much so. If she was tougher, especially on Jess, things might have turned out differently. "No! No, she's not like that. I can't believe she'd do this. She must be more stressed than I thought."

Jess watched as they wheeled Ward's stretcher toward radiology before leading her dad toward a chair in the nurses' station. "Let me get back to work," she said, then walked to room one to check out George. "What happened, Mr. Stiles?"

He shook his head, clearly shocked. "It was scary, Jess, the way she snapped. I've never seen anything like it. One minute she was eating her burger, and the next she was kickin' the shit out of Em."

"How much did she drink?" Jess asked as she went over him in the same fashion as her other two patients.

George looked at the sheriff and the ceiling as he seemed to weigh his answer. It was clear he didn't want to give one, and whether it was to protect Ward or himself, she wasn't sure. Nor did she care. His hesitation told her all she needed to know. Ward was drunk. "Never mind, Mr. Stiles. It's not important. Let me take a look at you."

Jess examined him, checking the wound and his brain function and found him to be in better shape than her other two patients. "This is just a small cut. I can close it with two staples. Does that sound okay?"

When he nodded, she cleaned the wound, and before he could protest, she was finished. "I guess there's just the matter of the police, Mr. Stiles. Are you going to press charges against her?"

He shook his head. "I like Ward, and I know she didn't mean me any harm. I'll be fine, if I can just get a ride back to the bar."

"I think the sheriff's going to play taxi driver tonight. Just give me a minute to do your paperwork, and Em's, and I'll let you get out of here."

"The CT is normal," the tech told Jess as she passed by, wheeling Ward back into the exam room. Ward was still out of it. Jeez, why would she do something so stupid?

"What about the labs?" the nurse asked, and Jess didn't turn to meet her gaze, trying to appear nonchalant. "No, I don't think they'll be helpful. But set up a surgical tray. I want to do a lumbar puncture."

Jess pulled up the X-ray of Em's nose and winced. It wasn't just broken. It was shattered, but she didn't tell him that. "Em, your nose is broken."

"No shit!" he said, with humor rather than malice this time.

Then she figured she'd better level with him. This fracture would probably need surgical repair if he ever hoped to breath normally again. She told him so.

"That bitch." The anger had returned.

Jess turned to see her father approaching, and once again he placed his arm around her for support. His words were hard to hear, but she knew they were true. "Ward isn't a bad person. She's just out of her element here. She's stressed, and tonight, she took it out on poor Em."

Jess didn't want to have this conversation in front of him, but he had other ideas, and when she heard them, she nearly fell over. "Em has agreed not to press charges, but only if Ward leaves town. He wants her gone. And, you have to go out for dinner with him. On Valentine's Day."

"Dad, that's ridiculous!" Jess looked from her father to her patient, but neither was smiling.

"Which part?" Em asked.

"All of it!" Jess looked at them. It was so preposterous an idea that Jess would have been suspicious these two had set Ward up if Mr. Stiles hadn't witnessed the attack.

"Listen to me, Jess. Even if you don't go out with me, you should think about Ward. This isn't her home, and she doesn't belong here. Tonight, that really showed. If I press charges, she'll probably lose her license and be in a whole heap of trouble. If I don't, who's she going to beat on next? Someone else who appreciates you like I do? Or someone totally innocent? Is that what you want?"

Jess couldn't believe this was happening. How had her life gotten so fucked up? "Let me think about it, okay?"

Jess discharged both George and Em, and then she went back to Ward's bedside. Her mental status was no better than it'd been earlier. She was barely responsive. Her breath smelled of alcohol. The more data she amassed, the clearer the diagnosis became. Ward was fucking passed-out drunk, in plain English. Still, Jess had to be sure. Could Ward have caught some strange infection that was taking over her brain? As an intern, she'd seen a case of viral encephalitis caused by the herpes virus. The patient had stabbed her husband, a Baptist minister, with a knitting needle and used more cuss words in a single sentence than she'd ever heard in her life.

With help from the nurse, Jess positioned Ward on her side and took her place on a stool behind her. After cleaning her skin, she carefully placed a long, thin spinal needle between the vertebrae in the low back and easily withdrew five tubes of clear, colorless fluid from the space around the spinal cord. Four were necessary, the fifth was a bonus. Ward didn't even flinch during the procedure. Jess instructed the nurse on the orders, but she suspected this test would also be normal. While germs and blood rendered spinal fluid discolored and cloudy, clear fluid usually meant no worries.

An hour later, Ward's status hadn't changed, but four tubes of normal spinal fluid satisfied Jess that she had her diagnosis. Alcohol intoxication.

Jess looked up from the lab reports to find her father walking down the hallway. "Well, everyone's all tucked in. George is going to forget about this, but I'm worried about Em. If he presses charges, what's going to happen to Ward?"

Jess nodded. "I know," she said, the words floating out on a huge sigh as she leaned against the wall beside Ward's room.

"How is she? Is she coming around?" he asked.

Jess couldn't speak as she fought tears, and the ER was eerily quiet, amplifying her silence. After a moment, she found her voice, faint but resolved. "I think she'll be fine. Would you mind taking her home?"

"Wouldn't mind at all."

"Just put her to bed, Dad. I'll get her shift covered for the morning. No matter what I decide to do, there's no way Ward's working tomorrow."

Chapter Seven
Penetrating Trauma

Abby finished the last bite of the cheeseburger she'd ordered from the hospital cafeteria, then headed into the private bathroom connected to her office. When she worked late, she usually patronized the cafeteria. As CEO, it was good for her to show the hospital employees that the hospital food was palatable. It was practical, too. The cafeteria was just two floors beneath the administrative suites.

After brushing her teeth, she touched up her makeup and her hair and then smiled at herself. For the first time in a week, her reflection smiled back. Dick Rave was out of the ICU and expected to make a total, if slow, recovery. The hospital staff, especially the ER physicians, had come together to cover the holes in the schedule left by Dick's illness, and Abby was proud to be their CEO. Now, a new physician was arriving to cover for Dick during the last weeks of January, and the agency Abby had hired was able to cover the ER for another six months, giving Dick plenty of time to recover from his illness. If he didn't recover, or if his convalescence was prolonged, she'd deal with the scheduling void then. For now, though, she could relax.

It was good to see her eyes looking bright instead of worried, and the light highlights in her long hair also made her look lively. She applied color to her full lips and made sure no hamburger was stuck between the perfect rows of sparkling teeth. Satisfied that she passed inspection, she pulled on the purple jacket that matched her skirt and headed to the lobby. Her new doctor was expected any minute.

"Done for the night?" Jake, the custodian, asked as Abby stepped into the hallway from the administrative suite.

"Actually, no, but if you need to get in there, feel free. Just let me grab my bag and you can have the place to yourself."

"Okay, thanks. I hear Dr. Rave is doing real good," he said, pausing the buffing machine that pulled him down the hallway.

Abby nodded. It might have been common knowledge, but she still felt some obligation to protect Dick's privacy.

"I'm sure glad about that. I've been praying for him. You have a good night, Miss Rosen," he said, then went back to work. She watched his bent form as she awaited the elevator, wondering if the prayer had helped Dick. It didn't hurt, anyway. Abby once again realized how happy she was to live and work in Factoryville, PA. Her hometown was famous as the birthplace of baseball legend Christy Mathewson, but Abby was less impressed by him than by the rest of the citizens of this humble town. They were all hall-of-famers.

Her elevator car stopped on the second floor, and she realized she wasn't the only one working late. "Dick looks great," she said to Dave Simpson, the surgeon.

"Yeah, I'm really happy with his progress."

"Just another testament to good, small-town medicine," she said, knowing how doctors loved a nice ego stroke. Abby was quite experienced in such matters.

He gave her an "aw, shucks" look. "I hear we have a replacement?"

"Yes, as a matter of fact I'm meeting with him now. His credentials are impressive, so I think the ER will be in good hands. I booked the agency for six months."

"Good move."

"Thanks for the advice," she said, and bid him good night before they exited the elevator.

The lobby was relatively deserted and Abby had no difficulty identifying her target. He was petite, if a man could be described that way. Slight. Certainly shorter than her, anyway, and thinner, too.

His dark hair was cut very short but was stylishly arranged. Dark-colored, thick-rimmed designer frames sat atop his slight nose. He stood, with perfect posture, hands clasped behind his back, staring out the window into the darkness. His charcoal suit was tailored and draped elegantly all the way to the brilliantly polished wingtips on his feet.

He would have been noticeable in any venue, but in the lobby of a small community hospital in the mountains of Northeastern Pennsylvania, he really stood out.

Abby, dressed in her own designer suit and fresh from her bathroom touch-up, felt an unfamiliar twinge of self-consciousness and smoothed nonexistent wrinkles from her jacket as she approached him.

Not surprisingly, his hand was cool when she shook it. "I'm Abby Rosen," she said. "The CEO. Welcome to Factoryville."

❖

"Edward Hawk. It's good to be here."

Abby Rosen would never know just how good it was. Immediately after his release from his prior position, Edward had contacted his personal assistant. "I need a job. Not in Florida or New Jersey." Edward had worn out his welcome in New Jersey, and his prior peccadilloes in Florida could come back to haunt him if he ran into someone he knew there. In his role as a doctor, anyway. He had no concerns about visiting the Sunshine State, and he immediately took off for his parents' house on the Gulf of Mexico, prepared to regroup there. They were away on an extended cruise, so he had the freedom and privacy to do as he pleased. He'd been too miserable to have much fun, worried about the mistake that had led to his termination in Jersey and restless about his future. Then, just as his razor stubble was beginning to resemble a beard, his phone rang. Some hick doctor in the middle of nowhere had gotten sick, and an immediate replacement was needed. The locum tenens agency was willing to hire him on the spot, if he could begin the next day. It was only a three-week assignment, but if it worked out, he wouldn't have to worry about a job for a while. The company had already offered him a one-year contract. A job meant many things. Money. He really didn't need it, thanks to his family money, but he liked it anyway. It gave him the ability to eat and dress and travel well, habits that would have been difficult to change. Impossible, actually. He was quite set in his ways.

The job also gave him company. He didn't really like to be with people, had never lived with anyone since he'd left his parents' home for college. Because of his discomfort with people in his personal space, and his unusual hobby, he never had guests at his house. He did get lonely, though. In the ER, he could be aloof enough to be left alone by the staff, but their mere presence pleased him. The background chatter was a familiar comfort, and the bells and whistles were soothing.

Mostly, though, a job meant exposure to patients, the sick and injured souls whose lives were placed in his hands. It was a dream, an opportunity like no other. Edward had been nervous before the phone call about the job in Factoryville. Like a heroin addict, all he'd been able to think about was his next fix. When would he be able to kill again? Hourly, his agitation grew so intense that he was beginning to plot the abduction of an undesirable tourist to fulfill his cravings. That was risky, though. Even undesirable tourists had friends and family members to report them missing, and if questions were asked, the answers might point back to Edward. Killing in the hospital was much safer. How could he get caught when no one even suspected a crime had been committed?

For a man with his agenda, Factoryville, Pennsylvania was a dream come true. Doctors came here because they couldn't cut it in the big cities, he was sure. They'd be too stupid to know protocols, too out of touch with modern medicine to understand his clever methods. Nurses, too. Not only were they inbred at the local schools, but they were trained to respect the doctors. They'd never question him. He smiled, knowing he'd be able to do whatever he wanted, and no one would even notice. He followed Abby Rosen to the administrative suite for his hospital orientation. It was indeed good to be here.

CHAPTER EIGHT

EXTUBATION

A soft knock roused Ward from her sleep, and she opened her eyes to a dark world interrupted only by the sliver of light permitted by the crack in the bedroom door. Sitting up, she wiped the sleep from her eyes and cleared her throat. "Come in," she said softly.

The swath of light grew wider as the door opened and Rosa Perez popped her head into the room. "I wanted to say good-bye," she said, then "I thought you'd be awake."

Indeed, Ward hadn't been sleeping well and had been up to enjoy coffee with her old medical-school friend every morning before Rosa left for work. Rosa practiced anesthesiology and was busy doing pre-op evals at the hospital while most people were still snug in their beds.

Sliding her legs to the floor, Ward crossed the wooden planks of the guest bedroom in a few strides and pulled the door fully open. "I must be feeling better if I'm sleeping past five," she said dryly.

"Beach therapy is quite effective," Rosa said as they walked toward the kitchen. The house was modern and huge, with an open plan suited for entertaining, and for the past two months, Rosa and her partner, Cindy, had had their hands full with Ward. She'd arrived a few days after Jess threw her out, needing a place to crash that didn't remind her of Jess. Ward had spent a miserable two days at their house in Philly before calling on her friends in Rehoboth Beach, and they'd tended her wounds and guided her through the chaos her life had become. Ward was by no means over Jess, but she was functional once again, and it was time for her to go.

She had a job!

"Can I make you one last coffee before I set out?" Ward asked.

"Of course. I'll miss you waiting on me. Can you possibly train Cindy to be a good wife like you before you leave us?"

Ward shook her head and frowned. Rosa and her partner Cindy were so similar it was scary. They both had long, dark hair, dark eyes, and dark skin. They were both intelligent and tended to take things a bit too seriously. They shared a love of the arts and food and fashion, and were both physicians. Both were pathetically lacking in home-repair and cooking skills. Any remorse Ward might have had about crashing at their house was alleviated by the payment she'd made in home improvements and food preparation.

"I'm sorry, my friend. She's a lost cause." Then she smiled. "But I promise to come back in the summer, and I'll cook for you."

Sipping the hot coffee, Rosa looked up over the cup and met Ward's eyes. They held for a moment, and then Ward closed the gap between them and wrapped herself around Rosa. "I don't know how to thank you," she said.

Rosa whispered into Ward's shoulder. "Just be okay. That's all I want."

"I'll be fine."

"I wish you weren't heading back into the devil's den. Why couldn't you have taken a job in Alaska or South America? Someplace safe and far, far away from Jessica."

"I'm not that close to her."

"I hear the Taliban needs doctors. Maybe you can get a job sewing suicide bombers back together. That would be better than being near your ex."

Ward broke the hug and pulled back, laughing. "Stop! I don't want to be far away. Whether it's over, or we start over, I have to get some closure with Jess. And until she's sure what she wants, I can't move on."

Rosa shook her head, angrily. "It's ridiculous that Jess should expect you to wait around while *she* decides what *she* wants to do with *your* life."

"I know. It's hard to understand." Ward had cried on Rosa's shoulder a dozen times since she'd been in Rehoboth, when she'd first arrived on her doorstep and, again, after every time Jess refused to talk and after every awful thing she said when they did. Jess was having a mid-life crisis, and while it wasn't fair that she was taking it out on Ward, it also wasn't fair of Ward to abandon her. Jess was emotionally unwell, and until she told Ward it was over between them, Ward couldn't give up on her. She loved her, and she still believed Jess would come through this and they would be together again.

Rosa swallowed a piece of blueberry muffin and washed it down with coffee before she spoke again. "Since she's not talking to you—"

"She is talking to me! Just not as much as I'd like—"

"Since she's not talking to you *as much as you'd like*, will you at least consider putting in your application for a Delaware license? Then, if it doesn't work out with her, you can come back here."

Ward studied Rosa's face and saw concern there. It was warranted. She'd been in bad shape when she arrived on Rosa's doorstep. Jess had asked her to leave Garden, had "suspended" her from her duties in the ER, and had put their relationship on hold while she evaluated what she wanted to do with her life. In addition, Ward was humiliated by the way she'd behaved at the bar. George had been a friend; to think she'd assaulted him mortified her. Even if she despised Emory Paldrane because of his feelings for Jess, he still didn't deserve to have his nose broken.

She had no excuse for her behavior, but the total lack of precedent really concerned her. She'd never acted violently in her life. Was something seriously wrong with her? Was she capable of hurting someone else, maybe someone she loved, like Jess?

And why couldn't she remember anything that had happened? Her mind seemed to have protectively blocked out the horrifying events, but instead of soothing her, the amnesia only worried her more. She had no recall after leaving the hospital that night—not the drive to the bar, nor the drinks she'd consumed, nor the assaults she'd perpetrated. She'd lost more than sixteen hours of her life, from the time she left the hospital a little after eight that night, until she awakened in her bed around noon the next day. That's when Jess had filled in the blanks and kicked her out.

Ward had been devastated, of course, and felt so fortunate to have the kind of friends who loved her unconditionally and helped her weather the storm. Rosa was one of them, and had been since they'd met early in their medical careers. If a simple gesture from Ward would ease Rosa's concerns, why not do it? All it would cost was a few bucks and a few hours of her time to complete the paperwork. And Ward suspected she'd have plenty of time in the coming months.

She smiled at her friend. "If it makes you happy, I'll apply for a Delaware license. Then I can work with you and live with you and cook for you…"

Rosa stood and hugged her again, smiling. "Thank you for admitting I'm right."

They walked to the door, arm in arm, and hugged again before Rosa climbed in and started the car's engine, and didn't move until the taillights faded into the darkness. She closed the garage door and glanced at the wall clock as she walked back to her bedroom. It was just after five.

She'd completed the majority of her packing the night before, and it didn't take her long to brush her teeth and her hair, and wash her face. Her eyes seemed tired, but all in all, she looked a hell of a lot better than she had when she'd arrived in Delaware. Grief and sadness still dominated her emotions, but she had moments of happiness, like the one she'd just shared with Rosa, and she was laughing once in a while, too. She was ready to jump back into life.

After slipping into her jeans and a sweater, Ward pulled on her sneakers and closed the smallest of the three suitcases she'd brought with her. The other two were already in the car, and she quietly carried their mate to the front door and softly closed it behind her. A note contained her final good-bye to Cindy, and she was on Route

One heading north to Philly just a few minutes later. She planned to shower when she reached the city and spend a few hours laundering and putting away the majority of her winter clothes. Although she knew March in the mountains could be cold, by April she'd need warm-weather gear. It seemed pointless to pack many sweaters.

Traffic was manageable until she reached Chester, but even then it still moved, and she pulled her car into her garage in Wayne only two hours later, next to the little red sports car that belonged to her tenant. Michelle Marker was a fourth-year medical student, worked constantly, and had agreed to live at Ward and Jess's place while they were away. It was a win-win situation for all parties, and Ward was happy to see Michelle's car.

"Welcome home," Michelle said at the kitchen door. Wearing scrubs, her short hair slicked with gel, Ward couldn't tell if she'd just finished work or was about to start, so she asked.

"Sadly, I'm just leaving. I wish we had more time to catch up," she said, seeming to choose her words carefully. Ward hadn't shared the details about Jess with Michelle, and she knew her tenant was curious about Ward's sudden move to Delaware. But until Ward knew what was happening with Jess, she wasn't sharing much with anyone. Only a few, very good friends knew the details of that night in Garden.

"Next time," Ward said, and they hugged as Michelle raced out the door.

When the garage door closed and the house was quiet, Ward took a moment to look around. She hadn't done that two months earlier when she'd been too blinded by tears, and even now it was hard. Jess was everywhere. Above their table hung a painting they'd purchased in Venezuela. On shelves next to the window lay trinkets from trips they'd taken and a few photos, all of the two of them together. It would be the same throughout the rest of the house, for they'd bought it together and painstakingly decorated and furnished it beautifully.

What would she do with this place if Jess stayed in Garden? She'd decided she'd wait six months, staying close by so she and Jess could see each other, and talk, and try to work this out. She owed that to Jess, and to herself. But for the sake of her sanity, she needed to have some sort of deadline for when she'd walk away, whether she was ready or not. If she didn't, she'd be lost, floating, waiting. On the first of September, either alone or with Jess, she'd be coming back to Philly and picking up the pieces of her life.

Ward spent a few hours as she'd planned—putting away clothing, sorting mail, inspecting the house. When she'd worked up a sweat, she washed it away with a shower. At eleven thirty she pulled out of the garage again and weaved her way along the back roads until she found herself on Henry Avenue in Philadelphia, at Dalessandro's, her favorite cheesesteak shop. A woman of sixty, with auburn hair and dazzling green eyes, was already seated at the counter. Ward stooped and kissed her cheek.

Dr. Jeannie Bennett stood and wrapped her arms around Ward in a gentle hug. They were just about the same height, a few inches taller than average, and about the same build, but somehow Jeannie's presence seemed larger. "Sit. I ordered for you," she commanded.

"How'd you know what I want?" Ward asked as she folded her coat and sat on it.

"You don't have many options, dear. So tell me how you are." Jeannie swiveled on her seat and faced Ward.

Ward spent a few minutes trying to convince her old mentor that she was doing well, but the skeptical look on Jeannie's face told Ward she wasn't a great actress.

"Well, the good news is, this company you'll be working for is quite reputable. I checked with a few colleagues, and they all thought the doctors they hire are skilled and competent. So, at least you won't destroy your reputation while you're off on your adventure."

Ward patted Jeannie's back. "I'm giving it six months, Jeannie. If she's not ready to commit by then, I'm coming home."

Their food arrived, and both of them dove in. "Tell me your plans," Jeannie said after chewing and swallowing and wiping sauce from her mouth.

"I have a meeting today at four with the HR person, where I'll get my ID badge and orientation and all that jazz. Computer passwords, policy manuals, you know the drill. I start work tomorrow morning."

"You ER docs don't know the meaning of the word Saturday, do you?" Jeannie deadpanned.

Ward smiled through the cheesesteak she was chewing, knowing well that most doctors, Jeannie included, had worked their share of weekends.

"So you'll be there for the whole month?"

Ward cleared her throat. "Yes, I signed up for five months with the locum tenens company. I'll spend a month at five different hospitals, all of them in the mountains, and then I'm taking August off. I'll start back here in September."

"Well, you're a skilled physician, Ward. You should be able to handle the medicine. My concern is your heart. How will you handle seeing Jess?"

Ward forced a smile. "I have to do this, Jeannie. Maybe it'll work out, and maybe not. But if I don't give it a chance, I'll never know, right?"

Jeannie looked skeptical as she chewed, and Ward spoke again, trying to convince Jeannie. Perhaps she was talking to herself, as well, trying to fortify her doubts. "I know you don't like her, Jeannie, but have you ever thought about Jess? What she's going through? She lost her mom, and she's unsure of her future. Of everything. I'm sure she feels awful."

"To answer your question, no. I haven't thought about her. We all lose our mothers one day, and it sucks. But you don't do this to someone you love. She could have seen a therapist, or taken some time off—"

"That's exactly what she's doing. She took some time to figure it out. I can't blame her for that."

"She's hurting you," Jeannie said softly, but then quickly changed the subject. "Anyway, I'm not here to preach," she said, and handed Ward a large mailing envelope.

Ward took it and read the words LAKE HOUSE printed on the front.

"It's self-explanatory. Directions, keys, alarm code, cable instructions, local restaurants, and shopping. All your questions should be answered when you read this."

Ward smiled. "I really appreciate this, you know."

Jeannie waved her hand dismissively. "I'm happy the house will get used. Bobby's the only one who spends time there these days, and since he travels so much for his job, his time is limited. But if you come home to find a tall, incredibly handsome young man who looks just like me, that's my son. I'll try to warn you if he's coming, or if anyone else is, but for the most part, you should have the place to yourself."

"Well, I don't know how much I'll use it. They do offer housing at all of these hospitals, but who knows what it'll be like. I could find myself in a dingy motel room."

"Exactly. If you need a place, it's there. If not, no big deal."

"Will I see you and Sandy at all?"

Jeannie laughed. "Maybe one weekend a month, but who knows. We have two houses in Philly, one in New York, two in the Poconos, and now one in Rehoboth. I never know where I'm going until Sandy tells me. But I'd like to see you, so let's try to make a date when you know your schedule."

Ward picked up the bill and left money on the counter, then walked with Jeannie out into the cold final day of February. "Spring's coming, Ward. New birth. New life. You'll be fine." Jeannie's hug was fortifying, and Ward was thankful for her and all the good people in her life.

Driving on the Pennsylvania Turnpike's Northeast Extension, Ward pondered Jeannie's words. She had no idea what they meant in her situation. What new life was in store for her? Starting over alone? Starting over with Jess? Jess had mentioned a baby. Was that in her future? She'd never seriously thought of it. Who knew?

Friday afternoon traffic was light, and Ward found herself at the hospital well over an hour early. The head of human resources seemed happy to see her, and Ward suspected the woman's weekend would begin as soon as she'd finished orienting her. Sure enough, an hour later, after processing an ID badge and filing paperwork, issuing computer codes and guiding a tour, the woman slipped out the door and left Ward to inspect the emergency department where she'd spend the next thirty-one days.

"Hi, I'm Ward Thrasher," she said to the slim, dark-haired man seated at the X-ray monitor. "I'm the locums doc."

"Edward Hawk. You're my replacement. Would you like to start now?" he asked, meeting her gaze, and Ward wasn't sure if he was joking. She was startled by the intensity with which he stared at her and his striking good looks. He was small, and his build was slender, but his demeanor suggested a confidence and competence that made him seem bigger. He wore a suit, which surprised her. Surgeons and ER docs tended to get messy, and cotton scrubs were a lot easier to launder than wool pants. Ward supposed the administration liked the suit though. He'd be a tough act to follow.

Responding to his comment, Ward chuckled. The Friday festivities seemed to have started, and Ward noticed a few patients hanging out of doorways and a pile of charts that needed attention. She wasn't credentialed to start until the next day, though, and she knew he understood that, so she didn't respond to his question.

"Did you have a good month?" she asked.

He nodded. "Yes, I did. It's a nice place to work. Steady volume, not usually overwhelming," he said, and waved his hand to the stack of charts. "Competent staff, good back-up. I can't complain."

"Where do you go next?" she asked.

"Carbondale," he said.

Ward smiled in recognition. That was the next leg of her journey, too. "So I guess I follow you, huh?"

"I guess. I don't know all the rules. This is my first month with the company."

"Gotcha. Well, I won't keep you. I just wanted to introduce myself. Have a safe trip."

He nodded as he walked away, and Ward talked to a few other staff members before heading out. The ER was busy, and no one had time to chat.

It wasn't quite five o'clock on a Friday night, and it took Ward only half an hour to unpack and settle in at the quaint home provided by the hospital. It featured a stellar view of the parking lot. There was off-street parking, and she could walk to the hospital and the corner store. If Edward Hawk had stayed at this house, he had already packed his bags, because the place was empty. Everything was in place, and the surfaces sparkled as if recently attacked with a dust rag. As the lone occupant of the ten-room house, she wouldn't be crowded, but she'd check out Jeannie's lake house when she'd finished the last of four consecutive shifts the following Tuesday. For the moment, though, she had nothing to do.

A pile of DVDs sat next to a small, flat-screen television, and Ward leafed through them, but none were appealing. In the study, a wall of bookshelves was filled with volumes of old medical books as well as works of fiction. Normally, the texts would have fascinated her, but not today.

Being this near to Jessica was upsetting her equilibrium, and she felt an inexplicable pull to her. She knew she shouldn't stop by without calling, but the fear that Jess would say no was too real to suppress. So Ward climbed into her SUV and programmed the GPS to direct her toward Garden. Forty-five minutes later, she was parked in the driveway of the Victorian that had been home for four months. Jess's car was in front of hers.

The back door opened before Ward even reached the porch, but instead of the warm welcome she'd hoped for, Jess's expression and her manner were neutral. "Hey," she said.

Ward heard no emotion in her voice—no anger, surprise, happiness. Suddenly she regretted her decision to drop by and scrambled for an excuse. "I needed to pick up some clothes," she said. "And my fishing pole."

"Oh," Jess said, nodding. She seemed relieved, as if Ward might have stopped by to assault her, or argue. Then she seemed to remember her manners and offered Ward a drink.

"No, thanks. I have a long drive."

Jess nodded. "That's smart. I guess you learned your lesson."

Ward's mouth dropped open in shock. They'd spoken of that night a few times during the two months since then, but it wasn't usually the opening gambit. Either Jess was in a rotten mood, or Ward's visit was really making her uncomfortable.

Ward shook her head, and when she spoke, her voice was low, choked with tears. "I still can't believe that happened, Jess. I've never done anything like that. You know that. I almost feel like I was drugged or something."

"Huh!" Jess said, and began to pace, waving her arms around. "You're unbelievable, Ward, do you know that? You get drunk and assault two men, and then you try to blame it on someone else."

Ward ran her fingers through her hair and studied the high windows looking out to the mountains beyond. They were still covered in snow, and in the fading light of day, the world looked as gray as she felt. "I guess it doesn't make sense. It's just so hard to understand. First the violence and then the blackout. There has to be a reason."

"Why would anyone drug you? Do you think George wanted to rape you? Or was it Emory?"

Ward looked up and met Jess's eyes. "No, Jess. Emory wants you, not me. If he was going to drug someone, it would be you."

Jess's head popped up, as if she'd been hit by the force of the words. Then she shook her head. "You're ridiculous. Now maybe you should get your things and go."

❖

Pulling back the curtain, Jess watched Ward pack her car and back out of the driveway. The reel of their conversation replayed continuously in her mind. *Emory wants you, not me. If he was going to drug someone, it would be you.* Pushing her memory back a little further, she thought of a night two weeks earlier. Valentine's Day and the dinner she'd shared with Emory to protect what little was left of Ward's reputation.

He'd insisted on picking her up at her house, and then after she'd endured mediocre food and a stale monologue of childhood memories, he'd refused to take her home. Instead, they'd stopped at George's pub, and he'd steered her to a table where some of his friends were celebrating the evening.

Jess knew most of them, but like the town, she'd left them behind when she went away to college. They were good people, though, and she quickly found herself engaged in conversation with two classmates who'd been together since tenth grade. While Em went to the bar to order beverages, they told her about their children, and she listened with interest. She was suddenly interested in everyone's children. She was surprised when Em returned and placed a beer before her. "I don't drink beer," she said, annoyed. She'd asked him for a Coke and wondered if he was trying to get her drunk. He'd ordered a bottle of wine at dinner, instead of the glass she'd requested, and they'd ended up wasting most of it.

"Hey, no problem. I'll take care of it for you," their classmate said, and reached for the glass. Before he could grasp it, Emory reached out and knocked it over, spilling the beer not only on the table, but on Jess's pants as well.

Fuming, she'd escaped to the bathroom and called one of her friends for a ride home. She hadn't spoken to Em since then, in spite of his many calls and visits to the ER. She'd told him politely she wasn't interested and hoped he was honorable enough to keep their agreement. So far he had.

Jess stared into the early night, focusing on the snow still piled against the sidewalk in front of the house. She'd assumed Em had reacted angrily at their classmate, not wanting him to drink her beer. But what if it wasn't anger? What if it was fear? *Emory wants you, not me. If he was going to drug someone, it would be you.*

Had Em drugged her beer that night? Shaky legs carried Jess down the hallway and into the kitchen where her phone was plugged into the charger on the wall. Picking it up, she dialed a number she now knew by heart. "Medical center, how may I direct your call?"

"Hi," she said. "This is Dr. Benson. Can I have the lab, please?"

Her call was answered on the first ring. "Laboratory, this is Dave speaking."

"Hi, Dave. It's Dr. Benson. Do you still have the spinal fluid on Dr. Thrasher?"

"Hold on, Doc. I'll check. We usually keep that stuff for six months, so I'll bet it's here."

Jess tapped the counter, waiting, wondering. How did her life get so fucked up? When did she become so unhappy? Why did Ward seem to make her so angry? Ward was never anything but kind to her, and other than the night she'd gone into attack-mode, she'd never done anything wrong. At least that Jess knew of. But everyone has secrets, right? She wondered if she was really mad at Ward at all. After all, Ward's behavior that night had given her the escape she needed. Why was she so angry? Why did she say the cruel things she did? Was it just easier to be angry than sad? And if she thought about it, she supposed she was a little sad about how things had turned out with Ward. Or was she really just sad in general? It was too exhausting to think about.

It wasn't so long ago that they'd been happy, that she'd wanted Ward. Back then she would have pulled Ward into her arms right there in the driveway and then offered her a coffee when she walked through the door. She would have built a fire in the living-room fireplace and spent an evening together, both of them doing their own thing, but with a comfortable companionship that Jess once enjoyed. Being close to Ward was dangerous, though. Ward's drinking made Jess edgy. Ward was too soft, too. Jess needed more definition in her life, not someone like Ward who went along with everything and didn't argue. Jess needed some accountability, someone who stood up for herself, stood up to her. Someone who cared enough to question her decisions, not just give in.

She longed for something else, too—to let her guard down and be free, to be herself. What would Ward say if she knew the real Jess? What would anyone say? Maybe being alone was her best option.

Shaking her head to remove the uncomfortable thoughts, Jess willed herself into the mind of Dr. Benson. Jess was really fucked up, but Dr. Benson was still a highly functional, exceptionally talented physician. Right now, Ward needed Dr. Benson. And if Ward was right about the drugs, Jess needed Dr. Benson, too.

"Doc?" Dave asked a minute later.

"Yeah, I'm here."

"We have a whole tube."

Jess sighed in relief. Suddenly, she needed to know the answer that spinal fluid was hiding. At first she'd resisted the tox panel, because of possible legal issues, but she was no longer worried about that. Ward had left town, and Em and George weren't pressing charges. It was time to know what really happened that night. "Can you send them out to the lab for a tox screen?"

❖

Edward glanced at the tires on the Porsche Cayenne, assuring adequate inflation, and climbed into the driver's seat, immensely pleased with himself. Happy. He had struggled for weeks after his termination, questioning his future, wondering when he'd work again. A deep depression—deeper than normal—had set in as he cruised the Gulf of Mexico aboard his father's boat. And then his assistant had called about the locum tenens work, and suddenly, a world of possibilities had opened to him.

Locums work allowed him to move around frequently without raising suspicions. It was ideal for him, and he wondered why it had taken him so long to figure that out. Sure, he had to work in Pennsylvania, and in small hospitals, without the benefit of coverage in most specialties. But because of that, he was given tremendous freedom to practice emergency medicine as he saw fit. His time passed quickly as he filled his days and nights with work, inserting endotracheal tubes to breathe for patients, huge IV catheters for transfusion of blood and fluids, and pacemakers to make their failing hearts beat.

Best of all, he'd had the opportunity to commit murder, not once or twice, but five times during the first weeks of work. He wondered if he might be doing too much, but then he watched his colleagues carefully and knew no one was suspicious. It was heavenly! The scent of the most recent death he'd caused still lingered in his nostrils, and the adrenaline flowing through his veins made him feel like he could fly.

Meeting Ward Thrasher had been interesting. She seemed so normal, but she couldn't be. Why would anyone normal do this kind of work, away from friends and family, drifting from place to place like a migrant worker? Only someone like him, who had no friends and despised their family, would choose this work. Or someone who had a secret to hide.

What was Ward's secret? He doubted she was a murderer like him. He was a student of murder, had read everything available on the great serial killers, and he thought it highly unlikely that a female physician would be grouped in his category. Drugs or alcohol? Highly likely. Impaired physicians often burned bridges, and starting over in a remote place where no one knew their secrets was a good idea. Or maybe she was just incompetent and trying to hide from the prying committees that constantly interfered in the practice of medicine.

Who knew? Likely, he'd never find out the truth about Ward. Then he felt a sudden chill as he realized she might be asking the same questions about him. Did people wonder why he was doing this sort of work, traveling instead of settling down, working in the country instead of the big city where he'd trained?

He'd have to think of a good story to tell people, something that would stop the questions before they started. Before people had a chance to become suspicious. A dead fiancé, perhaps? Or maybe just a bad breakup. Financial worries? He could hardly make that argument while driving the Porsche. He'd go with the girl problems; that made sense. He'd have to think of an entire story, like a screenplay. Names, dates, places. Maybe several sets that he could change monthly. It would be so exciting!

Edward started his car and pointed it toward New York City. Barring a catastrophe on the highway, he'd be home in a few hours, and then he'd shower, change into club clothes, and head out to one of his favorite bars. With any luck, he'd find a cute young college kid to spend the night with. Boy or girl, it didn't matter. He was so primed from his day at work, he could fuck anything. And he planned to, many times over the weekend.

On Monday morning, he'd pack his car again and head back the way he'd come. The good people of Carbondale, PA needed an ER doctor, and he was ready to heed the call.

CHAPTER NINE
RESPIRATORY ARREST

A rriving half an hour early for her shift allowed Ward to ease back into the murky waters of the ER. She'd found that to be a much more pleasant immersion than jumping right in. A locker was waiting for her, along with a stack of institutional-style blue scrubs, which pleased her immensely. They matched her eyes perfectly. After changing and securing her valuables, she walked through another door and into the staff kitchen. It was deserted but well stocked with a traditional coffee brewer as well as a Keurig, a toaster-oven and a microwave, a fridge, and a combination ice-and-water machine. And it was remarkably clean.

She found a corner in the fridge and stored her lunch. Then, after glancing in the mirror to confirm she still looked like a doctor, she took a few deep breaths and went to work.

The department was quiet, and Ward had to search for signs of life. A crew of three—a doctor, a nurse, and a clerk—ran the ER at night, and she found them all in the lobby, watching the news. A tall, unshaven man with black, curly bed head stood and smiled when he saw her, then introduced himself as the ER director.

"Did you bring your boots?" he asked, nodding toward the TV. "More snow tomorrow."

Ward tried not to cringe when she thought of the boots Jess had given her for Christmas. But they were indeed packed, and she had plenty of cold-weather gear to insure she didn't freeze on her fifty-yard trek across the parking lot to the hospital from the house where she was staying. "I did," she said simply.

After they exchanged pleasantries, he introduced her to his colleagues, and she learned she'd be working with them when she covered the night shift the following weekend. At this hospital, the weekend consisted of Saturday and Sunday evenings, and like most places, while the physician staff rotated shifts, the rest of the staff was dedicated to days or nights. Both the nurse and the clerk had young children waiting for them at home, and the few hours of sleep they'd had when the ER was slow was probably all they'd get until they put them to bed that night. Night shifts in a slow ER were a good way for working mothers to go.

The director gave her a little more orientation, made sure all of her passwords were in order, showed her how to use the software for ordering and reading X-rays. "Don't worry. You can always write the orders on an order sheet and give them to the clerk. And if you're too slow on the system, you can dictate a note and they'll scan it in, or you can handwrite the chart and scan that. Just write legibly." He smiled at his last words.

In the code room, he showed her his favorite toys—a fiber-optic system for intubating and a portable ultrasound to assist with IV access. Ward was familiar with both instruments and was happy to see them. They were like old friends, and she knew they'd have her back. Nothing could get a doctor's heart rate soaring like a crashing patient who couldn't breathe and had no IV access, and the equipment he showed her had helped her save more than a few lives.

Voices signaled the arrival of the day-shift team, and introductions were quickly made. An additional nurse was on day shift—the nurse manager, who also wore a few other hats and floated in and out of the department as needed. At nine, when business started to boom, another nurse would start her twelve-hour shift.

"It's nice to meet you," the clerk said in a friendly voice, but the nurse, a young androgynous woman with a scowl on her face, wasn't quite so welcoming. "Hi," she said, offering a reluctant hand. The grip, though, was powerful, and when Ward met her eyes, she saw a challenge there.

Great, she thought. Just what she needed as she started her new venture—a turf war with a young butch. And several hours later, after the nurse, Erin, had questioned her every order, Ward wondered if she'd made a huge mistake. The next few months would be like medical school again, changing assignments every month, learning new systems and new ways. And new people. There were always battles of wills among the staff: personality differences, cliques, and some downright nasty people to deal with.

Almost ten years had passed since she'd worked anywhere other than home, with the exception of Garden, which truly was an exception. She and Jess were welcomed there, hometown heroes of sorts, and everyone had been friendly. Experience told her that wasn't the typical case, but she hadn't even thought about that aspect of the job when she'd signed on the dotted line for the locums job. All that had filled her mind was the thought of Jess, the need to be near her, and the need to work and occupy her time. She'd thought the locum tenens work was ideal, but after only five hours on the job, she was questioning the sanity of that decision.

"I'm not comfortable giving that shot," Erin told Ward, her arms folded across her chest and her feet spread wide in a challenging stance.

Ward looked up from her computer and met Erin's icy gaze.

"And why is that?" she asked, leaning back in the chair, giving Erin some space. It sucked to have to deal with this sort of crap, and back in school Ward had just tried to blend in, do her job, not make any trouble. It was different now, though. She was in charge, and that meant she had to stand up to the bullies. She hated it, but she wouldn't let Erin know that.

"It causes bleeding, and people have died because of it. The pharmacy issued a warning about it, and I'm not going to risk my license because some hotshot doctor from Philadelphia comes in and starts ordering me around. You don't give a shit about the patients. You just want to collect a paycheck. You'll be gone at the end of the month, but I'll still be here, and I'll have to face the families of whoever dies."

Ward was speechless. She'd encountered challenges in her career, but never the open hostility Erin displayed. As tired as she was of Erin's attitude, and as much as she would have liked telling her off, this wasn't the time for a fight. "Wow, Erin. I'm going to have to think about that and get back to you. I'm not in the habit of killing my patients, and I feel comfortable with this medication, so if you just give me the vial and the syringe, I'll draw it up and push it myself."

Seconds later, the requested supplies were placed on the desk before her. "Thanks," Ward said, trying to maintain some appearance of professionalism. She picked up the bag and headed into the exam room where a thirty-five-year-old man with a history of kidney stones was moaning and rolling around on the stretcher.

"I have some medication for you, Joe. It's going to take a few minutes to work, but then you'll feel better." Ward popped the plastic tamper-resistant lid from the vial and drew up the appropriate dosage into the syringe, then slowly injected it into the port on his IV tubing.

"Aren't you going to get a CT scan?" Erin asked from the doorway.

"That's an excellent question, Erin," she said, then directed the answer toward her patient. "We know you've had kidney stones in the past, and the pain you're having now seems like a kidney stone, so why should we expose your body to all that radiation? We don't need a CT scan now, but if your pain doesn't go away with medication, or you develop a fever, or it doesn't resolve in about a week, then we should. Most stones will pass on their own, though, if we give them a chance."

"What if it doesn't pass?" the man's wife asked.

"The urologist can fish it out or break it up with ultrasound. Do you understand about the CT scan?"

"It makes sense to me. We know it's a kidney stone. It just seems like all the doctors want to get a scan before they even give him any medication. It's expensive and we have a high deductible, so it really sucks. And he has to wait a long time for his medicine."

"Controlling costs is important, and so is controlling radiation exposure." Ward turned her attention back to her patient. He wasn't quite so pale and didn't seem as anxious. "How're you feeling? Any better?"

He nodded his head. "A little."

"Good. Let's give the medication a little more time to work, and then if you need more, I'll give you another shot."

"An ambulance is here, we need you," Erin said as she rushed past the room.

Ward followed her to the large trauma room, which was really a multi-purpose room to take care of all critically ill patients—trauma and medical, adult and pediatric. Much of the equipment used was the same, and in a small hospital like this, it made no sense to have separate areas to treat the sickest patients.

One look at this one told Ward she was in trouble. A woman in her sixties was seated upright on the stretcher, arching her back and her head with each labored breath she took. A plastic mask and bag delivering high-dose oxygen was fastened around her head, but she held it tightly against her mouth, trying to get more air.

However, she couldn't. The bag was doing its job, but the woman's lungs weren't. The only thing that would help her was to force air into her lungs, either with a tube or a mask, and Ward sensed the woman would need the tube.

Ward looked at Erin and ordered the medications she would need to sedate the patient. Then she turned to the nurse manager, who'd arrived with a host of others when the cry for help had been announced over the hospital's intercom. "Bag her!"

"You're going to sedate her?" Erin asked. "What if you can't get the tube in?"

"I'll get the tube in!"

"What if you can't? Then she won't be able to breathe on her own and she'll die."

"If I can't get the tube in, we'll bag her. The meds are short acting and they won't hurt her."

"I don't feel comfortable with this," Erin said.

Ward was losing patience. She didn't have time to debate or educate the argumentative nurse. "Just give me the meds. I'll do the rest."

With a clenched jaw, Erin drew the meds and handed them to her. She pushed them into the IV port and watched the patient's face. The nurse was assisting her breathing with a large Ambu bag attached to the mask across her face, and, as a result, the oxygen levels were climbing, her skin color turning more pink than blue. After a few seconds, when it seemed the woman's face relaxed and she was sufficiently sedated, and her oxygen level more stable, Ward stepped behind her, opened her mouth, and used the laryngoscope to get a visual on her vocal cords. Without taking her eye off the target, she reached for a breathing tube and easily slid it into her trachea.

"It's in," Ward said after watching the tube pass through the vocal cords. Before moving, she used a syringe to inflate the air bladder that would hold it in place.

The respiratory therapist placed a small plastic sensor on the end of the tube, and the color change confirmed Ward's observation. It was detecting carbon dioxide from the lungs. If the tube had been in the stomach—the only other place it could go—the sensor wouldn't have changed colors.

The nurse secured the tube with a foam dressing, and the respiratory therapist connected the tubing to the ventilator that would breathe for the patient for the next few days.

After issuing orders to the lab, the X-ray tech, and the respiratory therapist, she turned again to Erin. "Can you get an EKG, or don't you feel comfortable with that?"

Erin's face turned red, but she didn't comment and immediately began attaching the EKG leads. A minute later, she handed Ward the sheet of thermographic paper that had recorded the electrical blueprint of the patient's heartbeat. The electrical signals were elevated from the baseline in places and depressed in others. In this situation, this could mean only one, very bad, thing.

"Shit," Ward said. "She's having an MI." The director had given her a set of instructions on how to handle such emergencies as heart attacks, like this one, that were better treated at larger hospitals with staff cardiologists, cardiac cath labs, and heart surgeons.

The clerk, Petra, was waiting in the doorway for instructions. "I need the hospital in Scranton on the phone for a transfer," Ward informed her.

She turned to Erin and, instead of giving any further orders, simply asked for the meds she needed. As an ER doc, she was quite capable of administering them herself, and she couldn't use her energy arguing with Erin. The patient needed her full attention.

"Cardiology on the phone for you," Petra said a few minutes later.

Ward took the proffered portable phone and shared the information with the cardiologist in Scranton. After agreeing to accept the patient for admission, she asked Ward how long it would take for the transfer. Ward wasn't sure.

"How long to get to Scranton?" Ward asked the nurse, Jim.

"By the time the ambulance gets here, and they get her loaded, I'd say fifty minutes."

Ward stared at him, confused. Wasn't the ambulance already there? It couldn't have been more than ten minutes since they dropped the patient off. Didn't they have paperwork to complete, supplies to replenish? They'd brought in a patient from a minor car accident early on in the shift, and Ward would swear they'd hung around for an hour, gossiping with Petra. Even though the delay bothered her, she didn't question him. She was sure he knew the routine better than she. "Fifty minutes," Ward informed the cardiologist.

After disconnecting the phone, she went to the patient's bedside and studied her vital signs. Oxygen level perfect. Heart rate slow and steady. Blood pressure holding. All she needed now was a balloon or a stent to open up a blocked artery in her heart, and she'd be fine. Ward had administered a clot-busting drug, and she asked for another EKG to see if it was making any difference.

"Where'd the ambulance go?" she asked Jim as he handed her the paper.

"Back to the station."

Ward glanced at the EKG. No change from the prior. "Why?"

"What do you mean?" he asked, his expression guarded.

"They brought the patient in. They knew she was having an MI and would need a transfer to Scranton. Why did they leave at such a crucial time? Time is muscle," Ward said, quoting one of the early advertising promotions that tried to illustrate the need to act quickly in treating heart attacks.

Jim shrugged. "I guess they had something to do."

Ward intended to ask them, but when the crew returned, they went straight to work preparing the patient for transfer, and before she knew it they were on their way. As the stretcher disappeared from view, she walked across the hall to check on her other patient.

"How's the pain?" she asked Joe.

"Gone," he said.

Ward smiled. Nothing felt better than making someone feel better. A long list of medications would help make sure the pain didn't return and would allow him to treat further episodes at home. That would save him time and money, and give him faster relief during his next attack. Ward discussed the plan with both Joe and his wife, then excused herself to prepare the discharge instructions.

When Ward finished, no more patients were waiting, so she headed across the department to the break room. She'd snacked on an apple earlier, but she was starting to feel a little hungry. If she didn't eat when she had the chance, she might not get to. Her peanut-butter sandwich was too cold from the fridge, but it still tasted great. Better still was the quiet and solitude of the room. She was tired of locking horns with Erin and would be happy when the shift ended at seven.

On cue, the break room door opened and Erin stepped inside. She procured a Keurig cup from the cupboard, and after she prepared her coffee to her liking, she leaned against the counter and sipped it, studying Ward.

Ward ignored her and tried not to hurry through her brief respite just to escape this nasty young woman. What was her problem, anyway?

Erin interrupted her thoughts. "They can charge twice," she said.

"Huh?"

"The ambulance. If they leave and come back, they can charge for two calls instead of one. That's why they left."

Ward felt her head drop a few degrees, but her eyes never left Erin's. The nurse was serious. How awful! In cases like this one, time truly was crucial. A few extra minutes might not seem like much, but they could mean the difference between life and death. One minute a patient was stable and the next in cardiac arrest. What kind of callous disregard for human life would dictate a policy that had trained personnel leave a sick patient's bedside only so they could charge extra?

"Does the administration know this?"

Erin shrugged. "It is what it is. The ambulance has to make money to stay in business."

Taking another bite of her sandwich, Ward reflected on Erin's words. Did the greater good trump the rights of the individual? If the ambulance company went bankrupt, then no one would have access to essential medical services, and many people would die. Yet, by skirting the rules like they were, they put every patient's life on the line.

"You did a good job with that tube," Erin said, yet Ward sensed a big "but" coming.

"Thanks," she said cautiously.

"And you were right about the pain medication."

Ward nodded and studied Erin for a moment. She leaned against the counter, shoulders shrugged and head hung, looking defeated. Why? She chose her words carefully.

"These are basic things ER docs should be able to do. Manage pain and manage airways."

"Well, they should, but that doesn't mean they do."

Ward sensed Erin needed to vent about something, and if they were going to spend the month together, it was better to get it out now. "Did you have a bad experience with another doc?"

She grunted in response. "That's an understatement. The last doctor who was here—I don't know how to describe it, Dr. Thrasher. He was smart. Really smart. He could tell you amazing facts like why you shouldn't give one drug with another because they utilized the same pathways of metabolism in the liver and could cause toxicity. And he'd name the liver enzymes that caused the reaction and the toxic metabolites that could build up. It was like chemistry class. He knew every muscle in the body. His patients didn't have neck strain. They had trapezius strain. They didn't have sprained ankles. They had lateral collateral ligament strains."

When Erin paused for a breath, Ward tilted her head and studied her. "That sounds amazing. I bet you learned a lot working with him."

"Yeah, but even though he was a wizard, his patients still died. And he didn't seem to care very much."

Ward was surprised. Hawk had seemed friendly enough. She'd met quite a few jerks during her career, and usually she could tell immediately. They didn't bother with the friendly banter the way Hawk had, just ignored you from the start or said something condescending by way of greeting. "What do you mean by that?"

Erin shook her head and closed her eyes, seeming to gather her composure, and she shook her head, as if trying to free herself of a bad memory. Ward wasn't sure Erin would say anything else, but after a moment, she did. "There was a little boy in a sledding accident. His only complaint was shoulder pain. But the doc made me put in an IV, and he ordered a CT of his abdomen, and sure enough, the kid's spleen was ruptured. That was a brilliant catch. Amazing diagnostic skills. But before the surgeon could see him—he was in the OR with another case—the kid coded. We couldn't bring him back. It was the most devastating code I've ever worked. We gave him blood, fluids, plasma, but nothing worked. And when it was over, Dr. Hawk just walked away. I mean he said the right things to the parents—he was sorry, and we tried everything, you know the deal—but he didn't mean it. Five minutes later he was eating sushi in the lounge, with his feet kicked up while he watched CNN on the television."

"Well—"

"And then last night, another awful case. It was a woman I know—I went to school with her daughter. She's diabetic, with known kidney disease. Her daughter found her unconscious and called the ambulance. All she needed was a shot of sugar and she came around. So when she got here, she was laughing with the medics, trying to fix her daughter up on a date with one of them. And a half hour later, she was dead. I went in to check on her, and she was unresponsive. I called a code, but she was already flat-lined. We got nothing back, except when Dr. Hawk put in a pacemaker. We got heart activity on the monitor but no pulse. It was devastating, and again, he just shrugged as if to say, 'Oh, well. You win some, you lose some.'"

"How old are you, Erin?"

"Twenty-four."

"So you've been a nurse for two years?"

"Yeah. I volunteered on the ambulance for six years, though, so I've seen it all."

"Well, then you must have some way of dealing with the emotional aspect of your job, right? Because if you live and die with every patient, you'll burn out. And the people who need you won't have a good nurse to take care of them. It doesn't mean you shouldn't feel compassion, or anger, or even sadness. You just have to learn how to feel without it pulling you under, or you'll drown. I suspect that's what Dr. Hawk does. And when you've been doing this for ten years, or fifteen years, you'll still cry—at least, I hope you will. But it won't be as often, and you'll learn to hide your feelings from impressionable young nurses."

A weak smile appeared in appreciation of Ward's humor. "I hear what you're saying, and I understand. But it's different with Hawk. Take the MI. You were worried about her, I could tell. Hawk wouldn't have been worried. He'd have been excited. He would have liked the challenge—but if she lived or died, he wouldn't have really cared."

Ward digested Erin's words along with the last of her sandwich before speaking. "I don't know him, and you could be right. But I suspect he's just learned to hide his feelings so he can stay focused. In this job, if you lose your focus, people die. So, keep your focus, Erin."

Erin looked at her and smiled, a real smile this time, and Ward thought perhaps she'd made a difference. She didn't have a chance to wallow in it, though. The door opened and Jim poked his head in. "Doc, we need you."

Erin turned to go, but he stopped her. "Finish your lunch. I've got you covered."

Ward walked out into the ER to find that three new patients had arrived, and the afternoon passed quickly as she did what she was trained to do. That evening, after the sign-outs were given and clothes were changed, Ward was wandering slowly down the hall that led to the hospital's side door and her house. The evening had been busy and she hadn't had a chance to eat, and she was contemplating her options. A few taverns and restaurants were scattered around town, and she thought a burger might be a good way to end her day. No beer, though. She'd learned her lesson.

"Hey, Doc! Wait up!"

Ward turned to see Erin running to catch up with her, and then they walked side by side.

"I was wondering if you have a girlfriend," Erin asked.

"Excuse me?" Ward turned to look at her.

Erin met her gaze. "A girlfriend. Do you have one?"

Ward hadn't seen that one coming, and she couldn't help chuckling at Erin's brazen approach. "As a matter of fact, I do."

"Well, do you wanna grab a burger anyway? Just as friends? Colleagues?"

Why not? Erin's demeanor had improved tremendously after their lunchroom chat, and she'd enjoyed their banter as they worked together during the afternoon segment of her shift. After she got over her worries, Erin proved herself to be competent and charming as well. In the end, it had been a good day. Ward had nothing but an empty house awaiting her, and she'd been thinking about the burger anyway. "Why not?" she said.

CHAPTER TEN
SUBARACHNOID HEMORRHAGE

Shifting his stance, Edward discreetly dropped his right hand and adjusted himself. The sudden erection was painful in the confines of his form-fitting underwear and slacks, and his reaction was somewhat adolescent, but he truly couldn't help himself. This was just too exciting.

The computer screen was like a silent movie, showing an animated feature as each picture changed slightly from the one before it. All of them combined to form the magnificent, excitingly erotic picture that had stimulated his manhood so completely. It might have been a difficult story for some to follow, but not for him. He was an expert at reading CT scans, and this one of the brain showed a layer of blood dissecting through the crevices of the most important of all the body's organs.

It wasn't a surprise, the blood. His patient, a thirty-five-year-old mother of three, had just dropped her children off at school when she felt an explosion in her head. It was so intense and sudden she didn't even have time to pull the car to the side of the road before the first wave of vomiting hit. As a result, her car had plowed into another vehicle, and the other car's driver had rapidly activated the emergency response system. If she'd hit a parked car, or been at home, the prompt care needed to save her life might have been delayed. It wasn't, though, and so even though a significant amount of blood was visible on the CT scan, the woman was still awake and functioning. With a subarachnoid hemorrhage—the medical term for this woman's condition—that fact was very important. She'd need emergency repair of the artery. A patient awake and talking at the time of the repair was likely to remain so afterward. Someone in a coma before the procedure might regain some function, but a full neurologic recovery was unlikely.

Her story was classic for a ruptured aneurysm, so perfect it could be written into a textbook or board question. Edward knew it and had anticipated the results of the CT scan, and so, just before following the patient to the radiology department, he'd slipped into the locker room and retrieved a small vial from his effects. He pulled the contents of the vial into a small syringe, which he concealed in the pocket of his lab coat, and carefully wiped the bottle to remove fingerprints. Before his trip to the CT scanner, he slipped into the critical-care area and deposited it in the biohazard bag, where it would attract no attention.

Edward reached into his pocket and caressed the syringe, knowing what its contents would do to his patient. He'd stolen the clear liquid a week earlier, rerouting it into his pocket instead of the vein of a man suffering a heart attack. The powerful clot-buster would have helped open the blocked artery in that patient's heart and might have saved his life if he'd been given it and not the saline solution Edward had left in its place. Instead, he'd suffered, sweating profusely as his choking heart tried to function without blood and oxygen. It had been a miserable forty minutes before the heart finally gave out, and no one could revive him. No amount of electricity could save a dead heart, and Edward had been thrilled that the man had died in his ER instead of in the ambulance on the way to see a cardiologist. He even kept a copy of the rhythm strip showing his fibrillating heart, just a quivering line really, the last vestiges of life, but one of the most exciting things he'd ever seen.

Now, he was about to have another thrill, a sort of two-for-one special. One drug—withheld from a patient who was clotting and given to another who was bleeding—could kill them both. A two-for-one special always delighted him, and this young woman was the perfect victim. Many people would cry for her, and he would be able to watch their mournful reactions when he gave them the news that she had died.

He reached for the phone and looked at the CT tech, who was busy copying the images to a disk. "What's the extension for the ER?"

She told him, and he dialed it and spoke to the clerk when she picked up. "I need whatever hospital takes care of brain aneurysms. This patient needs a coiling. And send a helicopter. We can't waste any time. She's critical."

"I just need a minute, Doc," the tech informed Edward. "Then we can get her back to the ER."

Edward smiled. "Thanks." The tech was a cute young thing and had done everything to indicate her interest, but it was too soon. This was the twelfth of April, and a bad time with her could mean a miserable eighteen days in the ER here. He'd wait until the twenty-fifth or so, and then he'd have some fun with her. He'd have only five days of hell to pay afterward.

"I'll talk to her," he said, referring to his patient.

He opened the door and entered the scanning room, where his patient quietly lay on the CT table, awaiting further news about her awful headache.

"Hi," he said, and she opened her eyes, winced from the bright lights, and immediately closed them. She was pale, and she looked to be in tremendous pain. Even though the nurse had removed her soiled clothing, Edward could still smell her vomit. It was sickening, and he had to force himself to stay close to her. He took her hand in his and, after checking to make sure the tech was still occupied, slipped the syringe from his pocket. He was able to conceal it in his closed fist, and after he quickly connected it to the IV port in the patient's hand, it appeared that he was simply holding her hand to comfort her. Since she wouldn't open her eyes, he leaned closer. "I have some bad news for you," he said, and then in spite of the pain they flew open wide and she stared at him in horror.

He loved the fear there, and he wished he saw some sign as he depressed the plunger and injected the clot-buster. Maybe a scream of anguish as the bleeding worsened, or a seizure as it irritated the sensitive tissue of the brain—anything to indicate the medication was working. But he saw nothing.

"What is it?" she asked.

He leaned forward and whispered, so the microphone in the scanning room wouldn't broadcast his words to the tech in her insulated booth. "You have a hemorrhage in your brain. You're going to die." He pulled back so she could see his face and smiled at her. As he watched, the light of comprehension faded and she simply closed her eyes. It was one of the most anticlimactic murders ever, and he couldn't help feeling a little disappointed.

"We better get moving," he said as the tech emerged with the disk containing the patient's CT scan. She handed it to Edward, and he placed it in his pocket, next to the syringe. He had no worries about the syringe falling out when he removed the disk, because he knew the disk wasn't going anywhere. The patient would be dead soon, so the helicopter ride would be canceled, and there would be no need to send images to another physician.

When they arrived back in the ER, Edward shook his patient gently but had no response. The bleeding was compressing the brain and function was diminishing by the second. Perfect! Her respirations had become irregular, in an effort to change the blood pH and lower pressure in the brain.

"She's crashing. We need to intubate," he informed the nurse, and the ER came to life as various hospital personnel came running to help.

Just as he secured the breathing tube, the clerk called out from across the room. "I have the doctor on the line." Edward briefly glanced at the monitor. Her heart rate had slowed and her blood pressure dropped, both reflexes aimed at decreasing the pressure inside the skull. He shined his penlight into her eyes and saw no reaction.

His pace was brisk and bouncy as he crossed the department to reach the phone. "Dr. Hawk here," he said. "I'm afraid I won't be needing your services after all."

When he was through, the unit clerk grabbed him by the arm. "The family is here. Her husband and a sister and a few others. They're in the counseling room."

Nodding, he turned and walked in that direction.

"I'm sorry—" He had to try very hard to suppress his smile when the woman's sister wailed.

"No, no, please, no," the husband begged him. Edward felt at that moment that he held the power of God in his hands.

❖

"Is it possible to get it out without cuttin' it, Doc? This is one of my favorite lures."

Jess chuckled at the patient who had a fishing hook poking through his eyelid. Miraculously, it had missed the globe and his vision was intact. "Not without ruining your good looks. I'd have to make a pretty big cut to pull this out."

He didn't hesitate. "Do it. I can't get any uglier."

Laughing again, Jess opened a cabinet and removed the equipment she knew she'd be using a few more times on this first day of fishing in the mountains. With anglers everywhere, they couldn't help hitting each other as they cast their lines into the lakes and streams of Northeastern Pennsylvania.

The procedure took just a few minutes, and Jess triumphantly handed him his prized lure after she'd rinsed it in the sink. He followed her to the nurses' station for his paperwork.

It was an unusually quiet Saturday morning in the emergency department, and Jess wondered why. Sure, many of the county's residents and visitors were fishing this morning, but where were the heart attacks and diabetic emergencies and car accidents? She feared this was the calm before the storm.

Sitting at her computer, Jess typed in her password and saw an alert flashing on her screen. Lab results were ready. That's odd, she thought. No patients were in the ER and she hadn't ordered any tests. Cultures of wounds and urine went into the general nurse mailbox, and someone in that role checked them daily, because the doctor schedule precluded them from responding to issues in a timely manner.

After handing her patient his instructions and wishing him a good day, Jess clicked on the lab icon. Her breath caught when she read her message. Lab results were back on her patient Ward Thrasher. More than a month had passed since she'd ordered the tox panel on Ward, and she'd been waiting. Jess knew it would take time for the results. The tox screen on spinal fluid was an unusual test and had to be sent to a lab with specialized equipment. Jess had checked for results just about every day and was expecting them, but still, she was shocked to see them. Or was it fear? What would she find?

She'd been trying hard to keep Ward from her mind. She'd been back in the mountains for six weeks, and they'd seen each other only three times. Jess still wasn't sure what direction her life was going, or what part Ward would play in it, and all Ward did was confuse her, with her questions and loving looks and pleading eyes. She loved Ward, but she wasn't sure she wanted a life with her. She didn't know what she wanted.

She'd been on a date with an accountant, a nice man with two kids in college and a beautiful lake home in the mountains. They'd enjoyed relaxed conversation and good food, washed down by an excellent bottle of wine. Yet when the night was over, Jess felt a dread like she hadn't had since her last date with a man—the fiasco with Emory didn't count—almost twenty years earlier. No matter how nice he was, she felt no spark and had no desire to kiss him good night, and feared he might try to plant a big wet one right on her lips. So, when they pulled into her driveway, she fled the car as soon as it stopped and told him she'd call him. She wouldn't. Once inside, she'd settled into a bath and thought about the county coroner, a very nice butch she'd met on several occasions in the ER.

Wendy, the coroner, had asked her out. It was common knowledge that Jess had lived with Ward, and common knowledge that Ward was gone, also common knowledge that Jess was dating again. Jess had told Wendy she'd think about it, and she had. Day and night. Wendy was adorable, with brown hair cut short and blue eyes that sparkled with mischief. She owned a funeral home, which she'd inherited from her father, and lived above it, just around the corner from the Victorian Jess was renting. In addition to seeing her on those unfortunate occasions when her services were needed in the ER, Jess had seen Wendy walking Cleopatra, her energetic little poodle. They chatted, and on mornings when Jess wasn't scheduled in the ER, she'd started taking her morning coffee on the front-porch swing just so she could see Wendy and Cleo as they walked by. Almost always, Wendy lingered, and the day before, Jess had asked her in for breakfast. She'd accepted, and now they had a date scheduled for that very night.

Jess was delighted and excited and nervous all at the same time, looking forward to her evening with Wendy more than anything since she'd come to the mountains. Yet she had to tell Ward. Somehow, the dates with Emory and John the accountant didn't seem like cheating, but going out with another woman did. Jess needed to be sure Ward understood her, because she didn't need any more guilt where Ward was concerned. She already felt like shit because of their breakup, because of the way she'd treated Ward, even though Ward's binge had precipitated it.

Moving her computer's mouse, Jess clicked on the appropriate box and Ward's file appeared. Before her the screen lit up with the results of the spinal-fluid analysis for toxins. No cocaine was in her system, nor marijuana or any other of the typical drugs of abuse. The alcohol level was minimal. Not what Jess had expected. Even more shocking, though, was the positive result for flunitrazepam, more commonly known as Rohypnol, the date-rape drug.

Roofies typically rendered women comatose and vulnerable, but like most drugs, sometimes people had strange reactions to them. Intense violence after use of Rohypnol had been reported, and Jess suspected that was just what had happened in Ward's case. It explained everything. Yet it explained nothing.

Why the fuck did she even order the test? She'd wanted answers, not more questions when she'd asked Dave in the lab to run the tox screen on Ward's spinal fluid. She'd always felt uncomfortable about that night. First, Ward's totally uncharacteristic violence. Then, George's hesitance in answering the question about her alcohol intake. Finally, the quick and easy solution her father and Em had concocted to solve the problem. She'd gone with it, and she was ashamed to admit that getting Ward out of her hair had been what she wanted. Yet she suspected she'd betrayed Ward just to solve her own problems, and that guilt had eaten at her since. So much so she'd ordered the testing. Now that she had the answer, what did she do?

Jess closed her eyes and rubbed her temples. What the fuck was this about? It made no sense. How did that get into her system? Why? According to what they'd told her, George and Emory had been the only ones at the bar that night. Rohypnol was quick acting; someone had to have slipped it into Ward's drink at the bar. If George and Em were the only ones at the bar, one of them had done it. But why? Neither had a motive for drugging Ward. What would they have done with her? Snuck her out of the bar under their coats to have their way with her, hoping the other didn't notice? And no way were they in on this together. Emory and George weren't even friends, let alone partners in crime. Besides that, George was a teddy bear, an older, happily married man who surely wouldn't do something like this. And while Emory might have despised Ward, why would he want to rape her? It was Jess he liked.

Jess leaned back in her chair, eyes still closed, and considered the possibilities. It didn't seem likely that rape was the motive. Robbery? Ward carried little cash—although most people wouldn't have known that—but neither man needed money. George made a good living at the bar, and Emory's landscaping business was flourishing. Then another idea came to her, and Jess's breath caught in her throat.

Murder. What if Emory wanted Jess so badly he was willing to murder Ward to get her out of the way? He would drug her, lure her out of the bar, and drag her into his car, and Ward would never be seen again. Or he'd run over her in the parking lot when she was too confused to jump out of the way.

A chill came over her, and she rubbed both arms to chase it. She should have been happy to have this news. It exonerated Ward. At the same time, though, it put someone else—probably Emory, and possibly her father—in a whole lot of trouble.

What should she do now? Jess knew Ward was concerned about that night. She knew she should tell her. But if she did, Ward would pursue the truth. She'd pursue Jess, trying to convince her she was worthy of another chance.

Jess couldn't deal with any of that. She clicked the printer icon on her computer screen, and instantly Ward's labs were permanently recorded on paper. She folded the copy several times and placed it in her coat pocket for safekeeping, until she made a decision. The one thing she knew with certainty was she couldn't share the lab results with Ward. Maybe eventually, but not yet. Jess wasn't ready. She needed to tell Ward about her date with Wendy, though. She picked up the phone and dialed her number.

CHAPTER ELEVEN
FOREIGN BODIES

Ward pulled her car to the side of the road and slapped the steering wheel. She was so overwhelmingly frustrated. Her GPS was useless. Gazing to her right through a break in the trees, she studied the weed-infested trail that led deep into a mature forest. On either side of this grassy lane, trees stood watch, and from the looks of things, they were successful in keeping out stray vehicles. She detected no hint of life or the lake that was supposed to be just off the main road. Glancing first down at her map and then at her car's odometer, she puffed out her cheeks in frustration and leaned her head against the headrest for a moment of peace.

What had started off well had turned into a miserable day. She'd worked the Friday overnight shift in the ER and managed to snag five hours of sleep. When the staff called her at six in the morning to see a patient, she ran into Melvin, the ER security guard, who invited Ward to go fishing on this first day of the season. It seemed like a perfect way to spend the few hours she had off before her night shift, and so she accepted his invitation. He'd drawn a map on a hand towel and told her he'd meet her there later in the day. Ward had been looking forward to the outing until just a few minutes earlier, when her phone rang. Actually, she was fine when it rang, but not so good by the time she disconnected the call from Jess.

Calls from Jess had been scarce in the past months, and Ward was always excited when she saw Jess's smiling face on her phone's screen. She kept hoping Jess would call to tell her she wanted to patch things up or try again. To talk about their relationship. But Jess didn't want to talk about it. She didn't want to talk about anything.

Ward had pressed the green icon to accept the call and promptly made a wrong turn. After a moment of small talk, Jess told her she was planning to start dating again, and Ward's world had been spinning in the wrong direction ever since. After hanging up the phone, Ward realized she was lost, and she'd spent the past thirty minutes trying to find her destination. After driving the same road a half dozen times, the local police pulled her over for speeding, and the officer was ready to ticket her until he realized she was the new ER doc. As happy as she was to be spared the ticket, she was pissed off, too. The news would be all over town by the time she made it back for her night shift. And now, frustration washed over her as she tried to decipher Melvin's map. He'd drawn a line depicting a dirt road "three miles or so" from the last major intersection. Melvin would never make it as a cartographer, that was for sure. Was this grassy lane considered a dirt road? It didn't look like it. But she'd traveled more than four miles from the intersection, doubled back twice, and it was the only road she'd come upon.

Could weeds wrap around car tires and destroy the car's engine? Or its transmission? Or some other important part? She knew little about automobiles, but she didn't think a car, even an SUV like hers, was designed to go down that road. It was meant for Hummers with drug runners hanging from the windows, not for exploration by mild-mannered physicians. She put her car in drive and forged ahead anyway.

Ward was tossed around in her seat until she slowed her car to a crawl. Thank God for four-wheel-drive, she thought as the wheels struggled for traction. Beneath all the grassy cover, the ground was wet. And scarring trees on both sides of the road, every hundred yards or so, Ward read signs. KEEP OUT. TURN BACK. NO TRESPASSING. PRIVATE PROPERTY. GUARD DOG ON DUTY. NO HUNTING. NO FISHING. NO TIMBERING. They were all hand painted in white, on planks of wood that had been nailed at odd angles. Ward shook her head. The way her day was going, some mountain man with a gun was likely to pop up in the road and shoot her.

After a bumpy mile, she saw the mirrored surface of the lake glistening through the trees. She didn't see any place to pull over and room for only one car along this thoroughfare. How was she going to turn around to get out? Backing up that distance wouldn't be much fun, and she didn't think she could make a K turn on the narrow road. Maybe she'd just keep driving forward until she ran out of gas, or into a tree, or a ravine, or found some other good excuse for calling AAA. And then, when she called them, she'd have no idea how to tell them where the hell she was, because Melvin's map sucked.

Stopping the car, she took another moment to lean against the headrest, and before she knew they were coming, tears were flowing freely down her cheeks, her chest heaving in great sobs that shook her body. What the fuck had happened to her life? A year before she was a successful emergency physician with a cushy job at a teaching hospital. She guided young residents, taught them the skills they needed to save lives, hobnobbed with learned colleagues and administrators at committee meetings. She was paid well to do it! And at the end of her days, she went home to a beautiful woman who loved her.

When that beautiful woman asked her to give up her career—or at least to put it on hold, Ward hadn't hesitated. Because, truthfully, she wasn't that ambitious. She had a good many commas after her name, but when Jess had asked her to sacrifice them for a year in Garden, working as a staff physician, she did it, not because of her own ambitions, but because of her feelings for Jess. Jess was what mattered most, not her career. Lately Ward had started to wonder if she'd somehow failed to let Jess know that, to tell her not only how much she was loved, but respected and appreciated.

Now it was too late, anyway. Jess was almost unapproachable, and it seemed ridiculous to speak of those things now. Ward thought herself pathetic. She'd spent the past months begging for attention from a woman who no longer wanted her, a woman who'd moved on and was now dating the local coroner. It had been bad enough to know she'd gone to a Valentine's dinner with Emory, but deep inside, Ward knew he wasn't a threat. Sure, it bothered her that the woman she loved was going out with a man, but if she needed to try dating a man, then Ward had to give her that freedom. Jess was gay and no man stood a chance.

The coroner, though, was a different story. The coroner was a sexy little dyke and just Jess's type. If Jess wanted to date her, it meant only one thing. She didn't love Ward anymore. She'd never said it—in fact, she'd reassured Ward of her love dozens of times in the past months. She'd used the words confused and scared and drifting and sad, but she'd also told Ward she still loved her. How could she date another woman if that was true?

It was all so strange. Jess was once the most decisive person Ward knew. She didn't ask, she demanded. She knew what she wanted—whether it was a specific medication for a patient, or a vacation destination, or a date with Ward. Ward always thought Jess was the perfect complement for her. She tended to be quieter and to let others make plans about restaurants and travel and other nonsense. She had enough responsibility at work, so why stress about the trivialities? She let Jess make those decisions, and manage their money, and organize their lives. It made them both happy. It had, anyway. Neither of them was happy now. And this Jess who didn't know what she wanted was a little scary. Ward didn't know how to deal with her.

"Arrgh!" Ward yelled, then opened her eyes. The sun was shining, and in spite of her personal emotional storms, the day was beautiful. The lake was visible through the trees, and the image was picturesque. Perfect. Taking a few deep breaths, she hummed a few exhalations and put herself into a kinder, gentler reality. A few minutes of meditation did the trick. Ward wiped her tears and vowed to enjoy her afternoon in the woods.

Should she wait for Melvin or begin without him? Deciding she needed a distraction, she hopped out of her car.

Jeans and sneakers were the attire of the day, and in spite of the bright skies, Ward needed them. Here, in the shade, it wasn't going to reach the seventy degrees the forecasters had promised. Her Phillies sweatshirt would probably not come off, and she'd brought a windbreaker, too. Just in case.

At the back of the car she pulled out her tackle box and her official fishing hat. Her license was attached, just as Zeke had taught her years before. The little box containing her portable fishing pole—another gift from Zeke—fit easily in her other hand. After stashing her valuables in the cargo bay, Ward closed the hatch and locked the car, then picked her way through branches and brush to the side of the lake.

Once in the clearing, Ward took a moment to just look. To listen. To smell. In thirty seconds her troubles were forgotten as she saw a bird—she had no idea what kind—swoop down toward the shimmering surface of the lake, then pull up, gliding back around and disappearing into the trees. All around the lake sentinel trees watched, their arms branching over the water, the lowest limbs flirting with its surface. To her left a patch of blueberry bushes hugged the shoreline, and beyond them, lily pads littered the lake's surface. Ward tended to measure everything in golf terms, and the lake was big. Wider across than two par fives, perhaps a thousand yards. She couldn't determine its length from where she stood— it disappeared around a bend to the right, five hundred yards from where she stood.

She was impressed that such a large body of water remained undeveloped, but Melvin had told her his family had owned it since they settled here in the mountains two hundred years earlier. The family vowed to keep the land whole, and Ward suddenly felt privileged for her invitation. She thought of Towering Pines and how wise Jess's grandfather and his friends had been to preserve that area for this generation.

She stood gazing, her arms resting on a low-hanging tree branch, relaxing for the first time in days. This had been a good idea, the fishing. She only threw her catches back, but it wasn't about hooking the fish. It was about the tranquility of the woods and the beauty of a silver-topped lake.

A ratchety-clicking noise, one she'd heard many times in the mountains, caused Ward to freeze. She'd been just about to bend down and begin assembling her rod, but instead she raised her hands in the air and turned slowly toward the sound.

The shotgun was expected. That ratcheting noise was unmistakable. But it was the woman holding the gun that stunned her. She was tall, with leathery skin battered by the sun and a shock of white hair. Intense blue eyes peeked out from behind prescription eyeglasses. She wore a loose, button-up work shirt, jeans, and fishing waders. A fishing hat dangled on its cord behind her head. Ward guessed she was in her seventies, but the gun she had pointed at Ward made her seem much younger.

"You speak English?" the woman demanded.

Ward couldn't find her voice. What the fuck?

"*Habla spanol?*"

Ward shook her head.

"Oh, Christ Jesus! *Spreken dutch?*"

Ward didn't move.

"*Per lay voo friend chase?*"

Ward cleared her throat, looked at her shaking hands, and willed them to stop. "I speak English," she said at last.

"Well, can't you read it? There are twenty-five signs posted along that road, missy, and all of them say 'stay out.'"

"I…I…I'm a friend of the owner. He's supposed to meet me here."

The woman cocked her head and looked at Ward through squinty eyes. "What owner? Who the hell are you?" she asked, turning her head but keeping the gun trained on Ward.

"My name is Ward Thrasher. I have my driver's license in the car, over there." Ward gestured with her head. "I'm supposed to meet Melvin here."

At the mention of that name, the woman looked heavenward and then shook her head. More importantly, she lowered the gun. "Why the hell does that old bugger do this to me? Can't he just pick up the telephone and call? Tell me he's sending a guest over?"

Why does he do this to *her*? You should be me, Ward thought. "I don't know. Sorry," Ward said, her vocal cords more relaxed now that she wasn't in the crosshairs.

The woman approached and held out her hand. She shook Ward's enthusiastically, as if she hadn't been aiming to shoot her a few seconds earlier. "I'm Frieda Henderfield. Melvin's sister. It's nice to meet you, Dr. Thrasher. I've heard good things about you. All the town says you're doin' a good job over at the hospital, so it's a pleasure to welcome you to my lake."

It didn't surprise Ward that Frieda knew her. Not anymore. Having a new doctor in town was kind of like having a celebrity. Someone special, and even with a shotgun in her hand, Frieda managed to make Ward feel welcome. "Thanks. Those are kind words."

"So you fish, do you?"

"A little," Ward confessed.

"Well then, follow me. You're not going to catch much over here."

Frieda bent and picked up Ward's equipment. All of it. Then she turned and began walking, pushing aside low branches and high bushes as she wove her way silently along the bank of the lake. Ward had no choice but to follow. A fleeting thought caused her to pause—will they ever find my body if I follow this woman deeper into the woods?—but she pushed it aside and decided it didn't matter. Her day couldn't get much worse.

There was no way for her to tell how far they'd walked when they reached their destination. They'd turned toward a mountain and climbed a bit, through densely packed trees and across a shallow stream, then headed back toward the lake and into the woods again before coming to the clearing where Frieda finally stopped. The vegetation had given up, and bare soil and rocks covered the ground here, at the edge of a quiet cove lined by more blueberry bushes and fallen trees.

Frieda sat on an old, overturned wooden crate and motioned toward a rowboat pulled into the woods. "Sit in there, if you want."

Opting for a socially appropriate response, Ward retrieved a crate for herself and positioned it a few feet from her hostess. "Will Melvin find us here? I figured he'd look for me near my car," Ward asked.

"I'll bet you a bottle of beer he's fast asleep by now."

Ward raised an eyebrow. "You mean I've been stood up?"

"Don't take it personally. He's older than he looks, and he needs his nap or he gets cranky."

Frieda nodded toward the crate as Ward sat. "I'm sorry, I've forgotten my manners. I should have gotten that for you. Can I give you a hand with your rod?" Frieda asked.

Shaking her head, Ward declined the offer. It was the little rituals of fishing, like assembling her rod, that made Ward like the sport so much. They shared bait but not much conversation as they pulled in fish after fish over the course of a few hours. Ward landed a few sunnies and trout, and one impressive bass. Of course, since Ward was releasing her fish back into the lake, she might have just caught the same fish over and over.

As Frieda had predicted, Melvin was a no-show.

When Frieda's bucket was full, she stood and locked her hook into the line to prevent it from snagging, and announced the end of the day. "You hungry?" she asked Ward.

Ward nodded. The peanut-butter sandwich she'd had for breakfast had worn off, and she'd left her lunch in the SUV, miles and miles away. "Come back to my place. I'll fry up one of these fish and teach you why you shouldn't throw 'em all back."

"What about my car?" she asked.

"I'll drop you off, and you can follow me home."

Ward was stunned that they were only a hundred yards from another dirt road, and she put her gear in the back and hopped into the front of Frieda's pickup. In seconds they were back on the main road and then on the grassy lane that led to her car. She hopped out of Frieda's truck and into her car and drove forward, and when the road curved around the next bend, it widened enough for Frieda to take the lead. After a few more turns, the trees cleared and plowed fields dominated the landscape, until a large barn and a silo took over. Beyond that, a classic farmhouse came into view, white and wooden with a stone foundation that matched the chimney that ran along the side from the ground, erupting through the roof as if trying to touch the clear blue sky. A chocolate Lab greeted Frieda's truck and followed the vehicles the length of the driveway.

She showed appropriate stranger anxiety, barking and jumping in the direction of Ward's car, until Frieda told Ward it was safe to exit the vehicle. Ward offered a hand, and after a few sniffs, the dog lost interest and went back to her owner for kisses.

Frieda held the door with one hand and her fish with the other, and Ward walked through a large sun porch into an equally spacious kitchen. With nimble fingers, Frieda filleted the fish and discarded the waste into a plastic bag, which she double tied, and then proceeded to batter and fry them as they talked.

"This house was built around 1810, when my great-grandfather came here from Scotland." Her ancestors had been farming the land for generations, until this one. Small farms, she explained, were expensive to run. She kept a large garden, and someone leased the land, but the majority of it sat unused.

Ward wandered the kitchen as they talked, looking at the variety of art and pictures hanging on the plank walls. Frieda identified a man in uniform as her father. He'd landed on Normandy Beach in 1944 and managed to survive. Beside his picture was the framed flag that had adorned his casket and the pocket bible that had saved his life by stopping the bullet still lodged in its pages. A picture of a younger Melvin, also in uniform, hung a few boards down. And then there was Frieda, with dark hair and no wrinkles, squinting in the sunshine beside a lovely young woman, fair and thin and carrying about two feet of hair teased straight up on her head. Ward laughed. She'd seen many such pictures of her grandmother and great-aunts, but they were usually buried in photo books and not displayed proudly on the walls. "Who's the girl with the bouffant do?" she asked.

Frieda didn't need to turn from the stove. "That's Ursula."

"Who's Ursula?"

"My friend. Okay, this is ready. Can you pour the lemonade?"

The trout Frieda cooked was delicious, served with a lemony butter glaze that surely neutralized any health benefit the fish otherwise might have had, but Ward didn't mind. Perhaps she'd start keeping a fish or two, if she could make it taste as good as Frieda did. She'd watched closely, and she was sure she could duplicate her success.

While they ate the fish and sautéed asparagus, an early gift from the garden, they talked. Frieda told Ward about the house, the work to modernize it and keep it up. She'd been forced to sell some land a few years earlier, to pay her taxes, and she might have to again.

"Do you work?" Ward asked. "Other than on the farm?"

Frieda laughed. "I've had so many jobs in my life, I probably can't remember them all. I've done whatever I had to do to pay the bills, take a vacation, put the kids through college."

"You have kids?" Ward tried to keep the surprise from her voice. Frieda had pinged her gaydar. Of course, in the mountains, it was sometimes difficult to distinguish the lesbians from the farmers. And, of course, there were still quite a few women who'd married before figuring it all out, and their children dotted the landscape like palm trees along a tropical beach.

"I used to. Two of them."

Before Ward could ask for clarification, a knock on the door interrupted their banter, and as she looked, she saw a man of fifty approaching. He was sharply dressed in a golf shirt and linen slacks, and his carriage and dress suggested to Ward that he wasn't a local.

"Come in, Joe," Frieda instructed him, when she saw him hesitate. Most likely because of her, Ward thought, because he seemed familiar with the place.

"Joe Harding," he said as he extended his hand to Ward and introductions were made. Joe was a local, once upon a time. He'd left home for college never to return and found himself back on the family farm to arrange for its sale after the death of his father.

"How'd the auction go?" Frieda asked.

"That's why I stopped over, Ms. Henderfield. It sold. I don't imagine I'll be coming back here, so I wanted to thank you for your kindness to my father over the years."

Frieda squinted, then cleared her throat. "He was my friend, Joe. One of the best I've ever had. I'll miss him. It was no trouble to look out for him. That's what neighbors do."

He nodded, and a blush crept from the collar at his neck to his ears. "Well, I'm grateful. If you should ever find yourself in Seattle, Washington, please look for me. I'll buy you a real cup of coffee."

Frieda laughed, and Ward suspected she'd missed a friendly joke. As they watched his retreating form grow smaller in the distance, Frieda spoke softly. "Did you hear about Joe, Sr.?"

"What?" Ward asked, confused.

"His father, Joe, Sr. Did you hear about him over at the hospital?"

Ward shook her head. "Did he work there?"

Frieda frowned. "No. He died there."

Before Ward could get more information, they were interrupted again, this time from the other direction. A whining, fragile voice was calling out Frieda's name from somewhere in the recesses of the house. Frieda seemed to ignore it, but the voice continued to call, growing louder as her footsteps signaled she was getting close. "Damn you!" Ward heard from just behind her a moment later.

Ward turned her head slightly to the woman standing there, a thinner, older version of Frieda. Her posture was stooped and her frame thin, and she looked fragile, until she spoke.

"Frieda, I don't want your women in this house!" she shouted.

Frieda was undaunted and continued eating. "This isn't one of my women, Mom. She's the doctor over at the hospital."

"I don't care if she's a preacher of the Lord! That sort of nonsense will not be tolerated."

"Mom, she's a friend of Melvin's. She came over to fish at the lake."

"So, she's not a lesbian, then?"

"Well, I can't say. I didn't ask."

Frieda's mom took a few steps toward Ward, pushing the walker as she went. "You a lesbian?" she demanded.

Ward sat straight and faced her accuser. She had never denied her sexuality, but looking at the combative old woman Ward found no point in confronting her. And the truth would likely cause problems for her new friend Frieda. Still, the traitorous words wouldn't come. She opted for a neutral response and hoped she wouldn't notice. "Your daughter's honor is safe with me, Mrs. Henderfield."

The woman's face broke into a wide, toothless grin. "Frieda, find me my dentures. It's not often I have a doctor in my kitchen!"

After Frieda located her mother's teeth and served her lunch, they were treated to a history of medicine in their town. And it truly was a treat. Irene Henderfield was less than a year away from celebrating her centennial, and she remembered most of those hundred years. Her tales included home childbirth (in the very kitchen in which they sat), setting broken bones, and fixing plasters from the herbs in the garden. Irene treated everything from an abscess to pain with balms and rubs she mixed right here in her kitchen.

"Do you sell any of this stuff?"

"Why would I sell it?" Irene asked.

"To help people," Ward suggested.

"Any of them that wants help, just send 'em over. I'll fix 'em up."

Ward couldn't help chuckling at that one, and most of the things Irene commented on. It seemed she had an opinion about everything and wasn't afraid to share it. By the time Frieda walked her to the car, Ward's stomach hurt from laughing. She felt wonderful.

"Well, Doc, let me say that you're welcome anytime. I promise not to greet you with a shotgun."

"I'd appreciate that. And thanks for the lunch, and the fishing, and the entertainment."

Frieda nodded. "My pleasure."

"I'm going to try my luck over at Lake Nuangola tomorrow," Ward said, "but maybe we can get together later in the week." Jeannie and Sandy were visiting for the weekend, and when she finished her shift this night Ward was making the drive to the other side of the mountains. She planned to spend her days off there, relaxing on the deck with a good book and hitting some golf balls at one of the local courses.

"Ah, I know that lake. Nice golf course right down the road."

Ward's pulse pumped. The weather hadn't been conducive to hitting golf balls. Even when the sun was out and the temperature up, the ground was so wet even the driving ranges were closed. In the next few days, though, the forecast was promising.

"You golf?" Ward asked.

"Anthracite Cup champion ten times." She pointed to her chest.

"Wow. I'm not sure I'm qualified to play with you, but if you don't mind a hacker, you're welcome to join me Monday or Tuesday. I'm planning to play both days. I'd be happy to have a golfing buddy."

"I'd love to!" Frieda said, and she gave Ward her phone number, as well as directions back to the main road. As she drove away, Ward marveled at how the day had turned around. She'd met a friend—an amazing, funny woman, who shared a few of her passions. Two bad Frieda had been born forty years too soon.

Even more impressive, Ward hadn't thought of Jess all day.

CHAPTER TWELVE
GUNSHOT WOUNDS

So, I noticed you didn't answer Irene's question," Frieda said as they waited on the first tee for the group in front of them to play their shots. Three out of four of the men hit their initial offerings into the woods. They all glanced at the women behind them and re-teed. It was going to be a long round, but the sun was shining and the company was good, so Ward didn't complain.

Although Frieda said nothing further, Ward knew what she was referring to. She turned to Frieda, dressed in perfectly creased khaki pants and a dark-blue golf shirt, and studied her for a moment. The decision was an easy one. Frieda's mother had already outed her, and even if she hadn't, Ward felt comfortable enough with her to share her sexuality. "I don't like to lie. But I thought the truth would ruin lunch," she explained.

"Aah. Probably a wise decision."

Ward shrugged. "Sadly, sometimes secrets are best."

"So is that why you're in the mountains? A woman?"

Ward had been having such a wonderful day. Days, really. The fishing and conversation at Frieda's had been lovely. Her ER shift was surprisingly uneventful for a Saturday night, and she drove directly to Jeannie's from the ER, in time for breakfast with the entire Bennett clan on Sunday morning. They'd all ventured to a local flea market and hunted for treasures. Before heading back to Philly, they'd barbequed ribs and chicken and enjoyed a feast. Ward had spent Monday morning foraging for essentials like shampoo and Jax and chocolate-chip cookies at the Wilkes-Barre stores, and she'd had time to hit a bucket of balls on the range before their round of golf began. It was a happy forty-eight hours, spent entirely Jessica-free, and she cringed for a second at Frieda's question.

Then she let out the breath she'd held and realized she didn't feel as awful as she had a few days earlier. "My ex is here. In the mountains."

"Yeah, so?" Frieda asked. "Why are you here?"

Ward shook her head and looked to the sky, cloudless on this April day. The temperature was near seventy and the conditions were perfect for golf—no wind, bright skies, and zero-percent chance of precipitation. The only cloud hanging over her was Jess, but that really did seem to be breaking up.

"I followed her. I thought we'd be able to patch things up."

"And?"

"She's dating someone else now."

Frieda patted her leg. "She doesn't deserve you."

For the first time in many months, Ward tended to agree. She didn't say it, though. The tee box had cleared and Ward advanced the cart to the second box, then got out and began to stretch. She was loose after the bucket of balls she'd hit, but they'd sat for fifteen minutes waiting for the men in front of them to clear out. "Show me the way," she told Frieda.

Frieda hadn't hit any balls on the range. She'd barely stretched a muscle. And she unceremoniously hit her drive nearly two hundred yards down the middle of the fairway. There was no preamble of lining up the ball or taking a practice swing. She just placed it on the tee and whacked it.

"Wow," Ward commented. "I think I'm glad we're not playing for money."

"Oh, come on, Doc. How about a dollar a hole?"

Ward nodded. She did like to gamble, and it would make the round more interesting. "Okay. I can afford to lose eighteen bucks."

"C'mon! Where's your confidence? You'll never win with that kind of attitude."

"I'm just trying to scam you. I'm really a pro. How's five bucks a hole sound?"

Frieda chuckled. "Just hit the ball."

Ward nodded and then began her pre-shot routine. She adjusted her visor, then her glove. She eyed the fairway before planting her tee in just the right spot. Then she pushed it in a bit farther, placed a brand-new, shiny white ball atop it, and then checked the alignment from the back of the box. After several practice swings, she addressed the ball, carefully began her backswing, and hit a long drive deep into the forest along the right side of the fairway. "Fuck!" she murmured.

White stakes lining the out-of-bounds area meant she had to hit her next shot from the tee box. After switching clubs, she did, and her ball safely landed on the fairway thirty yards behind Frieda's. "What club did you hit?" Ward asked when she saw Frieda's tee shot so much farther than hers.

"A three wood. How about you?"

"Driver."

"These woods are unforgiving, Doc. You should leave your driver in the bag."

Ward couldn't help whining. "But I hit it so well on the range."

Frieda laughed. "That's why I don't go to the range. I don't want to waste all the good shots there."

The green cleared, and they both hit off target but managed to finish the hole without losing another ball. Ward took Frieda's advice and played sans driver, and she managed to avoid the woods for most of the round. They snuck past the foursome of men at the turn and sailed through the back nine. When they added up their scores, Ward ended up paying Frieda three dollars in winnings.

"You're not so bad, Doc," Frieda said as she took the money Ward offered. "But we're going to have to up the stakes. This won't even pay for my gas."

"You're three hundred years old, Frieda. I should be able to split with you, don't you think? Instead, I'm paying you three bucks. I think I need more practice before I up the stakes."

"Don't they pay you at the hospital?" Frieda deadpanned.

Ward shook her head. It had been a delightful day, and she didn't want it to end. It wasn't quite dinnertime, but she decided to extend the offer. "They do. How about I use the other fifteen bucks I had set aside to buy you dinner?"

They enjoyed juicy burgers and fries in the clubhouse, and then Ward invited Frieda over for a beer when they were done.

The view of the lake from Jeannie's deck was spectacular, but after the sun settled behind the mountains, it was too cold to sit out. They walked down a level, where a stone fire pit stood in the middle of the patio. Wrapped in sweatshirts, they sat beside the fire and talked, foregoing the beer for hot tea and cookies.

"Tell me about Ursula," Ward suggested.

She could see Frieda's expression change, but Ward couldn't name the emotion Frieda hid behind it. She ate a cookie and swallowed some tea before answering. "She's dead. Heart attack, right on the kitchen floor."

"Oh, Frieda. That's awful. When?"

"Ten years or so."

"How long were you together?"

"A long time. We met in junior high."

That was impressive. "So you started dating then? What was that like?" Ward estimated Frieda was in her seventies. Junior high for her had to be in the 1950s. Not exactly a good time to come out.

"No, not then. We both knew we felt something, but there was no *Modern Family* then. We had no idea what it was, or what to do about it. So, our senior year, she got engaged and married right after graduation."

"Oh, no. What did you do?"

"I joined the service. The navy. And I went off to Washington, D.C. and figured out what it was all about."

"So what happened to Ursula?"

"She stayed here. Her husband owned a farm, and she worked it a bit, ran the farm stand out by the road, had a baby. All the normal stuff."

"So what happened to you?"

"I was a stewardess." Frieda chuckled and shook her head. "Can you believe that? Me, in a dress and pumps?"

Ward nodded and looked at Frieda in her khakis and plain gray sweatshirt. "That is hard to imagine."

"I'll show you a picture. Anyway, I was the stewardess on Navy One. Did you ever hear of Navy One?"

Ward shook her head no.

"Did you ever hear of Air Force One?"

Ward nodded.

"Navy One was its predecessor."

Ward opened her eyes in wonder. "So you were the stewardess to the president? Of the United States?"

A sweet smile of recollection appeared on Frieda's face, smoothing out the wrinkles and making her look younger. Or perhaps it was the fire casting its red glow. "Yes, ma'am."

"Which president was that?" Ward tried to do the math, tried to remember American history. Obama, homophobic Bush, Clinton, other Bush, Reagan, Carter, Ford, Nixon, Johnson, Kennedy, Eisenhower, Truman.

"Eisenhower," Frieda said.

"Holy shit! What did he drink?"

"Coffee. Gallons and gallons of coffee."

"Oh. My. God! Frieda, that's amazing. So you just flew around with the president?"

"Yeah. That's how I learned to play golf. The crew would have time off at bases when he landed. He'd get escorted off base by limousine, and we'd stay with the plane and kill time. Sometimes for days."

"Wow. How long did you stay in the navy?"

"Oh, a little over three years. Then the pilot decided to land the plane in the Potomac, and that was enough for me. Nothing will cure your love of flying like a plane crash."

"Holy shit! The president's plane crashed? Was anyone hurt?"

"The president wasn't on board, and no one was seriously hurt. But I got off that plane and took the first bus home. I never flew again."

Ward nodded. She also hated to fly, but for other reasons. "So you came home to Ursula?"

Frieda took another chocolate-chip cookie from the container and thought for a moment. "She heard I was home and invited me to lunch. Her son, Mark, was just a toddler. She put him down for his nap, and, well…" Frieda smiled broadly.

"So she left her husband?"

Frieda shook her head. "No, nothing was that easy, Doc. The navy came looking for me, and they hauled me back to Washington. I flunked my psychiatric testing, and they didn't make me get on a plane again, but I did have to stick it out for another year."

"What happened to Ursula?"

"Well, baby number two came along. A girl, Brenda. When I was discharged from the navy, I had no job, no money, and she had two kids to support. She wasn't going to risk losing custody of them or letting them go hungry so she could live with me."

"So she gave you up?"

"No. Hell, no. We snuck around for a year, mostly those long lunches when the kids went for their naps."

"And then she left him?" Ward was eager to know the story. She knew Frieda got the girl, but how? How did it work fifty years ago?

"No. I killed him."

Ward leaned forward in her chair, grateful her mug of tea was nearly empty. "What?"

"I killed him."

Ward remembered the shotgun at the lake and realized just how little she knew about Frieda. "Holy shit, Frieda. Did you go to jail?"

"Nah. He shot first. Fortunately, my aim was better."

"Are you making this up?" Ward asked, meeting her gaze. It was hard to believe.

"No, Doc, I'm not. He came home, caught us in the act, and pointed a gun at me. I jumped out the window, ran across the porch roof, and jumped into the flowerbed below. On my way to my truck, he hit me in the shoulder. I knew if I stopped running, I was dead. I got the door open, somehow pulled my shotgun off the rack behind the seat, and managed to hold it with my left arm. My right was hanging, useless. I felt faint, from pain or blood loss, who knows? But the adrenaline kept me alive. Fear. I didn't want to die. Not naked in Ursula's driveway, anyway."

"And you managed to shoot him? And kill him?"

"Yeah, I did. He kept coming toward me, pointing his rifle at me, not aiming it—walking carefully, conscious of the ruts in the dirt drive. I rested the gun across the hood of my truck, aimed it at his chest. When he stopped, I told him to put his gun down. When he sighted it, I pulled the trigger. Hit him in the heart. He never got his shot off, other than that first one that hit my shoulder."

"Wow."

"So Ursula got the farm, and I moved in with her and helped her run it. Paid the bills doing photography and running the cutting floor at the underwear factory. Put both kids through college."

"Where are they now?"

Suddenly Ward remembered the question she'd asked about kids when she'd been at Frieda's house. She used to have them. A sense of dread filled her heart.

"Can't say. When their mom died, they kicked me out. Sold the farm out from under me, left me with practically nothing."

Ward didn't know what to say. Were there words of comfort to offer in such a situation?

"Maybe we should have that beer," she said.

CHAPTER THIRTEEN
SNAKE BITES

Ward's car was full as she pulled into the driveway of the house she once shared with Jess. Garden had bloomed in the late spring, and everywhere she looked bright patches of color filled her eyes. This small town showed no evidence of a recession or decay; every property was lovingly maintained, from the paint on the shutters to the fresh mulch in the flowerbeds. It was the end of June and the town was bright and alive, as it had been when they moved here the summer before.

It was a stark contrast to the bleak, freezing day when she'd left. Nearly six months had passed since that horrible day when Ward had awakened to learn she'd assaulted her rival for Jess's affections and her life had changed forever. Back then, she'd never thought she was leaving for good. Jess would come to her senses, Ward thought, and they'd be back together before the snowdrifts on their street had a chance to turn black with mud.

It was hard to believe that had been the end, but after all these months, it was likely they'd never patch things up. That was okay, really. Back then Ward had thought she'd never recover from the loss of Jess, but now as she sat beside their former home, she knew she would. It had taken time, and tears, and a few new friends, but she was beginning to heal. She thought she could see Jess without crying, without begging for another chance. At least she hoped she could, because she didn't want to humiliate herself before Jess yet again. She had to face her though, and she couldn't help wondering what was going on.

Jess had asked her over to talk, calling the night before as Ward was packing for the weekend at Jeannie's house. She'd spent the month of June in the bustling town of Venley, half an hour north of Scranton on Interstate 81. It had been a busy month as she patched up gas workers injured on the job and in drunken brawls. With the explosion of the natural-gas industry in the mountains, the small hospital had tripled its volume nearly overnight and was ill equipped to handle the increase in patient flow. It seemed much like the inner city, with men of every race and religion, speaking several languages, all demanding instant attention. Thankfully, June was behind her. Only one more month until her contractual obligation with the locum tenens company was fulfilled, and then she could enjoy some R&R. She'd head back to Philly and her former life. Or was it her future life? She didn't know what to think, but somewhere in the mountains she had found herself again, and she knew she'd be okay.

In the meantime, she had four days off before she began her new assignment. She'd turned down an offer of golf from Frieda and the unbelievable opportunity to visit a rattlesnake roundup in Noxen in favor of a few days of rest. She planned to spend her time relaxing on the deck with a good book. If Jess hadn't called, she'd already be there, but she'd waited so they could talk. She'd been waiting six months to talk, so what the hell did Jess want to talk about now?

Part of her hoped Jess wanted to reconcile, and part of her hoped she wanted to end it once and for all. All of her hoped for an explanation for Jess's strange behavior. She wasn't optimistic on any front.

Jess had been dating Wendy, but that relationship seemed no more fulfilling for Jess than theirs had been. She was still searching and Ward was tired of waiting. She'd done a lot of thinking during the lonely six months she'd spent without Jess, and although her heart was still broken, she no longer looked at her as the angel she once worshipped. Jess had flaws, many of them, and Ward had allowed her to walk all over her in their time together.

Their separation had been no different—Jess had made the decisions, and Ward was forced to live with the consequences. So, if Jess decided it was over, she was ready. If Jess decided she wanted to try again—well, Ward wasn't so sure what to do about that. She wasn't willing to go back to the way things were, and she didn't delude herself into thinking Jess could change. As much as she loved Zeke and Pat, they'd spoiled their only child and created a monster that Ward had been forced to contend with. She wasn't willing to do it anymore. Jess had said she'd changed and used that as the excuse for ending their relationship. Perhaps that was true. But she could never change in the ways Ward needed her to. At least Ward didn't think she could. The sliver of hope alive in her heart that Jess could be the woman Ward wanted and needed was indeed a small one.

Other parts of Ward's brain argued that Jess's call was completely unrelated to their relationship. After all, Jess hadn't hesitated to discuss things on the phone before, little bits of gossip like she was dating the coroner, so why make her come all the way to Garden now if that was the reason for the visit? Perhaps Zeke was in poor health. Considering his behavior, that wouldn't have surprised Ward. Or maybe Jess was sick. That thought gave Ward her own set of physical symptoms. Maybe she needed to ask for a favor. Who knew? If she didn't get out of the car and knock on the door, she'd never find out.

"I thought you were going to sit in the car all morning," Jess said as she stood back to allow Ward into the brightly painted kitchen. Sunlight blazed through the dozens of panes in the tall windows, lighting up the yellow walls. White wooden cabinets, extending from the granite counters to the ten-foot-high ceilings, were original to the hundred-year-old house, and Ward looked at them, and the rest of the kitchen, with a sense of loss. She'd once dreamed of living in this house forever, on the quiet street with the huge yard in the small town where Jess had been born.

Shaking off the sadness, Ward took the proffered seat at the small wooden table but declined the coffee. She'd stopped for breakfast before leaving Venley, and a second cup would only agitate her already friable nerves. "I was just thinking about our move here. It's almost a year."

"Yeah," Jess admitted, but seemed uncomfortable at the subject. Ward didn't have a chance to wonder why.

"I want to stay here, Ward. I love this house and this town. I want to sell the house in Philly and move here."

Ward had known this was a possibility, and Jess spoke softly and with all the care possible under the circumstances, but her words were still a hard blow. She physically felt the force of them push her back in her chair, felt her eyes fill with the tears she swore she would never cry again for Jessica Benson.

Jess said nothing but handed Ward a tissue and poured the unwanted cup of coffee. Her mind was blank as she watched Jess move around their kitchen, the vision broken by a million film clips of their years together. Good years. Mostly good times. But not good enough, she supposed.

"I suppose you mean without me," Ward said, just to clarify. Just to be sure Jess really meant it was over.

Meeting her gaze, Jess answered gently. "Yeah. Without you."

Ward sniffed. "What have you done? About this?"

"I don't understand. What do you mean?"

For some stupid reason, they still shared a bank account, and both of their salaries were directly deposited into it. The mortgage on their Philly house and all their other joint bills came out of that account, and although Ward had access to it, Jess had always managed the money. She could have written a check for a hundred thousand dollars and wiped out the account, drained all of their savings, and Ward wouldn't have known about it. Only her retirement account was protected. Even she couldn't get money out of that without a presidential decree.

"I mean, our money. Have you drained the accounts? Have you sold all of our furniture? What am I looking at here?"

Jess sighed. "I guess I deserve such a malicious accusation, but the answer is no, and no." Then she shook her head. "I don't hate you. This isn't about you. It's about me and my needs. I wrote myself a check for half the money in our joint accounts. I need it for the down payment here. The other half is yours. The bank will need both of our signatures to close the accounts, but it won't matter if there's no money in them. We can take care of that when I come to Philly."

"Oh, okay," Ward said, as if it all made perfect sense, when in fact nothing seemed to make sense anymore. Jess had taken her half of their money! Wow. Ward had never felt so stupid in all of her life, and she was grateful at the moment that Jess had left her anything.

She thought about the house in Philly, their house, and felt a surge of anxiety. What had Jess done with their things?

"What about the house? Did you raid it?"

Jess shook her head and frowned. "I wanted to talk to you before I take anything. Other than a few things I had before we moved in, most of it we bought together. If you're planning to keep the house, you might want to keep the furniture. It all goes so well with the house. "

Ward was stunned. Did she even want the house without Jess? They had purchased it together, lovingly decorated it to make a home, spent much of their time there. It was a great house, twenty-five hundred square feet of wood and stone and glass, with a magnificently landscaped yard ideal for reading on a bench swing beneath a shade tree or cooking out on a summer evening. She might like to keep it. Or she might not. She wasn't sure if she could live there with Jess's ghosts, and at the moment, she was certain Jess would haunt her forever.

Why hadn't she thought about this possibility sooner? She knew it had been heading this way, but Jess's words still shocked her. No matter what she told herself, the truth was, she'd been hoping Jess would want her back, and she would have said yes. Or at least maybe.

Somehow Ward managed to clear the clouds from her mind and find her voice. "I can't deal with the house right now, Jess. I'll think about it. Maybe I might want to buy you out. Can you give me until the end of August to figure out what I want to do?"

Jess nodded understandingly. "Of course, no hurry. As long as we can get it on the market in the next few months, I can afford both mortgages. I'm going to make an offer on this place next week. The owner dropped the price, and I'm afraid it'll get some attention now."

Ward laughed, bitterly. None of this was unexpected, but the reality still stung, as it had on that cold January day when Jess had said very awful things to her and pushed her out of her life. Why did she feel like she was watching a bad reality show? Like this was happening to someone else and not to her? Her life had always been so good, so blessed and wonderful, and now, it just wasn't anymore. And she didn't even think she'd done anything wrong. Suddenly, she lost the composure she'd been fighting to keep together for six months.

"What did I do, Jess? I just don't understand."

Jess stood, walked to the counter, turned, and leaned against it, facing her. "I'm just not happy. You're married to your job as much as to me, and then when you're off, you're always on the go. Skiing, hiking, golfing, tennis, whatever. It's always something. You can't just relax. I want to slow down and enjoy myself, not race through life as if I have to cross a finish line."

Jess's words stung. "Jess, I do all those things with you, or to keep busy when you're working. What would you have me do with my free time, knit? What's your idea of relaxing? Watching television? We're outside, enjoying nature and getting some Vitamin D, for God's sake. And I gave up my career to come here with you, to be with you. How much more married to you could I be? You're what's important."

Jess looked angered by Ward's comments, but she held her tongue. "Like I said, Ward—it's me."

"Is there someone else? Is it serious with Wendy?"

"I don't know. And I'm not in a hurry to find out. I'm just going to take things as they come and try to be happy. But I need to move on the house, because this one won't stay on the market long."

"Well, I don't want you to miss your golden opportunity, Jess." She jumped up

Jess met her, grabbing her arm as she turned to leave. "Ward, stop! Don't do this."

"Don't do what?" Jess had already done it all.

"Don't leave mad. Can't we be friends? After all we've been through together, can't we still be friends?"

Ward shook her head. "No, Jess, we can't," and she didn't look back as she walked through the door. Nor did she bother to close it behind her.

Ward drove without really seeing the roads, not fast, for she wasn't in a hurry. Where did she have to get to, anyway? Only Jeannie's empty lake house awaited her. Before she knew where she was going, Ward found herself on the newly familiar roads leading to Frieda's house. As she pulled into the long gravel drive, she drew Hershey's attention, and the Lab came racing toward the car. Frieda followed at a more leisurely pace.

Hershey jumped at the car door, nearly preventing Ward from opening it, but backed down at Frieda's command. Still, when Ward stepped out of the car, she danced excitedly until her master told her she could pounce, at which point she bathed Ward in kisses. In an instant, if only for a little while, she forgot all her troubles as she felt the dog's love.

"Yes, I missed you, too," she said as she scratched the fur behind Hershey's ears.

"This is a pleasant surprise," Frieda said as she snuck around her dog to steal a hug.

"Yeah, for me too. I didn't really know where I was going, and somehow, I ended up here."

Frieda laughed. "I guess you're worse off than I thought. But don't fret—you're in good hands. I'm going to take you out golfin', and then we're going to play the ponies and win some money." Frieda rubbed her hands together enthusiastically as a wicked grin spread from ear to ear.

Ward debated for a nanosecond. What did she look forward to today? Nothing. Perhaps that's why she'd come here. Frieda's friendship had been a bright orb of sunshine in her dark world, and right now, Ward surely needed that. Another idea came to her, though. "Did you ever go to the rattlesnake roundup?" she asked.

Frieda puckered her lips in concentration. "Over in Noxen?"

"Yeah, that's the place. One of the nurses I know invited me, and I have to tell you I'm very curious."

"Well, it's been years since I've been there, but if they still have a beer tent, I'm willing."

After depositing Hershey in the kitchen with Irene, Ward sent a text message to Erin, and then she and Frieda headed to the golf course. Frieda called ahead and made a tee time, and they were paired with a father and son who were blessedly clean-mouthed and competent on the course. It took until the third hole for Frieda to begin interrogating Ward.

"So what's the story?" she asked.

Ward was enjoying the day, the bright sky and the chatter of birds. The scent of freshly mowed grass and evergreen filled her nostrils. Her mind had buried its burdens, and it took a second to divine the meaning of Frieda's question.

Sucking in air through her bottom teeth, she made a bizarre whistling sound. Then she spoke. "Jess ended our relationship."

Frieda squinted. "I thought she already did."

Ward shrugged. Was it obvious to everyone but her that it had ended back then? Rosa, Jeannie, and now Frieda all seemed to think so. "I guess she did, Free. I took this time to work in the mountains because I hoped she'd change her mind, but you're right. It was already over."

"What now?" she asked as they pulled up to the place on the fairway where their tee shots had come to rest. She seemed to be taking her frustrations out on the golf ball and had bested Frieda by a dozen yards.

"I have the weekend off, and then I start in Factoryville on the second. It's my last month working in the mountains. Then, vacation for the month of August, but I guess I'll use that to pack. Or house hunt. Or maybe I'll just stay at the beach and let Jess take care of it. I don't know yet. All I know now is that on September one, I'll be back in Philly, at my old job, and start putting the pieces of my life back together."

Frieda stood waiting while she listened, and when the men in their group finished hitting, she used an iron to put the ball on the green. "Slow down, baby. Slow down!" she cried to her ball as it hit hard and rolled toward the back, threatening to find the edge and disappear into the rough. "Yes!" she said when it stopped on the flat surface, a few yards from the pin.

"Nice shot," Ward said. They drove to her ball, a few yards ahead, and she chose a club. Miraculously, she'd managed to clear her head enough to hit nice shots and make par on the first two holes. She lined up her shot, positioned her feet, and took her practice swings with an eerie calm. Her life was disintegrating, but she was focusing on golf. It felt good. Her seven-iron shot landed short and ran up toward the pin.

"Oooh, baby!" Frieda exclaimed. "I think that's close."

The men applauded as well. "That's a gimme," the father said as they drove up to the green. Sure enough, Ward's ball was inches right and just a foot short of the hole.

Fourteen more holes went much the same as the first three, and Ward, who was a very enthusiastic but not necessarily talented golfer, stood on the last tee box looking down the fairway toward a record score. She'd never broken eighty. Hell, sometimes, she didn't even break ninety. But all she needed was a five on a rather short par four, and she'd have the first seventy-nine of her career.

A driver off the tee left her less than a hundred yards from the pin. It wasn't a difficult shot, but the trampled grass near the trees on the right of the green told what a challenge this one could be. Not for her, though. Not today. Her pitching wedge landed softly and stopped, and her two putts gave her another par and a seventy-eight. Also a hug from Frieda and the offer of a beer in the bar from the father and son they'd played with.

As they walked to their cars after their drink—Ward chose water—Frieda put an arm around her and pulled her a little closer. "See, all you needed was to shake the albatross from your neck and your talents emerged."

"I was just lucky."

"Maybe we should go watch the ponies instead of the snakes."

"You really are a gambler, aren't you?"

Frieda shrugged. "I'm just hoping to win back all the money I lost to you on the golf course today."

They continued to talk in Frieda's truck on the way to Noxen.

"Have you thought of staying here?" Frieda asked.

Ward shook her head. "No. Not without Jess. She's the reason I came here."

"But you love it here. At least I think you do. You seem to enjoy the things they don't have in the big city—like trees and golf and kayaking."

Ward hesitated to point out that she could find all of those things without much of a drive from her house in Wayne. The truth was more complicated than that. But Frieda was right. She did like it in the mountains. Maybe someday she'd find a place here, someday when thoughts of Jessica Benson were no longer painful. For the moment, though, she was looking forward to the rattlesnake roundup.

The line of cars, SUVs, and pickups wound through the town of Noxen, and it took them twenty minutes to reach the back of the field where they were directed to park. It was a long hike back to the festival, and they were parched when they finally made it through the crowd of children at the bounce house and the teenagers playing carnival games. Erin accosted them at the gate of the fenced-in area where the kegs were set up.

Ward had been very cautious about her alcohol intake in the months since the incident at George's bar. That night still haunted her, and it scared her to think she could drink so much that she'd become violent and suffer a blackout. On top of that, Jess had outright accused her of being an alcoholic. She didn't think she was, but she wasn't so foolish as to ignore something as significant as the night she'd nearly killed Emory. She'd listened to Jess's criticisms and examined her life completely after their split. She admitted she enjoyed a cocktail in the evenings, especially after a difficult day at work. But she wasn't a drunk, and she wasn't abusing alcohol, no matter what Jess said and despite the fact that she'd nearly killed a man in a drunken rage. She hadn't had a drink since the day she'd left Garden in January, but now perhaps it was finally okay to enjoy one again. A few beers with her friends would be harmless, a way to relax on a beautiful summer's night, and besides, now that it was officially over, she didn't really care what Jess said about her drinking.

After they all hugged, Ward and Frieda followed Erin to a corner where a group of women had gathered. Ward recognized

Erin's new girlfriend, but the other five faces were unfamiliar. Each of them, though, was young, like Erin, and suddenly Ward felt very old.

She might just drown in the dating pool. She was thirty-five years old and could hardly remember the blur her life had been at their age. She'd been in medical school then, spending her days in class and her nights in the library—studying, learning, achieving. From medical school until Jess, she'd dated only women her own age—classmates in school and residency. Their lives revolved around work, and they talked shop and managed to squeeze in sex between shifts in the ER and night call in the ICU. What did people even do on dates?

In spite of the age gap, the crowd warmly welcomed her and Frieda. They were all members of Erin's softball team, and most of them were teachers, off for the summer and looking forward to the championship games when softball would end and their real vacations would begin.

"So where are these infamous snakes?" Ward asked after she'd adequately quenched her thirst. It had been only one beer, and she really didn't need another. She didn't want one, either. Fuck Jess. She was not an alcoholic.

"C'mon. I'll introduce you," Erin offered.

Frieda declined the invitation, but Ward eagerly followed Erin to a clearing beneath a huge maple tree. A small grandstand seating area stood in front of her, and Ward couldn't help smiling as she looked around. On the perimeter, burgers and hot dogs were being served from a counter on the right. Behind her, she spotted halushki and potato pancakes. In the middle, dozens of poisonous snakes slithered around the grass of a twenty-by-twenty-foot snake pit enclosed with a fence made of fine mesh. Men, women and children gathered at the edge, chowing on their picnic food as they ogled the snakes and listened to the game commissioner discuss their merits.

A particularly fierce-looking rattler in the dark phase (whatever that meant) was paraded around the pit, the upper half of his body stuffed into a clear plastic tube that resembled a narrow sewer pipe. The handler held the tube with one hand while the other secured the lower half of the snake's body. He shook the snake, and the telltale rattling sound echoed around the pit, to the delight of the rather large crowd gathered to gawk at the captives. Even Ward smiled, but she tried to hide her expression by lowering her head. She detected movement and jumped back as a four-foot-long black snake slithered to the fence in front of her.

"Holy shit!" she said, laughing, and Erin caught her.

Ward breathed deeply at the contact of Erin's strong arms, and for just a moment she was tempted to sink into Erin's embrace. From the moment they met she'd felt a chemistry between them. It had been sour for the first few hours, but after that, their relationship had been friendly and fun and supportive. Erin was obviously interested, and if Ward was honest with herself, she was too, on some level. Erin was smart, and capable, and cute. But she was too young, and the attraction would soon fade. Then they'd be left with nothing. So Ward shook the temptation from her brain and steadied her legs, easing herself up and subtly shifting away from Erin.

They both laughed. "You're not afraid of snakes, are you, Doc?"

"Petrified," she confessed. "But I'm determined to conquer all my fears before I die. Do you think they'll let me touch it," she asked, then quickly added, "while its head is in that tube thingy?"

"I don't think so. But if you want, I'll catch one for you and you can have all the fun you want."

Ward turned to her, incredulous. "No way! You catch snakes?"

"Sure. There's tons of 'em in the woods."

"I think I'm going to faint," Ward proclaimed. "Most of my tee shots end up in the woods."

Erin responded with a hand on Ward's back, and suddenly Ward thought better of the plan she'd had to tell Erin about her breakup with Jess. Her touch felt too good, and Ward thought she'd better put up some walls rather than tear any more down.

"Erin!"

A booming voice from behind startled them, and they turned simultaneously in that direction. Ward noticed the smile on Erin's face before she saw the cause—a tall, dark, and handsome woman wearing a paramedic's uniform. Her dark eyes were keen and penetrating. She was older than Erin, probably older than Ward, too, but looked neat and fit and impressive. And vaguely familiar. Had they met?

The other two shared a quick hug, and Ward caught the newcomer checking her out even while her arms were wrapped around Erin. Before Erin could introduce her, the woman stood back and blatantly studied Ward. "If it isn't the rent-a-doc. You look good with clothes on."

Erin howled, and Ward held out her hand in introduction. "Ward Thrasher. Have we met?"

"Our eyes met, across a crowded trauma room."

Ward searched her memory. This woman was totally hot, and she was sure she'd have remembered meeting her, but since she was obviously flirting with Ward, maybe it was better that she didn't. Better not to seem too interested because, quite honestly, she wasn't sure she was ready to be interested at all. Perhaps, though, it was good that she was even thinking about the possibility of being interested. There might be hope for her future yet. Not love—she would certainly never do that again. But hot sex? Maybe. Just maybe she could do that.

"I don't remember. When was that?"

"Oh, a few months ago. I was working a transfer. You sent a trauma to Scranton. Snowmobile vs. tree. No helmet. Tree won."

Ward nodded. "I remember. That was Erin's case." Then Ward frowned. "I heard that guy died."

"Yeah, I heard that, too. A lot of dying going on with the rent-a-docs around." Her posture stiffened and the playfulness left her voice as she caught Ward's eyes.

Ward recoiled, as if one of the snakes wandering just a few feet away had bitten her. "Excuse me?" she asked.

The woman shook her head. "Oh, sorry. I didn't mean that."

Ward knew she should let it go, but she couldn't. "Well, what the hell do you mean?" Who was this woman, and what gave her the right to say such a thing?

Her face fell and she reached a hand out to Ward, but Ward stepped back. "Doc, I'm really sorry. I shouldn't have said that."

"Don't be sorry. Just tell me what the hell you're talking about."

"Why don't we get a beer?" she asked.

Ward looked to Erin. "I'll get you a pet snake, don't worry," she said as she protectively guided Ward back to the beer cage.

They found Erin's friends where she'd left them, and they quickly filled glasses from a pitcher and handed them over. Ward met the stranger's eyes over a beer she had no intention of drinking and realized she didn't even know the woman's name. But she knew she didn't like her.

Ward took a few steps toward her and leaned in. "So, why don't you tell me why you felt the need to make that disparaging remark about me? Don't you know how damning words can be, especially from a professional like you? People trust your opinion about medical issues. They listen to what you say."

The medic gulped her beer and then leaned close, so only Ward could hear her. So close Ward could feel her breath tickling her ear when she spoke. "Look, I really am sorry. And I know you're right. But there's this other doctor. Hawk. He's been all over the mountains in the last six months or so. And because I work per diem, I get around too. I've never seen so many dead patients as I have when he's taken care of them."

Ward turned to face her and they were nearly nose-to-nose. Ward hoped the woman could feel the fire burning within her, threatening to erupt. Without serious evidence of wrongdoing, saying such things was flat-out unprofessional and inexcusable. Such remarks could ruin a physician's career, or at least derail it. Every doctor lost patients, sometimes for no obvious reason, and sometimes there was nothing to be done but mourn and move on. To have professional colleagues speculate about patient care was difficult enough, but to hear one smear a physician's reputation with a patient's blood was inexcusable. Ward couldn't contain her anger.

"How dare you? Who the hell are you, anyway? What's your name? I want to know who you are so when I call the state board I know who to report!"

Apparently, the volume of Ward's voice had risen above the whisper where it started, because everyone in the group had stopped

• 126 •

talking and turned to stare at them. Everyone except Erin, who stepped closer and wedged herself between them. "Hey, guys, calm down!"

Ward realized she'd been out of line, and she stepped back. "Sorry, everyone." She didn't apologize to the medic, but instead reached for the nearly empty pitcher of beer on the tall table in the middle of their group. Erin followed her to the counter where Ward requested a refill.

"Moira really isn't a bad person, Ward," Erin said. "She's just been burned."

"Not by me!" Ward retorted.

"Yeah, I know. She's still angry, though. It was a guy she knew. Third-degree heart block. Lyme disease, they said. Moira saved him, but then he coded in the ER. Same story, you know? The staff said Hawk went through all the motions but didn't really seem to care that the patient died."

Ward shook her head. "She still shouldn't be talking like that, Erin. This is a physician, a man who's sacrificed his life to study and train to do this job. Little comments like that are harmful. Just the suggestion of malpractice can plant the seed and bring a lawsuit that shakes the whole hospital. It wouldn't just be the doctor. It's the medic's judgment in question. If he was so sick, why didn't she take him to Scranton where there's a cardiologist? The nurse's work is questioned. The hospital is questioned. And truthfully, Erin, tell me how much closer to death could the guy be than third-degree heart block? His heart was practically stopped. Whatever caused it to stop didn't go away just because he arrived in the ER. Maybe she gave him some medication or put on an external pacemaker, but there's only so much you can do with a sick heart! It could have been Hawk, or me, or the chief of cardiology at Mass General, and the patient still would have died."

"I know what you're saying, Ward. It may not be malpractice at all, but it seems to happen again and again when Hawk's around. You remember the stories I told you? Moira has a dozen more. And he's just so creepy he makes people's skin crawl."

"And so Moira blames me for this? Why?"

"Well, duh. You work for the same company."

Now it made sense. "Guilt by association."

"Exactly. It's not you. As a matter of fact, I think she likes you."

Ward rolled her eyes. "Not if she was the last woman on the planet!"

Erin's smile grew wide. "Oh, so does that mean there's hope for me? I'm only second to last?"

Ward closed her eyes and shook her head. Erin was relentless. Good thing she didn't know about the breakup.

"But listen," Erin said. "Chances are you're going to run into her again, so you should just make peace. The last thing you want is an enemy on the medic unit."

"Since I'm only going to be here for another month, I really don't give a shit."

The startled look on Erin's face told Ward she'd said too much.

"What? You're leaving? Where are you going?"

Ward had never told Erin the whole story about Jess. She'd simply said she was taking a few months off from her relationship. Erin knew Jess was the director at Garden, though, so it was only a matter of time before Erin realized they'd split up. Ward had to tell her the truth.

"I'm going back to Philly," she said simply.

"What about Jess?"

Ward didn't look at her and concentrated on the tune her fingers were tapping on the countertop. It was covered in plastic with a red-and-white checked pattern, and her fingers danced from color to color in time with a far-away musical tune. "She's staying here."

The world seemed suddenly still, and the chaos around her seemed to grow quiet as Erin touched her gently on the arm. "You're better off without her."

Ward didn't know if that was true, but with so many people saying it, maybe it was. Unfortunately, she'd have a chance to find out.

Chapter Fourteen
Central Lines

Edward stood in the darkness, leaning against the door of the physician's lounge. His breathing was ragged, and he needed the door to support his weak legs. Killing sometimes had that effect on him. When he felt he could walk again, he made his way to the bathroom and washed his face, careful to keep the water from his clothes. He hated dirty clothing. The CPR had been disgusting, and after only a few minutes, he'd been wet with sweat. He was tempted to change into hospital-issued scrubs, but who'd worn them before? His own sweat was far less foul than someone else's.

Feeling better after the cool water on his face, Edward reflected on his kill. It was a child, a little girl with a femur fracture. She'd been seriously injured, and in the hands of an incompetent or inexperienced emergency physician, she might have died anyway. He had the knowledge and skills to save her, if he'd wished to. But he hadn't. Even before she arrived in his ER, he'd been excited by the prospect of murdering her. The medic's report detailed her injuries and unstable vital signs, and he knew she would be his from the moment he'd taken the call.

It was a tremendous pleasure in the end, the murder. She was a whiny little thing, crying for her parents from the moment she reached the hospital. In spite of her low blood pressure, she'd managed to punch him in the face when he unfastened the restraints holding her to the backboard, and she did worse damage to one of the nurses. When she'd stopped breathing, it had been a blessing for all of them.

Of course, the death of a small child was something he had to aggressively fight. He'd gone through the motions with more enthusiasm than was warranted, even under the circumstances. In the end, it was all futile, as he knew it would be. There was no bringing her back, and he had to admit, the thrill of her death was worth the cost of dry-cleaning his suit.

Reaching into his bag, Edward removed his toothbrush from its case and brushed his teeth. He straightened his tie and combed his hair. The reflection in the mirror smiled at him, and he realized he should be happy. His month in Factoryville, PA, had been very productive. God, he loved locum tenens work.

CHAPTER FIFTEEN

ARRHYTHMIA

They'd told Ward she couldn't miss it, and they hadn't been lying. *They* were the entire ER staff. The entire hospital staff, really—at least the ones she'd met during her first three days of work at Endless Mountains Medical Center in the metropolis of Factoryville, Pennsylvania. It seemed they all knew and loved Dr. Judi Rosen, the energetic senior citizen who still practiced medicine-full time and served as the hospital's chief of staff. The entire hospital work force had been invited to this annual Fourth of July celebration at her home, and from the number of cars parked along the stretch of country road leading to a mailbox marked with a dozen red, white, and blue balloons, all of them were at the party.

Ward had debated coming; she was tired after her third consecutive twelve-hour shift in a busy ER. The tourists had arrived in the mountains in record numbers, or so it seemed, and had discovered a variety of interesting ways to injure themselves. She'd cast arms and ankles, dressed burns, stitched wounds created by knives and bicycle pedals, and after more than forty hours of that nonsense in just three days, Ward was exhausted.

But.

There was always a *but*, she thought. No matter what the situation, she'd learned long ago that the answer to the question never came without a big fat *but*. She always had something or someone else to consider. For the past six years, Jess had caused her to think twice, and after all that had happened in the past six months, she was beginning to wonder if she should rethink her philosophy. Instead of going along and getting along, maybe it was time to just say no.

She'd been a loving, accommodating partner, sacrificing her own wants and needs to make Jess happy, and where had that gotten her? Jess was dating another woman, buying a house, and moving out of the one they'd shared. Ward didn't know why, what she did or didn't do, or what she should have done. She didn't know what she might have said or when she should have kept her mouth shut. Was she too "out" for a small town like Garden, or should she have been more aggressive in demanding acceptance and respect from Zeke and all the others at the hospital who seemed to like her, but in the end weren't unhappy to see her go?

She'd never flaunted her sexuality, but she didn't have to. Everyone knew Sheriff Benson's daughter Jessica's *friend* Dr. Ward Thrasher. And they all knew the nature of their relationship. They'd seemed friendly to her, and supportive of her as the ER doctor, yet none had called after she left to see how she was doing, to ask if she was coming back, to wish her well.

If she'd walked away with the girl, she wouldn't have really cared. Under the circumstances, though, she couldn't help wondering what she'd done wrong. She wished she had the answers to all her questions. She would have liked nothing more than to crawl into the old claw-foot, porcelain bathtub and soak away her frustrations before returning to the hospital for yet another twelve-hour shift the next morning. Twelve that would likely become thirteen, as the others had.

But.

Dr. Judi Rosen, who seemed to not only run the medical staff but the county as well, had personally invited her. Twice. She'd stopped in at the ER two days earlier, fifteen minutes into Ward's first shift at the hospital, offering an unofficial orientation to the ER protocols and to invite Ward to join her and the rest of the county at her home as they celebrated the country's birth. Then today, as Ward was covered in sterile garb and inserting a needle into a dead man's heart in an attempt to restart it, Judi had poked her head through the door and told her again about the shindig. "Doesn't matter how late," she'd said, and winked. "The fun doesn't even start 'til after dark."

It wasn't wise to ignore such a request, at least if one had any political aspirations. It wasn't polite, either, and certainly no way to treat a colleague. And Dr. Rosen was quite an exceptional colleague. The first this and the first that, with a whole lot of letters after her name and awards on her resume. As a female, and a physician, Ward couldn't help but admire her. And so, she'd sacrificed her bath and her sleep and now found herself wedging her car onto the shoulder of this country road so she could celebrate the holiday with hundreds of people she barely knew.

Ward chuckled as she locked the car. This was the middle of nowhere, and a thief would have had a grand time with all the cars deserted along the road for as far as she could see. No nosy neighbors or even a casual bystander were nearby to report a break-in. Industrious thieves could have brought a car carrier, loaded it, and driven away without raising an eyebrow.

Oh, well, she thought. If someone wanted her collection of Broadway show tunes in the CD changer, she could make more from her originals at home. And she wouldn't miss the few dollars' worth of change in the cup holder. Thinking it smarter than paying a five-hundred-dollar deductible to replace a broken window, Ward turned around and unlocked the car. It was just easier. At the hospital in Philly, some people placed signs in the windows saying the car was unlocked and had nothing valuable within. Although she'd never done it, she'd thought it a brilliant idea, until the day one of her colleagues found a vagrant sleeping in her backseat at the conclusion of her overnight shift.

Ward crossed the street, at least ten miles from the place she'd seen the balloons, and wandered back toward the house. A stone wall, three feet high and with a dusting of wildflowers at the base to add a splash of color, guarded the property along the front border. It curved gracefully at the drive, where the flowers were concentrated in a lovely, mulch-topped bed. In front of her loomed a house of wood and stone in palatial proportions, with accent lighting showing off still more landscaping. A dozen miniature trees dotted a front lawn that would have dwarfed a football field. She followed the wall for several hundred yards along the left edge of the property, noting that it disappeared into a mature forest near the mountain to the rear. Along the mountain's base, more trees were scattered, each landscaped with flowerbeds and benches connected by stone pathways.

Directly behind the house, dozens of chairs and tables were set up, some beneath tents and others under the fading light in the early night sky. To the far right, in a clearing of appropriate size, a softball game was underway. Ward wondered how they could see the ball and hoped she wouldn't be needed for any emergency services. Dozens of people sat on the sidelines cheering. And along the wall to her left, in what Ward assumed was normally a field of grass, still more cars were parked. Five rows of them, to be exact.

This gathering resembled the county fair more than a house party, and Ward hesitated, reconsidering her decision to attend the party. Was she really up for this much excitement? As the chief of staff, Judi would know how busy the ER had been and that Ward had left the hospital an hour late, and would forgive her bad manners. As she stood debating, she was spotted. Frankie, the ER nurse manager, began waving frantically at her. Resigned to staying, she waved and began walking again, toward the crowd rather than the road.

The quiet hum she'd detected from the front of the house grew steadily louder. She wove through statues and sculpted shrubs and, of course, dozens of folding tables set up on the lawn and on the patio beside an Olympic-size swimming pool, complete with a fountain and a sliding board. She grinned as she noticed the line for the slide on this warm evening. Most of the people queuing were adults. Twenty others were already in the pool, and hundreds of people had gathered around it, enjoying the fading warmth of the sun's last rays. They all seemed to be having a good time.

Frankie approached and hugged her.

"Some party!" Ward said.

"You're not kidding. Wait till you see the fireworks. I bet they don't do it this well in Philly."

Ward didn't argue but turned to another voice. "Hey, Doc! Over here!" someone yelled, drawing her eyes to one of the many tables. This particular one was occupied by the people she'd spent most of today with, and clearly they'd been looking out for her. She made her way toward them.

"I'll catch you later," Frankie promised before he headed toward the portable restrooms tucked behind the trees.

She stopped at the table and greeted her colleagues, then proceeded toward the food tent, glancing as she walked, hoping to see a sign of her hostess in the crowd. If she could just find Judi, she could say hello, thank you, good-bye, and then make her exit. There were just too many people, though. But she did find the food, and her growling stomach reminded her that the peanut-butter sandwich she'd hastily swallowed at lunchtime had been digested long ago.

This was an All-American picnic, and the burgers and hot dogs were grilled while she waited. Ward made use of the time by filling a plate with a variety of salads cooling on a bed of mostly melted ice. Pasta, fruit, potato, and green beans were piled high on her plate before she chose a water from a large tub. Before she could take a sip, Judi Rosen patted her on the back.

"Thrasher! Glad you could make it!" Ward had noted Judi's tendency to address everyone by their last names and wondered if she'd been in the military. She certainly carried herself like a commanding officer.

"It's a pleasure to be here," she replied. "Thanks for the invite."

Judi waved a dismissive hand. "Everyone comes. I don't even know some of these people. Since you're new in town, I had to make sure you got a decent burger on the holiday. Lord knows you've been working up a good hunger in the ER the past few days."

Ward chuckled before sipping her drink, then nodded. "This certainly isn't the sleepy little country hospital I was expecting, that's for sure."

"Well, you're doing a great job, and we're all very pleased to have you here. Any chance you'd think of staying on? You know,

Dick Rave isn't recovering from his surgery as we'd hoped, and I'm not sure he's ever going to come back. He has a sweet disability policy that pays full salary until the age of seventy-two. Why work?"

Ward had heard about the ER chief, who'd suffered a ruptured bowel from diverticulitis and had every complication known to man since then. She didn't know him though, and had no comment about his disability, and certainly no designs on his job. In a month she'd be at the beach, on vacation, and in two months she'd be back to work in Philly. That was her home. She had a great job. And she loved it there. Still…there was something to be said for the type of medicine she was practicing now, and if Jess had asked her to stay in the mountains, it wouldn't have been a hard decision.

Judi walked with her toward her table, and a dozen people nodded to her as she made her way there. Some faces were familiar, but most weren't. Still, they all seemed to know her. The new ER doctor.

"They let you out!" someone said as Ward reached the staff table, and the man sitting on the end stood and offered Ward his seat. He took beverage orders before he walked away, and Ward had to decline half a dozen suggestions for alcoholic beverages. Since she'd been watching her alcohol intake, it amazed her how much everyone else drank.

She was introduced to the people around the table as she ate. Most of them were ER staff, but about every third face was unfamiliar and belonged to the spouses. Judi excused herself, and Ward made the usual small talk as she tried not to eat too quickly. Either she was really, really hungry or the food was exceptional, because she consumed about half her weight in a span of ten minutes, and could have kept eating if she hadn't looked down and found her plate empty.

Deciding to give her stomach a break, she joined the conversation. Hundreds of patients had demanded their attention in the ER, and she hadn't had much opportunity for small talk with the staff. Now, though, her coworkers began the interrogation. They asked the typical questions—where she was from, where she'd trained, did she know so-and-so, how she liked their town and their hospital. It was always the "What are you doing here?" that caused her to pause. She'd been out since the age of six, when she announced at her aunt's wedding her plans to marry her best friend from school, a girl, and not some disgusting boy. Zeke had pushed her toward the closet, though, and since January she'd found herself more cautious with her remarks than she'd ever been. After all, if you couldn't trust your father-in-law, who could you trust?

So, for the fifth time in as many months she found herself talking about needing a change and taking to the mountains for some time in the outdoors. Natives every one, they all agreed with her decision and were full of suggestions about how she could fill her free time while in town. When someone mentioned the good fishing on the local river, Ward held up both hands defensively and told them her funniest fish tale. They all roared as she described Frieda emerging from the forest pointing a shotgun at her.

"I'm going to stick to the parks from now on!" Ward said, and everyone laughed.

The fading light brought an end to the ball game, and Ward recognized more faces as both fans and players came back, some moaning and others bragging about the contest. As they all moved to accommodate the new arrivals, Ward found herself squeezed uncomfortably close to a nurse anesthetist whom she'd met during the treatment of a cardiac-arrest victim. The woman, Gianna, had done everything short of tattooing her phone number on Ward's body to let her know she was interested.

Ward wasn't, though. She supposed she might be ready to date if she found the right woman, but it wasn't Gianna. There was nothing unattractive about Gianna, but Ward was inexplicably not interested. Gianna's sudden appearance, and the pressure her left hand was putting on Ward's right thigh, changed the jovial atmosphere at the table to an uncomfortable one. It was time to leave.

"Excuse me," she said to the crowd, avoiding Gianna's gaze. "I need to use the restroom."

She was directed to the pool house—set aside for the female partygoers—and prayed Gianna wouldn't follow. She was tremendously relieved when she didn't. Ward emerged a few minutes later to find the hordes of guests migrating toward the softball field, where preparations had begun for the fireworks display. During the course of the dinner discussion, it had grown dark enough for the show, and Ward understood that Judi liked to end the fireworks at a reasonable hour, since so many of her guests would have to be at work in the hospital early the next day.

The table where she'd been sitting was now vacant, and Ward was relieved. She'd had a long day, and if the fireworks display wasn't imminent, she might have skipped it altogether.

But.

Here she was, on a warm, clear, gorgeous summer night, and could think of no better way to fill the remaining hours of her day.

She glanced around and grabbed a fresh water from one of the many ice-filled tubs scattered around, and then, instead of joining the masses, she walked in the other direction, toward the mountains and the fruit trees at their base. She kept her head down as she followed a stone pathway, careful not to trip on the uneven surface in the near darkness. Just as she reached the stone bench beneath the tree, the crunching sound of footsteps startled her. She looked up to see someone approaching. She couldn't discern any features from a dozen feet away, but the approaching shape was unmistakably feminine, with wavy hair that met the tops of her narrow shoulders, and a small, thin frame that was curvy in all the right places.

"Oh," a light, female voice said as she noticed Ward, and Ward could hear the surprise. The stranger was just as startled as she was.

"I'm sorry," Ward said, with a hint of laughter in her voice. "I didn't mean to scare you." It was sort of comical, though, to nearly run into another human being in such a deserted place in the near darkness. And then she added, "I didn't realize this tree was taken."

The stranger overcame her shock and apparently also found the humor in their situation. "Well, I did have a reservation, but since my date didn't show up, I'd be happy to share my bench with you. There's a perfect view from here, and it's not quite as loud as it is by the softball field."

The stranger sat and patted the bench beside her.

"So, I guess you've been here before?" Ward asked as she took the proffered seat.

The stranger laughed, a deep chuckle that suggested a long story was meant to accompany her answer. Ward found herself waiting, eager to hear the tale. She was disappointed by the stranger's simple reply. "Yes. Many, many times. How about you?"

"First time," Ward confessed. "First time I've seen fireworks in years." She didn't go into detail, didn't explain about her strange job that didn't end on holidays, or the hassle of fighting traffic to see a fireworks display in the city.

The stranger was polite enough not to ask questions but instead patted Ward softly on the shoulder. Her voice was like a caress in the darkness. "You're in for a special treat, then."

"Yeah?"

The stranger cleared her throat. "Oh, yeah. Judi goes all out for this. The guys who do the show are pros."

Ward leaned back and slid down, slowly stretching her legs in front of her as she rested her head against the back of the bench. She turned to face the stranger. Now that her eyes had adjusted, she could see her features more clearly. The wavy hair was one length, tucked behind the ears at the moment, but only because she persistently redirected the strays that managed to escape. Her eyes were fair, like her hair, and her nose was long and straight, with a small bump at the bridge that looked invitingly kissable. As did her full lips, which were parted at the moment. The sight of them caused Ward to suck in a breath, which seemed obnoxiously loud in the quiet beneath their tree. A softly curving chin led into a long neck, partially hidden now by the hair that seemed to have a life of its own.

Lovely, Ward thought. This woman is lovely.

Ms. Lovely seemed to sense Ward staring at her, and she herself turned, pulling a leg beneath her on the bench as she pushed another stray lock behind her ear.

Their eyes met, and Ward could feel them searching hers. "Who are you? What are you doing here?" they seemed to ask.

"Well, thanks for sharing your bench. I'm Ward, by the way."

Ward could see the smile spread across the woman's face, and she imagined a twinkle in the eyes. "Abby. Nice to meet you," and the eyes held for just a moment longer than necessary before Abby turned back toward the distant sky.

"So was it a man or a woman?" Ward asked, not believing her boldness. Ten minutes earlier she'd practically ran away from Gianna for her brazen behavior, and here she was doing much the same thing. She couldn't help it though. Something had drawn her to this place, and she might just have found someone to help take her mind off Jess. The question came out before she even knew she'd been thinking it.

"Excuse me?" Abby asked.

And now Ward had an excuse, an opportunity to run away from a potentially embarrassing situation. For her, if the woman was straight. For both of them if she wasn't. Fresh from the sting of Jess, though, Ward didn't take the easy way out. If she wanted to meet women, what better place than at a fireworks display? What a story that would be, years later, when people asked how they'd met! And so she asked again. "Your date. The one who didn't show up, leaving room on this bench for me. Was it a man, or a woman?"

Abby seemed to study her in the darkness, her eyes burning a path toward Ward's mouth, down her neck to the curve of her breasts, along the flat plane of her stomach, and all the way down her legs to the toes sticking out at the bottom of her sandals. Ward sensed the answer coming but, instead, heard the distant whistle as the first firework was launched. Ward turned and caught the streaming light of the missile as it shot up from the ground and exploded in a burst of white, lighting both the sky and the earth. Each tiny burst of light exploded yet again, and each daughter danced her way back to the earth, melting into the darkness along the way.

"Wow," Ward said. "That was just like Disney World." Before Abby could reply, another missile was launched into the darkness, and the explosion colored a large swath of sky red. Abby hadn't been kidding when she said this was professionally staged.

They sat side by side, commenting on the magnificence as each new display seemed more beautiful than the one before it. "Ooooh," Abby said as a green, fuzzy light filled the sky.

"Aaah," Ward responded.

And then they looked at each other and said, simultaneously, "Wow!" and burst into laughter.

Before the next display began, Abby spoke. "So did you crash the party, or did you get an actual invitation?"

Ward could tell Abby was teasing and decided to play along. "Caught me! I was just driving along and saw all the balloons out front, and I figured with all those cars, no one would even notice me. So I grabbed a burger and a beer and snuck back here, and well, you know the rest."

Again, Abby responded with that deep, throaty chuckle that was like a song in Ward's ears. "Well, as long as you stay away from the pasta salad, I won't turn you in."

"The salad with the blue cheese and olive oil?" Ward asked.

"That's the one," Abby said, a scornful look on her face.

The salad had been delicious. "It looked disgusting, really. Moldy. Are you sure you want to eat that stuff?"

"I'll take my chances," Abby proclaimed, and this time Ward laughed. It felt good, like seeing an old friend after a long absence. Not like laughing with Frieda, though. This was different. It was fun and...flirtatious. Ward swallowed hard at the realization.

"I like you, Abby," she said, so softly she wasn't sure she really spoke the words, instead of thinking them.

But Abby responded. "I bet you say that to all the girls," and their eyes met and held, again, for just a bit longer than innocence allowed. And even though her question about Abby's date went unanswered, Ward suspected Abby preferred to spend her time in the company of women.

Another explosion happened in the sky, and her peripheral vision caught the shower of red rain, but Ward thought the sight before her was even more spectacular. The light from the fireworks bathed Abby in its warm glow, and Ward's heart skipped a beat. She'd thought Abby attractive in the dark, but she was even more beautiful in the light. Perhaps it was the mischief in her eyes, or the smile that seemed to show off all thirty-two teeth, or the splendor of the night. Ward couldn't say; she only knew that Abby was gorgeous and she hadn't felt such an attraction in a long, long time.

"Oooh," Abby said, still looking at the sky.

"Aaah," Ward replied, looking at Abby.

And their eyes met again. "Wow!" they said softly.

Somewhere in the sky, the grand finale was happening with bursts of noise and color, but their eyes held as they studied each other, with only intermittent peeks at the spectacular display of fireworks. And then there was darkness, and applause replaced the thunder of the fireworks. People screamed, and clapped, and shouted, and landscaping lights came on all around the property, illuminating their hiding place.

On cue, Abby stood. Ward debated what to say as she stretched her legs and stood as well. She was tempted to ask for her number, but maybe this was just meant to be a magical moment in the darkness and nothing more. Besides, if she wanted to, in a few days, she could find the number from Judi. How many thirty-something gorgeous woman named Abby could there be in Factoryville, Pennsylvania, population three hundred?

Abby seemed to be waging the same debate as she turned and began walking back toward the house. "Well, party-crasher, it's past my bedtime. Thanks for a lovely show."

As they walked silently toward the house, Ward felt inexplicably happy. How could meeting a woman who she might never see again have that effect on her? Then she realized it didn't really matter if she ever spoke to Abby again. They had shared a brief, beautiful moment. It was important that she'd talked to her tonight, that she'd felt an attraction, that she was alive. And if she could meet a beautiful, funny woman beneath a tree in the middle of a field in the darkness, there was hope for her still. She wouldn't call Abby or ask Judi about her. What they'd shared was enough. It was a gift, the message to Ward that she was ready to move on. What a great gift that was.

Always the ER doc, Ward touched Abby's shoulder. It was hot, the fabric of her shirt soft and comforting. "Drive carefully," she said as she turned and followed the parade of headlights back to her car.

❖

Abby stopped before she reached the crowd, watching Ward as she disappeared into the flow of pedestrian traffic heading back toward the road. Back toward reality. They'd shared a spectacular moment, but it was over, and although Abby had the resources to track down this woman and possibly pursue her, she wouldn't. The spark between them had been totally unrelated to the fireworks, but if Ward had been interested, she wouldn't have walked away. And Abby wasn't desperate enough to resort to stalking women who weren't interested. Yes, she was single. She wasn't sure she wanted to change that status. Freedom was a wonderful state that allowed her to enjoy a spontaneous treat, a moment of magic under a tree in the night. If she had a girlfriend, she suspected the moment with Ward wouldn't have happened.

Still, she couldn't help wondering about the attractive new-comer. The only certainty was that Ward was new to the area. Abby had lived in Factoryville most of life, save for a decade in the middle carved out for graduate school and smoothing out the rough edges on her fledgling career. If Ward had ever stepped foot in town before, Abby would have known about it. She was definitely not a native.

Ward. First name, last name, nickname? The uncertainty would make it more difficult to track her down, if Abby were so inclined. Ward had walked away, and so would Abby. End of story.

But what was she doing here, this beautiful woman with a sense of humor and no date on the Fourth of July? Natural gas, probably. The business had doubled the population of Pennsylvania overnight, it seemed, and not all of them could live in the small towns where the gas wells were drilled. Especially not attractive women like Ward, who'd be natural targets for the scores of men lurking about. Better to drive a few miles to an upscale town like Factoryville where it was safe, where she could find restaurants and a grocery store and a quality dry cleaner's. Yes, that had to be the answer. Ward was an engineer, or an attorney, working with a gas company. Perhaps she was a laborer, but Abby didn't think so. She seemed too sophisticated.

Since she opposed gas drilling, she was now resigned to never trying to find out where Ward was living during her stay. That would only complicate matters. Still, they might be able to have some fun together, right?

Abby chastised herself for both the thoughts and the poor willpower that allowed them to continually resurface. It had been too long since she'd had sex, and that was her problem. Her last significant girlfriend had moved out of state with her company two years earlier, and in spite of a few lovers in the interim, she hadn't had anyone substantial in her life. That meant infrequent sexual liaisons, and she was sure infrequent sexual liaisons caused everything from heart disease to cancer. She was destined to die young.

She was happy, though. Her life was good and exciting, even if she didn't have one special woman to share it with. A cadre of friends was always available to travel or have dinner, hike or play golf. That was enough, right? It always had been, but as she searched the darkness that held the mysterious woman called Ward, she feared it wasn't anymore.

Chapter Sixteen
Mass Casualties

"Excuse me?" Ward replied, sure she'd misheard the perky young ER nurse who'd grabbed her arm.

Shayna repeated herself, more slowly this time. "Twenty girls are coming in from one of the summer camps. There was a bat attack."

Ward tried to keep her horror from showing on her face. It was her job to be strong, after all. She was the top-ranking staff member in the ER, and since it was Saturday, the day after the Fourth of July holiday, it was very likely she was the only doctor in this small community hospital. "Was it some sort of terrorist?" she asked, incredulous that someone would attack small children with a weapon like that.

Shayna looked at her as if she were speaking in tongues. "Huh?"

"The guy with the bat? Was he a nut job, or a terrorist, or what? Do they even know who it was?" Suddenly Ward was concerned. Would there be more attacks around the county? Would they have a mass casualty situation on their hands? Not that twenty patients wasn't already a mass casualty.

Shayna broke into a fit of laughter, throwing back her head and holding onto the counter for support. "You're funny!" she said as she walked away. Ward watched her for a moment, confused, then grabbed the first chart in the rack. She'd better get busy. If twenty trauma victims were arriving, the ER would soon be crazy.

After diagnosing a case of poison ivy, she emerged from a room to see the ER overrun by an army of pint-sized invaders, dressed in matching kelly-green T-shirts with an emblem for Camp Shickshinny across the chests. Because of all the camps in the Poconos, campers boosted the summer volume in the ER, and the green shirts were about the tenth different color she'd seen since arriving in Factoryville. They were usually in the ER for the trivial injuries their parents would have ignored but camp directors couldn't take chances with. Judging by the noise level, that was probably the case now. None of them appeared to be seriously injured. Several adults tried unsuccessfully to herd them. Another woman, similarly clad but much older than the others, approached her.

"Are you the doctor?"

"Yes. I'm Dr. Thrasher." Ward stood tall, sensing she'd need to.

"I'm the director of Camp Shickshinny. How long do you think this will take? We're supposed to be going to Knoebel's today, and we should be on the road already."

Reflexively, Ward glanced at the large atomic clock on the wall. It was just after nine, and already the department was hopping. She'd seen half a dozen patients since her seven o'clock start, but four of them had been in the previous thirty minutes, and at last glance, she'd seen several additional charts in the rack. She began to mentally calculate how far behind she was before she realized she had no idea what the woman standing before her was talking about.

"I'm sorry," Ward said, "but who are you?"

The woman tried unsuccessfully to cover her irritation. "Marsha Evans. Director of Camp Shickshinny. How long is this going to take?"

Ward tried to do a better job than Marsha Evans at concealing her frustration. The patient always comes first. That mantra had been drilled into her head since the first day of her residency, and no matter how rude or obnoxious they were, Ward had trained herself to ignore the demanding patients and focus instead on their issues. Issues were usually manageable. People weren't. "I'm confused, Ms. Evans. What are you talking about?"

Marsha Evans threw her hands up in the air dramatically and shook her head. Ward imagined she was accustomed to getting her way, for her theatrics to draw some reaction. But Ward had trained in Philadelphia, and nothing anyone said or did surprised her. Marsha's little display didn't compare to some of the things she'd witnessed during her decade in the ER in the big city.

"I can't believe this place!" the woman said. "Didn't they tell you we were coming?"

Suddenly it dawned on Ward. "Are you the camp that had the bat attack?"

Marsha smiled. "Yes, that's me. Can you take a look at this girl so we can get out of here?"

Frankie, the nurse manager, saved Ward from answering. "I'm going to triage your camper now, Mrs. Evans, and then the doctor will be right in."

Ward smiled her appreciation and pulled a chart, then left to evaluate a child with abdominal pain. When she emerged from the room fifteen minutes later, Frankie was waiting for her. Already summoned from home on his day off because of a sick colleague, he seemed to have a day destined for chaos.

"Hey, Doc, can you do me a favor and see these kids from the camp? It should be a quickie. They're on their way to a field trip, and I'd hate to see their day ruined."

"What's going on?" Ward asked.

"They were attacked by a bat. Didn't Shayna tell you?"

"She did mention that." Ward looked around. The campers had disappeared. "None of them looked hurt," Ward said.

"That's just it. You can get them out of here quickly, and everyone will be happy, including the hospital board. The woman who owns the camp is a member."

Ward resigned herself to moving the pushy Marsha Evans and her tribe to the front of the line. She was well schooled in hospital politics and knew this wasn't a battle worth fighting. She'd need her own favor at some point and wanted Frankie to owe her one. There were terms, though. "Sure, Frankie. But while I'm in there, I need you to find me a surgeon. This kid has appendicitis." She offered him the chart.

Frankie winced and stared at the chart as if it were poisonous. "How old is the kid?"

"Ten."

"Not gonna happen, Doc. They won't operate on a ten-year-old here. We'll have to transfer him."

"Fine. He's not critical. Get me a surgeon somewhere. Anywhere."

Frankie finally reached for the chart and Ward released it to him, then headed toward the trauma room and the entire population of Camp Shickshinny. The room, equipped with three stretchers and enormous square footage for an ER with only ten beds, seemed suddenly small. It was like walking into the primate building at the zoo. Girls were on and in everything. One of them really was hanging from the overhead OR light.

"Hey, hey! Girls!" she shouted above the roar, forgetting for a moment to be politically correct.

Marsha Evans ignored Ward's comment and wore a victorious smile. "Dr. Thrasher, thanks for coming straight in."

At least her tone was more pleasant. "No problem, Ms. Evans. What happened? Someone attacked the girls with a bat?" Ward looked around, confirming her initial impression that none of them seemed to be hurt. From the looks of things, the bat-wielding intruder had met his match.

Marsha looked perplexed. "No, they weren't attacked *with* a bat. They were attacked *by* a bat. You know, like a vampire bat?"

Ward couldn't control her laughter as she realized what an idiot she was. "Oh. Okay. So what happened?"

"Lillie Spencer," Marsha yelled, circling the room, scanning it for some sign of the girl. "Lillie! Where's Lillie?" she shouted to no one in particular. Then, spotting the girl, she yelled even louder. "Oh, there she is! Lillie, come here!"

Ward saw no sign of the girl emerging from the masses, but apparently Marsha was satisfied because she turned her attention to Ward once again. "She awoke this morning with a bat in her hair. A vampire bat," Marsha emphasized with a wink. "So she says. I can't find any bite marks, and none of the other girls saw it, but the camp doctor said we'd better get her checked. In fact, he said I should get them all checked." Marsha rolled her eyes to let Ward know just what she thought of his medical advice.

"Oh, Lillie, good. This is Dr. Thrasher. Tell her what happened."

Ward looked down at a skinny ten-year-old with red hair and freckles, the twin of the young Jess she'd seen in pictures. A wave of nausea hit her and she fought it down.

"So, I felt something funny. It was in the back of my hair, 'cuz I was sleeping on my stomach. And I thought it was a bug, 'cuz sometimes they get into our cabin." She swallowed before continuing. "And then, I sat up, 'cuz I hate bugs, and I felt my hair, and it was all soft, but it moved, and then I yelled, and I sort of jumped a little bit, and then I saw it fly up to the top of the ceiling, by where the door is." Lillie swallowed again, staring intently at Ward, who nodded to indicate she was listening. "And then I just kept screaming, and then everyone woke up, and they were screaming, too, and then Melody, she's our cabin counselor, she made us leave out of the emergency exit, and then she killed the bat."

During the duration of her dialogue, Lillie had shrugged, made faces, and patted her head as she demonstrated the bat's discovery, jumped around, and shrieked. Ward couldn't help laughing, but Marsha wasn't amused. Ward put her doctor's face back on and interviewed her patient. "Did you feel anything like a bite?"

Lillie shook her head emphatically. "No, just like a tickle."

"How about any blood? In your hair, or on your pillow?" Ward knew that bat bites were often so small they were undetectable and usually left no blood, but she had to ask the questions and go through the motions for the sake of the camp director, who was listening attentively.

"Well," Lillie said as she ran her hands through her hair. "I do have a scab on my head. But it was from before. It bleeds if I scratch it."

"No blood today?" Ward asked.

"Nope."

"And your pillow?"

"I didn't check my pillow, 'cuz I had to run out of the room, and then when we went back, I forgot." Her tone was very serious now, matching Ward's.

"How about if I check you, to be sure?" Ward asked, not because she thought she'd find anything, but because it was her job to look. She scooped Lillie up into her arms and deposited her onto the stretcher, then pulled the otoscope from the wall and used the light and magnification to examine Lillie's scalp. Other than a crusted lesion, which could have been from anything, the tissue was clear.

"How about you ladies? Any bat bites for you?" Ward asked the girls sitting in a row on the stretcher beside Lillie.

"Well," a dark-haired girl with matching eyes said. "I did kind of think something was in my hair while I was sleeping, but I was having a dream, so I didn't wake up."

Ward chuckled softly but stopped when Marsha scolded the girl. "Eva! Don't be telling tales!"

"So, Lillie's scalp looks good," Ward said.

"Thank God," Marsha exclaimed. "Can we get the paperwork and get on the road?" she asked, and then as an afterthought, she added a smile.

"Let's talk in the hallway, Mrs. Evans," Ward suggested as she nodded in the direction of the door.

When they reached the corridor, Marsha crossed her arms as if preparing to stand her ground against an invading army. Ward braced for the impending confrontation, wondering if the camp doctor had prepared Marsha for what she was going to say, or if she'd left Ward to be the bad guy.

"We need to treat all these girls—and the counselor who was in the room. We need to vaccinate them for rabies."

"What?" Marsha demanded. "They weren't even near the bat."

"You don't know that, Ms. Evans. Bat bites are often too small to be seen. But they're deadly. If that bat bit one of these girls, and it gives her rabies, she'll die. There's no treatment. Our only chance is to give her the vaccine to prevent it."

"You've got to be kidding me," she exclaimed as she slapped herself in the forehead.

Ward shook her head. "No, I'm afraid I'm not."

Marsha turned in a circle, cradling her head in both hands, sighing dramatically. "How. Long. Will. This. Take?"

Ward hated to use an excuse like *I'm new here*, but it was true. She didn't have an answer. Bat attacks weren't frequent in her part of the state—except for the wooden kind of bats. Ward could count on one hand the number of times she'd treated rabies, and in those cases, it had taken hours to procure the vaccine and immunoglobulin needed to prevent the virus from taking over the body. That was in the city, though, with only one victim. How long would it take to procure two-dozen doses of both medications in this rural area? She was afraid to guess, but the process would be lengthy. Twenty-one patients had to be registered, triaged, and examined by a nurse and then by a physician. And Ward was the only doctor in the ER. On the best of days, it would take hours to get these children treated. Today, with the department already under siege from the region's tourist population, it would be next to impossible.

"Let me check with Frankie," she told Marsha. "He's the nurse in charge." Frankie would know the protocols and obviously had a relationship with Marsha. Better if the news came from him.

Marsha marched back toward her campers and Ward headed in the opposite direction, looking down at her phone as she walked. She pulled up her favorite ER app and read about rabies. She didn't treat it often enough to remember details like medication doses, and she wasn't cocky enough to fake it. She also reviewed the protocol for the vaccine, which she hadn't forgotten. It was still the same, all these years later. It was good to know she was right, because she was sure Marsha was in the other room Googling the same information. She needed to be prepared for battle, and knowledge was the best weapon. After jotting down the correct doses for both medications, she looked up and saw Frankie talking with a medic who'd just delivered her next patient, a young man sitting upright in the stretcher holding his upper arm and moaning. He was shirtless, and the hollow in his upper arm told her the shoulder was dislocated. It was one of the few orthopedic diagnoses that could be made without an X-ray.

"Did you give him something for pain?" Ward directed her question to the medic.

"Not yet," he said defensively.

Before Ward could criticize him for torturing the man, Frankie interrupted her. "I was just coming to get you, Doc. I have the surgeon on line three."

"Okay." Ward nodded toward the man suffering on the stretcher before her. "Get him an X-ray stat and set him up for sedation so we can pop that shoulder back in," she said. "And please give him four of morphine before he passes out." She pulled the phone across the counter and said hello to the pediatric surgeon on the other end. After exchanging credentials, she quickly explained the case. She grinned when he immediately agreed to accept the care of her patient. He didn't ask any questions about insurance and tests, just the facts about the case. This child needed his help, and he was willing to give it.

Wow, how refreshing, she thought. No haggling, selling her patient, trying to convince him her diagnosis was correct, as was often the case with transfer patients in the mountains. Lately she'd found doctors, especially specialists, reluctant to accept transfers. They were no longer men and women called to help people in need. They were like factory workers, punching a clock and passing the buck. It wasn't their problem. She'd been dealing with that issue since she started working at Garden, and it was frustrating. This encounter had been different though. Maybe it was an omen. She could only hope.

She looked up to see Frankie waving his hands frantically in front of her face. "Don't hang up. The clerk needs to talk to admissions with insurance info and then someone will call for a report." Ah, Ward thought. Maybe not so easy after all. She handed the phone to the unit clerk and turned back to Frankie.

"I have to talk to you about Camp Shickshinny," she said.

"What's up?"

Ward handed him her notes. "We need twenty-one doses of RIG and twenty-one doses of vaccine. And of course, all the kids and the counselor need to be signed in, etcetera."

Frankie laughed. "Ha, Ha. You're such a comedian."

"Yeah, I know. But I'm not joking. They woke up in a room with a bat, and any one of them could have been bitten in her sleep. We need to treat them all."

Frankie's face dropped, and Ward thought the white walls were suddenly darker than his complexion.

"You're not kidding?"

Ward shook her head for emphasis. "No."

He looked down at the note she'd given him and then back up to her, even paler now. "I'll get right on it. And Shayna's hunting down everything for that shoulder."

"Super. I'll go back to work."

Ward walked into a patient's room, and when she emerged ten minutes later, she looked for Frankie again but saw no sign of him. She completed transfer orders and talked to the boy with appendicitis about what to expect. Shayna had set up everything for the patient with the injured shoulder, and with the right combination of pain medication for relaxation and brute force for moving bones, Ward popped the shoulder back into the joint. The patient thanked her a hundred times in the two minutes she'd spent explaining how to take care of the arm to prevent future injuries.

She examined and discharged four more patients, and still, she saw no sign of Frankie. She wasn't surprised; she'd given him a Herculean task. Still, she wished she had some news to report to Marsha Evans, who was pacing the corridor across the way, her phone pressed to her ear as her mouth moved a mile a minute. Soon, she'd come looking for Ward, demanding answers and action, and it would be nice to have something to tell her.

She glanced at the chart rack. The number of patients waiting for her attention had climbed to five, and that didn't count the twenty-one victims of the terrorist bat. She laughed to herself as she realized how stupid she'd been, then turned at the sound of her name.

A gorgeous woman of her height, with shoulder-length auburn hair and blue eyes, stood before her. A concerned look had replaced the smile that had enchanted Ward the night before, but she couldn't mistake the fact that this was the woman from the fireworks. The angel who had come and told Ward she'd be fine—that she'd find a woman attractive again, and once again laugh and enjoy a simple pleasure like a fireworks display.

Her eyes, Ward noticed, were darker than she'd thought, and her hair lighter. It was streaked with gold and now pulled back and up, and not a single strand broke free. She'd exchanged the T-shirt and shorts for a suit—navy blue, with a blazer tailored to fit her curves and a skirt equally flattering and hemmed to the knee. Ward's eyes kept going past the skirt, down Abby's legs to the tips of her red-painted toes, then back up across the low-heeled sandals, the legs, the butt, the curve of her back, and the narrow shoulders. Finally she met Abby's eyes, which registered surprise and then seemed to laugh at a joke only the two of them shared.

"Abby?" she asked. Ward's heart pounded as she spoke, and her stomach did a little somersault

Abby's appearance in the ER wasn't unwelcome, and Ward might have laughed, too, if she knew what the hell was going on. She didn't know why, but she suspected Abby's appearance here wasn't a coincidence.

"Ward? *You're* Dr. Thrasher?" Abby asked.

Ward pursed her lips and took a step back, even as Abby stepped closer. "Well, not if you say it like that!"

Now Abby laughed out loud, her eyes twinkled, and she stepped forward again, offering her hand in introduction. Her handshake, Ward noticed, was crippling, but her smile was gentle. "I'm Abby Rosen, the CEO."

Ward shook with what she hoped was an impressive strength. "The CEO?"

"Yes. The CEO. Of the hospital."

Ward shook her head and bit her bottom lip to control her laughter, but she couldn't stop the smile. "Well, talk about a small world."

Abby's hand still held hers, gently now. "Yes," she said softly. "I should have known. Not too many strangers show up for my mom's party."

"Your mom?"

"Yeah. Judi's my mom."

Ward nodded, amazed. "Smaller world, but nice. What a delightful surprise. I didn't think I'd see you again." And then Ward grew concerned. "Is everything okay? Are you sick?" Why else would the CEO be in the ER on a holiday weekend?

"No, I'm fine," Abby said, but Ward detected a shift in her posture, as she seemed to grow taller and her eyes darkened to black.

Suddenly Ward grew alarmed. What *was* the CEO doing here? Preparing for some battle, no doubt, and it had to do with her. Which really sucked, considering how much she'd liked Abby and how much she'd thought about her before falling asleep, and then upon waking in the morning and in the shower. Before she'd left for work she'd actually made up her mind to find out who she was, so she could call her. Maybe explore the possibilities that had presented themselves in the explosion of color lighting the night sky.

Well, no need for that now.

"So, how can I help you?" she asked, assuming her own fight stance, standing tall, squaring her shoulders, picking up her chin.

"Shed some light on this bat problem. I had calls from a frantic camp director and another from a frantic nurse. I expect a board member will be next."

Ward squinted at Abby, studying her, assessing the threat. Surprisingly, she saw none. Abby's smile was warm, her stance softer.

Abby's stance didn't soften Ward. She couldn't afford to let it. She'd been facing enemies of all sorts since that first day in the ER months earlier, and she knew such battles wouldn't stop until she was back home, on her own turf. She wasn't surprised Marsha Evans had pulled rank and called Abby. She could, and it was her job to take care of her campers. But for Frankie to turn too miffed her. The ER was supposed to be a team, and his call to the administrator amounted to treason.

Seeming to sense her angst, Abby grabbed her arm. Ward looked down to where Abby's manicured thumb, painted a brilliant red, seemed to caress her arm. Their eyes met, and despite the situation, Ward's belly flopped and a flood of heat surged lower into her abdomen. Wow.

"Relax," Abby purred. "It's okay. Everyone's just panicking, and they called me. It's my job to help out in a crisis, and I think twenty-one patients on the same bus fits the definition."

Ward let out a breath. Abby wasn't looking for a fight. Not yet anyway, the little voice in the back of her head said. While she didn't have much experience with rabies, she'd gone toe-to-toe with administrators of all kinds, on many occasions. The encounters weren't always pleasant.

"Can you tell me what's going on?" Abby asked, with no hint of confrontation. Her grip eased, and her hand slipped from Ward's forearm.

She missed the contact before it was even broken. Refocusing, she explained the situation, about the need to treat for rabies, conscious of the frustrations that seemed to be growing in spite of Abby's professional demeanor. Why did she have to explain medicine to the administrator? What did Abby know about this, anyway? She tried hard to calm herself, trying to believe Abby really was there to help.

"And you're sure about this?" Abby asked when she finished.

Ward's jaw clenched, again, and she purposefully unclenched it before answering. "One-hundred-percent sure." She didn't mention that she'd double-checked the protocol for rabies exposure before issuing her orders. But should she? The CEO didn't have the authority to question a medical decision, but Abby had to know this wasn't a typical situation, and Ward supposed she had a right—even an obligation—to make sure the staff was doing things the correct way. Perhaps the information she'd learned would help ease Abby's concerns. For some reason, that thought comforted her. She didn't want Abby to worry, especially if she had the power to prevent it..

Putting her ego aside, she spoke again. "I double-checked the CDC protocols on my smart phone. All the kids need to be treated, and the counselor, too. It's just too risky to ignore."

The rewarding smile Abby offered made Ward feel ashamed that she'd hesitated. That news was all the ammunition Abby needed to stand beside her and fight. To stand in front of her, really. "Let me break the happy news to Miss Evans." Abby winked.

Ward offered her a supportive pat on the back. "Good luck with that."

Both of them turned and walked away, Abby to deal with Camp Shickshinny and Ward to deal with the citizens of rural Luzerne County. Before she made any progress, though, Frankie was in her face. She suppressed the urge to question his manhood and was immediately relieved she had.

"Okay, here's the situation. We can't find enough vaccine for these kids. There's some sort of shortage. I called the Department of Health and they're going to try to locate the doses for us, but they may not be able to. Worst-case scenario is we send them all home to Massachusetts and Ohio or wherever, and let the local ERs treat them. I called Abby Rosen, the CEO, to deal with the camp director, because this is going to be a nightmare."

Filled with a mixture of relief and shame, she patted Frankie's back. "Thank you, Frankie. Good job."

He nodded. "Yeah, well, I have a feeling I won't get a bite of lunch today, and probably not any dinner, either, but the good news is, I'm off at seven. Only nine more hours to go."

Ward glanced at the clock. Eight and a half, really. She could do this.

CHAPTER SEVENTEEN

HYPOGLYCEMIA

An amazing calm descended on the ER in the early afternoon. All of the men, women, and children who'd been injured on sports equipment or contracted communicable diseases were miraculously cured as the day grew older, and Ward found herself sitting in the unfamiliar rolling desk chair in the physicians' work station, catching up on charts. If she could sing just one praise of the hospital's electronic medical-records system, it was the ability to cut and paste, a feature she used twenty-one times, allowing her to finish in record time the notes on the crew from Camp Shickshinny. When her replacement arrived half an hour early for the night shift, he bid her farewell, and she stood in stunned silence, wondering what to do with the remainder of her evening. A Saturday shift had never ended early before.

She made her way to the physicians' lounge, grinning all the way, knowing she'd figure something out. A good book sounded delightful. Perhaps a burger, first. The memory of the juicy, fire-grilled delicacy from the night before was still making her mouth water. And as she walked into the deserted doctors' retreat and eyed the large bathroom, another idea occurred to her. A shower. Blissful, comforting, hot, hot water.

Over the years, she'd been in some decrepit hospital call rooms, so dingy and dirty she hesitated to change her socks and step on the bare floors. Leftover food and linens had littered the floors and counters, and a collection of forgotten personal items collected dust. Some of the bathrooms had facilities where the water in the shower wasn't even connected. In others only cold water came spraying from the showerhead, testing her inner strength. But the physicians' lounge here was perfect—clean, well appointed, and with both hot and cold water working fine. A supply of full-sized towels was neatly stacked on a shelf, and she saw no evidence of fungus.

Throwing her used scrubs into the bin, she stepped into the shower and imagined the germs washing down the drain, felt the tension leaving the muscles of her shoulders and back, and finally, her mind. She emerged from the lounge ten minutes later, shiny and clean, her wet hair brushed by her fingers, and nearly collided with Abby.

They both laughed.

"What happened to the ER?" Abby asked. "I've never seen it empty before."

Ward raised an eyebrow. "I believe you just jinxed them."

"Good. As the CEO, I'd prefer it to be busy."

Ward couldn't help laughing. "Well, at least you're honest," she said as they began walking in the general direction of the parking garage and Ward's house. "Usually, the administration pretends to commiserate with the staff but screws them anyway."

Abby nodded. "We're fighting the same war, but I have to fund it, too," she said simply. "But lucky for you, it's an early night. What do you plan to do with yourself?"

Ward was tempted to stop, to stare. Was Abby hinting at something? Or was that wishful thinking? And why was she skulking in the hallway beside the physicians' lounge at seven o'clock on a Saturday night? Ward kept walking, wondering how to answer. "No plans, except food. I'm famished. Have you eaten?"

They'd reached the exit, and Abby held the door for her, and when she walked through, Abby stopped, finally looking at her, searching her face.

Ward stared back, waiting for an answer to her subtle invitation. Abby's eyes held delight and invitation of their own, and they locked on Ward's for a moment before she answered. "I haven't. I was planning to get some work done, but food sounds much better. Would you like to join me?"

Panicked, a hundred thoughts flashed through Ward's mind. Abby had replaced the business suit she'd worn for her battle with Marsha Evans with another T-shirt and golf shorts, which matched Ward's attire perfectly. She didn't need to worry about how she was dressed. But what did Abby like to eat? Who would drive? Was her car clean enough for company? And that Yankee Candle Christmas Cookie air freshener was still kind of strong—would it be too much for Abby? What are you thinking, she asked herself after a second. None of that mattered. A beautiful woman wanted to have dinner with her. They could eat candy worms in a smelly car and it would still be perfect.

"I was fantasizing about a burger," Ward said, although suddenly she didn't think she could eat.

"That's some imagination you've got, Doc."

Ward took the teasing in stride. "Long day. Four days, really. I don't have any energy left for creativity."

"Yes, I hear it's been busy. I was away for a few days and just got back last night. Otherwise, I'd have been here to meet you and orient you. I'm sorry about that."

"No worries. If I'd known who you were, I don't think I'd have enjoyed the fireworks so much."

"Really?"

"Well, yes. Fraternizing with the administration can be dangerous."

"Should we cancel the burger?"

"No, this is eating. It's much different."

"So it's settled then? We'll eat?"

Ward met Abby's eyes and saw the warmth there. "I'd love to."

They agreed to walk, with Abby promising a guided tour through town en route to the best burger joint around. Not surprisingly, tables at the best burger joint in town were in demand on a Saturday night, and they sat on a bench overlooking the gardened terrace while they waited.

"How long have you lived here?" Ward asked when they'd settled on the hand-carved bench. The name of the craftsman, along with his phone number, was engraved in the headrest. Once again, Abby pulled her legs up under her and turned to face Ward as they talked. It reminded her of the fireworks, and she smiled.

"Basically, my whole life. I was born at the hospital, raised here, left for college and worked for a few years in Philly. When my predecessor keeled over and died at a board meeting, the hospital was scrambling for someone. I agreed to take over temporarily. That was eight years ago."

"Your predecessor's fate might have discouraged some."

"I really needed the money."

Ward smiled and Abby shook her head. "No, I'm serious. I'd just bought a Porsche, a cute little convertible, which I'd convinced myself and the bank I could afford. And then I had to make that payment every month, and…"

Ward squinted at her. "And the hospital trusts you with its budget?"

Abby nodded again. "Absolutely. If I could figure out how to buy a Porsche on my former salary and not starve to death, I'm surely a financial genius. I can do anything."

Ward was silent as she studied Abby. She was beautiful with the sunshine bouncing off the golden highlights in her hair and reflecting off the smooth surface of her sunglasses. Her pose was relaxed and confident. Ward suspected she *could* do anything. Lost in her thoughts, she nearly missed Abby's question. "How about you? Where's home?"

Ward gave her the synopsis of her family and her career, carefully omitting the name Jessica from her tale. It wasn't a lie, Ward thought. It just wasn't relevant any more.

Abby's name was called, and they were seated at a picnic table just a few feet away from the bench they'd been enjoying. After they took care of the business of studying menus and ordering food, they went back to talking.

"So what kind of work do you have to do on a Saturday night? Are you still trying to pay off that car?"

Abby squinted. "It's all mine, finally. No more car payments." Then she cleared her throat. "I actually came back hoping to run into you. So I could ask you out for dinner."

Ward studied her for a moment. "Do I look that lonely?"

Tilting her head, Abby seemed to study Ward for a second, weighing her answer. "No. You look that cute."

Ward thought back to the night before, when Abby had said that her date stood her up. Abby had just answered the question she'd asked her last night. Ward looked at her sitting there and tried to reconcile the conflicting images in her mind—the playful, flirtatious woman in shorts and a T-shirt with the hard-nosed executive wearing the business suit and heels. Abby seemed to be a delightful combination of tough and kind, serious and playful. And being with her felt good. Ward felt as good as she had in ages.

She blushed. "Thanks." Her grin quickly spread to Abby, and they were still smiling a few minutes later when the server delivered two cheeseburgers and a heaping basket of fries with vinegar on the side.

"So where'd you go?" Ward asked.

"Hmm?" Abby asked, her mouth twisted in confusion.

"You said you were away. Where'd you go?"

"Rehoboth Beach, Delaware."

Ward couldn't help smiling. "I love Rehoboth. I've spent a lot of time there over the years."

Abby nodded. "My ex has a house there." Then she said, "I have my own bedroom. Separate from hers."

Ward bit her lip to stop the emerging laugh. "I understand. I pretty much have my own room there, too. In my friend's house. Not my ex's."

"Your ex doesn't want you around?"

Ward sensed Abby was fishing for information about her sexuality. She didn't hesitate to tell her. "No, I don't think she does," she said, laughing at the absurdity of life. A few days earlier, she'd been crying about Jess, and now she was sharing a burger with a beautiful woman who seemed to be flirting with her, and Jess seemed like a distant memory.

They were quiet for a moment as they enjoyed their food. Ward's, covered with mushrooms and Swiss cheese, was so tasty she didn't even bother adding any of the various condiments the waitress had offered. She tried not to moan as she tasted the wonderful blend of flavors. When she'd finished, she deposited her flag-adorned napkin onto her plate. Resisting the urges to burp and pick her teeth, she folded her hands politely beneath her chin. "Thank you for today," she said after a moment.

Abby wiped her mouth and looked at Ward, a question in her eyes. Ward saw them light with recognition as she divined what Ward was talking about and how she felt about the day. "It's important to you to do the right thing, isn't it?"

Ward shrugged.

"You must make enemies." Abby leaned against the wall behind her. The sun was beginning its descent into the mountain behind Ward, and the last rays were bathing Abby. She seemed to relish the warmth on her face, and even though she wore sunglasses, Ward could tell her eyes were closed.

"Sometimes. But you do it anyway. The right thing, I mean. You did today." Abby had been the one talking to the officials at the Department of Health so that Ward and Frankie and the other staff members could take care of patients. In the end, they'd managed to locate all forty-two shots, and Abby had arranged for the entire group to have their second doses at the hospital-owned clinic to reduce the logjam in the ER.

A frown appeared on Abby's face. "I do try. But it's sometimes difficult to determine what the right thing is. It can differ from day to day. And working with physicians can be trying. They all have an opinion, and everyone's version of the right thing is a little different, so no matter what you do, someone is unhappy about it."

"So you just do your best, right?"

Now Ward could tell Abby's eyes were open. "It's all you can do."

The conversation had somehow gotten serious, and as the waitress came to clear their table, Ward decided to lighten it a bit. "So what are you best at?"

Abby took Ward's teasing tone and ran with it. "Oh, now that's a loaded question."

Ward laughed. "It wasn't meant to be. I mean…what do you do for fun?"

They split the check and began the short walk back to the hospital. Ward found herself walking slowly as she listened to Abby, trying to prolong their time together. "I like to work in my yard, play around with landscaping a little. I like to spend time on the river, fishing and kayaking. And then there's my love-hate relationship with my golf clubs. I spend a good amount of my time with them. How about you? Do you golf?"

"I do."

Abby stopped and turned to Ward, grabbing her arm. "Are you free next weekend? I need someone for the hospital tournament. This could be perfect!"

Ward chewed the inside of her lip. She was supposed to play with Frieda, and as tempting as the invitation was, she couldn't stand her up. "I wish I could, but I have plans to play with a friend."

Instead of the disappointment she'd expected, Abby's face became even brighter. "You have a friend? Who plays golf?"

Ward nodded and laughed. "Don't sound so surprised."

"Ha, ha. No, this is perfect, perfect! Dick Rove still isn't ready to play, so he and his wife pulled out. I need two people. If you and your friend could play, you'd really make my day."

Ward liked the idea, too. "I'll call her in the morning and check. If she's willing, I'd love to."

They'd reached the hospital's parking garage, but instead of heading in that direction, they turned toward the house where Ward was staying. Abby grinned when she saw the kayak atop Ward's car. "Is that yours?"

Ward nodded and patted the battered blue plastic affectionately. "Sure is."

Abby grinned mischievously. "I was thinking of going out tomorrow. Wanna join me?"

Ward was taken aback by the invitation, not because it should have surprised her, after their night under the fireworks and the burgers they'd shared, but because it had been so long since she'd spent time with a woman who wasn't Jess. If she'd taken time to think about it, she might have actually declined the invitation, just out of habit. But before she could think, the response was out of her mouth, and Abby was asking the next question.

"Would one o'clock work for you? I really do have some work to catch up on in the morning, but if we go out in the afternoon, I'll have it all done and can just relax. And have fun."

Ward agreed to the time. She could use the morning to catch up on her own errands, tasks ignored while she worked four consecutive, very long days. But was she really ready for this? She had no doubt what Abby had on her mind. She was obviously single and had been flirting with her from the moment they'd met. She'd waited for her to ask her out for a burger and told her she was cute. Abby was definitely interested.

As she watched Abby walk away, her sculpted ass swaying seductively, Ward had to admit that she was, too.

❖

An unpleasant combination of fear and anticipation surged through Ward's body, not by turns, but instead sharing attention and threatening to short-circuit her neurons. For the hour since Abby had left her, she'd thought of nothing but the next day, and the more she thought about it, the more anxious she became. It took her awhile, but she finally figured out what was bothering her. She feared the possibility that dating Abby would mean it was really over with Jess.

Yes, Jess was dating. But Ward's heart was still true, and until she herself moved on, until both of them had moved on, it wasn't truly over. Jess was still real to her, and if she went kayaking with Abby—on a date with her—that would truly mean the end of the most significant relationship she'd ever had. She didn't feel ready to make that turn, yet at the same time she envisioned a day on the river with Abby, laughing and soaking up the sunshine, relaxing as her kayak glided along the surface of the water.

It had been forever since she'd really enjoyed herself, yet in just a couple of days, Abby had managed to bring her more joy than she'd felt in the past year. She wanted that—to be with Abby and laugh. Perhaps she wanted even more. She hadn't really had time to think about it. Yet, now, she couldn't avoid the difficult decision before her or pretend it was insignificant. Kayaking together wouldn't be a chance meeting; it was premeditated and full of promise. The promise of happiness, at least for a few hours. But if she wanted to have any fun with Abby tomorrow, she needed Jess's blessing.

Jess's number was first on her favorites' list, and she dialed it as she paced the kitchen. It was already after ten, and normally she wouldn't have called so late, but she had to. If she didn't, she'd spend a sleepless night worrying about making the call in the morning. No way was she spending a day on the river with Abby if Jess made her a better offer. Hell, any offer.

Waiting was torture, and Jess made her listen to several rings before answering. She envisioned Jess staring at the phone's screen, deciding if she wanted to talk to her, and the thought made her sad.

"Hi, stranger," Jess greeted her, and Ward thought it an odd choice of words. If they'd become strangers it was only by Jess's design. Why rub it in? She heard no emotion in Jess's voice, neither happiness nor anger. She was annoyingly indifferent.

"How's it going?" Ward asked, fighting tears. It was difficult to make this call, and even harder to hear everything unspoken in Jess's response. Yet she needed to hear Jess tell her their relationship was over. Again. She just needed to hear the words so they might register, finally, in her heart.

"Good. Really good, in fact."

Jess didn't offer, but Ward had to ask. "Wendy?"

Ward heard Jess take a deep breath. "Ward..." she said, stretching the monosyllable into three.

Ward sighed. Was she that annoying that Jess couldn't bear to deal with her? Or was Jess that much of a jerk? The way Jess was acting, and had acted, suddenly pissed her off. And angry felt a whole lot better than sad.

"Listen, Jess. I just need to ask you one thing, and I'll never bother you again. If I want something after this, I'll have my lawyer call you, okay? So, are you sure about this? Because..."

The anger evaporated as she realized what she was about to say. Lowering her voice, softening her rage, she said, "I met someone, Jess. Someone...fun. And beautiful. And she asked me out. But I can't say yes if I'm worrying about you. So if you tell me it's really over, I'm ready to move on and start dating. If you tell me to wait, because you're not sure—well, I'll wait. Because..."

Even though it was still true, Ward couldn't say I love you, not after what she'd been through. After what Jess put her through.

"What's her name?" Jess asked, and Ward heard more kindness in her voice than she'd heard in a long while.

She stopped pacing and looked out at the hospital parking garage in the distance. It was brightly lit and gave the eerie appearance of daylight even though it was late. Then she imagined a face, with eyes that held laughter and tremendous warmth, and it suddenly softened the view from her window. "Abby."

"What's she like?"

Ward ran a hand through her hair, anxious. She hadn't called to talk about Abby. "What the fuck is this, Jess? An interview?"

"Ouch. Sorry. I was just trying to be friendly."

Closing her eyes, she swallowed a tear. "Hmmm. I guess I didn't recognize friendly."

Jess gasped. "I guess I deserve that. And you deserve some happiness. So go out with your Abby and have fun. If things change on my end, I'll let you know."

The coldness was back in Jess's voice, and it was just what Ward needed. Anger was definitely much better than sadness. "I can't do that, Jess. I can't be with her and think I might have a chance with you. I can't use her for entertainment while you're making up your mind."

"I don't know what else to say. Go out with her. I'm dating, and you should, too."

"So, it's really over?" Ward put a palm to the forehead that suddenly throbbed, wishing she could retract the words, knowing how pathetic they sounded. She reached for a glass and turned on the water.

"I hope we'll always be friends."

"I have no interest in friendship, Jess," she said and hung up.

CHAPTER EIGHTEEN
CARDIAC CONTUSION

Why have a GPS when none of the roads show up on it? It seemed like the device was useless in the mountains, and Ward turned around for the third time on a deserted stretch of road, searching for Abby's driveway. She thought back to the last time she'd been in this situation, driving in circles around Frieda's lake. That day had started off terribly but ended well. She could only hope this one was half as good.

She pulled off to the side and dialed Abby's number. Thankfully, she had cell-phone service.

"I ran out of gas driving in circles. What do you suggest?"

"Give me landmarks, maybe I can help."

She looked around. "I see trees. Green ones. Oh, and a bird. A big one. Big and black."

"Well, you're very close, then."

Ward chuckled. Abby made her laugh, and at the moment, Ward loved her for that. She'd spent a restless night after talking to Jess, had called several friends to cry with in the middle of the night, and awoke in the morning with a migraine.

Yet, she'd vowed to move on. Her date on the river with Abby was the first step in her new journey, and with Abby's wicked and delightful sense of humor, Ward thought it had the potential to be a great trip.

"Help me! Please!"

"Okay, okay. Lock your doors so a bear doesn't attack you, and I'll come rescue you."

"Do you know where I am?"

"I have no idea, but you sound so pathetic I have to at least try."

"Gee, thanks."

"Tell me the last thing you saw that was man-made."

Ward thought for a moment. "I saw a sign for boats. Gondola something."

"Great! You're on the right road. That's the company that sells and fixes boats on the lake. Is that sign in front of you or behind you?"

"I have no idea. I've turned around a few times."

"What direction are you facing?"

Ward looked at the compass on her mirror. "East."

"Okay, stay put. I'm heading east, and with that kayak on your roof, I should be able to spot you. So, how was your day?"

"What?"

"How was your day? What did you do?"

Ward couldn't tell her. She didn't want to talk about Jess, or how she'd spent much of the morning thinking of her as she'd shopped for groceries and laundered her clothes. "It was okay. I bought some food and washed clothes. Nothing special."

"Well, I'm glad about the clothes. I don't want you smelling funny. Look to your left."

Ward did as directed and smiled at a waving Abby. She wore a huge grin beneath a Phillies cap and sunglasses, and Ward could see it all clearly because Abby was driving a sporty little red convertible.

"We have to turn around," Abby said, and made a K turn right in the middle of the road. Since Ward hadn't seen any other vehicles in the time she'd been lost, she figured Abby, in her tiny Porsche 911, was probably safe.

"How far are we? Are we close, or were you driving around looking for me before I called?" Ward executed a similar turn on the deserted road, although not as gracefully as the sports car had.

"About thirty seconds away."

"Well, at least I was close."

"Very close," she said, and Ward saw her blinker signal a right-hand turn.

She saw a guardrail beside the driveway, and an old stone bridge over a stream, just as Abby had indicated, yet somehow Ward had missed the gravel road. She followed it now for several hundred yards, into a clearing in the woods where a small log cabin with an attached two-car garage was set among landscaping shrubs and flowerbeds. In front of an open garage bay, a pickup truck sat, a kayak dangling over its tailgate. Abby pulled the Porsche into the other garage bay and hopped out.

"Nice ride." Ward nodded toward the convertible. "I might go hungry for that, too."

Abby grinned. "Thanks."

"I kind of like the truck, though, too."

"That was free. I inherited it from my father."

"Oh, I'm sorry."

Abby laughed. "Oh, no, don't be. He didn't die. He moved to Florida and bought a convertible of his own. The truck's twenty years old and not worth much, so he gave it to me."

"My parents fled to Florida, too, but all I got was a couple of boxes of junk from my childhood bedroom."

"Those greedy bastards." Abby shook her head and frowned.

Ward laughed. Again.

"Do you need to use the bathroom before we leave? We won't see anything but woods for the next few hours."

"No, thanks," she said, and climbed up on her car seat to loosen the restraints holding her own kayak in place. Abby helped her slide it from the roof, and then they put it beside hers on the truck bed. After retrieving her life vest, paddle, and a small cooler, she joined Abby in the cab of the truck and they headed out.

"Did you remember your sunscreen?" Abby asked playfully.

Ward would stop shy of calling Abby a control freak, but she certainly felt comfortable giving orders. Ward had listened quietly that morning, writing quickly as Abby dictated a list of essential items for their short excursion on the river. After a minute, Abby had stopped and asked her to repeat it.

"I've kayaked before, you know," Ward had told her, and reminded Abby again now. "I'm an ER doctor, Abby. I've taken courses in wilderness medicine. Sunscreen is first on the list of essentials."

"Am I being too controlling?" she asked. Her eyebrows rose above her sunglasses.

"Maybe a tad."

"I'm used to ordering everyone around. Sorry. Sunday mode, Ab, Sunday mode," she said, and Ward cracked up.

"Do you always talk to yourself?"

"Always."

Their playful banter continued for the duration of the ride to the park where Abby backed the truck into the boat-launch platform. They easily lifted the kayaks from the truck, and Ward waited with the boats and their gear while Abby parked her truck in the lot a hundred yards away. While she waited, she surveyed the river. Stream would have been a better descriptor, she thought, although not unhappily. She could have thrown a baseball across it, but even though the river was narrow, it also appeared calm, with little visible white water. It wouldn't be a challenging voyage, but it would be calm and peaceful, and she needed calm and peace at the moment.

She looked around, happy to see nothing but a few scattered pieces of evidence proving the existence of man. A few vehicles in a gravel lot, a sign or two, but otherwise, nothing but green. Above her, a canopy of trees offered nearly complete cover, with only scattered areas of dappled sunlight shimmering on the water. In spite of the cars in the lot, the area seemed abandoned, devoid of human bodies and noise, the quiet broken only by the calling of birds above.

Abby appeared, breaking her reverie. "It's nice here, isn't it?" she asked as they pulled the kayaks into the water. After quickly donning their life jackets, they easily cast the boats into the gentle current of the river and were carried downstream. Ward used her paddle to guide her craft toward Abby's.

"Shouldn't we start off going upstream? So we can float back down later?"

Abby shook her head. "Trust me, we'll be fine."

"Okay." Ward pulled her paddle across her lap, allowing the current to guide the boat. She too wore a baseball cap and sunglasses, as well as a T-shirt and nylon shorts, which had already suffered a splash from her paddle. Her feet were protected by hiking sandals that had gotten drenched during the launch but felt fine.

They coasted quietly for a few minutes, only using the paddle to steer and not to propel the kayaks, and she allowed herself to soak up the peace of her surroundings. It was amazing.

"Look," Abby said softly and nodded to the left. Just around a gentle bend in the river, three young deer frolicked in the water as their mother watched from the shelter of the forest. The youngsters noted the kayaks but continued to play as Ward and Abby steered opposite and latched onto a fallen tree to anchor. The deer reminded Ward of her and her brothers as kids, splashing each other as they played in the waves at the Jersey shore. As children she and her brothers had watched strangers warily, just as the deer observed them. Finally, their mother decided they'd had enough fun and called them back into the woods. Ward and Abby pushed back into the water and watched as the smallest of the deer held back. It seemed curious about the humans, determined to introduce himself. And then, like a flash of lightning, he bolted after his siblings. Ward followed the white of his tail until he tucked it down and disappeared.

They smiled at each other and steered back toward the center of the river, where the current was strongest, and after a few minutes, she finally needed her sunscreen, as the river widened and the overhead cover parted as if offering the river to the heavens above. Suddenly, beads of sweat formed as the full force of the July sun beat down on them, and she was happy for the cap and sunglasses, and for the icy water in her cooler. As they floated along, they pointed things out to each other—wildlife in the forest, ruins along the riverbanks, occasional people and the detritus they'd left behind. Abby pulled out a squirt gun and blasted Ward, who retaliated with a significant paddle splash that soaked Abby's top.

A peaceful silence had fallen over them as they looked to the trees and the forests, listening to the birds and other animals scurrying about the woods. In addition to the deer, they'd seen dozens of squirrels and chipmunks, one snake sunning on a flat rock at the water's edge, and dozens of fish in the clear waters beneath their kayaks.

Ward couldn't remember the last time she'd had so much fun. Not that it was all fun...it was relaxing, and that was truly a luxury. With all the twists and turns her life had taken in the past year, relaxation seemed a foreign concept. First she'd taken care of business at the hospital in Philly in preparation for her leave. Then she'd had to pack and find a suitable house sitter. Moving to Garden and adjusting to small-town life had been stressful, even though she hadn't realized it at the time.

Yet she and Jess had been under the microscope, and her life had played out on the stage of the streets and restaurants of the town, the townspeople witnessing everything they did. Then, of course, it really got stressful. Her mother-in-law died, her father-in-law asked her to leave town, and she'd beaten the crap out of two innocent men. She was banished and spent six months hoping and praying and trying to regain Jess. Now, all that was behind her.

In a way, Jess had done her a favor by telling her about Wendy. It gave her an extra month to enjoy herself before she packed her clothes and her kayak and headed home to Philly. And when she got back from the beach in September and headed back to work, well—then she'd worry about selling her house. Hell, maybe she'd even tell Jess to take care of the details, since it was her idea. It didn't matter. It would all work out, and just as the birds circling in the sky above her somehow found their way, she'd be fine in the end, too. Somehow, she'd end up where she was supposed to be. The beautiful woman beside her on the river had shown her that she still had a heart beating in her chest, and eyes to appreciate beauty, and ears to appreciate the song of the birds. Yes, it would all be fine.

Ward's only worry now was the return trip up what, at her estimation, was ten miles of river. They'd been in the boats for a few hours, and though the current was gentle, it was still moving them farther from the boat launch. It was a long way to paddle, and even though Abby had told her not to worry, Ward couldn't help but wonder about her aching arms when they finally reached Abby's truck. She decided to share her thoughts.

"I was thinking the same thing. Why don't we pull the boats out up here." Abby pointed to a clearing in the trees a few hundred yards ahead. "I could use a drink, and then we'll head back."

Ward didn't tell her how she dreaded the return trip. She would still say it was worth it, four hours from now when they got back, but would she have the energy for even a shower later? Probably not.

Directing her kayak toward the left bank of the river, Ward followed Abby, amazed as she pulled her kayak up and into the backyard of a secluded cabin nestled in the clearing between the water and the forest. The cabin was two stories tall, with a chalet-style pitched roof on one side. The stone of the foundation seemed to flow outward, to a patio, and then across the lawn where large boulders sat scattered about, marbles thrown by the hand of God. Each was landscaped with flowers, the only color in sight.

Ward stayed in Abby's shadow as they pulled the kayaks through the grass and finally rested them beside the stone patio at the base of the steps that led to a wrap-around deck above. She stopped short of following Abby into the house, but stood staring as she opened a door in the foundation and stepped inside.

Instantly, Ward heard the telltale screeching of a triggered alarm, then a series of five beeps as Abby deactivated it.

Suspicious, Ward studied her surrounding—the property, the house, the river. Of course! She thought. Abby had driven upstream to the boat launch, and they'd floated down. They'd have to drive back to retrieve Abby's truck, but that sure beat paddling upstream.

"Do I get to drive the Porsche?" Ward asked when Abby peeked back out the door.

"No one but me has ever driven the Porsche. Sorry."

Ward took advantage of the indoor plumbing, and when she emerged, Abby reset the alarm and they walked around to the front of the cabin where Ward's car awaited them. "No one else has ever driven it?"

"Well, no one that I know of. It's technically possible, though. It had seven miles on it when I bought it."

They climbed into Ward's car and headed down the long drive. "And you're not even taking into account the mechanics and the valets. I'm sure they've all taken it for a spin."

Ward stopped before turning onto the road and smirked at Abby, who was glaring at her.

"Not funny."

Ward patted Abby's leg. "I'm just kidding. They never do that."

"If you keep this up, I'm not going to feed you."

"Oh, I didn't realize food was involved. I'm sorry for my insensitivity."

"You should be, and you're forgiven. But don't let it happen again."

They quickly found themselves at the launch area, and she dropped Abby off at her truck and then followed her home. She parked behind the Porsche and stepped out of the car. As she surveyed the house from the front, she was amazed at the difference in the two points of view. The construction of wood and stone was the same, but the front and side yards here were a meadow of wildflowers. It was just as picturesque, but so very different from the back of the house with its rustic charm.

Abby pulled the leash on her kayak, and Ward helped her carry it to the garage and cradle it in the hanger in back. "Are you serious about dinner?" Ward asked as they worked to fasten her craft to the roof of her car.

Abby's eyes twinkled. "I have veggies and chicken marinating. I'll turn on the grill and throw together a salad, and we'll be eating in twenty minutes."

Suddenly Ward was filled with a wonderful joy. The warmth of Abby's smile and the welcome in her eyes did more than her words to let Ward know the invitation was genuine. "What can I do to help?" Ward asked.

Abby motioned with her head, and they walked through the garage and into the basement of her house. It was vacant, except for a few gardening items stored neatly against one wall and the bathroom Ward had just used. "The basement is known to flood, so I try to keep it empty."

"That must be hard," Ward said as she followed Abby up steps she hadn't noticed before. They entered a large, open kitchen with vaulted ceilings. To her right was a spacious living area, with the same high ceilings. On one wall, huge glass panels flanking a fireplace gave a glorious view of the river at the side of the house. A door beyond presumably led to a bedroom. The house was small but magnificent, with natural wood and windows to let in the light and the view.

"It's the price you pay for this," Abby said, waving her hand toward the yard and the river beyond.

"I guess it's worth it then." Ward took a moment to look across the yard of boulders and flowers.

"It is."

"So what can I do?" Ward asked.

Abby assigned her the menial tasks of pouring water and setting the table, and as she did, she couldn't help peeking at Abby's perfect ass bending down to turn on the tank feeding gas to her grill. When she finished, Abby stood and turned, catching her in the act. She felt the blush flash across her face and it seemed to spread through all of her. She looked quickly away, but not before she caught Abby's answering smirk.

Rather than face her in the kitchen, Ward took a seat at the table and admired the view from the deck while she waited for Abby to emerge. The smell of chicken wafted through the air, birds sang yet again, and across the yard the river hummed faintly through the trees. They were in full bloom and surrounded her with a shield of leaves, and other than the man-made things in view, everything was green.

A moment later Abby emerged from her kitchen, carrying a tray bearing everything they needed to complete their meal—salad, dressing, salt and pepper, barbeque sauce. After placing the tray on the table, Abby checked on the food grilling nearby. Seeming satisfied, she removed everything and placed the food on a plate in the middle of the table. "Help yourself," Abby said.

"Oh, wow," Ward said when she bit into the chicken.

Abby looked pleased but blew off the compliment. "It's just chicken."

After swallowing, Ward wiped her mouth and leaned back into the cushioned seat. "But really, really good chicken. Do you like to cook?"

Abby chewed and swallowed before answering, then leaned back too, matching Ward's pose. "It's a necessity when you live alone."

Ward swallowed the thought that she would soon understand the routine of living alone and nodded, then busied herself with a bite of grilled red pepper.

"I take it you don't cook?" Abby asked, refusing to let Ward off the hook.

Ward looked up to meet Abby's gaze. Her eyes seemed to soften in the late-afternoon sun, as if she understood all of Ward's secrets and liked her anyway.

"No, I do. A little. It was too expensive to eat out in school, so I figured out how to make a few things to get by."

They finished their food with harmless conversation about baseball and fishing, and the golf outing planned for the following weekend. Frieda had enthusiastically agreed to join them, and Ward had to admit she was looking forward to the day. When Abby rose to clear the table Ward tried to help, but she dismissed her with a wave of her hand, stacking everything into a pile she was able to carry on the tray in one trip.

"So may I presume there's no Mrs. Ward?" Abby asked when she returned.

Ward closed her eyes. The large umbrella shaded her from the late-afternoon sun, but she still felt its warmth, and suddenly Abby's inquiry made her feel uncomfortably hot. She'd known this question would come up. She wanted to see Abby, to be with her, yet Jess was still there. She was a part of Ward's life, her world, her heart. Saying no, telling Abby there was no one in her life seemed like such a betrayal. It seemed dishonest, untrue. Yet it was true—Jess was no longer her partner. Jess had told her to move on, as she had.

It was time for Ward. Even if it was only for one night, or one week, or for the twenty-four days she had left in this town, she was going to enjoy herself.

"No," she said without turning to face Abby. "No Mrs. How about you? Do you have anyone special in your life?"

Abby didn't sound disappointed when she answered. "No."

"That surprises me."

Abby rearranged the place setting before her as she seemed to ponder Ward's comment. "I'm like an onion, with lots of layers. I like the arts and I like sports. I like to hang out at home sometimes, and travel, too. I like to cook, but I love to eat at five-star restaurants. I enjoy a cocktail or a glass of wine, but I don't want to get drunk. And I don't want to be with a drunk. I can listen to any kind of music—and I like to listen to all of it. I'd get bored if I listened to the same thing all the time. It's sort of the same with women. I've never found one that I thought could hold my interest, and I'm realistic enough to admit it. If I meet someone absolutely perfect, maybe I'll get serious. Until then, I'm going to have fun. Does this make sense?"

Ward nodded, her mind spinning. After the comments about alcohol, she hadn't really paid much attention to Abby's words. Why bother? Abby would be sending her on her way soon, when she learned she'd recently gotten so intoxicated she assaulted two men. And when she figured out how boring she was. In spite of what Jess said, she didn't feel like she needed much. She liked to do things and keep busy, but she didn't need those things. What she needed was what she'd always had—a partner to come home to, a few books to read, a bike to ride or a boat to paddle. If Abby was an onion, with many layers, she was more like a strawberry. Sweet, but with no depth, no layers at all. She was simple, really, and she suspected Abby would grow bored quickly.

"Perfect sense," Ward said.

"Okay, so what would you do if I turned on an opera right now?"

Ward focused on the music playing in the kitchen, a soft rock song on a popular channel. It was probably what she would have chosen for the night on the deck as well. But could she handle opera? Sure. "Well, I wouldn't sing, that's for sure. I have trouble with the high notes."

Abby laughed. "So you're not a fan?"

Ward shook her head. "No, it's not that. I actually think opera's beautiful. But I can't sing for shit."

"Well, thanks for the warning."

Her voice had dropped a measure, and Ward turned her head to meet Abby's gaze. "What?" she asked, self-conscious as Abby's eyes bore into hers.

Instead of an answer, Abby stood and bent forward so they were nose to nose. Ward might have turned away, moved slightly to give Abby the answer to the question asked in the form of her brief delay. Instead, Ward stood her ground and silently told Abby it was okay.

Abby cupped Ward's chin with two fingers, and Ward turned slightly, closing her eyes. Their lips barely met, and she could feel Abby's breath on her mouth. It wasn't so much a kiss as a caress, the softest of touches that caused a tingling that began at the site of contact and shot quickly to her toes. An instantaneous throb began between her legs, as if her pulse was beating there.

Just as quickly, Abby pulled back and offered a hand.

Ward took it, grateful because her legs seemed to be numb and her head was spinning from the kiss. She needed direction, and Abby seemed to be a compass.

"I'd like to show you the rest of the house."

The proffered hand pulled her up, held her steady, drew her nearer until they were face to face, and Ward wrapped both arms around Abby's waist and pulled her closer still, until they were one. They were the same height, and everything seemed to fit perfectly as their hips locked and breasts mashed and mouths crashed into each other. This wasn't the same tender caress, but a needy, demanding kiss, and both of them asked much of each other with their tongues battling and conquering. Ward felt all of Abby against her, and the heat of the contact seemed to melt her. Her brain was foggy, her muscles like mush, and her center a pool of lava.

"Okay." She didn't even care that she sounded so lame.

Abby pulled back and grabbed her hand again. "Come with me."

She followed Abby through her cabin, across the kitchen and great room and through French doors on the other side. Once through the threshold, they turned left, into a huge bathroom with marble tile from floor to ceiling. The colors were all earthy and blended with the natural woods and stone she'd seen throughout Abby's home. Abby pushed her gently onto a supple leather bench and then knelt on the floor, carefully removing the sandals from Ward's feet. She bent and silently demanded another kiss, and Abby complied. It was minutes before they pulled away, breathless from the mingling of tongues and breasts.

Then Abby stood before her, her breasts at eye level, and reached down, pulling Ward's shirt free of her shorts and up and over her head. Without missing a beat, she slipped off her own top. Ward stood and turned Abby gently, kissing her as she spun. Her forehead, her ear, the back of her neck, down to her shoulder. Her skin was salty, her smell musky, and Ward's heart pounded with anticipation. They faced the mirror now, and she looked up to see Abby's eyes closed but her mouth slightly open, a look of wonder on her face. Then she looked at herself and smiled.

The bra holding Abby's breasts was off in a second, and Ward removed her own. The feeling of Abby's bare back against her breasts was intoxicating. Closing her eyes to the vision before her, she moaned with the simple pleasure of a soft touch. It had been so long since she'd touched a lover this way, and she savored the sensations. Who knew when this might happen again?

She moved slowly, allowing Abby's skin to caress her nipple much like that first kiss on the deck, barely touching yet causing an explosive reaction. She reached around and opened her eyes to find her hands appearing on Abby's chest, watched her fingertips find the stiff peaks of Abby's nipples, then felt the quivering of Abby's entire body as she sank back into her. Abby opened her eyes, and as they locked gazes, Ward thought she'd never seen anything so beautiful as the desire she saw now.

Abby turned then and knelt again, this time to remove Ward's shorts. The underwear only came down to mid-thigh when Abby buried her face in the triangle there, pulling Ward into her, seeking with her tongue to know all of her. Then she pulled back, and as Ward shed her shorts and underwear with a swift kick, Abby removed her own, turned on the shower, and beckoned her inside.

The water was the perfect temperature and felt like hot raindrops on a summer's day, falling from the overhead fixture. And as Abby once again stepped into her arms, the water caressed them as they devoured each other. Abby pulled back, reached for shampoo, and then spilled a huge puddle into her hand. Then she palmed Ward's head, and Ward closed her eyes and allowed her to have her way. Fingers firmly massaged her scalp and the water cascaded over her. The pressure lightened across her forehead and her face, in her ears and behind them, along the muscles of her neck, one side and then the other. Then her head gently tilted forward as Abby rinsed the shampoo, and soapy hands slid down her arms and back under them, across her chest, beneath breasts and between them, and then lower, slowly down her belly, through the curls of hair at the bottom, and through her legs, across her ass, and up her back. Abby paused briefly to kiss her stiffened clit before sitting cross-legged to wash her legs. Picking up her right foot, she washed from toes to thigh, then repeated her efforts on the left, until every inch of Ward was covered in soap and thoroughly rinsed.

Abby shifted to her knees and gently guided Ward down, against the wall of the shower, so her sex was under the falling rain of the showerhead. Using both hands, Abby pushed her legs apart and knelt between them, then put her mouth on Ward. The wetness at her center had nothing to do with the falling rain and everything to do with Abby, and she quickly drilled a finger into the puddle at Ward's entrance. Ward gasped, and Abby stilled the finger as her mouth devoured Ward's sex, licking and sucking her clit and her labia as Ward rose from the floor to meet her mouth, then grabbed her head to hold it in place. Abby still moved, though, both her finger and her tongue, and very quickly the orgasm she was trying to coax from Ward came crashing down on both of them. Ward clenched her vaginal muscles, squeezing the thrusting finger, and arched back and into Abby's mouth. Her cry was soft and quickly turned to a laugh of pure joy.

With her head on Ward's belly, Abby rested for a moment, and then, to Ward's surprise, she grabbed the bottle of shampoo and began washing her own hair. Mesmerized, and exhausted, Ward could do little more than stare at the magnificent woman who so brazenly had claimed her on this beautiful day. Abby tilted her head back, and Ward imagined her mouth leaving a trail of kisses along her graceful neck. Her eyes followed Abby's hands and she imagined her mouth there, and when Abby soaped her breasts, Ward thought she saw her abdomen clench. It happened again when Abby reached between her legs. Ward thought she spent much more time spreading soap than was necessary, and her expression suggested she was taking much pleasure in this cleansing. Suddenly fearing Abby would bring herself to orgasm without any help at all from her, Ward sat up and demanded the soap.

Abby handed her a thick washcloth, and Ward finished the job in much the same way Abby had done earlier, first with one leg and then with the other, and then by pushing her back onto the shower floor as she dove into her pussy. Ward's face was filled with Abby and she had to pull back to take a breath, then began again, rubbing Abby's clit with her nose and her eyes and her mouth as two fingers worked their way inside and began circling each other around the tight walls of Abby's vagina. The combination of sensations appeared to be too much, and Abby suddenly clenched her legs and her pelvis and held Ward's head in place as she cried out in pleasure.

Only the cooling water forced Ward to move, and she reached up and turned the knobs until the flow trickled and then stopped. Collapsing next to Abby, she kissed her triumphantly. Ward should have felt exhausted from the day on the river and the powerful orgasm, but she didn't. She was happy and excited and energized, and wanted to spend what remained of the day with Abby, doing just what they'd done in the shower. "Any chance there's a bed in this place?" she asked, as she trailed kisses from Abby's ear to her mouth.

Abby bit the smile from her lower lip as she slid out from under Ward and stood, offering her hand once again. "A great big one," she said.

Ward allowed Abby to pull her up, and into her huge bed, and they stayed there until Abby had to leave for work in the morning. For the second consecutive night, she didn't sleep, but this time, she didn't mind at all.

CHAPTER NINETEEN
DEAD ON ARRIVAL

Subtle indentations in the wooden surface of the desk told Edward it had been well used over the years. Like the craftsman home that housed it, the desk had been around a long time. Did it have tales to tell? If he placed a naked paper over it and etched with a pencil, what would it say?

Nothing as interesting as what he wrote this day, he was sure.

Looking down at the elegant sheet of linen paper, printed especially for him, he felt his pulse began to race. Nearly a hundred similar documents had piled up in his collection over the years, but he treasured every one. Each new acquisition was as exciting as the first. That first victim's name was Helise, and she was once his babysitter. Edward had strangled her in an act of rage after he discovered her fucking her boyfriend. He had watched from the shadows, first the sex, and then the escape as the boyfriend jumped to the garage roof and then onto the Ford Bronco hidden beside it, then drove away with the headlights off. Edward had been tempted to kill him, too, but in a flash of genius he'd realized the police would find cause to blame him for her murder, setting Edward free. What better revenge could there be?

As the Bronco's taillights had disappeared into the night, Edward snuck into her room, following a path he'd taken hundreds of times before, when Helise preferred his cock to her boyfriend's. For almost three years, they'd been lovers. Sure, they'd never acknowledged it in public—she was five years older than him, after all—but he'd had exclusive rights to her. Wherever, whenever. Three, four, sometimes five nights a week they'd get together for tutoring sessions where she taught him cunnilingus and how to fuck, how to give her multiple orgasms.

Life after Helise wasn't much fun. His body had grown accustomed to hers, and suddenly his hand wasn't at all as satisfying as it once was. And most sixteen-year-old girls from Rumson, New Jersey did not put out. At least not to nerds like him. He'd even tried guys, because they were perpetually horny. At a rest-stop bathroom on the Garden State Parkway South, he'd eventually earned his second certificate. He'd planned the sex but not the murder. The guy got creepy, though, so Edward hit him with a rock from the ground beside the picnic table where they'd just fucked.

It had been a long year between those first two victims. He'd examined his conscience, denying himself the satisfaction of killing again until he knew he wouldn't be implicated in Helise's murder. The wait was torture, but during that time he came to understand himself better. He was a killer. A murderer. He loved committing homicide more than he loved sex or power or money, and he'd chosen a career path that gave him access to a bountiful garden of potential victims. He'd come to embrace his murders as some admired their art or music. Each death certificate, like the one before him on the desk, represented a masterpiece of cunning and planning and execution. He was now at master level. Number one hundred.

Even the most notorious mass murderers didn't reach a hundred kills. Gacy had only a few dozen bodies beneath the floorboards, and Bundy had scattered perhaps forty bodies across the Pacific Northwest. Yet everyone knew them! They were famous. One day, he would be, too.

Picking up his pen, he began the process of completing the document. Name. Date of Birth. Sex. Time, Date, and Place of Death. And then, the part he loved most. Writing the deed almost gave it life. Cause and Manner of Death. The causes varied but still gave him shivers. Writing the word homicide made him tremble so violently the pen shook in his hand.

When he finished, he read it over for the sheer pleasure of it, and to proof it as well. When he was satisfied, he pulled out his smart phone, photographed the document, and then uploaded it to his iCloud. In seconds, the document was safely stored, away from prying eyes and hot flames and all other conceivable methods of destruction. He immediately deleted the photo from his phone, then began scrolling through the photos saved in cyberspace. One hundred of them, arranged in chronological order, dating from that first one more than twenty years earlier. One hundred deaths made possible by his hands, nearly a quarter of them in the past six months. He shuddered as he did the math. His recent career change had put him in a most wonderful position to see a record on the horizon. A macabre record, a dubious pathway to celebrity, but a means nonetheless. If he continued at his pace, he'd have the opportunity to become the first serial killer to earn a comma. One thousand victims!

Then, he'd do something spectacular to announce his achievement. Perhaps an interview on prime-time television. He'd have fun with that. Or a front-page story in *The New York Times*. That would get the attention of all the people in New Jersey who'd thought he was a nobody. He'd furnish the newspaper with copies of all the death certificates, but he'd save the originals for posterity. Perhaps the national crime museum would want them. They had Bundy's car, after all. Closing his eyes, he imagined it all—the national-television interview, and later a spread in the *National Enquirer* or *People* magazine, featuring him. He would include a high-school-graduation photo, and perhaps an anonymous acquaintance would contribute a more recent one. Multiple photos of the victims with catchy little captions beneath them would fill the pages. They'd come up with a clever nickname for him, too, he was sure. Dr. Death? Emergency Monster? Caduceus Killer? It was so exciting an erection began to stir. He touched himself with one hand as he caressed the paper on the desk with the other.

"Better keep you safe, little guy," he said to the paper, mocking the death of Christian Cooney, who'd died of a venous air embolus. "You could be famous one day!"

He carefully tucked the paper into the secret compartment of his briefcase against another that hadn't yet made it to the safety of the bank box where the first ninety-eight were stored. He liked the sound of that. He said it out loud. "The *first* ninety-eight victims of the world's most prolific mass murderer, Dr. Edward Hawk."

He retrieved his car keys and his wallet from the briefcase, locked it, and headed toward the door. The local sheriff had offered to take him shooting, and the idea intrigued him. He'd never used a gun before. Perhaps it was a way to broaden his horizons a bit. He'd used his hands on the first dozen victims, varying the details enough so police in Rumson and the Jersey shore communities wouldn't suspect the same man was at work. Hell, no one even knew about him! Later, when he had ready access to hospital patients, he took full advantage. After all, hospital patients were supposed to die, and other than that incident at his last job, he'd managed to kill hospital patients for over a decade without detection. But maybe changing things up would be good. Or adding to them. Maybe a hunting accident would be fun.

His mind spinning with ideas, he whistled as he walked to his car.

CHAPTER TWENTY
GOLFER'S ELBOW

"Nice shot!" Ward watched her drive soar into the clear blue sky and land in the middle of the fairway, two hundred and fifty yards away. The lush green fairway was surrounded by even more green—the rough, at first a few inches high, and then taller until it melted into the forests lining both sides from the tee box to the putting surface. She turned back to the three women standing behind her, framed by tall trees, and nodded. "Someone has to carry this team," she told them.

"Cocky one, aren't you?" Abby whispered as Ward stood beside her and Frieda teed up her ball.

Ward said nothing, but she tilted the left corner of her mouth upward. She felt cocky. Since the moment she'd first seen Abby and felt the attraction, her self-confidence had returned. It hadn't started to come back as a slow process, like drips of water filling a bucket. It had returned suddenly, like a fire hose shooting the container full in a split second, overflowing the edges.

"Good ball," Ward said as Frieda's drive landed somewhere close to hers.

"Let's get back in the cart, Abby. Save your energy for the next one. How many holes have we played, anyway? I have to pee."

"We've played eight holes, Mom. If you can hold it, you can use the indoor plumbing on the turn." The tournament format was a shotgun start, but their group had started on the first hole.

"Oh, I prefer the woods, but I guess I can wait."

Abby followed her mother to the cart they shared, and Ward walked beside Frieda. "Five bucks says I outdrove you," Frieda said.

The balls sat so close together and were hit so far, it was impossible to tell from this distance which was actually the longer drive. "Do you gamble on everything, Frieda?" Ward asked.

"Pretty much."

"Okay, five bucks it is."

Ward took her spot behind the wheel and began driving along the cart path, her eyes on the little white spheres floating on the sea of green far ahead of them. Her ball lay to the right of Frieda's, and as they drew closer, it became sadly apparent to Ward that the ball on the left had come to rest a few yards ahead of the other.

"Fuck," she said softly, prompting a laugh from Frieda.

"Well, youngster, we can go double-or-nothing on the approach shot."

"Oh, no. That shot's not in my bag. How about a putting contest?" Her strength was on the tee box. Her drives usually went a long way and often landed on the fairway, but her game fell apart after that. She had a slim chance of hitting the green on her second shot. Once she did, though, her putter was a great weapon.

"I may be a dumb farm girl, but I'm not stupid."

Everyone climbed out of the carts, and Abby stepped next to Frieda's ball to check the yardage to the pin. As she pushed her sunglasses onto her head and brought the GPS device to her eye, Frieda called out. "Eighty yards."

Judi countered her estimate. "Eighty-four."

Ward checked Abby out as she measured the yardage. Long, tanned legs stretched from beneath neat white linen shorts. A button-up cotton top in various shades of blue and green draped to her waistline. Her feet were planted hip-width apart, and she arched her back a little as she rested both elbows on her breasts and held the distance finder to her eyes. Ward imagined her arching her back in another situation, but before she had the opportunity to dwell on that vision, Abby dropped the device to her side and glared at her mother and Frieda. "Eighty-two yards."

Frieda hooted as she held up her palm, and Judi smacked it enthusiastically. "We could have saved you a few hundred bucks," Frieda said to Abby.

She just shook her head and grabbed the pitching wedge from her bag. With club in hand, she took the spot beside Ward at the front of her cart. They waited. And waited. The foursome in front of them was still chipping.

"Frieda, do you have a gun in that truck? Maybe a few shots at their feet will move them along."

"Mom!" Abby chastised her. "Don't even joke about that."

"Oh, be quiet! You're too politically correct."

Frieda nodded but frowned. "This whole generation. That's their problem."

"That and a few other things." Judi sniggered, and she and Frieda laughed.

Abby looked to Ward for support, and Ward studied the two older women. They'd really hit it off, and Ward was delighted to see Frieda having such a nice time. Ward suspected she was lonely living in the farmhouse with only Hershey and Irene for company, with no close neighbors to nag her and no job to occupy her time. Maybe when Ward went back to Philly, Judi would take her place as Frieda's golfing buddy.

"Behave, you two, or I'll have to separate you," Ward said as she wagged a finger at them. Then she leaned against the front of her cart and looked toward the green. "And stop complaining. The slow play seems to favor us. We're five under par through eight holes, and this one looks like another birdie opportunity to me."

At eighty-two yards, both Abby and Frieda had the ability to land the ball close to the pin. Judi would likely be in the woods, and Ward would be in the sand, but they would still have two balls on the green, close enough to one-put. Oh, the joy of team golf! Their well-balanced foursome was doing what they were supposed to do. Ward got off the tee, Abby got them onto the green, and Judi could putt. Frieda did everything. They'd mixed and matched shots for eight holes, and the results had been great.

"Don't jinx us!" Abby warned them.

"While we're waiting," Judi said, "I should talk to Ward about the ER committee meeting."

"Oh, Mom, knock it off. We're having fun," Abby said.

"Abby, a doctor is never off duty," Judi retorted.

Ward decided to intervene. This was the first time she'd spent time with Abby and her mother, and she was unsure of their family dynamics. Maybe bickering was typical of them, but she was picking up a hint of frustration from Abby and didn't want it to ruin their day.

"It's okay, Ab." She winked, then looked at Judi. "What's up?"

Judi looked smugly toward her daughter before turning her full attention to Ward. "As you know, our director has been out sick for a few months. The QAs are starting to pile up. I was hoping you could take a look at some of the charts and give an opinion."

"What are QAs?" Frieda asked.

Abby spoke first. "Quality Assurance. When there's a bad patient outcome, we always review the chart to see what happened. What did we do wrong, what can we do better next time."

"What do you mean by bad outcome?" Frieda asked.

Abby didn't look the least bit uncomfortable. "Unexpected deaths."

"What's unexpected? Isn't everyone expected to die?"

Ward fought her smile but turned toward Abby, who didn't. Behind her, the sun hid behind a cloud and Ward could see her features clearly. Her sunglasses were still atop her head, and her squint produced tiny lines at the corners of her eyes. Ward found them incredibly attractive. Her cheeks had a slight blush, possibly the result of the day's warmth, or perhaps it had been applied with a brush. Either way, it defined them and made her look so alive. The gold streaks in her hair seemed even brighter against the backdrop of the clouds. Her beauty startled Ward. Abby seemed to be growing more lovely every day.

Suddenly feeling the heat, Ward looked away, toward the green. The flag had been pulled, and the four men were studying their putt as if a green jacket from the Master's Championship were on the line.

"If they have a pulse when they arrive but not when they depart, we review the case."

Ward turned back to Abby and shook her head, dropping her chin to her chest to keep from laughing at Abby's colorful description.

"Humph. I wish they'd review my neighbor's chart. I'm telling you, something funny happened there."

Ward watched Frieda shake her head and Judi place a comforting hand on her arm. "Were you close?"

"Knew 'im since we were kids. He was healthy as a horse one minute, and the next he was dead."

"Probably his heart," Judi said.

Frieda leaned forward slightly, resting her weight on the golf club in her hands. "That's the thing. He had some sort of weak spell, and they took him to the hospital. My brother works there so I got the whole story. He said they checked his cardiogram and his blood, and he definitely wasn't having a heart attack. They called me to come get him, and when I got there, he was dead in his room."

Ward cringed, not only at hearing the terrible story, but at the way Melvin had violated the patient's confidentiality.

"It sounds dreadful, Frieda, but unfortunately, it does happen," Ward said sadly. In fact, it had once nearly happened to her. Only the hand of God had saved her patient, whose paperwork had gotten jammed in the printer. Twenty minutes later, as the patient was walking out the door, she collapsed. The new EKG revealed a heart attack, and Ward and the rest of the team were able to revive her. The heart team went to work and opened a blockage in one of her coronary arteries. She lived to see her fortieth birthday.

"Well, I still think they should investigate."

Abby tried to reassure her. "You might not be aware of it, but I'm sure they did. The hospital has a huge stake in patient survival."

"At least until they pay the bill, right?" Frieda said.

Everyone was silent, but when Frieda started to laugh a second later, the tension was broken. On cue, the men in front of them began their trek off the back of the green.

Their rotation had been established on the first hole, and it had been working. Judi, the weakest golfer, always hit first off the fairway. After allowing an appropriate few seconds for the men to clear the green, she stepped up to the ball, took a choppy backswing, and whacked the ball. It flew half the distance to the green on a soft line drive, then hopped on, and to the utter astonishment of everyone watching, it struck the flagstick and dropped into the hole.

They mobbed her amid hooting and hollering, and when the foursome behind them started cheering, Judi faced them and politely bowed. As they walked back to their carts, Frieda patted her on the back. "You know what this means, don't you?" she asked.

Judi looked perplexed. "I buy the drinks?"

"No, silly. That tradition is for a hole-in-one. It means we have time to pee."

Everyone laughed, and they did indeed stop at the restrooms before beginning the back nine. When Abby and Ward emerged a few minutes later, to their shock, Judi and Frieda were rearranging the golf clubs on the carts.

"What are you doing?" Abby asked.

"I decided to ride with Frieda on the back nine. You two don't mind, do you?" Judi asked.

Abby looked from her mother to Ward, a question in her sparkling eyes. Ward shrugged. "I don't mind."

When they were out of earshot, Ward nudged Abby. "Don't take this the wrong way, but I think your mom is flirting with Frieda."

"Why would I take it the wrong way?" she asked. "I think they'd make a cute couple."

Ward's jaw dropped. "Abby, is your mom gay, too?"

Abby nodded.

"Wow. What a team."

Chapter Twenty-one
Sepsis

Ward awakened gradually, ignoring the assault on her senses that tried to pull her into the day. The sun bathed her eyelids with a warm wash of light. Birds chirped outside her window, gossiping back and forth, then singing together in chorus. Silky, soft sheets caressed her naked skin. The sweet scent of sex filled her nostrils. Among her senses, only taste was denied satisfaction this morning, and if she concentrated, she could still imagine the tangy taste of Abby on her tongue.

It was Sunday afternoon. Two weeks had passed since her first visit to Abby's, or was this still the first visit? She'd left a few times, but only for the essential tasks like work and grocery shopping, golf and kayaking. She hadn't been home to Philly, or to Jeannie's, and the bed in the house beside the hospital had been essentially undisturbed. She had spent all of her nights—the ones outside the hospital, anyway—at Abby's house. She'd messed up her own sheets only to catch some sleep after her night shifts. On one of those mornings, just as she'd been about to pull on her mask and crawl into bed, a knock at the door had surprised her. Abby had warmed her bed for an hour before heading to work. They hadn't made love that morning, just spent an hour talking before Abby's first meeting of the day. They tended to spend a good deal of their time talking—about everything.

Stretching, Ward rolled onto her side and studied the room. It was Abby, and the more she knew of her, the more Ward liked both her and her house. For fifty hours each week Abby dressed in skirts and heels and roamed the sterile world of the hospital, but when she came home, she was a jeans-and-T-shirts girl, warm and cozy in the woods of her home and the woods that surrounded it.

Slipping from between the sheets, Ward located a T-shirt that looked familiar as well as a pair of shorts. After pulling them on, she peed and brushed her teeth, then wandered into the living room. Abby sat on the couch, her laptop perched on her knees as she peeked at the television and the Phillies' game being broadcast.

"Hi," Abby said, a smile exploding on her face.

Ward was exhausted. She'd just worked three consecutive night shifts, nearly forty tough hours in the ER. Although she'd slept after the first two shifts, she'd cut this nap short. If she didn't, she'd have difficulty sleeping tonight, and her body wouldn't swing back into day shift. So, she'd crawled into bed around ten in the morning, and even though it was only two in the afternoon, she'd forced her eyes open and her body upright. She'd stay that way until the rest of the world went to bed later tonight.

"How was your nap?"

In spite of the lack of sleep, she was invigorated by Abby's smile. Sleep was totally over-rated. "Wonderful."

They spent the afternoon on the couch, watching the game and talking, sharing a few kisses. It was perfectly relaxing, and in spite of her lack of sleep, Ward felt good. Great, in fact. Being with Abby felt great.

The ringing of Ward's cell phone broke their peace. She stood and looked at Abby apologically. "I need to take this call." She placed the phone to her ear as she eased through the sliding door onto the deck. It had been difficult to pull herself out of the comfortable arms of the couch, but she had to. Michelle was calling, and while Ward touched base with her tenant regularly, it was unusual for Michelle to initiate contact. Ward needed to make sure nothing was amiss.

"Howdy," she said. Since Michelle had started teasing Ward about her retreat into the rugged terrain of the mountains, Ward had been playing the part of cowgirl when they talked.

"Howdy. Do people really talk like that where you are? Do they have guns? I mean, out in the open, on their trucks? 'Cuz that sort of scares me more than the knife-and-gun club here. At least I know these guys just want my money. Who knows what guys in pickup trucks want?"

Instead of settling into one of the cozy chairs on Abby's deck, she leaned against the plank railing, looking out at the breathtaking view of the river. It was early evening, and the cloudless sky afforded the sun full access to the deck. It heated her skin as she imagined the cool of the forest and river at the end of her line of vision.

Some people might question Abby's decision to live close to the water, to tolerate its fits and floods, but Ward wasn't one of them. She could marvel at this beauty forever. The trees lining the banks at the rear of the property were hundreds of years old, the boulders scattered around the yard and the woods and the water thrown there by the same violent forces that created the heavens and the earth. The ferns and moss along the water's edge and under the trees were tenacious species that tolerated both the water and lack of light under the great canopy above them.

Gazing back from the path of the water, Ward recognized Abby's touch. Her hands had laid the pockets of vibrant color between the rocks there, and that knowledge gave Ward much satisfaction. Abby was truly talented. Her yard, her whole house was put together to meld woman and nature, and it amazed Ward that it was so beautiful and technologically advanced at the same time. The colors and designs Abby chose just seemed to flow into each other, peacefully. And that was just what Ward felt when she was here—serene.

A click made her turn, and she was surprised to see Abby walk out onto the deck. More surprised that Abby walked over to her and rested her head against her shoulder, and she couldn't resist the urge to turn just a fraction and pull Abby against her. Just the touch gave her goose bumps. Michelle hadn't even revealed the purpose of her call, and Ward wanted to end it so she could take Abby back to bed.

"I know how you feel. The guns take some getting used to. But you kind of caught me at a bad time," she said, as Abby began flicking her tongue along the muscles of her neck, working her way toward her ear. "What's up?"

"The dryer stopped working. I'm going to have the guy come out and check it. I'm off tomorrow. Just wanted to let you know."

Ward swallowed, fighting to focus on the conversation as her body was flooded with the sensations of Abby—her smell, her softness pressed against her, her hot mouth on her skin. "Okay, just let me know what it costs and I'll reimburse you."

"No worries. I'll take care of it."

Ward disconnected the call and tossed the phone onto the chair behind her, then pulled Abby into her arms. She arched her neck, giving Abby more space, and gasped from the electrical shocks those tiny kisses were producing. Her skin tingled, her breath caught, and her heart pounded. The flood of wet heat in her sex made her knees grow weak.

Abby broke the kiss long enough to guide her back to the lounge chair.

❖

"So, who was on the phone?" Abby asked as she circled Ward's nipple with her silky fingertip.

"Hmm?" Ward asked, trying to shake the fog from her brain.

"On the phone. Roommate?"

Blinking a few times, Ward cleared her eyes and tried to look at Abby, but she couldn't focus. Abby was too close, her head resting on Ward's chest. "No, umm, not roommate. Housemate, I guess."

"Housemate? Ex-roommate? Girlfriend? Partner? Wife?"

Abby's tone was inquisitive, not demanding, and Ward kissed her gently on top of her head.

"Just housemate, Abby."

Abby pulled back and smiled sadly at Ward. "C'mon, Ward. Beautiful women don't just appear on my doorstep every day. You must be running from something. Or someone."

Two weeks earlier, when she'd asked if there was a Mrs. Ward, Ward hadn't been ready to talk about Jess. Her time with Abby had been healing, though. Abby was like an elixir that had soothed all of Ward's wounds and breathed life into her again. She wasn't sure where their relationship was heading, but if it was going anywhere—even to the bedroom from the deck—she needed to be honest. She pulled Abby back to her and wound her fingers into Abby's. "Not running *from* someone, Abby. Running *to* someone."

Abby looked up and searched Ward's eyes. "I don't understand."

"Her name is Jess. I followed her here, from Philadelphia. I wanted to be close by, in case she changed her mind about us. But she's made it very clear that it's over, and so..." Ward shrugged.

"You've moved on?"

Ward nodded and smiled.

"So I'm the famous transition girlfriend?"

Ward looked into Abby's eyes. She saw no judgment, only concern, and found her courage in their warmth. "Are you my girlfriend? I'm not sure what it is we're doing here, but I think it's time we give it a name."

Abby sat up but looked down. "You're leaving in a few weeks. We'll probably never see each other again. We don't need to give it a name."

Abby sounded defensive, and Ward found that reaction oddly comforting. Jess hadn't really cared what Ward did, where she was, or what she'd planned. It seemed that Abby did, though, and Ward had to admit she cared, too. She'd wanted nothing from Abby at the start, nothing except the sex she knew was on Abby's mind when she'd taken her hand and guided Ward to her bedroom. Unexpectedly, they'd created something wonderful together, and Ward had slipped into this...what was it called, if not a relationship...and it felt as good and as right as anything she'd ever felt.

Ward grabbed Abby's wrist, a little more tightly than necessary, and Abby looked up. Ward loosened her grip and offered a small smile, then opened her arms. "Come back here, Ms. Rosen."

When Abby had settled against her once again, with Ward's face in her hair, Ward spoke. "Abby, a few weeks ago, I couldn't even think about someone else. And then I met you under that tree and saw fireworks. Literally. I haven't been able to think of anything—or anyone—but you, since then. You're beautiful." Ward turned Abby's face toward hers and kissed her softly on the lips.

"And funny." They kissed again. "And smart." Another kiss, this one longer.

Abby pulled back a hair and whispered into Ward's mouth.

"And insatiable. God, Ward, I've never felt like this before. I really can't get enough of you. Let's go back to bed."

"What's wrong with out here? It's certainly private enough."

Abby looked down at the lounge chair, intended for one. "I'd like to...spread out."

"I can't argue with that."

They made love, not passionately, but slowly and tenderly. When they were face-to-face on Abby's pillow an hour later, Abby ran her fingers through Ward's hair and kissed her softly on the nose. "So tell me about Jess."

"What about her?"

"Everything. She's officially my competition, and I want to know what I'm up against."

Ward laughed. "You're not up against anything, Ab. I told you, it's over with Jess."

"And I told you, I'm not that stupid. I want to know everything you're willing to tell me. Maybe talking to a neutral third party will help you realize she's an idiot and doesn't deserve you."

Ward laughed and pulled Abby closer. "I already know that," she said, "and I have a feeling you're not very neutral." She told Abby her story anyway. Maybe Abby could make sense of it all or offer some insight no one else could. Or maybe she just needed to be honest with Abby, because if she was honest with herself, she was beginning to feel like she wanted the month of July to last forever. She wanted her time with Abby at this little cabin by the river to never end. And in spite of the fact that Abby had never had a serious relationship, Ward suspected she felt the same way.

CHAPTER TWENTY-TWO
VENOUS AIR EMBOLUS

Meetings had always been one of Ward's favorite things. From the time she was a Girl Scout, she'd loved the power that filled a room full of people coming together with common goals in mind. She loved the idea of it, anyway. It didn't take her long to realize little was accomplished at meetings, that most of the negotiating and discussing took place in the high-school cafeteria and on the basketball court. It didn't matter how far she climbed up the ladder, nothing ever changed. It was now a hospital cafeteria, and a golf course instead of basketball court, but it still worked the same way.

Ward had agreed to review charts and attend the hospital's Morbidity and Mortality meeting as a favor to both Judi and Abby. She didn't relish the task, but understanding that it had to be done and that no one at Endless Mountains was qualified to do it, she'd agreed. And so, on her day off, she'd come to work and quickly became engrossed in a game of politics.

She'd arrived early to peruse charts, and as she walked the halls from the ER to the board room, no fewer than three physicians on staff had gone out of their way to speak to her about the patients whose care she was reviewing. All three held professional ties to the patients—two were the primary-care physicians, and the third was a surgeon who'd recently operated on one of the deceased. It quickly became evident that none of the three were as interested in the outcome of her probe as they were in vindicating themselves.

All three spoke of non-compliance—missed appointments, failure to adhere to treatment plans, skipped medication doses—all factors that could have contributed to the patient deaths.

Two other physicians had also approached Ward. Both predicted the conclusions she would reach and wondered why the hospital bothered with such matters as peer review. "We all know hindsight's twenty-twenty," one of them had said. "At least you'll get a free dinner out of it," the other told her.

After four months of rural medicine, Ward was no longer shocked by the comments and coercion. The attitude among medical staff members was still frightening, though. Instead of regarding the process as it was intended—as a way to improve patient care and educate physicians and nurses to help them save lives—they were all threatened by it. Is this what malpractice suits had done to everyone? They'd become afraid to admit their mistakes, even to themselves, and lobbied their colleagues for reassuring pats on the back. Or was it worse than that? Was it all just about fragile egos?

Ward listened to them, all five respected physicians, and thanked them for their help in the matter. And then she promised herself to disregard everything everyone had told her, and all the gossip she'd heard, and to formulate her opinions based on the information contained within the pages of the medical records.

Confidentiality concerns made it necessary for her to do this work within the four walls of the hospital. While she might have taken advantage of Abby's secure system at home, Ward knew that when she began probing into restricted patient files, an electronic fingerprint would be generated. That could create problems. If she accessed those charts under Abby's name, would people question Abby's motives for reading the charts? After all, her background was in business, not in medicine, and she couldn't add much insight. And if Ward signed in using Abby's online connections, would people speculate about the nature of their relationship as well as Ward's motivations in the probe and the integrity of her findings?

Although both scenarios were ridiculous, she'd seen so much petty bullshit during her medical career that nothing surprised her. Therefore, she went into the hospital a few hours early instead of reading the records at Abby's place. This way, there would be no questions about anything other than the medical care provided to the unfortunate patients who had died in the ER. And in the end, it was still much easier than during the old days. Back when she was a student, chart review meant spending hours in the medical-records department of the hospital, in a tiny cubicle with an uncomfortable chair, flipping through hundreds of pages to find the data she needed. Computers made it so much easier.

Ward's list contained eleven names, the total of all the patients who'd died in the ER during April, May, and June. After the ER director's illness, some others had picked up the slack, but apparently, they'd quit when the warm weather rolled around, leaving three months' worth of charts to review.

First Ward asked Frankie for a list of all the patients who'd died in the department in the preceding year. Since she was only seeing a tiny snapshot, she thought a bigger picture would give valuable information. Since she was so new to the hospital, she wasn't sure what was normal. Eleven deaths in the ER in Philly in one day wouldn't have been unusual, but perhaps it was here. Of the eleven, Ward figured ten would have been from heart disease, drug overdose, and trauma. In the mountains, she didn't think drugs would be a top killer, but nothing surprised her. Not since the bat attack, anyway.

Thanks to the wonders of modern technology, the list Frankie produced was beyond Ward's expectations. As requested, the inquiry went back a year, and he'd sorted the deaths in the department into every conceivable category: first, by month, and then by cause of death, age, race, religion, time of day, attending physician, attending nurse, mode of arrival (ambulance or personal vehicle), time elapsed between arrival and death, and primary-care doctor. With all of that data, patterns were likely to emerge, patterns that would give her an idea of what was normal at Endless Mountains Medical Center.

Before even looking at the individual patient charts, she studied the data and started making sense of it. Forty deaths had occurred in the ER during the twelve-month period under review, an average of three-and-a-third deaths per month. The previous October had seen the lowest number, one. June had kept the undertakers busiest. Six people had died then. Three seemed to be the norm. Time of death favored dayshift by a two-to-one margin, and Ward didn't know if that was significant. She'd have to look more closely at the causes of death with regard to day and time. More heart attacks and strokes happen during the morning, but more car accidents happen on the weekends, when more cars are on the road. Sex didn't seem to be a significant variable—the split was about even, with twenty-two men and eighteen women on the list. Almost all were white and Christian, just like everyone else in the mountains. Most of the patients were older, with a variety of medical conditions that explained their deaths. Some, though, were young. Too young. The chart of an eight-year-old caught her eye, and she deliberately pushed it aside. She'd died in June, and if she completed her task in a chronological manner, Ward could avoid that one for at least a little while longer.

Three-quarters of people who died in the ER had taken their last ride in an ambulance rather than a car, and most of them had died within an hour of arrival at the hospital. Their family doctors and the ER docs who cared for them varied: fifteen different family doctors, and seven from the ER. When Ward broke down the numbers for the ER docs, nothing looked out of the ordinary. One doctor had seen eleven of the patients, another ten, one eight, one five, and the remaining docs had split up the others. She assumed the disparity had to do with the number of hours worked. The more patients a doctor sees, the more patients he's going to pronounce dead. She would expect a full-time physician to have treated the majority of the deaths and a part-timer a smaller number, unless that part-time doc was seeing all the trauma victims on Saturday nights.

Glancing at her watch, she pushed the pile of paperwork aside and stood to stretch. She'd set aside four hours for this task and was beginning to fear she'd grossly underestimated the time she'd need. It was three thirty and she'd already been at it for more than an hour, though, and she hadn't even touched the actual charts yet. Bending from the waist, she let her shoulders and head fall, feeling the stretch in the muscles of her neck and back. Touching her toes with her fingertips, she tried to force her head to her knees. Not even close.

Daily yoga wasn't enough to make her that flexible. Smiling, she stood, arched her back, and returned to the computer station.

Ward had camped in the boardroom, fearing the interruptions she'd face in the physicians' lounge and the ER, and so she wouldn't have to move when the meeting began. She took her place at the computer and logged in. She had three more hours before the room started to get noisy, giving her about fifteen minutes to review each chart. Some would be easy to get through. Reviewing massive brain hemorrhages and dissecting aneurysms and other catastrophic illnesses didn't require much time. She would make sure the basics had been done—patients were seen promptly, proper tests were ordered and the results documented correctly. Other disease processes weren't so straightforward, and she might need to spend more time going through them. There are always questions when someone dies, and Ward had to ask them. Was time wasted? Were the proper medications given and the proper tests ordered? Were mistakes made, such as giving the wrong medication or putting a breathing tube into the stomach? Was the doctor successful in his or her attempt to insert the tube or the IV? Was the correct diagnosis made?

Ward took her list, a pen, and some sheets of notepaper and got to work. The first patient on the list was a ninety-year-old man who'd developed indigestion after eating his nursing-home hash on the morning of April Fools' Day. His heart rate and blood pressure were tanking by the time he got to the hospital, and he'd suffered a cardiac arrest within minutes of arrival. Everything conceivable was done, but nothing helped. After reviewing the chart, Ward decided that his care had been first rate and appropriate. She moved on to chart number two. A week later, a teenager was brought in, also near death. He'd hit a telephone pole and suffered massive facial and head trauma, so much so that the paramedics were unable to secure his airway with a breathing tube through the pools of blood and broken facial bones. Anticipating trouble after the medic's radio report, the ER doctor had paged the surgeon, who was waiting in the ER when the patient arrived. In spite of the emergency airway the surgeon inserted into his trachea, the patient coded and couldn't be revived.

Not much could be done to force oxygen through his bloody airway, and Ward sensed his care had gone above and beyond the standard.

The final patient seen in April was another heart-attack victim, and this one was completely unresponsive to every medication and maneuver the medics and the ER team had given him. Ward couldn't find a single fault in the patient's care.

She logged into the next chart and checked the time. She'd spent forty-five minutes on the three patients who'd died during the month of April. Right on schedule. Fortunately, the May cases were straightforward as well. She made it through most of June and couldn't avoid it any longer. It was time to look at the eight-year-old's chart.

Her name was Hailey, and Ward was unable to shake her sadness as she finished reading the notes that documented her final minutes of life on earth. A car had hit her when she'd run into the street, fracturing her femur. The medics had successfully inserted an IV and given fluids, but the IV had shifted at some point and stopped running. Her heart rate was fast and her blood pressure was low—a complication of the massive blood loss associated with femur fractures—necessitating another IV. The ER doctor had successfully inserted an IV into her subclavian vein, but within seconds of that maneuver, Hailey had coded. An extended course of CPR was unsuccessful, and after more than an hour of trying, the code was called.

On autopsy, a significant amount of air was found in her heart, a fatal complication of insertion of the subclavian catheter.

Ward leaned forward onto the computer table, rubbing both temples. It was hard to argue this case. Unlike the eight charts she'd reviewed before this one, where she could place no clear-cut blame, Hailey's death could be directly attributed to the insertion of the line. No line, she lives. Line placed, she dies. Did that mean the doctor was at fault in her death for failing to check the line? Or was the nurse at fault for failing to purge air from the IV tubing? Was a venous air embolus an acceptable complication of IV insertion? Ward wasn't sure. She knew it happened, but did that mean it was okay? She'd have to research that a little more. She also needed to decide if the line was really necessary in the first place. If the risk of a procedure is death, the procedure better damn well be a lifesaver. Yes, her blood pressure had been low, but had they tried other IV sites before jumping to the subclavian vein? If not, that would be the first recommendation she made to the board.

Picking up the phone, she dialed the ER. Shayna had been the nurse taking care of Hailey, and Ward had seen her earlier. Perhaps she'd have a minute to talk and share her take on the events.

"Hi, Ward, how's it going?" Shayna asked in greeting.

"Great. I need a little help, though. I'm reviewing cases for the M & M meeting, and you took care of one of the patients. Hailey Conrad. Can I ask you a few questions?"

Shayna gave a deep sigh and was silent for a moment. "That was the most fuckin' awful code I've ever been on," she said a few seconds later.

"I can imagine," Ward said softly, beating down her own little ghosts.

"We gave her blood, fluids, all the right meds. Nothing worked. We tried for like an hour, and we never even got a blip on the monitor. Once she coded, it was a like a fuse got tripped. Nothing."

"I could see that from the chart, Shayna. You did all you could."

Shayna sniffled. The cocky young nurse, with spiky hair and tattoos on her tattoos, was really a softy at heart. "Thanks."

"Can I ask you a question?" Ward asked.

"Sure."

"Why did Dr. Hawk put in the central line? Was there no other access?"

"Huh! That's what I told him! I'm great at IVs, and he practically pulled the needle out of my hand so he could put in that subclavian. It was like he had an agenda, ya know? Do doctors have to do a certain number of procedures on kids to keep your licenses? 'Cuz that's what it seemed like to me. Nothing was going to stop him from putting in that line. He got the kit out, opened his own gloves, even pulled out the bag of fluid and hung it himself."

"So you didn't prime the tubing for him?"

"No. He was on a mission, and he did it all himself. As a matter of fact, when I tried to help, he glared at me. Told me to check on the transfer, since we were going to have to send her out to have the fracture repaired. Our orthopedics wouldn't even come in to see her."

"Did he seem like he knew what he was doing?" Ward asked. Injecting air was a rookie mistake or one made in haste. Clearly, he wasn't in a hurry if he was gathering the equipment and priming the IV tubing by himself.

"Oh, yes. His technique was flawless. He gowned up and had the sterile gloves on in seconds, found the vein on the first try. He bragged that he was an expert on IV insertion. Said he was the one they called when no one else could get the line in."

"So, he wasn't a rookie," Ward murmured, almost to herself.

"No, definitely not."

It wasn't a rookie mistake. And he wasn't in a hurry. So what the hell had happened to little Hailey? Her conversation with Shayna didn't tell her why it happened, but it clarified one thing for Ward. The source of the air embolus was the doctor, and no one else.

"I appreciate your help, Shay." Ward disconnected the phone and stood again, going through her familiar stretching routine. She hadn't finished by the time the first arrivals began walking through the door for the Morbidity and Mortality Committee Meeting. Damn, she thought. She still had two charts to review. Hailey's had taken so much time she hadn't had a chance to finish the others. Glancing at her watch, she contemplated sneaking back to the ER. A half hour remained before the start of the meeting, and if she hurried, she could finish those two charts and be done with it. She hadn't counted on the early birds.

"Joe McGee," a man said and held out his hand, interrupting Ward's thoughts. He was short and morbidly obese, with thinning hair and pale skin. His smile was warm, though, and his greeting friendly. "I'm the pathologist. Thanks for helping out with these chart reviews. It's always beneficial when you can have the opinion of a neutral expert, and you certainly qualify."

"I'm not so sure about that."

"On the neutral or the expert?"

"Yes," she said, and he laughed as he turned and waddled away.

"I have to agree with you!"

Turning slightly from Dr. McGee, Ward caught the glare of Dr. Marc Pierce, one of the hospital's three radiologists. She hadn't noticed him as she'd focused on the pathologist. Ward had met Pierce only once, in the lounge, and he'd seemed cordial enough. Likewise, whenever she'd spoken to him on the phone about imaging studies, he'd been professional and receptive to her questions. Now, though, he seemed quite confrontational.

Ward looked around. No one else in the room. "Are you talking to me?"

"Damn right I am, and as soon as the rest of the group gets here I'm going to propose removing you from this committee. I'd say sleeping with the hospital CEO is a conflict of interest, wouldn't you?"

Ward was momentarily stunned. It wasn't like she and Abby were hiding their relationship or that they needed to, but still—were they ready to be out? Too late for that question, she realized. More germane, did her relationship with Abby in some way conflict with the interest of the committee, as he suggested?

Joe McGee's eyes bulged, and Ward wondered if it was homophobia, surprise at the information, or shock at Pierce's gall.

Deciding to ignore the gossip and address the potential problem, Ward looked at Pierce. "In what way does my relationship with Abby affect this committee?"

He laughed. "She's the administrator, and she has an agenda!"

"And what would that be, Dr. Pierce?"

Ward wasn't sure who was more surprised by Abby's question, her or Marc Pierce. She knew who was the most relieved, though, and was grateful to have Abby in her corner. The fire in her eyes and the steel in her posture told her Abby was poised to do battle.

Pierce's chin shot up and he looked down his nose at Abby, puffing out his chest as he did so. "To control this medical staff like we're your puppets. Ever since you came here, you've been using this committee to pull the staff apart, to position us against each other, making us place blame for patient deaths on each other's shoulders. United we stand, and divided...well, you get to be in charge, then, don't you?"

Abby calmly walked to the head of the long wooden table in the center of the room and, dismissing her detractor, placed her briefcase on the table and sat down. When she did, she met his glare. Her posture had softened, but the fire remained in her eyes. "You are most welcome to share your thoughts and opinions, Dr. Pierce, but perhaps you should practice before a mirror first. It would give you an idea of how idiotic you sound."

A man from the kitchen walked in at that moment, pushing a laden cart. Food was always a good way to attract committee members, and suddenly Ward's growling stomach reminded her lunch had been long ago. Abby had promised her the spread would be worth her wait, and as she spied each plate being uncovered, she had to agree. There were the customary salads, of course, but also colossal shrimp in a white wine sauce, salmon with a dill dressing, and beef tips in gravy. Mixed veggies and red potatoes rounded out the dinner menu, and on a separate table, Ward glimpsed crème brûlée with a strawberry garnish.

As happy as she was for the food, she was more thrilled that the confrontation with Marc Pierce had ended. Sure, the respite would be temporary, but it gave both her and Abby an opportunity to form a battle plan, and with the element of surprise gone, Pierce was in for a fight. Personally, Ward didn't really care much about the committee. A few hours of her time would be wasted if she was dismissed, but in the end, it didn't really matter. To Abby, though, this was a huge moment. How would she defend herself and her relationship with Ward to the committee? Abby's words and actions at this meeting could have serious repercussions in her future as CEO.

When the dinner plates were cleared and while the coffee was being poured, Abby called the meeting to order and didn't waste any time addressing the matter. "Dr. Pierce made some comments this evening about my interest in this committee. I'd like to address them. A committee such as this is vital and necessary to the quality of care provided at a hospital. It is our job to make sure our professional staff is giving the most appropriate medications and using the most current protocols in caring for our patients. If someone is behind the times, it is our job to point it out to them and to educate the rest of the staff as well. It is not about pointing fingers or blame. It is about improvement. It is what modern institutions such as ours do. It is also a requirement of our malpractice insurance policy to conduct such reviews."

"The malpractice requires it?"

The question came from Ham Jarrod, a young internist just out of residency. How did he get roped into this committee?

His question echoed around the room in a variety of forms. *Really? Wow? Get out!* and *You've gotta be kiddin' me* came from the ten members of the committee. Any who might have questioned Abby's personal motives seemed to resolve the issues on their own, as no one mentioned it, and Marc Pierce sat in stunned silence, his crème brûlée untouched before him.

"That is correct, Dr. Jarrod. Insurance companies reward good behavior and penalize bad behavior. In our case, the findings and recommendations of this committee are submitted along with a ton of other data required when our policy is reviewed."

"Why are we with this company if they make us jump through so many hoops?" Joe McGee asked.

"Good question. The malpractice crisis in Pennsylvania caused quite a few companies to stop doing business here. Our choices are limited. Of those companies large enough to insure us, the requirements are similar. They mandate certain guidelines for us to follow and standards to uphold. I'd be shocked if all insurance companies didn't have a similar requirement."

"Damn insurance companies," someone said, and everyone murmured in agreement.

"Dr. Pierce is concerned because I have a personal relationship with Dr. Thrasher, who has agreed to review the ER cases for April, May, and June. Does anyone else share his concerns?"

No one did.

Way to go, Ward thought as she pulled out her notes. Abby had handled a room full of powerful men with ease, and she sensed they all respected her. When she glanced at Abby she couldn't help smiling. Abby, though, had already moved on.

"Okay, then. Let's get to the business of this meeting." Physicians were present representing every department in the hospital, each of them having reviewed patient deaths and complications according to the standards written for their departments. Since they held this meeting monthly, most had only a few cases to review. One patient had received a medication she was allergic to, but the error seemed to be on the patient's end, since she'd told the ER, the primary doctor, and the nurse who gave the med that she had no allergies. Another patient had died of sepsis, and the question of transfer was debated. Would the patient have lived if she were sent to a larger hospital with a more experienced team? Who knew? Ward suspected the policy for treating septic patients would soon include an option for early transfer.

They'd made their way around the table, and finally, it was Ward's turn. She'd purposely sat next to Abby, because it would have looked strange if she didn't, and besides, she wanted to. That meant she was the last to present her findings, though, and she suspected the committee members were eager to get home. At last glance, the meeting was more than two hours old.

"I've reviewed all of the cases except two," she said. "And I'll finish those as soon as I can and send all of you a memo about my findings. I found no problems with the care on any of the April and May cases." Ward listed the names to be sure everyone was clear on her conclusions. She listed the cases from the month of June, explaining her findings. "Hailey Conrad," Ward said, leaning forward. "This is a tough call. She died from a venous air embolus, and I don't know enough about it to say anything at this time."

"That was Hawk, wasn't it?" Ham asked.

Ward nodded, and Ham shook his head, a scowl on his face.

"None of us likes to point a finger, but he was bad news."

Ward looked at him. What did everyone have against Hawk? "Whatta ya mean by that?"

"I can't explain it. But I'm glad he's gone. Any chance you can stick around awhile longer? You seem to know what you're doing."

Ward blushed, not at the compliment, but at the invitation to stay at Abby's hospital. The head of pediatrics saved her from answering.

"Hailey was my patient. How long before you can get an answer for us?"

"I'll have it by tomorrow," Ward said.

CHAPTER TWENTY-THREE
CARDIOGENIC SHOCK

Jesus," Ward whispered as she scanned the pages of yet another scholarly article on venous air embolus. Before taking on this task, she'd known next to nothing about the matter. Now, though, her knowledge was causing a considerable sense of angst. She'd seen the most accomplished and capable physicians whacked in the kneecaps by the hammer of peer review. Sadly, as with malpractice, a bad outcome such as death often causes suggestions for changes that might not be necessary. The challenge is to know when changes need to be made for the sake of safety, rather than for the sake of politics. Typically, Ward could review this case in a matter of an hour. Nothing about Hailey Conrad's case was simple, though. Should she have been transferred directly to a trauma center? Or a hospital with pediatric critical care? Should a protocol be devised for starting central lines? Or just for central lines in children? Should doctors be prohibited from priming IV tubing, a task normally left to nurses who were more experienced and capable?

"Hmm?" Abby asked.

They were both working, seated on opposite ends of the couch, Ward with her legs propped up on the hassock and Abby sprawled out so her feet rested against Ward's thigh. In spite of her preoccupation with the case she'd been reviewing, she couldn't keep from smiling, once again, at the domesticity of the scene. She'd lived with Jess for nearly six years and could count moments like this on one hand. With Abby they were piling up so rapidly she needed to remove her socks and shoes to count toes in addition to fingers.

"What?" Abby asked.

Ward turned and looked at her, and for a moment, she forgot what she'd been reading. Abby's auburn hair was tucked behind her ears, and the lamp behind her cast her in a halo that made her look angelic.

"God, you're beautiful," she murmured, surprising them both.

The smile that spread across Abby's face told Ward she'd said exactly the right thing, though, and she was awed by how good it felt to put that smile on Abby's face. She knew it was unfair to compare Abby to Jess. This was a new relationship, devoid of the trials and monotony of the six-year affair she'd had with Jess. She could argue the newness caused the pure joy she felt just to be in Abby's presence. That they laughed so much because they were simply giddy from frequent, fabulous sex. That they talked so much just because they had so much to learn about each other. She'd told herself all those things, but she had difficulty remembering a time she'd ever felt as comfortable with Jess. Abby and Jess were such different women that the relationships they created were equally dissimilar. Yes, they were both intelligent and attractive and successful, but that was about all Ward could see in common.

Jess tended to be serious, while Abby was playful. Jess took even play seriously. Her golf clubs were clean and shiny and organized within her bag. She took lessons and watched videos to perfect her game, arrived early to stretch and hit balls, and still shot the same score as Ward, who barely gave the game a second thought when she wasn't on the course. Abby was much like Ward in that regard, confessing she'd never have enough time to be a great golfer, but she wanted to relax and enjoy herself when she did play.

Both Abby and Jess had perfected the art of sarcasm, yet Jess's shoulder was dusted not only with freckles, but with a few significant chips, and Ward couldn't figure out why. Six years later, she still couldn't understand the mechanism that made Jess tick. Jess came from a wonderful family, and while Ward didn't understand Zeke's recent streak of homophobia, he'd always been a great father. Hands-on. Loving, caring, and supportive. Jess's mom had been the same. They'd always had enough money and never seemed to need to worry about it. Yet Jess always seemed a bit discontented, questioning her decisions, wondering how she could be better. Would she have looked nicer in the dress she'd left on the rack at the store instead of the one she brought home? Would they have been happier with the other house, if they'd taken the other vacation, if they'd eaten at the other restaurant? And in the end, she questioned the girl, too.

Abby was so different, and Ward was refreshed by her optimism, by the pure joy she found in simple things like the sun setting over the trees behind her cabin or the flowers exploding in her garden. Looking at things with Abby, Ward felt like she was seeing in color again for the first time in a very long time.

The strangest thing for Ward was the way it was all becoming so clear to her now. None of her friends had ever liked Jess. They'd tolerated her, for Ward's sake, but had no real connection to her. Ward had always thought her friends had been lacking, but as she stepped away and the video of her life with Jess came into focus, she realized how self-centered and demanding Jess had been. At times, which were coming more frequently now, Ward had to remind herself why she'd ever loved Jess in the first place.

"Why. Are. You. Smiling?" Abby asked.

Ward felt herself blushing, thankful Abby couldn't read her mind. "I suspect I'm just happy."

Abby leaned forward and put her papers onto the table, then set her glasses atop the pile. "It's legal, you know," she said softly.

"Are you happy?" Ward asked, afraid of the answer. It was too soon to ask for more from Abby. Too soon after her breakup with Jess. But their relationship felt good, and right, and she was beginning to dread packing up her car and heading south when her time in the mountains was over. She didn't want this to end. So what if she was going back to Philly? Her ER schedule allowed flexibility, enough to spend at least a few days a week with Abby. If Abby wanted the same thing. If Abby wanted her.

A smile danced across her face. "I am."

"Are you ready to talk about August?"

"I am not," she said, but nothing but a light air carried her words. She was teasing.

"We're running out of July," Ward said simply and, closing her eyes, leaned into the cushion of the couch, allowing the buttery soft leather to engulf her.

Abby's response reached across the couch to her, across the fear and anxiety and uncertainty, and erased them all. "It'll always be July, Ward. If we want it to be."

Ward couldn't keep her eyes closed. She needed to see Abby, to look at her. Their eyes met. "It seems so fast. We hardly know each other. But—"

"We know everything we need to, don't we?"

"I know that I like everything about you, and I want more."

"I like the sound of that, Ward. I want more too. And Philly isn't so far away that we can't work something out. We both have cars and free time. Let's not worry about it, okay? Let's just see what happens. Is that what was troubling you?"

Ward looked at her, confused. "Huh?"

"Before this conversation. What were you reading?" Abby nodded toward the computer perched on Ward's lap.

"Oh, that," she said, drawing out the words into three syllables before turning her attention back to her laptop and the pile of notes she'd made. "What do you think the odds are of developing a venous air embolus from insertion of a central line?"

Abby stared, her face contorted into a look of confusion.

"You know what a central line is, right?"

Between her childhood with two physician parents and her career as an administrator, Abby evidently understood a good deal about medicine. Sometimes Ward forgot Abby didn't actually practice.

"A big IV inserted into the heart?"

Ward had to suppress her smile. Abby had conceded to August, and just the thought was thrilling. Now she looked so adorable as she tried to maintain her professional image.

"Close. A big IV inserted into a big vein that goes into the heart."

Abby waved a dismissive hand in Ward's direction. "Close enough. What about it?"

"So, when you're injecting medication into an IV, there's always a chance of injecting a little bit of air. What are the chances of injecting enough air that it causes harm?"

Abby bit her lip and shrugged. "One in a million."

"I think that's close. It's one in eight hundred catheters placed."

"That seems kind of high."

"Actually, it's not. Since central lines aren't so common, it's a rare occurrence."

Abby still looked confused, but it didn't matter. Ward's next point was even more profound. "So what do you think the odds are of dying from an air embolus created during insertion of a central line?"

Abby held out her manicured hands in surrender, an annoyed look on her face. "One in a million?"

Ward reached out and tickled her. "I'm about to state something profound and you're not taking this seriously."

"Well, then state it, and quit torturing me with trivia questions."

Ward backed off, but not before placing a kiss on Abby's nose.

"Okay, let me put it this way, so you can understand the significance of what I'm saying. In my career, over ten years of practicing in the ER, I'd guess I've inserted a couple hundred lines. So about twenty a year. To have a fatal embolus, I'd have to insert twelve thousand lines. I'd need to practice for six hundred years."

Abby was quick to reply. "Wow," she said, and then she was quiet, thinking. "Or you'd have to be very unlucky."

Ward grew somber. "Yes, Abby. There's a lot of luck in medicine, both good and bad."

"So Hawk could have done everything right, been a perfectly good doctor who had bad luck."

"Yes, exactly," she said, then laughed. "I don't know. I'm just not sure how air accidentally ended up in the vein. A little air is explainable. You can have a little mixed into the fluid getting injected, and the doctor wouldn't even notice unless he checked carefully."

"So it would be an oversight?"

Ward bit her lip as her mind raced, trying to figure it out, picturing IV tubing and fluids and syringes. How could a large volume of air accidentally get into the vein? "Well, that's the confusing part. I can understand missing a small volume of air. Less than a CC. Half a CC probably could get by without noticing. But a fatal bolus of air would be huge. Like a big syringe full. I don't know how that happens without someone noticing."

"So someone injected a syringe full of air into this child's heart and didn't know it?"

Again, Ward shook her head. "I'm not sure, Abby. But the air had to get in there somehow."

"Why would you inject air? Is there any medical reason? Don't you need air?"

Ward shook her head. "You'd never inject air. The air we need—oxygen—goes into the lungs and gets absorbed in tiny amounts into the blood. Air injected into the vein acts like a clot. It forms a blockage and shuts down the circulation."

"So what do you think? How did this happen?"

"I don't know? Maybe from the IV tubing?" Abby looked confused, so Ward elaborated. "There's air in the tubing, just like in a hose. Before you connect the tubing to the IV, you run fluid through it. That flushes the air out."

"So it could really just be bad luck, and we don't need to make any changes to our protocols."

Ward sighed. She didn't know what to think. Perhaps Hawk had neglected to flush the tubing but was too afraid to admit his mistake. That would go along with what she knew of him, learned through the rumor mill. He was uncaring and unremorseful. Why would he admit to a mistake? Ward wasn't sure if she should tell Abby that Hawk had taken care of the tubing himself. She wasn't so sure it was important, but perhaps it was.

"There's one more thing. Normally, when a central line is placed, the doctor focuses on the doctor parts—prepping the skin, setting up the sterile field, inserting the needle into the right place. The nurse opens the fluids and connects the tubing. But in this case, Hawk did it all. He took care of the tubing."

"So no matter how the air got in there, it was Hawk's fault," Abby observed.

"Yep."

"Even if it only happens once every six hundred years, it still happens, right? So perhaps we should create a protocol that only nurses flush tubing."

Ward shrugged.

"What?"

"I'm beginning to think Dr. Hawk is...not a good person."

Ward turned to face her, and she knew her own expression matched the somber one Abby wore. Then Ward did something she'd never done before. She talked badly about a colleague.

"It's just talk, Abby, you know? I've been following him around since March. That's when I started with the company. And at every hospital, the ER staff makes little comments about him. No one blatantly accuses him of malpractice, but they've certainly hinted at it." She thought of Erin. "It was also suggested he's quite indifferent to the fates of his patients."

Abby nodded, her look still closed, as she seemed to search carefully for words. "I have to listen to the gossip, Ward. It's my job, to know everybody's business. But I have to decide what's bullshit and what's real. And as the product of two physicians, I'm very hesitant to pass judgment on medical errors. But you're reviewing these cases because those same questions were raised here, not just by the ER staff, but by the medical staff as well. And you know when doctors question one of their own, it warrants a closer look. I didn't want these cases to wait until Dick Rove comes back."

"Really?" Ward asked, surprised. "I got the feeling that every doctor on staff perceives the peer-review process as a witch hunt."

Abby chuckled. "Well, if you were looking at one of the staff physicians, I'd say that's true. They'd defend each other to the death. But Hawk was an outsider and therefore fair game. Notice that no one pointed a finger last night except when Ham Jarrod said he didn't like Hawk."

"Scapegoat?" Ward asked.

Now Abby sighed. "I don't think so, but I guess it's possible. That's why your opinion is so important. You're neutral."

"I don't know if I have an answer for you, Abby. I don't think we'll ever know what happened to Hailey Conrad. I just can't help feeling like I'm missing something important."

"Like what?"

Ward glared at her. "If I knew that...No, seriously. I have a bad feeling about Hawk, but I really don't have any proof of malpractice. An air embolus is an acceptable complication of central line insertion. Even if it's rare, it does happen."

"Okay, we have an answer then. Remember our mission— we're not pointing fingers, right? We'll use the information you've gathered to make everyone smarter. Set up a protocol for insertion of lines, perhaps a check list to make sure tubes are flushed and syringes are checked for air."

Ward felt all warm and fuzzy inside. Abby really was good at what she did. "Case closed, then." Ward quickly typed up recommendations for the insertion of central lines and sent the document to Abby via e-mail.

"I have two more cases to go. Can I use your computer to pull up the files?"

Since they'd been outed at the meeting, using Abby's secure connection to access patient records was no longer a concern.

"Of course."

Abby logged in using her password, then handed her laptop to Ward, who logged in to the medical-records section.

She pulled up the chart on the tenth patient under review. This was a sixty-year-old heart-attack victim, with a terribly abnormal EKG. He'd died shortly after arriving in the ER. Ward spent half an hour reading notes and labs, noting times that orders were given and completed. Perhaps Dr. Hawk had done something inappropriate in the man's care, but if he had, Ward couldn't tell by reviewing the chart. Jeff Jacoby had been seen promptly, had an EKG and chest

X-ray within minutes of arrival, was quickly given aspirin and the correct dose of clot-buster drug, but had suffered a cardiac arrest and died anyway. Hell, Hawk had gone so far as to mix up the clot-buster and administer it himself. It sucked, but nothing else could have been done to save the poor man.

Hawk was really a hands-on doctor, Ward noticed. In every case she'd reviewed, the nurses' notes indicated that he had performed procedures that were normally the nurse's responsibility. Probably just his training. Many inner city hospitals where residents train are inadequately staffed, placing the burden of nursing and janitorial duties on the residents. The habits learned then often stayed, and she'd seen many doctors inject their own medications and start their own lines. None to the extent Hawk did, though.

Ward told Abby her findings and noted the look of relief on her face. "Finished, then?" she asked, with a twinkle in her eye.

Ward frowned. "One more to go," she said, and began reading the next chart. She was only a few paragraphs into it when she experienced an eerie sensation of déjà vu, and before she'd finished, her mouth had gone dry. Kim Sparks was a forty-year-old diabetic who'd been vomiting for several days and become lethargic at home. She perked up when the paramedic gave her an IV shot of sugar, but shortly after arriving in the ER she was found dead in her room.

"Fuck," she whispered. This was the patient Erin had told her about. Her friend's mom. Only that woman had died in February, in another hospital fifty miles away, where Dr. Edward Hawk was working at the time. It sounded just like Frieda's neighbor, too. He'd died just before she met Frieda. Ward couldn't help wondering if Hawk had been his doctor. She suddenly felt clammy, found it hard to swallow. These cases were too bizarre and too similar to be a coincidence.

"Did you find something?" Abby asked.

"This is really strange," Ward said as she relayed her thoughts. Then she stared into the distance as she tried to recall the details. At the time she'd talked to Erin, she hadn't been too concerned about it; she'd simply been trying to make peace with Erin and offer her some solace. And she knew nothing about Frieda's neighbor.

"Who's Erin?"

"She's a nurse I worked with a few months ago. She was really upset over the death of one of her patients. It was the same history as the patient who died here last month. The woman came in with a low blood sugar, seemed to be doing fine, and was found dead in her room."

"Isn't that very unusual? Like more than one in a million?"

Ward could see that Abby wasn't kidding, just trying to get a handle on the information she was sharing. "I'd bet it's even steeper than that."

Ward met Abby's gaze, saw the question there, and answered before Abby could put it into words. "Yes, Abby. It was Dr. Hawk's patient."

"And Frieda's friend?"

"I don't know. But Hawk was there that month."

"This sounds worse than bad luck, Ward."

Ward had to agree.

With a shaking hand, she picked up her phone and found Erin's cell phone number in the contacts. It went straight to voice mail. "Damn," she said. "Erin's phone's off."

"Can you try the ER? Maybe she's working. And what about Frieda?"

Ward turned to Abby. She looked frightened. Ward wanted to find the answers and change that, but she suddenly feared she might not be able to. She'd begun this mission with good intentions, never once thinking anything would come of it other than a few recommendations like the ones she'd just e-mailed Abby. Now, though, she feared something else might be happening. Something much worse than incompetence or malpractice. What if Hawk had done this intentionally?

The signs were there. He drew up his own medication, which gave him opportunity to inject something, like air, into an unsuspecting patient. He'd prepped his own IV tubing, creating the perfect scenario for an air embolus. Ward thought of the other two patients who'd died on Hawk's watch. Their charts seemed clean, with nothing significant or unusual coming to mind. One had suffered a pulmonary embolus, a large blood clot in the lung, just after stepping off a tourist bus. She was quite unstable on arrival and died shortly afterward. Hawk had given clot-busters, but they hadn't helped. The other patient was also a heart-attack victim. Perfectly understandable, both deaths. Yet they made Ward uneasy. There were just so many deaths in June. So many on Hawk's watch.

Suddenly, she felt like she'd been thrown into the path of a tornado. Everything was moving around her, and the air seemed to get sucked from her lungs. She closed her eyes to calm herself.

"Are you okay?"

Instead of her calming Abby, the roles were now reversed. She opened her eyes, nodded, reached for her notes. She began computing something else.

Five of the six patients who'd died at EM over the year had succumbed on Hawk's watch. Ron Farley had seen eleven; Mario Litzi, ten; Al Briner, eight; and Dick Rove, five. They were all full-time docs. It was Rove's five that bothered Ward. He'd seen five, just like Hawk. Only Dick had seen them over the course of a year, and Hawk in just a month. "Abby, this isn't adding up." She handed her the data Frankie had extracted. "Look at the provider column."

Abby studied the data. "Hawk and Rove are tied."

"Exactly! But it's the data that's missing that's really important. How many hours did each provider work?"

"Oh, shit," Abby said as she began to understand. Her jaw dropped and she turned to look out the window beyond Ward. She spoke in a hushed tone. "At the rate he was going, Hawk would have sixty dead patients in the year. That's five times more than Ron Farley."

"It's almost twice as many as the rest of the staff combined."

Picking up her phone, Ward made the call to the ER. After an endless minute of catching up with the clerk, she asked for Erin, only to learn she was on vacation. Backpacking out West, with no cell-phone service. "Damn," she said as she turned to Abby and mouthed the news.

"Is there anyone else you can talk to?" Abby whispered.

Ward asked, "Who's the nurse?"

A minute later, a friendly voice greeted her. "Hi, Doc. It's Kelly. How the heck are you?"

Ward gave a generic reply before getting to the purpose of her call. She needed to gather information, without rousing suspicion. Small sparks of gossip tend to explode into infernos in fertile ground like an ER. "I'm doing a research paper," she lied. "About deaths in the ER. How they affect the staff."

"Wow. That's a great topic."

Suddenly Ward realized it actually was a great topic. Maybe she'd write it one day. "Yeah, you know how it is. Especially those unexpected deaths—the traumas, the sudden cardiac deaths. It really is hard."

"Don't I know it," Kelly said softly.

"I was hoping to talk to Erin. I know a few months back she had a patient who died. A diabetic. It was a woman she knew, and she took her death hard."

"It's awful when it's someone you know, Dr. Thrasher. And, unfortunately, in a small town like this, you know almost everybody."

"Do you remember that case? Erin's patient?"

There was a pause, as if Kelly was debating her response. "I wasn't here, so I only heard secondhand." But Kelly relayed what she'd heard, anyway.

Ward sat forward as she listened, pinching the bridge of her nose to chase away the threatening headache. It was similar, Erin's case. Too similar. It was unbelievable bad luck when a patient died of something strange, something difficult to anticipate and prevent. What was it called when the same thing happened three times? And then you have another patient, who dies of something equally bizarre? Is that just really bad luck, or something else, something far worse?

Abby had been watching Ward, listening to her side of the conversation, apparently hearing and understanding enough to look concerned.

"Well?" she asked when Ward disconnected the call.

"There are similarities."

Ward dialed Frieda, and before she could say anything else, Frieda answered. Another minute of gossip followed as Ward wondered how to phrase her questions. She wouldn't be able to bullshit Frieda as easily as Kelly. She decided to be as honest as possible. "Remember that committee Dr. Rosen assigned me to?"

"The unexpectedly dead people?"

Ward chuckled. "That's the one. I'm working on it now, and I couldn't help thinking about your neighbor. You said you found him in his room at the ER. Do they know what happened?"

"Just that his heart stopped. They didn't know why."

"Do you by any chance know which physician took care of him?"

"It was the one who came before you. From your company. Dr. Hawk."

Ward wasn't surprised, but the news was still numbing. What the fuck was going on with Hawk? She closed her eyes and leaned back as she disconnected the phone.

Suddenly Abby leaned forward and touched Ward's leg. "What are you thinking?"

She didn't want to tell her what she was thinking. That maybe there was more to this than bad luck. "There are too many similarities in these cases, Abby."

"Similarities? Is that a coincidence? Like the million-to-one thing? Can a few million-to-one things happen to the same person? Can this guy be that stupid? Or unlucky? What if it wasn't an accident?"

"It had to be, Abby. Right? Because if it wasn't…it was intentional."

Ward wasn't surprised that Abby had voiced her thoughts, nor was Abby's suggestion unexpected. "Maybe you should make some more calls."

Ward kept dialing the phone and talking to people long after Abby went to bed. She was just too preoccupied to rest. Her exercise proved to be futile, however. The ERs were staffed with new employees she didn't know well enough to talk to, old ones too busy to talk, and people with no information to share. Her only consolation as she looked at the clock at three in the morning was the promise two people had made to call her the next day. That and the fact that she didn't have to get up for work in two hours.

❖

Abby's hair dryer awakened Ward a few hours later, and she marveled at the difference a day had made. Twenty-four hours earlier she'd awakened feeling calm and peaceful, but the peer reviews had left her anxious. She was truly frightened about what her investigation would reveal. It saddened her that people died because of someone's incompetence. It horrified her to think of other possibilities, but the more she reviewed the things she'd heard over the months, the things she'd automatically dismissed because, really, almost everything could be explained away, the more tense she became.

She stepped from the bed and pulled on a sweatshirt to chase the morning chill, then made her way to the kitchen. Abby consumed large volumes of coffee every day, starting with a cup in the morning while she read the newspaper. Ward made herself a cup and one for Abby, then carried both back to the bedroom.

Abby smiled and held out her arms, one for a lop-sided hug and the other for her coffee mug. "Morning. And thanks for this."

"My pleasure."

"What time did you come to bed?"

"Don't ask." Ward collapsed onto the bed.

Abby hummed as she dressed and then kissed Ward passionately once again. "I think I can make it an early night. Any chance you're free for dinner? You can update me on your findings."

Ward rolled over and leaned onto her elbow, resting her head in her hand as she stretched out on the bed. She was off for another twenty-four hours, until beginning the first of three consecutive day shifts. "People are going to start talking, Abby."

Abby used her small finger to spread something shiny across her bottom lip, then rubbed both lips together. "Fuck them."

"I'd rather keep fucking you."

"Then I guess you're free for dinner." Abby didn't risk smudging her lipstick and blew a kiss instead, which Ward caught and placed gently on her own lips. She didn't move and didn't stop smiling until the sound of the Porsche's engine faded in the distance and she finally had to face the day.

After brushing her teeth, she headed into the kitchen and picked up where she'd left off the night before, calling the ERs at the hospitals where Edward Hawk had worked in March and April. Her memory was correct, and her friends confirmed that Hawk had been the doctor on duty when some unexpected deaths occurred. Other than the fact that he was there, though, the deaths weren't at all unusual for an ER. One patient had died from a heart attack, another from a blood clot, one from a brain hemorrhage, and two from trauma. The best doctor in the world might have lost those patients as well. Only Frieda's friend stood out from the winter months.

Ward had taken this assignment merely to help Abby and pass the time, and she'd expected to find nothing other than incompetence on Hawk's part. But she hadn't. In fact, he appeared to be a very knowledgeable physician, with good skills and a trail of dead bodies following him. Was it all just bad luck? The deaths gave her an uneasy feeling, and knowing Hawk's reputation fortified her anxiety.

She wished she could talk to Erin. She could tell her what had happened and bounce her thoughts off her. She couldn't trust anyone else with the nagging thoughts that had been hounding her since she read about the diabetic patient who died in the ER. Technically, her job was done. She'd reviewed the cases and made her recommendations. So what was she looking for now? Why was she still digging?

Because of the uneasy feeling. She wouldn't rest until she knew everything possible about these deaths.

She stood and stretched, then took her cup of coffee onto the deck and simply enjoyed a peaceful hour, listening to the birds and stretching her muscles in the early morning sunshine. Feeling refreshed, she picked up her pile of notes and began flipping through them. She read and reread, trying not to focus on any pattern, because it didn't seem there was one. The patients who'd died were young and old, male and female, and afflicted by a variety of illness and injury.

She'd just decided that she couldn't reach a concrete conclusion when her phone rang. A glance at the screen showed Abby's beautiful, smiling face, and Ward's expression instantly mirrored hers. Why did it feel so good just to see Abby's picture on her phone?

She accepted the call. "Hello, Abby."

"Hello, Doc. How's the detective work going?"

Ward relayed her findings.

"Well, that's good then, right? I mean, we don't actually want a psychopathic doctor on the loose, do we?"

"Yeah, you're right." Ward agreed reluctantly. "I was just so sure when I read that case about the diabetic patient. I thought if I started asking around I'd find the proverbial smoking gun."

"Well, I'm relieved. Because, truthfully, if you'd have found something, what would we have done?"

Ward smiled at Abby's use of the word "we." They were in this together. And they had no proof, not even enough evidence to revoke Hawk's hospital privileges. Abby was right, of course. Finding nothing was good.

CHAPTER TWENTY-FOUR
COMPOUND FRACTURE

In spite of many telephone calls, a few texts, and hours spent on the Internet researching probabilities and diseases, Ward made no further progress in her unofficial investigation of Dr. Edward Hawk. A handful of patients were dead under Hawk's watch, some from relatively routine causes, others from bizarre factors. Ward had no idea if Hawk was a good doctor with bad luck or a homicidal maniac with a literal license to kill. She'd met him, although briefly, and he'd seemed normal. He was handsome, well dressed, and polite. The nurses thought he was creepy, but that didn't mean much. Ward had worked with many physicians who hadn't managed to find themselves in the good favor of the nursing staff, and that didn't mean they were murderers. They just lacked personality, and while that wasn't ideal, it wasn't illegal, either.

Hawk's profile was available on the Internet, and Ward read the reviews from multiple sites that rate physicians. She knew the sites well. She'd been warned at conferences and by administrators about the power of the Internet, where anonymous posters are able to make comments about physicians they don't like. Yet in spite of his bad reputation amongst his peers, Hawk's patients seemed to love him. All of his scores were high, ranging from four to five stars out of a possible five. Either Hawk wasn't what he seemed to the nurses, or he'd really managed to snow the patients.

Erin was still out of cell-phone range, and Ward was waiting on a return call from another colleague, but she was beginning to accept the fact that she might have to just forget about this little investigation and focus on other things, because it wasn't likely she'd ever have any more answers than she already had.

With so much happening in her career as a detective, it seemed like weeks had passed since her last ER shift. Yet she quickly got into the flow of things when she reached the hospital the next morning, taking care of a wound and a broken toe before her coffee had a chance to grow cold.

It was after nine when Abby called her. She was straight to the point and all business, which turned Ward on. "What's the name of the app you told me about? The one that logs business expenses?"

Ward's accountant had informed her of the phone app, and she was using it to track the expenses she incurred on her travels through the mountains. Since so many doctors traveled for conferences, Abby told her it might be helpful info to share with the medical staff. "Let me look at my phone," Ward said.

She pulled the device out of her backpack and turned it on. "So how's your day going?" she asked as it powered up.

"Ah…" Abby practically moaned. "It started out great."

Ward tried hard to suppress the grin that threatened to erupt as she recalled their morning. Multiple orgasms before breakfast, again. A beep made her glance at the phone in her hand. She had a text from Kathy Henderfield, Frieda's niece and the head nurse at the hospital where Ward had spent the month of April.

Call me. Important.

Ward checked her apps and gave Abby the information she'd requested. "So, what's for dinner?" she asked.

"Oh, so you're available?"

"Oh, yeah."

Abby giggled, and Ward imagined the twinkle in her eyes and the smile on her face. They made plans to drive to Clarks Summit for sushi, and as soon as Ward disconnected the phone, she dialed Kathy's number.

"Hey, Kath, what's up?"

"I don't know, something kind of weird. Frieda told me you'd asked about her neighbor, and when I mentioned your call, the unit clerk reminded me about another patient."

"Oh, really?" Ward sat upright. Kathy had her full attention.

"Yeah. The patient was here in the beginning of March, during one of those freak late-winter snowstorms. He came in at the change of shift and Dr. Somerset was listed as the doctor of record, but actually Dr. Hawk took care of him."

"So what happened with the patient?"

"Well, that's what's weird. He suffered a compound fracture of his leg in a snowmobile accident. He seemed stable, but then he coded. Something you hear about but never, ever, see."

Ward's mouth went dry. She clutched the phone with a choking grip. "What did he die from?"

"A venous air embolism."

Chapter Twenty-five

Vertigo

Her ER was empty, and Ward was happy. As she hung up the phone, Kathy's words rang in her ears. She was dizzy, her mind overwhelmed. Kathy had confirmed that Dr. Hawk had placed a central line in the dead snowmobiler and that he'd coded immediately afterward. That made two patients in four months with fatal venous air emboli, when the odds dictated it should have taken Hawk more than a thousand years to accumulate such bad luck. When Ward considered the fact that his colleagues thought he was creepy, in addition to the two diabetic patients who'd died for no apparent reason, and Frieda's neighbor who was found dead in a similar manner, she could no longer wishfully suppose this was just bad luck or incompetence. This *had* to be intentional. Hawk was murdering his patients, using a syringe of air instead of a knife or a gun, but he was murdering them, she was sure. The odds simply didn't support any other conclusion.

What to do now? Ward had no proof of any wrongdoing, just this circumstantial evidence, but she had to stop Hawk. If she didn't, the body count would continue to climb. Should she call the state medical board? It had been her sad duty to report a physician colleague once before, when he refused to step down in spite of multiple appearances at work while visibly intoxicated. The process had been rather benign. As soon as the state launched their investigation, the physician in question had admitted he had a problem and voluntarily entered a rehab program. A year later, he sent Ward a card of thanks for her intervention.

Something told Ward it wouldn't go the same way this time. It was hard to imagine Hawk taking a call from the medical board and admitting to murder.

Thankfully, she'd never found herself in this position before. Pulling up the state board's Web site, she read about handling a physician suspected of illegal behavior. It suggested making a formal report to the local police in addition to a complaint with the board.

Ward picked up the ER phone and dialed the direct extension to Abby's office. "Abby Rosen," she said a second later.

Normally, Abby's voice brought a smile to her face, but not this time. Ward was nervous. "I really need to talk to you. Do you have a minute?"

"Absolutely. Your place or mine?"

"We need privacy. Should I come up?"

Sixty seconds later, after telling the smirking ER clerk she'd be in Abby's office, Ward walked through the door.

"He's murdering people, Ab. I know it. There was another venous air embolus," she said as she paced the room.

"Where? When?" Abby asked, breathing deeply and folding her hands that seemed to be shaking. Her skin seemed to pale before Ward's eyes.

Ward gave her the details.

"And there's no chance this is coincidence?"

Ward shook her head. She stopped wearing out Abby's carpet, but instead of sitting, she stood, leaning against the bathroom door and closing her eyes against the light.

"He was here in January, too."

"Huh?" Ward asked as she opened her eyes and stared at Abby.

"Hawk. He was the emergency replacement for Dick when he got sick. He was only here for three weeks, but do you know there were six deaths in January? It was a little high, but nothing that raised suspicions. Not at the time, anyway."

"Can we look at those charts?"

Abby nodded. "Of course, they were already reviewed, but in light of current events, I thought another look was warranted. I had the list pulled this morning and e-mailed it to medical records. Someone's going to get me the causes of death and attending docs."

"When will you have it?"

Without replying, Abby turned her attention to the screen on her laptop, perched on her desk. Her fingers flew across the keys and Ward saw her smile. "It's ready," she said as she typed away. An instant later, the printer beside Ward came to life and spit out a sheet of paper.

Abby stayed seated as Ward reached for the paper and scanned the document.

"January ER summary of causes of death by attending physician. Number one—January first, Marion Jones, MI, Dr. Rove. Number two—January fifth, John Fitzgerald, CHF, Dr. Litzi. January fifteenth, Stella Miles, MI, Dr Farley. January twenty-first, James Dutton, heroine overdose, Dr. Hawk. January twenty-fourth, Valerie Vincent, MI, Dr. Farley. January twenty-ninth." Ward stopped speaking, looked at Abby, and closed her eyes again. It was hard to breathe. She was dizzy. This was really happening.

"What?"

"Benjamin Moss. Dr. Hawk."

She felt Abby's hand on hers pulling the paper from her shaking fingers. She opened her eyes just as Abby began scanning the document. "Venous air embolus," Ward said softly.

Abby was silent as she walked to the leather couch against the wall adjacent to her desk. Ward followed and sat beside her, numb.

"So what should we do?"

When their eyes met, Abby's looked confused. Ward could understand that. Abby's parents were both physicians, healers. She'd grown up at this hospital, knew all the great men and a few women who'd practiced medicine here since her childhood. Most of them did an outstanding job, and even the ones who weren't stellar clinicians at least had their hearts in the right place. Ward had spent more time in the city than Abby had, and she knew that careless, reckless, even malicious physicians existed, but she'd never known anyone like this. She'd never even heard of anyone like Hawk. She thought for a moment, pushing the numbness from her neurons, and remembered what the state board's Web site had said.

"The state board suggests calling the police. And obviously reporting him to the state board." She laughed halfheartedly and frowned.

"Ward, I'm going to ask you again. Are you sure about this? Because once I call the police, I can't take these accusations back. If we're wrong, I'm setting the hospital up for the slander claim of the millennium."

"Well, I wouldn't want you to go out on a limb here, Ab. Just because people are dying."

Abby turned her head and glared at her. "I don't believe that attitude is necessary. I'm just trying to come up with a solution, the same as you."

Ward closed her eyes again and pinched the bridge of her nose. Abby was right, of course. They were in this together, and in their solidarity they'd find the solution.

"Abby, I know he murdered those people. I know it. But can I prove it? No, I can't. There's just a tremendous amount of circumstantial evidence pointing at Hawk. From an ethical standpoint, we have no choice but to report him. As long as we stay professional and keep this to ourselves, perhaps we can spare the hospital a lawsuit. We just hand over our information to the police and let them investigate. Ditto for the state board. What else can we do?"

Abby bit her lip. "I guess we can do that. But how long will it take the police? If he's murdering people, shouldn't we do something more to stop him?"

Ward stared out the window. Abby really had a magnificent view. The sun was out today, shining in a bright-blue sky over the Endless Mountains beyond the town. It was picture perfect, this scene. How could she look upon such beauty while discussing murder?

"I don't know what else to do, Ab—"

Someone knocked at the door, and Ward turned in that direction. Abby's secretary stood in the doorway, her hand poised to knock again.

"I'm sorry to interrupt you, Ms. Rosen. Dr. Thrasher is needed in the ER."

"Thanks," Abby said.

"Thank you," Ward added.

Their eyes met and Abby's seemed to pierce hers. Her voice was soft when she spoke. "I'll call the police. The chief is a friend of mine. He should be able to give me some guidance." Abby stood and pulled Ward to her feet, into her arms. She hugged her tightly. Nothing had ever felt so good as Abby did right now. She wished she could take her home, crawl into bed again, and wake up to find she'd dreamt all this nonsense. She knew better, though. "What about the state board?" Ward asked.

"I'll call them, too. The least they can do is evaluate his competence. Perhaps they can prohibit Dr. Hawk from inserting central lines."

Abby's tone was teasing, and Ward felt a welcome sense of relief, as if this was going to be all right. How, she hadn't a clue. But Abby just made her feel that way.

A minute later she was back on solid ground, in the comfortable chaos of the ER. A motor-vehicle accident had summoned her, and seven victims from two cars were being escorted through the department on stretchers and in wheelchairs. It was an hour before Ward even had an opportunity to think of Edward Hawk again.

Everyone's injuries had been minor, but one patient had suffered a significant laceration to the thigh, and as soon as all the paperwork was complete to release the other six, she went about the business of stitching.

Within moments she felt calm, the concentration needed to sort out the planes of tissue and plan the repair essentially shutting everything else from her mind. Once she knew where layers of fascia, fat, and skin were supposed to go, she inserted the needle into its holder and drove it home. One well-placed stitch told her the wound would close easily, and after a few more passes of suture through flesh, the actions became so routine her mind began to wander.

Abby's words came back to her. Could they do something else to stop Hawk? She had virtually no knowledge of police work, but investigations seemed to be time-eating monsters that often disappeared back into the forest before any real progress was made. That happened when real, certain homicide victims existed. In this case, murder was just speculation. How hard would the police pursue this case when they weren't even sure there was one?

In the meantime, Hawk would keep killing. Where was he now? Wherever he was practicing, patients were going to die, from bizarre diagnoses that should never be written on death certificates. It was so frustrating to think she had no proof, no weapon with which to stop him.

Or did she? The medical community in the mountains was relatively small, and while she might not know the ER directors at every hospital, she knew enough of them to be able to talk about this. People like Erin, nurses who worked with Hawk, suspected him of wrongdoing. Paramedics were uneasy around him. How much would it take to cause an ER director to show Hawk the door? Especially if they'd developed their own suspicions. She would have to work quietly, of course. If Hawk got wind of it, she would be signing over the house, the car, and the kayaks before his lawyers were done with her. But if she could keep the campaign very informal, off the record, perhaps she could convince someone to put Hawk out of work until the state board and the local police had a chance to investigate. Perhaps it would only take a week or two for them to complete their investigations, and then Hawk might be grounded for good.

Hopefully, he was still somewhere in the mountains. Ward felt pretty confident she could reach out to one of the small, local directors. If he'd headed to a big city, where no one knew her, or Erin, or Abby, they'd likely just dismiss her for lunacy.

How to find out? She'd met Hawk only once, even though she'd been following him for nearly five months. Did he keep in touch with the nurses? She doubted it. Nothing was endearing about the man. The nurses were happy to see him go and not likely to take his number when he did. Would Abby have it? Was he required to leave contact information in the event a chart needed a signature or something? No. Abby would just contact the…of course! The locum tenens company would know his present location. Just how would she convince them to share that information with her?

With the task of suturing nearly complete, she returned her full attention to her patient. Other than a coating of blood that seemed baked onto his skin, the leg looked great. She gave him verbal instructions and told him she'd write them down as well, pulled off her surgical gown and gloves, and headed back to the nurses' station.

"You're only seven patients behind, Dr. Thrasher. It could be worse."

Ward chuckled. "It could always be worse, so don't jinx me."

After completing the instructions, Ward chose the most critically ill patient and got busy. After another three hours, sans lunch, she had a break in the action. As she sat at her computer, hastily consuming a hospital-grade turkey sandwich, the unit clerk told her Abby was on hold for her. "You certainly earn your paycheck, Dr. Thrasher. What's that, fifteen patients and you're only halfway through the day?"

Abby could track the ER and OR schedules from her computer, and although it might have seemed like spying to some, Ward understood it was just another way for Abby to keep a handle on everything happening in the hospital. It was her job.

"I think it's seventeen, but who's counting?"

"Well, I know you must have a dozen charts calling your name, so I won't hold you up. I just wanted to update you. I called the state and they will review the cases. And the police chief just stopped in. He'll look into it."

"Humph."

Abby whistled out her sigh. "Our hands are tied, Ward. We have to let these people do their jobs. We've done ours—you've done great work, far beyond what anyone could have expected. You're responsible for bringing this guy to the attention of the police and the state board. You. But now you have to be patient."

"While he kills someone else?"

Abby didn't answer for a moment. "What would you like to do? 'Cuz if you have a brilliant idea, I'm all ears."

"Maybe I do."

Ward shared her thoughts about contacting the local hospitals to warn them about Hawk.

"I'll call the locums agency right now," Abby said.

"Don't you think I should call? After all, I work for them. They'd probably be more forthcoming with me."

"Hmm. I don't know. I can always say something like I need him for a peer review or to sign incomplete charts. I can ask if he's close by, so he can come back to the hospital, rather than having to mail confidential documents. What would your approach be?"

"I didn't get that far," she admitted.

"Well, then let me call them. But you should start working on Plan B."

"'Kay. Keep me posted."

"Will do."

Ward kept busy with charts and patients while Abby conducted her inquiry. She hurried to the phone an hour later when the clerk told her Abby was on the line. "That was fast," she said by way of greeting.

"And I have good news. I found him."

Ward was surprised. In the era of patient confidentiality, she would have hoped the locums company would have guarded *employee* privacy a little more carefully. "You're amazing. What'd you say to them?"

"I just said I needed for him to sign some confidential papers and asked if he was in the vicinity."

Ward couldn't help smiling. What a relief. Hopefully they could warn their friends and colleagues about their suspicions. The authorities might not be able to stop him, but maybe she and Abby could.

"So where is he?" she asked when Abby stopped talking.

"Close, actually. He's about forty-five minutes away, at a little hospital in Garden."

Chapter Twenty-six
Post Mortem

C'mon, Jess, answer the phone."

It was the third time Ward had made that request in the ten minutes since she'd disconnected her call to Abby. First, she'd dialed the ER. It seemed Jess spent most of her time there. The clerk had told her Jess wasn't working but had been kind enough to tell Ward she was expected at seven. It was nearly four, and if she was working the night shift, she would be waking soon. She hadn't answered her cell, though, and Ward didn't have time to sit there pressing redial all day. A patient had been waiting when she'd left the ER for the privacy of the physicians' lounge, and at four in the afternoon, more like him would soon be piling in. If she didn't get to talk to Jess now, she might not have a chance until midnight, when the ER in Garden slowed down. She didn't want to wait that long.

"Hello."

Ward nearly collapsed in relief. "Hey, can you talk?"

"Sure, just give me a minute. I just got out of the shower. I work tonight."

Ward paced the lounge while awaiting Jess's return.

"I'm back," she said after an eternity.

"Jess, you have a huge problem. Edward Hawk."

"What about Hawk?"

Ward detected the edge to Jess's voice that she'd noticed so often lately. It seemed so long ago that she could have made the same statement and a receptive Jess would have been concerned. The defensive Jess just sounded…defensive.

"He's murdering people. His patients."

The laughter preceding Jess's response was a response in itself. "Are you drinking?"

The barb stung, mostly because Jess knew how much it would. Ward swallowed a retort that might further the argument. She needed Jess on her side, and she couldn't risk alienating her.

"Plenty of water, Jess. I'm totally serious about Hawk. A little kid here with a femur fracture died of a venous air embolus after Hawk put in a central line. The chances of that are slim to none. Another patient—"

"That should be on the consent form. One of the complications of central lines is venous air embolus. It's expected."

Ward chuckled. "Sure, Jess. We tell people all that stuff so they don't sue us when there's a complication, but have you ever seen it?"

"That doesn't mean the guy's a murderer. I've been watching him for the past few weeks and he seems quite capable."

"I'm not arguing his abilities, Jess. But have you asked the staff about him? He's creepy. And his patients die, for no reason. Stable patients just crash and die when he's around."

"I'm sure there's an explanation. I mean, femur fractures bleed. The kid probably lost a lot of blood."

"They did an autopsy and found air in the girl's heart. Her hemoglobin was low, but not deadly low. It wasn't blood loss."

"Well, that doesn't mean it was intentional. As I said, air embolus is an accepted complication of the procedure."

"You have to put in twelve thousand lines to have a fatal complication. What are the chances of it happening three times?"

"Three?"

"Yeah. There was one in January, and another one, in March."

"You didn't say there were three."

"You interrupted me."

Ward heard Jess sigh into the phone. "It doesn't matter. One, two, three, who cares? It doesn't mean the guy is murdering people. Maybe he just sucks at lines."

"Seriously? If one of your patients died after you inserted a line, would you let that happen again? I mean, you have to ask yourself, why and how and what I should do differently next time. You don't let something that happens once every thousand years happen three times in six months."

"Maybe. But maybe he didn't know the cause of death. I don't know, Ward. It's just a completely illogical conclusion to jump to."

"There's more. Two other patients, both of them diabetic, mysteriously died in the ER. Both were ready for discharge, waiting for rides, when they were found dead in their exam rooms. Both were Hawk's patients. And another one was found dead, but had no autopsy to say why. Hawk had more deaths in two months at the hospital than the others had in an entire year." That was an exaggeration, but it was close enough to the truth that Ward didn't regret the words.

"Are you listening to yourself? You sound paranoid, like one of the patients from the hood we used to treat in Philly."

She heard Jess's tone and wanted to scream. Jess was quiet and calm, as if she were talking to someone irrational. On the other hand, Ward was loud. The psychology was infuriating.

"I'm not paranoid, Jess, and I'm not the only one who's concerned about Hawk. I just thought since I know you, I'd call. I thought I might get further than with a complete stranger, but I guess I was wrong."

"Is this an attempt to get me back? If you can get Hawk into some trouble maybe I'll think you're a hero or something?" If Jess's words weren't enough to push Ward over the edge, the condescending tone certainly was.

"Fuck you, Jess. Just. Fuck. You."

"Well, that's mature."

She'd managed to calm her pulse and her voice by the time Jess started to speak again. She cut her off before she could say anything further.

"Don't, Jess. I've heard enough. I've called the police, I've called the state medical board, and now I've called you. If Hawk kills again, it's not on my conscience."

❖

Jess heard the click as Ward disconnected the call. Ward had gone off the cliff, and Jess was sorry for her part in it. She still thought of telling her about the drug in her system on the night she attacked Em and George, but each time she debated it, she decided against it. It might make Ward feel better, but it would make the situation worse for everyone else. And her own situation wasn't great. Things weren't going well with Wendy, and though she suspected they'd be great friends, she knew they wouldn't make it as lovers. Her father was doing and saying things that concerned her, and she'd been trying to get him to the doctor for weeks. Dementia was a big concern. The ER was slammed with summer visitors, and she was working two or three hours extra every day to help the staff keep up. As the director, it was her job. Yet it all weighed heavily on her. It took all her strength to make it through her days, to keep it together, to get to work, and to not crack up. Being responsible for Ward, too, was just too much to ask.

Reaching into the bedside table, she pulled out her pill bottles. First, she opened the Xanax and swallowed two tabs with the water sitting there. Carefully, she closed the lid. She couldn't afford to lose pills. Yes, she could still get them, but since leaving Philly, it was much harder. Next, she opened the bottle of Percocet. She'd managed to convince the pain-management specialist that she needed six of the tablets daily, and mostly, she did. She'd spent the last two years of her life as small segments of time passed between narcotics doses. Through sheer force of will she'd managed to wean herself down to six tablets a day, but at times like now she definitely needed more. She tapped the bottle against her palm until three tablets sat in her hand. For a moment, she debated putting one back but then threw back her head and swallowed them before she could change her mind.

She definitely needed a new source. For years she'd been able to find pills through her regular patients in the ER, mostly the guys with sickle-cell anemia, who made regular appearances in the ER for crises. After getting to know some of the faces, she'd developed the sort of relationship with one or two that allowed her to exchange money for the thirty extra oxycodone tabs she needed every week. The cost was a little higher when she used her patients, but she didn't need to worry much about money. As long as she had her drugs, she could function, and she often needed as many as ten tablets a day to keep her that way. But then, the owner of the Happy and Healthy Pharmacies was arrested for distributing narcotics, and overnight the supply on the streets of Philadelphia ran dry.

Jess had been able to painfully wean herself down, and she would do well for weeks on end, then crash. Her needs would rebound and she'd need a dozen tabs to recharge. Now, she was mostly stabilized on this dose, and she'd found a reliable doctor to prescribe the pills. All she needed was a little insurance, for stressful times, like when her ex-girlfriend called to tell her one of the doctors on her staff was murdering patients.

Jess pulled on a pair of shorts and a T-shirt and sat on her bed. It had once been their bed, but the relationship had become too much for her. Her addiction to pain pills took all of her energy, and she just didn't have enough to share with a partner. At times she'd contemplated telling Ward about her problem, but in the end, she'd decided against it.

Jess had always been the prude, criticizing Ward for drinking too much, when, really, she was just having fun. Then, when her wrist surgery didn't go as planned, Ward had nursed her gently, cautioning her every day about the use of pain pills, until one day, Jess just went out and got another prescription from her family doctor so she could take them without Ward's knowledge. Her dependence on the drugs happened so quickly she'd never seen it coming. As her wrist healed, she'd tried to cut back, but within hours of taking a tablet, she started to feel the misery of withdrawal—anxiety, muscle aches, diarrhea, profuse sweating. It was hell, and just a single Percocet could make her normal again.

For a moment, she wished she could have shared this trouble with Ward. But she was too good, too perfect. She would have insisted on something like rehab, or random urine drug screens before bed. It was much better for Jess to be alone with this problem than to deal with Ward. It took all she had to function as a doctor, and that was her first priority, her true love. Women were emotional and taxing, and medicine really wasn't.

It was unpredictable at times—patients didn't always respond the way they should have to treatment, but that made it challenging. Almost always, she could solve their riddles and diagnose their problems. Almost always she could make them feel better. And in the chaos of her life, that one little sliver of joy kept her alive. Ward couldn't do it. Her career could. She'd had to let Ward go.

Jess didn't know what to make of Ward's accusations. Ever since learning Ward had been drugged on the night she attacked Emory and George, Jess tended to sympathize with her. Not enough to tell her the truth—what was the point? The lie gave Jess the perfect excuse to break up with her, and that had been just what she needed at the time.

What about now, though? Things with Wendy weren't working out, and she could never be with a man. She'd been foolish to even entertain that idea, but her life was in the sort of state where foolish ideas seemed logical. Was her breakup with Ward another folly? Was it time to rethink Ward? She'd never find anyone kinder and better for her—better to her, either. Yet that was part of the problem. Ward enabled her, and Jess couldn't help taking advantage. Ward was just an easy target.

What about Hawk? Could Ward be right? He was a little strange; the staff had mentioned that. What would make Ward label him a killer? It sounded like bad luck more than anything. Still, three fatal air emboli—that was a bit hard to comprehend. It was rare to see a doctor make a fatal mistake more than once. Doctors were healers—they buried their mistakes but learned from them.

I'll have to keep an eye on him, she thought as she sat before her computer. She liked to scan her e-mail before work, just to know what was happening. After logging on, she scanned the list. Junk, junk, junk, Wendy.

Jess clicked on the e-mail. She liked Wendy. She was cute, with rugged dark looks, but her personality attracted Jess the most. Serious, quiet, introverted. With Wendy, Jess felt at peace, unlike with Ward, whose energy left her feeling edgy. Wendy was like a balm, a drug to ease her suffering. Too bad there was no sexual attraction. The message was brief and to the point, like Wendy.

Autopsy report on Christian Cooney says cause of death venous air embolus. Probably from central line. Call me later.

CHAPTER TWENTY-SEVEN
PARALYSIS

The typical mid-afternoon lull in the Garden ER had stretched, and the entire staff of four had grown bored. They'd finished notes and cleaned and restocked rooms, organized supplies. Nothing was left to do except socialize.

The smile plastered on Edward's face hadn't changed in twenty minutes, when he'd first sat down with the staff to look at the menu from the Chinese restaurant. Listening to their stories and smiling at the simplicity of their lives wasn't easy, but he'd come to understand its necessity. If he wanted to avoid suspicion, he had to appear normal, just like all the common, ordinary people he encountered every day. It was difficult, but he could do it. He had to.

When he'd first taken the job with the locums company, he'd assumed he'd continue to move around. But that wasn't the case. The company was pestering him to return to Endless Mountains Medical Center, where he'd had a prolific month of June, but he hesitated. Five people had died at his hand. Wouldn't someone get suspicious if so many deaths continued? There'd been two deaths in January at Endless Mountains as well. If he went back, he'd have to tone things down. That wasn't ideal if he wanted the world record for serial killers. To earn that trophy, he had to keep moving to new places, where there were no watchful eyes or prior incidents to raise questions when he struck down his next victim.

Moving was ideal. He wasn't sure it was going to happen, though. He'd started thinking about the things he'd seen over the years, the way his peers handled those bad outcomes. He'd seen it happen hundreds of times in his career. Incompetent doctors and nurses lost patients all the time, and their professional colleagues would rally beside them, heads held high and mouths held closed while inquiry boards got nowhere. The staff stood together and supported each other. At least the ones they liked. The colleagues and staff who dared to be different—or just were different—were left on their own to face the firing squad. The ones with friends rarely had worries.

Edward began to wonder about friendship, a social arena into which he'd never ventured. Sharing, exchanging, compromising weren't comfortable concepts. He'd never really gotten close to anyone except his family, and barely tolerated them for the obligatory holiday functions. He used his job as an excuse and worked his way out of much of that, too. He was trying now, though. If he befriended his coworkers and a question ever came up about his character or his motives with a patient, would they stand beside him? Maybe. Stranger things had happened.

Sitting there wasting valuable time making friends, Edward was bored senseless. The ER was quiet, and the inactivity made him nervous. Edward looked up at the security-camera monitors. One of the six screens caught the image of Jessica Benson opening the door to her office, just outside the main ER doors in the hallway leading toward the hospital's back entrance. What was she doing at the hospital? Her shift didn't start for two hours. She typically came in on her day off to do paperwork, but not before shifts. The twelve-hour days were long enough without further extending them.

Was something wrong? He'd had a strong month, sending four patients out of the Garden ER in body bags. Had one of them betrayed him? Filled with a sudden sense of dread, he leaned back and stared at the benign image on the monitor. An empty hallway and a closed door, with no signs of life at all. Jess had disappeared into her office. What was she doing in there?

The call to the ER an hour earlier replayed in his mind. Ringing telephones annoyed him, and so he'd picked up the receiver and answered when the unit clerk was busy with another call. It was Dr. Ward Thrasher, calling for Jess, and she'd said her message was urgent. Thrasher had been following him on his journey through the mountain hospitals. Was it possible she'd learned something about him? Perhaps heard some nasty rumor?

Edward had always been careful, choosing methods of murder that were hard to identify. Most times his victims didn't even have autopsies because their deaths weren't outside the range of possibilities for people of their age and with their particular medical problems. Even so, someone had figured something out in New Jersey, and someone might have gotten lucky again. With his particular hobby, he could never be too careful.

Dozens of thoughts ran through his mind as he reached into his pockets, pondering his options. Confront her? Spy on her? Kill her? He needed to know what she knew, but how to get that information? He closed his hand on the syringe in his pocket, and an idea came to him. He could take advantage of the empty ER and disappear for a few minutes, then hopefully convince Jessica Benson to cooperate.

"I need to use the restroom," he informed the staff. They barely acknowledged him as they studied the menu. "Shrimp with broccoli," he said as he stood.

He walked in the direction of the restroom, checked to see that no one was watching, then turned toward Jess's office. His fingers slid over the syringe of succinylcholine in his pocket. It was a powerful medication used to paralyze patients before inserting breathing tubes. He'd used the sux earlier in the day, mostly as an excuse to open the vial and pilfer the leftover medication to have on hand for later use. What a wonderful way to kill someone! The sux paralyzes all of the muscles, including those responsible for breathing, but doesn't do a thing to change the level of consciousness. A person is wide-awake but can't move a muscle. He remembered the scenes he'd orchestrated over the years, his patients staring straight ahead as he told them they were going to die. Unfortunately, people become a little foggy when they go without oxygen for too long, so they're not usually aware of their heart slowing and stopping as it cries out before death.

He would have loved to see it all play out on a heart monitor, watching the oxygen level drop, and then the erratic pattern of the heart's rhythm—perhaps extra beats, or a fast rate, but eventually it would all end with the beautiful flat line of death.

When he'd drawn up the syringe of sux earlier in his shift, he'd had no idea who he'd use it on. If his concerns were founded, he had his answer, and nothing could have made him happier. He didn't like Jessica Benson. She was too controlling, always reminding him of the stupid protocols in place at the Garden ER. She'd come to Garden from the big city and had made endless changes, and challenged everyone who questioned them, including him. It was hard to murder people when he was forced to follow a standard guideline for medical care, but he'd managed it anyway. Just to stick it to Jessica Benson, Hawk planned to make his month in Garden a record breaker. Maybe he'd even add her death certificate to his collection.

❖

Jess didn't know what to do. After reading the e-mail from Wendy, she'd tried the cell phone of the hospital CEO, hoping for some advice, but he hadn't picked up. With no real plan in mind, it seemed prudent for her to review the chart of the patient who'd died of the venous air embolus. Perhaps she'd find something there she could use to help her determine what to do about Hawk, but she doubted it. If Ward was correct, and he was murdering ER patients, he was clever enough to cover his tracks. The proof wouldn't be in the chart of this particular patient but in the pattern of the deaths that had happened while he was working. And four patients dying of rare diseases on his watch was all the pattern she needed to be convinced. Still, she'd look anyway, at the chart of Christian Cooney and the other patients who'd died at Garden since Hawk had arrived.

After quickly putting on her makeup and pulling on her sneakers, Jess packed some food for her overnight shift and began her walk to the hospital. It had been a humid day, and even though it had cleared into a pleasant afternoon, the streets were deserted as her neighbors sought relief inside their air-conditioned homes. She let herself in through the hospital's employee entrance with her ID badge and headed for her office.

She supposed she could just show up early for work and tell Hawk to take off early. After he finished this shift, he had three days off and usually headed to his apartment in New York to enjoy his downtime. She could call the extra two hours a gift, but would that gesture draw his suspicions? A murderer probably had his antenna finely tuned to other people's behavior, and letting him go earlier would have been atypical. No, best to let him finish the shift. She'd sort out what to do sometime during the next three days. She only hoped no one died in the next two hours.

Jess unlocked her office door, turned on the lights and the computer, and sat down in front of it. She wanted to review all the ER and hospital deaths that had occurred since Hawk came to Garden, just to see if anything seemed unusual. She'd look for Hawk's name everywhere, because in a small hospital like Garden, he might have been called to care for a patient outside her department. If someone was in labor and no obstetrician was available, the ER doc would be summoned. If someone was in cardiac arrest in the cafeteria, Hawk would have gotten that call, too. Just by scanning the files she remembered, she came up with four ER deaths connected to him. Why hadn't that concerned her before? God, maybe her personal issues were affecting her job. The whole ER usually saw four deaths in a month; why did Hawk have so many? Whether bad medicine or murder, the situation certainly warranted review. Jess only hoped she found no evidence of cases outside the ER to pad the total.

Her computer asked for her password, and she entered it and quickly found the file she needed. As ER director, she was on the M & M committee. Each department head from pediatrics to surgery entered information about hospital deaths into this file for the process of review. At a monthly meeting, those chairs would meet over dinner and discuss the cases. The departments were listed alphabetically, and she began with the Department of Anesthesia. There were no deaths due to anesthesia in the month of July. The Emergency Department was next. She skipped that file. ICU was next. Jess clicked on that file and scanned the names of a dozen people who'd died in intensive care. Each of them had a death certificate, and if Hawk was the physician caring for them at the time of death, she'd see his name listed on the paper, but it was nowhere on the list. She'd just clicked on the ER patients when a knock on her door interrupted her. Strange. No one knew she was here. Perhaps they'd seen the light beneath the door, or someone saw her walk into the hospital.

She opened the door to find Edward Hawk standing before her. She tried not to let the fear spreading through her show on her face.

"I saw you come in," he said, a warm smile on his face. "Can I talk to you?"

"Sure," Jess said. "How about the staff lounge?" she suggested, attempting to divert him out of the private space of her office and the list of patient charts on her computer screen.

"No, here," he said, and pushed through the door.

"Hey," she said as she saw him walk right to the computer screen. It took a fraction of a second to see what she was reading, and his reaction was sudden and violent. He lunged at her, and before she could react, she felt the bite of a needle tearing into the flesh of her thigh. She screamed, batted at this hand, and attempted to jump from his grasp. They landed on the floor, his weight pinning her, his hand suffocating her. He finished with the syringe and discarded it on the floor with a flick of his hand, then focused on subduing her. Wrapping both legs around her lower body, he effectively immobilized her. His right arm managed to somehow pin hers and grasp her left, and the left hand over her mouth was like a vise. She tried biting but couldn't open her mouth enough to do any damage. Her muffled moans were a waste of the precious breath she could barely siphon through the narrow gap between her nose and Hawk's hand.

Even though Jess was in good shape, Hawk was too much for her. But something else seemed odd. Her body was betraying her, refusing to fight, and even as her mind yelled, "kick, buck, thrash," she seemed to just melt into the floor and collapse.

As he sensed this, his hold on her eased, except for the hand across her mouth, which held tight. His rapid breaths against her neck made her sick, but not so sick as the sound of his voice or the content of his message.

"It was sux in that syringe, Jess. An elephant dose. I can leave you on this floor to die and then come back later for your body, or I can breathe for you now if you promise to cooperate. I'm going to take my hand from your mouth. If you scream, I'll let you die. Now, do you want to live, or not?"

Hawk eased his hand from Jess's mouth, and she tried to suck in air, but she had no strength behind her effort. "No," she managed to choke out and thought for sure it was over.

He abruptly stood, opened the door a fraction, and peeked outside. He walked through it and she began counting as it closed behind him, wondering how high she could go before she lost consciousness. The sux itself wouldn't knock her out, but after a minute or so, her brain would begin to malfunction.

One. *Where the fuck did he go?* Two. *What the fuck is he going to do with me?* Three. *I'm going to die!* Four. *How could I have been so stupid?* Five. *Fucking stupid!* Six. *Ward. I've been so rotten to her.* Seven. *Calm down.* Eight, nine, ten…she pictured a clear blue sky and a still lake as she counted. If her last thought went with her to the next life, she vowed it to be a happy one.

She was at fifty, going on fifty-one when the door opened. Even if he planned to kill her, Jess had never been happier to see anyone. The fact that he held an ambu bag in his hand made her even happier. He quickly knelt beside her and placed a mask over her face. Then he connected it to the football and began squeezing, and suddenly he was helping her to breathe. He gently laid her onto the office floor and tilted her head back, pulled up her chin, and squeezed the bag. Jess couldn't feel the air rushing into her lungs, but she could hear the sound of the bag as it squeaked to herald the breath.

He'd paralyzed her with sux, and now he was breathing for her, keeping her alive! Why? The needle in her thigh confirmed her suspicions about Hawk. He was a murderer. Why wasn't she already dead? What did he want from her? She couldn't move, not even to blink, yet she was trembling with fear. She wished he'd let her die the easy way. She was too much of a coward to take torture.

She couldn't feel anything. Her hearing seemed hypersensitive, and she listened intently for sounds from the hallway, the sounds of someone who might be coming to save her. She heard nothing, though, except the rhythmic whistle of the bag as he squeezed it, maintaining her life, at least until he decided not to.

Suddenly he dropped the bag and stood, then took a few steps toward her computer screen and scrolled down. "I knew you figured it out. How?"

Jess couldn't answer him; she couldn't speak. She couldn't even stare him down; her eyes wouldn't move. She was aware of him at the corners of her vision, but he was just a blur, a form in an impressionist painting, vaguely resembling a man. Her fear level mounted with each second that passed, each second without the breaths that would deliver oxygen to her brain. The edges of her awareness grew fuzzy as Hawk scrolled through her computer files. When he dropped to the floor beside her, she was on the edge of consciousness.

He began bagging her again, staring into her eyes as he did so. He waited a moment before speaking. "So, Dr. Benson, this is how it's going to happen. I'm going to breathe for you until you can do it on your own. It will probably take twenty minutes for your muscles to recover. Then, I'm going to ask you some questions, and you're going to answer them. I'll tell you them now, so you have a few minutes to contemplate your answers. Then, I'm going back out there and finish my shift, and we're going to pretend this never happened. Because if you were ever to say anything about this, I'd have a lot more work to do. Kill your dad. Kill your little coroner friend. Kill some more people in Garden. So, really, all of their fates will be up to you. If you tell me what I need to know, your friends and family will live, and I'll move on. If not, they all die. And you do, too. Understand?" Hawk laughed. "Of course you can't answer. I'll assume you understand."

Hawk stood and opened the door, scanning the hallway. Before he knocked on Jess's door, he'd bent the clamp on the security camera. It was now pointing straight down. No one was in sight. How long had he been gone, though? What if someone came looking for him? He needed another fifteen minutes with Jess before she started breathing on her own. If he left her early, she'd die. He didn't particularly care if she did, but he hadn't planned for that, and it would be difficult to explain her body here in the hospital.

Could he really let her go when he was done? Fuck! He knew he couldn't. He had to kill her, but how?

Closing the door, he knelt beside her on the floor. Her eyes stared at the ceiling, and he squeezed the bag rapidly a few times, trying to build up the oxygen level in her blood. "I'm going to hyperventilate you and run out to check on things. I'll only be gone a few minutes."

Hawk squeezed the bag rapidly a dozen times, grabbed Jess's keys, and once again scanned the hallway. When he ascertained it was clear, he opened the ER doors using the wall button, then walked back into the ER.

"I'm not sure about Chinese food," he informed his coworkers. "My stomach is a mess."

"Well, we just called it in. Should we cancel?" Betty asked.

Betty was about ninety years old and a hillbilly, and probably the smartest nurse Hawk had ever worked with.

"I guess I'll risk it," he said. "Gotta run," he said, and scampered back toward Jess's office.

Checking the camera, he quickly opened the office door. "Miss me?"

Jess could go a few minutes without oxygen, and he figured he'd been gone only ninety seconds, but her eyes looked a little foggy. Unfocused. He hyperventilated her again and saw her come around.

"Okay, here are my questions, Jessica. First, what do you know? I know you're on to me, but what do you think I did, and what can you prove I did? Second, how did you figure it out? Did someone see something, or notice something, or did you figure it out yourself? Third, do you have any proof? Fourth, who did you share your information with? Fifth, how do you think I can prevent this from happening in the future? I like killing and don't want to stop, so if you can help me, I'd appreciate that."

Hawk stopped squeezing the bag keeping Jess alive, stood, and checked the hallway. Nothing. He knelt and resumed bagging, quiet as his mind raced. He had a huge problem to solve, and it would require some thought. He definitely had to kill Jess. But how? Could he murder her here without casting some suspicion on himself? He was in the building, after all, and that was bound to cause some troubles for everyone working tonight. If Jess didn't show up for her shift, someone would check her office, so he couldn't just leave the body here. He could always hide it somewhere in the hospital, but it would eventually be found. That meant he had to kill her in a way that suggested natural causes. Not an easy task for a healthy woman of her age.

No, that wouldn't work. He had to get her out of the hospital and dispose of the body so no one would discover it. At least for a long time, allowing decomposition to destroy any information about the manner and cause of death. How to get her out, though? He couldn't very well carry her. He'd figure out what to do with her later. He'd have the next three days off, plenty of time.

The ringing phone startled him, and he nearly panicked as he considered the possibility that someone in the hallway would hear it. Fumbling with the zipper, he tore open Jess's backpack to find the phone. The stern face of the county coroner greeted him.

Edward knew Jess was dating the coroner. That could be a problem. She'd start looking for Jess. And Jess's father was the fucking sheriff. He'd look for her, too. He didn't have much time to come up with his plan.

Unless—oh, wow. Maybe he could enlist the coroner's help! His brilliance sometimes amazed him, and now was one such occasion. He could call the coroner to take Jess's body out of the hospital, and then he'd steal it from the funeral home. It was the perfect solution.

No, he thought. The perfect solution was to remove all suspicion from him—to make it look as if the coroner had killed Jess. A deadly lovers' quarrel. *That* was perfect. It was his first murder all over again. Helise's boyfriend had gone to jail for murdering her, and no one had ever suspected him. If he could pin Jess's death on the coroner, he'd be safe.

Hawk heard noise in the hallway and stood to listen at the door. Voices, and then a rattling stretcher being maneuvered outside the door. The sound of the doors opening. An ambulance had arrived with a patient. Fuck. He was running out of time.

Lifting the bag from Jess's face, he watched her. "Try to breathe," he commanded. Jess didn't move.

"Dr. Hawk to the ER," the operator's voice cried out over the intercom. "Dr. Hawk to the ER."

"Fuck, fuck, fuck," he murmured to himself. Then to Jessica, "Give me a minute."

He opened the office door and surveyed the hallway. Empty. Three giant steps to the other side and he was through the door to the staff lounge a second later. The phone on the wall speed-dialed the ER. "It's Hawk, what's up?"

"We have a patient with chest pain."

"Oh, wow. I'm having trouble getting out of the bathroom," he said, trying hard to add the agony he felt to his voice. "But I'll be right there."

The hallway was clear and he was beside Jess a minute later. "Let's try the breathing thing again."

He watched her still chest, then picked up an arm and watched it drop limply to the floor. "I'm needed in the ER. I'll be back in a few minutes."

Hawk bagged Jess for a minute and then practically ran to the ER. He found the patient looking pink and comfortable in the resuscitation room. An EKG was sitting on the machine. He saw changes but no MI in progress. Under other circumstances, this seventy-year-old woman might have been a fun patient to play with, but not today. "Are you having any pain now?" he asked.

"No. That pill under the tongue took it away," she said.

"Chest-pain protocol, okay? I'm so sorry," he whispered to the nurse. "I gotta go."

Hawk ran back to Jess's office. Her eyes were still open, but she wasn't breathing. He squeezed the bag and then checked the muscle tone in her arms. To his delight, it seemed to be returning. "Thank God," he sighed, then chuckled. "Remind me not to do this again!"

After another minute, he stopped bagging Jess. "Breathe," he ordered her. It might have been just a twitch, but Hawk was elated. She'd be breathing on her own soon, which meant he could go back to the ER and take care of his patients, so the staff wouldn't come looking for him.

Hefting Jess up to her office chair, Hawk noted her improved tone. She'd be strong enough to kick and fight and scream in just a few minutes. He had to act quickly.

He opened the office door and quickly closed it. A Chinese man carrying a brown bag was walking in his direction. When he passed through the doors into the department and they closed behind him, Hawk sprang into action.

Holding the door open with his foot, he pushed the chair and Jessica through it, then jogged down the hallway, guiding the wheeled chair before him. At the end of the sixty-foot-long corridor, he turned left. This was the ground floor, and the loading dock for the morgue was in that direction, near the lab. While the lab was open around the clock, few staff members were here at this time. Edward had watched the autopsy on one of his patients and retraced his steps through the department. Thankfully, it was deserted—and unlocked. He wheeled Jess through a series of outer rooms, through the autopsy suite, and into the closet.

Utilizing the materials at hand—gowns, masks, and tape, Hawk restrained her, covering her mouth with tape and tying her to the chair and the wall. By the time he was finished, she'd regained enough strength to fight him.

"I'll be back for our little chat in just a little while. Be a good girl while I'm gone."

❖

Fear coated Jess in a blanket of sweat. She'd never been so scared, and the muscles that had so recently been limp now trembled uncontrollably.

Why hadn't she listened to Ward? When Ward had told her about Hawk, she'd reacted to Ward rather than her news. It wasn't exactly a case of shooting the messenger, but she'd allowed her mixed feelings about Ward to cloud her judgment. That might prove to be a fatal error.

And the pain she was in was agony. One of the side effects of succinylcholine is severe muscle pain, and if anyone ever debated that, Jess would be willing to offer testimony. Every movable muscle in her body was cramping, a tight pinching that wouldn't release. Perhaps if she could change position, or walk it out, stretch a little. Those weren't options, though, and as the tears flowed freely down her face, she pondered her fate.

What was she going to do? Hawk would kill her. He had no choice, really. After what he'd done to her, he'd have to kill her to stay out of jail. If he didn't want information from her, she'd probably already be dead. He could have let the sux do its job and she would have suffocated, leaving only a body to dispose of. Maybe not even that. He might have just taken his chances. Who could have proved it was him who'd stabbed her with a syringe full of poison?

He needed something though, and perhaps if Jess denied him the answers he sought, he'd keep her alive long enough for someone to come to her aid. Wendy would miss her. And her dad. They'd both start looking. It was only a couple of hours until she was due for her night shift. If she didn't show up then, the hospital would probably call the state police out to investigate. All she needed was a little time. If she could stay alive for a few hours, she just might survive.

She squirmed a little, trying to find a weakness in the bonds that held her fast to the chair. Nothing, except a little rocking of the chair. The tape cutting into her mouth was effectively cutting off her voice. Attempts at calling out were muffled and seemed to crawl back into her mouth in fear.

Looking up, she studied the shelves of supplies. A box of scalpels was promising. If she could reach the fourth shelf while bound with her hands behind her back, then open the box and the plastic sealed pouch, she might be able to saw her way through the bindings. Not.

She couldn't escape this mess. She just had to wait it out, hold on to the information that would be her death sentence, and hope for a miracle.

For the first time in twenty years, she began to pray.

❖

What an ordeal! The ER exploded after that first patient, and then, to the surprise of everyone on staff at Garden Memorial Hospital except Edward, Dr. Jessica Benson failed to show up for work. He'd dutifully stayed late, seeing patients without complaint, offering the appropriate words of concern for his missing boss. At ten o'clock, after one of the other staff doctors came in to spell him, he was finally free to take care of Jess.

Between casting a fracture and draining an abscess and taking care of a few other minor emergencies, he'd come up with a plan.

Back in Jess's office, he straightened up its appearance a bit. Her chair was missing, so he swiped one from the staff lounge. It wasn't a desk chair, but hopefully no one would notice. He ignored the computer. If he shut it down, someone would be able to use metadata to track it, putting Jess in her office just as he was leaving the hospital. The fact that she'd logged on at five that afternoon placed her at the hospital, and he couldn't do anything about it, but why give the police more information?

He picked up Jess's phone and dialed Wendy's number, immediately disconnecting the call. That would give the police the idea that Jess had called Wendy. Picking up Jess's office phone, he immediately dialed Wendy from that line.

"Garden Funeral Services, this is Wendy, how may I help you?" she answered in a professional and comforting voice.

It was time to put his plan in motion.

"This is Edward, from Garden Memorial Hospital. We have a patient, I mean, body. The family has requested your services."

"Okay, Edward, I can help you. I just need some information."

After Edward supplied the vital statistics, he asked about the protocol. "I'm new, and it's my first time dealing with a corpse."

"No worries. I'll be over in a few minutes. I'll ring the buzzer at the morgue door, and the hospital operator will call you. What extension are you at? It didn't come up on my phone."

Edward was happy about the new privacy feature on the phones. It didn't give the extension, just the hospital switchboard number. "Oh, I'm in the morgue now. I'll just wait for you."

Wendy laughed. "Okay, then. I'll be there in five minutes."

In spite of all the murders he'd committed, Hawk had yet to meet the county coroner. He wasn't worried that she'd recognize him.

He made his way to the lab and into the garage bay with the double, oversized hanging door. Pressing the wall plate, he opened the door and sat, waiting.

Edward figured his easiest option was to murder Wendy first and then steal her hearse. But he might need her alive, to motivate Jess to talk. Instead, he'd give her the same treatment he'd given Jess. When he had what he needed, he'd kill them both.

A minute later, a hearse appeared at the garage entrance, and the driver carefully backed it in. When it was in place, the driver killed the engine, opened the door, and stepped out of the car. Edward closed the garage door and walked toward the car.

"Hi, I'm Wendy. I'm from the funeral home," she said and extended a hand in greeting.

His was sweaty, and he wiped it on his slacks before extending it. "Edward."

"Where is she?" Wendy asked, wasting no time.

"Oh, in the autopsy suite. Do you want to follow me?"

"Just let me grab my stretcher," she said.

Wendy walked around to the back of the hearse, with Edward beside her. She turned to open the rear door, and Edward chose that moment to lunge at her, depressing the sux into her upper arm before she had a chance to fight him. No one was near enough to hear her screams, but he quickly covered her mouth to keep it that way. Just like with Jess, the medication began to take effect within a minute, and soon Edward had her positioned on the concrete garage floor, where he breathed for her with the mask and bag. He briefly explained the situation. "I may need your help to convince Jess to tell me what she knows. She trusts you, I think. If you convince her to cooperate, I'll let you live."

After a few minutes, Edward left the garage bay and walked quickly to the closet where he found Jessica bound and looking quite anxious. "You have a visitor," he exclaimed.

He used his utility knife to cut the tape holding Jess's chair to the storage shelving, then quickly pushed her back out the way they'd come in. The autopsy suite was just across the hall from the garage where the hearse and Wendy were waiting.

He left Jess at the doorway and hustled back to Wendy, who'd gone without oxygen for a minute or so while he'd been gone. She pinked up after a few breaths, and with both of them listening, he began to explain his plan. A few minutes later, Hawk put down the bag and pulled the stretcher from the hearse, then wheeled Jess next to it. He paused his project to breathe for Wendy for a few minutes, then cut Jess's bindings and lifted her onto the stretcher. Her mouth, hands, and feet were still bound, and she landed with a thud when Edward pushed her backward. He breathed for Wendy for a few more minutes, then lifted her onto the stretcher next to Jess.

It was a tight fit, but he made it work. "Breathe," he ordered her as he carefully watched her chest for signs of movement.

"Remind me not to use sux when I'm in a hurry," he said as he resumed the monotonous, rhythmic squeezing of the bag.

After a few more minutes, Edward stopped his efforts and watched Wendy's chest. It was moving. "Good enough. Now, ladies, I know you like being close to each other, so this will be perfect for you. We're going for a little ride."

Edward pulled on latex gloves before touching anything else. He loaded the stretcher in the back of the hearse, closed the door, and opened the hospital's garage door. After pulling the vehicle out of the garage, he ran back inside, closed the door, and hurried back outside before it fully closed. His car was parked at the apartment, which wasn't convenient, but it would have to do. For now, he was leading the funeral.

The hunting club was only twenty miles out of town, but on the dark, winding roads, the trip seemed twice as long. Careful to adhere to the posted speed limit, he found himself parked at the cabin forty minutes later. Edward appropriated the key from the fake rock in which it was stored, and after unlocking the door and verifying that no other members were lurking about, he picked up his cell phone and called the sheriff.

"It's Dr. Hawk," he said when Zeke answered. "I need you to come out to the cabin at the hunting club. It's Jessica. She's having some sort of crisis and I think she needs you."

"Thank the Lord she's with you. They told me she didn't show up for work, and I've been lookin' for her since. What kind of crisis is she having, Doc?"

"I think she had a fight with the coroner. A lovers' quarrel. Can you come right away?"

"Ah, jeez. Of course. I'll be there in twenty minutes."

"Perfect. And Sheriff, keep this under your hat. I'm not sure she'd want the entire hospital knowing why she didn't show up for work. It's rather unprofessional."

CHAPTER TWENTY-EIGHT
ALTITUDE SICKNESS

Ward tried to suppress a grin as she successfully eliminated the *X* from her rack of Scrabble tiles. Triple-word points coming her way.

After her conversation with Jess, Ward had been stressed. She and Abby had changed their dinner plans and had take-out pizza on the deck, and Ward shared her conversation with Jess and gave a brief synopsis of their history. Afterward, Abby had hugged her and suggested a game of Scrabble to help them relax. It was working splendidly.

"I don't think you should be able to use medical words," Abby complained, referring to the word *axon*, which netted Ward forty-nine points.

"It's in the dictionary. Suck it up."

Ward's phone interrupted their banter. The call was from the ER at Garden. Why was Jess calling? Hadn't she made her point when she'd berated Ward earlier?

"Would you mind if I answer this? It's Jess."

Abby's eyes flew open. Clearly, she hadn't been expecting that call either. "Please."

"Hello."

"Hi, Dr. Thrasher. It's Deb Carver, the nursing supervisor at Garden Memorial Hospital. I'm sorry to bother you, but do you know where Dr. Benson is?"

"What? Isn't she at work?"

"No, she didn't show up tonight, and we're all worried about her."

Ward's heart had stopped beating and was now correcting that pause by pounding at lightning speed. She'd just talked to Jess a few hours ago, and other than her anger, she'd seemed fine. Glancing at her watch, she grew even more alarmed. She and Abby had managed to burn three hours eating and playing Scrabble. That meant Jess was three hours late for work. Jess was never late. Something was wrong.

"I have no idea where she is, Deb. I talked to her about four o'clock and she seemed fine. Did you try the sheriff?"

"Yeah. Zeke doesn't know where she is either."

"How about the coroner, Wendy? They're friends. Maybe she knows something."

"No. Wendy hasn't heard from her."

"Well, Deb, I don't know who else you could call. I'll try some of our friends in Philly, but you know more about Jess's friends in Garden than I do."

"Okay, Dr. Thrasher. If you talk to her, tell her we're all real worried about her."

"I'll do that."

Ward looked to Abby, who seemed to know what was going on even though she'd only heard Ward's half of the conversation.

"Jess is missing?"

"Yes. And I don't feel good about this. What if she confronted Hawk and he did something to her?"

"Don't think the worst, but you're right to worry. Jess doesn't seem like the kind of person to skip work. Is it possible she had her schedule mixed up?"

Ward shook her head. "When I talked to her she told me she was working tonight."

"What should we do?"

"Well, since her father is the sheriff, I'm sure he's handling this. But, truthfully, I think he's getting a little confused. I don't trust him. Should we call the state police?"

"I'm not sure. They'd probably defer to the locals, especially if the sheriff is territorial. They won't want to step on his toes until they have to."

"I better go to Garden. I still have a key to her house. Unless she changed the locks."

"I'm coming with you."

"No, Abby. That's not necessary."

Abby grabbed Ward's arm and searched her eyes. "It's late. You're going to drive too fast, on dark country roads, and you're stressed. Who knows what you'll find when you get there. I want to come with you. I want to be with you, Ward."

Abby's gesture and her touch comforted her. She nodded. "Thank you. I could use the company. And I probably should get coverage for tomorrow."

"We'll phone from the car."

Both of them packed overnight bags and were in Ward's car fifteen minutes later. Abby took the wheel while Ward took the phone. She called Jess's cell phone first. It went unanswered. Next, she dialed the house in Philly. Why did they even have a house phone? That was the first thing she'd get rid of when she got back home. Michelle answered on the fourth ring.

"I don't think I've ever heard the house phone ring. It took me a few seconds to find it."

"Jess didn't show up for work tonight. Did she drive home?"

"No. I've been here all day. She hasn't been here." After making a few suggestions and wishing Ward well, Michelle said good-bye.

Zeke's was next. Ward dialed his house number, but he didn't answer. "He's probably out looking for her," she murmured, and Abby reached through the darkness to place a warm hand on her jeans-clad thigh. Ward placed her hand atop Abby's, thankful for the contact. She willed her heartbeat to slow, willed the breath to make it to the bottom of her lungs.

Zeke didn't answer his cell either. That wasn't unusual. Next Ward started scrolling through the contacts on her cell phone, dialing each in turn. No one had seen Jess in ages—some since she'd left Philly, some when they'd come to the mountains for her mom's funeral the previous winter. Each of them had suggestions, but after twenty minutes of phone calls, she'd proved most of the theories wrong.

Forty-five minutes after they left Abby's house, Ward directed her into the driveway of Jess's house in Garden. The landscaping lights were on, as expected, and a light above the kitchen sink leaked through the large window into the night. Ward hopped out and checked the garage. Jess's car was parked safely inside. Racing up the stairs, she tried the door handle and found it locked. Her key remedied that problem, and with Abby right behind her, she walked into Jess's kitchen.

"Jess? Jess, are you here? It's Ward."

From room to room they walked through the immaculate house: kitchen, dining room, den, family room, sitting room. Nothing was out of place, and they saw no sign of trouble, no evidence of struggle, no sign of Jess. They mounted the stairs and headed for Jess's bedroom. This room was also in order, except for some rumples on the patchwork quilt Jess's mom had made for her. Ward picked up the orange prescription bottles on the bedside table. Was Jess sick? Ward had never known her to take any medication.

"Jesus," she said as she read the first bottle. Xanax, 0.25 mg tabs, three daily. It was a low dose but a very addicting medication used to treat anxiety. Was Jess anxious? Fuck, Ward thought. Did my phone call push her over the edge? Then she looked at the date on the bottle. It had been filled three weeks earlier and still had twenty pills inside. Jess hadn't overdosed.

Ward picked up the second bottle, speechless. The huge bottle had once contained Oxycodone, one hundred and eighty tablets. Ten milligrams each. That was six tabs a day. What the hell was Jess doing taking that much oxy? Nothing was wrong with her! At least, nothing Ward knew about. Obviously, she didn't know Jess as well as she once had.

They briefly searched the rest of the second floor, then the third-floor attic, finding nothing.

"What now?" Abby asked.

"Would you mind a midnight visit to the funeral parlor?"

They pulled up to Wendy's a minute later. The old colonial's first floor housed the business. Security lighting shone from within, but the lights in the apartment upstairs were out. Abby pulled into the circular driveway and parked before a four-car garage. Ward jumped out and peeked through the glass. A jeep occupied the end space. The next space was empty. The third and fourth spaces housed limousines.

"The hearse is missing," Ward said. "At least, I assume a funeral home should have a hearse."

They rang the bells to be sure, but Wendy wasn't home.

"Let's try Zeke's place," Ward suggested. Fifteen minutes later, they pulled into the long driveway of his house on the outskirts of town. Every light in the house was on, but Zeke didn't answer his bell. "He must still be out looking for her," she said again. Another call to his cell phone went unanswered, though.

"What now?"

"Should we stop at the hospital?" Ward asked.

"Will it look strange that you're here?"

"It might. Maybe I'll just call. How about heading over to Frieda's? She's only about twenty minutes from here. Maybe we can crash there. It beats driving an hour back to your house."

Twenty minutes later they were sitting in Frieda's kitchen. It was just past midnight, yet Frieda poured them all coffee, and they all drank it as they sat around her kitchen table. Ward filled Frieda in on their suspicions about Edward Hawk and Jess's disappearance.

"Should we call the police?" Ward asked. "I mean, other than the sheriff?"

"Why don't we ask my nephew? You know Kathy, the nurse? Her husband's a statey."

"Should we bother him at this hour?"

"Oh, he's workin'. He won't mind."

A minute later, Frank Henderfield was on the phone. Ward relayed all the details. "And now you can't find the sheriff, either?" he asked.

"That's right."

"Let me look into this."

Fifteen minutes later, Frank was on the phone again. "I just talked to Zeke. He says he's headin' out to the hunting cabin to talk with Jess and her friend. They had some sort of argument, and he's helping them straighten it all out, but everything's fine."

Ward's entire body relaxed. "Thank you, Frank. I really appreciate it."

"I feel like an idiot," she said, shaking her head and frowning. Jess was having a lovers' quarrel with Wendy, that was all. Ward knew her nerves were fried, but this was a pretty extreme case of jumping to conclusions.

"Who woulda expected that?" Frieda asked.

"I was worried," Abby said, "and I don't even know Jess. We did the right thing, coming here."

Ward was happy to hear their reassurances. Relief swept over her, and over all of them, bringing exhaustion with it, so they decided to spend the night at Frieda's. Ward had switched her shift for the morning, and Abby had nothing pressing, so they'd awaken and head back to Factoryville after they bought Frieda breakfast. Before they could leave the kitchen, a high-pitched voice from the upper floor of the house startled them.

"Frieda!"

"Oh, no, we awakened the beast," Frieda said as she lowered her head and cringed.

"Do you have lesbians down there?" Irene screamed.

"Yes, Mother. We're having an orgy."

"Well, send them home and come to bed. It's the middle of the night."

They all laughed. "Okay, Mom," Frieda said as she guided them toward the stairs.

"Thanks, Free. You're a gem," Ward said and hugged her.

Ward collapsed into the old four-poster bed, thinking about Jess, feeling an odd mixture of sadness and concern. In spite of Jess's indifference, Ward would always care for her. It had been a rough couple of years for Jess, first with her mom's illness, then their move and a career change, and finally Pat's death. But now Jess was taking pills and missing shifts. It worried her, and she wished she could do something to help, but she felt too distanced from Jess to bring it up. Shit, now that she knew Jess was all right, she wouldn't even tell her she'd been to the house. Jess might file charges against her for entering the house uninvited.

Her sleep was restless, even with Abby's calming presence beside her. She was startled into consciousness by the ringing phone. It was light outside, and it took her a few seconds to realize where she was and to find her phone in her backpack. The familiar ring tone caused Ward's heart to race. "Jess," she said as she answered. "Thank God." And then she accepted the call.

"I've been worried about you," she said, trying to keep the fear from her voice, stopping before she said anything else. Jess already thought she was a drunk, and violent. What would she think if she knew she'd driven to her house, broken in, stalked Wendy's and Zeke's place, and spent the night at Frieda's house? Shit, she'd think Ward was really crazy. Shit. Maybe she was really crazy.

"Hi, Ward. Where are you?" Jess asked. Her voice was far away, like she was talking on a speaker phone, and it sounded hoarse, like she'd just awakened. Well, since it was only six in the morning, maybe she had. But what an odd question, Ward thought. Did Jess suspect? Yes, she'd left Zeke a few messages when she couldn't reach Jess, and she'd called and texted Jess a dozen times before Frank had put her fears to rest, but Jess didn't need to know Ward was hovering just a few miles away at Frieda's place. She still had some pride.

"I'm in Philly," she lied. "How about you? The hospital said you didn't show up for work last night."

"That's right."

Ward's heart stopped. The voice that answered this time wasn't Jess's. It was a male voice, and although Ward had spoken to him only once, she had no question it belonged to Edward Hawk.

"Hawk!"

"Very good, Dr. Thrasher. You're smart. Perhaps too smart for your own good."

"Jess? Jess, are you there?"

"She's here, Dr. Thrasher, but she can't talk right now. I'd like to talk, though. Maybe you should come over and we can discuss your suspicions about me. Your accusations are too serious to discuss over the telephone, don't you think?"

"Where are you?"

"At the hunting club. In the cabin. When I program your address in Philly into my GPS, it tells me you should be here in two hours and thirty-eight minutes. I'll expect you then."

"Hawk, wait. I need to take a shower and eat something. Stop for gas!" Ward was stalling, but she didn't know what else to do. She couldn't let him hang up. If she kept him talking, kept him occupied, he couldn't possibly hurt Jess, right?

"Too bad. Two hours and thirty-eight minutes. And if I see anyone else coming up the drive, your girlfriend's going to die."

"Hawk, calm down! It's a hunting club. People come and go constantly. I can't control that."

"I've been in the Poconos for a few months now, Dr. Thrasher. I can tell the difference between the locals riding in their SUVs and the local sheriff. Who, by the way, is also my guest. Anyone else shows up, and I'll kill them all. And I think you know I'm quite capable of it."

The hairs on the back of her neck stood up. "I understand. I'll be there." The phone went dead.

Abby placed a hand on her back. "Hawk?" she asked.

"He has them at the cabin. He says he'll kill them if I'm not there by eight thirty."

Abby looked at the clock beside the bed.

"What do I do?"

"Let's get Frieda. We'll call Frank and ask him."

Frieda wasn't in her room. They found her at the kitchen table, looking fresh in spite of only five hours of sleep. Ward filled her in.

"You have to call the police, Ward." The voice of reason was Abby's.

"Hold on for a second," Frieda said. "This guy is an egomaniac. Maybe he just wants to talk and find out what you know. You can't prove anything. Maybe he realizes that. Maybe he'll just tell you to back off, threaten you."

"So you don't think he wants to kill me?"

Frieda shook her head. "He's been getting away with murder because he's been sneaky about it. No one suspected a thing. Well, nothing they could prove, anyway. But if he puts a bullet in you, there's not much room for speculation."

"He could make it look like an accident. Or a murder-suicide," Abby suggested.

"It still draws attention to him, doesn't it?"

Abby shrugged. "Unless he just slips away and pretends he wasn't there. Shit, Ward, I don't know. He seems like a coward—killing helpless people. He's used a syringe to do his work, never a gun. But maybe he has to do something drastic now, because he's scared."

"I guess we can't be sure of anything he'll do. But he's in real trouble if the police show up. I think he'll kill Jess and Zeke, and himself. And Wendy, too, if she isn't already dead. No, guys. We can't call the police."

Abby seemed to read Ward's mind, and she shook her head. "Ward, no. You can't go there. It's too dangerous. You don't even own a gun."

Something Hawk had said triggered an idea. "No, but I know a lot of people who do."

She told Abby and Frieda her thought. "It could work." Abby agreed, though reluctantly. "But I still think you should call the police."

"He thinks I'm in Philly. We have a two-hour advantage, and a surprise could work in our favor."

"If you're wrong, people could die. One of them could be Jess. Or you."

Ward reached out for Abby, pulled her close. "Ab, he's a psychopath, and he's killed dozens of people already. If he's caught, he's going to prison. He won't allow that. If the police show up, Jess is dead. Her only hope is for us to surprise him. Now are you with me?"

Abby gazed at Ward, who was astonished by what she saw in her eyes. Love. Abby had never said it, but there it was, written in the clouds of concern. The realization was startling, but not quite as amazing as the understanding that she loved Abby, too.

The nod was almost imperceptible, but Abby's voice was strong. "Let's go get 'em, tiger."

CHAPTER TWENTY-NINE
GUNSHOT WOUNDS

Tom Billings, whose cell-phone number had been stored in Ward's phone under the first name *Quad*, held up the arm Ward had set six months earlier and twisted it enthusiastically. "Good as new," he boasted.

In spite of the circumstances, a smile spread across Ward's face. Tom was just as she'd remembered him, and that was exactly why she'd reached out to him for help in this mess. He hadn't been put off by the early morning call or skeptical of the information she'd relayed. He believed her story, and if three citizens of his town were in trouble, he and his friends were more than willing to help get them out of it.

And so, twenty men and their all-terrain vehicles were parked along the old road that led to Towering Pines, and Ward, Abby, and Frieda watched as they unloaded their ATVs from pickup trucks and trailers. Their plan was simple. The men would ride over the mountain and down to the lake, making enough noise to capture Edward Hawk's attention. Then Frieda would drive up to the cabin in her truck. If the three prisoners were in the cabin, Hawk wouldn't be able to let Frieda inside. He also wouldn't shoot her, with those twenty witnesses lingering so close by. Hopefully, he'd leave the shelter of the cabin and meet Frieda outside. That's when Ward and Abby and a few of the sharpshooters in the bunch would take him down. They were all armed with rifles, loaded with tranquilizers. Ward and Abby would hitch rides over the mountain on the ATVs, then wait with the other shooters in the woods behind the cabin for Hawk to emerge.

It seemed so simple. Ward didn't want to imagine what would happen if Hawk panicked and decided to shoot everyone and just flee down the mountain. She didn't think he would, though. He clearly thought he was smarter than everyone else, and Ward hoped his ego would hold out awhile longer, that he'd continue to believe he could outsmart everyone and get away with this. He wanted her, because she knew what he'd done. Hopefully, he'd wait. She glanced at her watch. It wasn't even seven thirty. He didn't expect her for an hour. This posse was going to be a surprise.

When everyone was in formation, Ward hugged Frieda and wished her well. "Don't approach the cabin until you see the guys heading down to the lake."

"I got it," she said, and saluted Ward. "Try not to shoot yourself, Doc."

Frieda had thought she should have been the one with the gun in the woods, but they all agreed she was the least threatening of them all to approach the cabin. Hawk wasn't likely to panic at the sight of an elderly woman with a fishing rod in search of indoor plumbing. He'd recognize both her and Abby, so they weren't possibilities. The men, though, would be a threat, and who could predict what would happen if he suddenly felt threatened?

Frieda pulled away in her truck, and Ward and Abby climbed onto their assigned ATVs. Ward rode with Tom, and Abby with his son Tommy. The roar of engines soon filled the quiet, and then they were off, a single line of hunters out on a deadly mission.

The sun hadn't reached this side of the mountain yet, so it was still cool at this early hour, and as they ventured deeper into the forest, Ward was glad she'd worn jeans and a hoodie for their mission. On the other side of the mountain the sun shone brightly. Would that help or hurt them? A blanket of fog would have been good for cover, but not so good for eyeing a target. Perhaps the bright sun was a good omen.

Years of neglect had caused the road to fill in with weeds, but the drivers seemed unfazed as they climbed the rugged path that zigzagged up the mountainside. In ten minutes they were at the top and began the descent without pause. Halfway down, four of the quads stopped and allowed the others to pass. The six marksmen—Ward, Abby, Tom, Tommy, and another father-son team named RJ and Rex—readied their guns and gathered around Tom for instructions.

Tom pulled a paper out of his pocket. He and Ward had drawn a rough sketch of the hunting club as they'd developed their plan, and now he used it to show them the positions he wanted them to take.

"Tommy, you're here," he said, pointing to a spot in the tree line several hundred yards to the right of the cabin's front door. "You're going to have to hoof it to get in position, so start moving. You'll be shooting from behind Hawk, but we have to be prepared that he might come out a window or something like that. Please don't hurt yourself, or your mother will never forgive me." Tom winked at his son, who gave him a thumbs-up and began jogging through the woods.

"RJ, you're going to be here." His position was to the right, and he'd be shooting just over Frieda's shoulder as she stood in the driveway at the cabin.

"The rest of us are here, behind and to the left."

"Can he escape out the back?" Abby asked.

Tom shook his head. "The cabin is built into the mountainside, with no windows on the back side. He has to come out the front door or the door on the left. We can't cover the front of the cabin, except from this bank of trees where Tommy's going to be. There's nothing but open space between the front porch and the lake, so we won't have anywhere to hide. Hopefully, he comes out and walks left toward Frieda."

Their approach down the mountain was hundreds of yards to the right of where the SUVs had gone, and they stayed well back in the woods to keep under cover. When the cabin was in sight, they stopped. Ward scanned the area for movement but saw none. Two vehicles were parked next to the cabin, and she recognized them both. The missing hearse from the funeral home and Zeke Benson's truck.

At Tom's signal, they fanned out. Ward was grateful for the thick, low-lying pine branches that hid them from view. They were nearly at the clearing behind the cabin before she could clearly see it, and if she was having trouble seeing the cabin, Hawk would surely have trouble spotting her posse sneaking through the woods. They took cover behind a line of pines and waited as Frieda's truck slowly made its way up the long drive. In the distance, Ward could see the ATVs parked by the lake, the drivers gathered around them.

Show time.

Pushing aside the dusty curtain, Edward looked past the rocking chairs, across the massive front porch of the cabin and the expanse of flowered field beyond. The convoy of ATVs that had come up over the mountain was now parked, and it looked like the riders were preparing for a day of fishing. Fuck! Just what he needed. It was only a matter of time before one of them had to use the bathroom and headed up to the cabin. He had to get out of here.

Glancing at his watch, he weighed his options. It was 7:45. Ward Thrasher would be here in less than an hour. But did he have that long? He didn't think so. He'd have to kill these three now and then intercept her on the road. There was only one road to the cabin, so she'd have to use it. He could meet her there, at the entrance to the hunting club, a mile away from the prying eyes of the guys on the ATVs. She'd have to slow down to make the turn from the main road onto the dirt and gravel driveway into the property. He'd shoot her then, head straight to JFK, be in Florida in six hours and out of the country by nightfall. What other choice did he have?

He sighed. How had this gone wrong so quickly? He'd been successful for twenty years because of intelligence and meticulous planning. Other than the first time, when he'd been driven by anger, his kills had been well orchestrated and unemotional. He'd deviated from that pattern by spontaneously abducting Jess, and now he was in trouble. He had three witnesses to get rid of, and his avenue of escape was closing quickly.

He'd planned on a shooting, a double murder-suicide, but he could hardly start shooting with the riders so close. They'd be raiding the cabin before he had a chance to get out of the driveway. If only he hadn't brought Zeke, he'd have had one less headache to deal with. He might have been able to sneak the women out of the cabin, but not the six-foot-tall, two-hundred-pound sheriff. But Zeke was a talker, and he'd given Edward a lot of useful information on that day he'd brought him to the cabin to go shooting. Jess was in a lesbian phase. She'd been involved with Ward Thrasher. Jess adored the lake and had spent much of her free time here when she was young.

When Jess disappeared, Zeke had been bound to show up at the cabin looking for her, possibly with reinforcements, so he'd figured it was better to get him out of the way from the start. At least then, the sheriff wouldn't surprise him at an inopportune moment. Who knew his plan would turn into such a disaster.

It had taken hours of intimidation before Jess finally told him what had aroused her suspicions. It was so ironic that, under other circumstances, Edward might have laughed. He'd killed a hundred mostly innocent patients, and the one that tripped him up in the end had been one who really deserved to die. Anyone stupid enough to ride an all-terrain vehicle in the dark forest while under the influence of alcohol should be killed before having a chance to reproduce and make more idiots.

Christian Cooney had been alive when he came in to the ER but had multiple broken ribs and a collapsed lung. His heart was bruised and beating irregularly. He was in shock, with pitifully inadequate veins. The paramedics had tried multiple times to insert an intravenous catheter but failed. Edward had inserted a large catheter into the subclavian, the large vein beneath the clavicle, just a few inches from the heart. When the nurse turned her back, he injected a large shot of air into the tubing. It only took a second for the air pocket to make its way to the heart, and the air lock it created instantly shut down the man's circulation. Blood couldn't get out of the heart to the lungs for oxygen. There was no blood for the lungs to send back to the heart, no blood to feed the brain and coronary arteries. Almost instantaneously, the heart rhythm went from normal and steady to a fatal, fibrillating dance of death.

Edward had worried as the nurse began CPR. Sometimes, the chest compressions squeezed the air bolus through the circulation or broke it up into tiny, more manageable bubbles of air, and the patient survived. Fortunately, that good luck had never befallen his patients. On one prior occasion when he'd killed with air, he'd had quite a scare when the patient experienced a transient return of his pulse, but the heart had quickly tired and given out. This time, he'd watched the monitor intently, ordered meds which he knew would be useless, even volunteered to do compressions himself, which he was careful to do incorrectly. However, the broken ribs had made CPR difficult, as the full force of energy wasn't transmitted into the heart. The resuscitation efforts were futile, and Edward had another death certificate to add to his collection.

No one could prove he'd murdered Cooney. But Ward Thrasher, following him on his journey through the mountains, had seen some sort of pattern. That wasn't truly a mistake on his part, was it? How many ways were there to murder a medical patient without leaving evidence? He only had so many options. Repeating his methods was necessary if he wanted to continue killing. And he wanted to continue killing. As soon as Ward arrived, he'd kill all of them and then get out of town. He'd move someplace far away and start over.

Then another thought occurred to him. What if Thrasher had somehow arrived in Garden early and come over the mountain on those ATVs? What if she hadn't been in Philly but was still in the mountains and was out there now, waiting for him? He looked down the hill, trying to get a better look at the riders, then snagged a pair of binoculars hanging on a hook. He couldn't see their faces clearly from this distance, but they all appeared to be burly men. Thrasher looked a little boyish in scrubs, but she wasn't that tall, and she was thin. Still, he wondered. Could she have disguised herself? He looked around the cabin suspiciously.

"Who are they?" he demanded of Zeke as he reached over and brutally pulled the gag from Zeke's mouth.

After swallowing a few times, Zeke finally found his voice. "I imagine it's the guys who ride up here all the time. Mostly retired guys, some of their sons. They ride and fish."

Edward used his knife to slice the tape that bound Zeke's legs to the chair, then roughly pulled him to his feet. "Take a look. Tell me who they are."

Zeke took the proffered binoculars and raised his hands, still cuffed, and gazed through them. "Can't say. They're too far away," he said as he set the binoculars on the windowsill.

"There was no one fucking here that day we came to shoot!"

Zeke shrugged and backed up as Edward motioned him toward his chair. As Edward was about to retape the sheriff's legs, a noise drew his attention back to the window. "What now?" he asked as he pulled the curtain aside and peered out. A red pickup truck had pulled up at the side of the cabin. "I don't fucking believe this. Who the hell is that?"

He looked at Zeke. "Come here and tell me who this is!"

Zeke struggled to his feet.

"I don't have all day, Sheriff!"

"My balance isn't so good. Don't forget, you put quite a lump on my head."

"I'll do more than that if you don't move a little faster."

Zeke swayed and reached out to grab the counter as he walked that way, resting a moment.

"Move it!"

A second later, he stood beside Hawk at the window and pushed the curtains aside. "Looks like Frieda Henderfield to me," he said, and in a flash he raised his right elbow and jammed it into Hawk's nose. He followed the initial blow with a whack to the head, using the binoculars, and several swift kicks in the groin.

With Hawk kneeling on the floor, bleeding profusely, Zeke opened the cabin door. "Frieda Henderfield, I've never been so happy to see someone in all my life. Could you do me a favor and call the state police?"

CHAPTER THIRTY
TRAUMATIC ARREST

Ward ran toward the cabin as soon as she heard Zeke's booming voice, with Abby and the two men right behind her. The men below had been carefully watching from their place by the lake, and Ward saw them all racing to the ATVs for the trip up the hill. As she burst through the door of the cabin, she nearly cried with relief.

Zeke had his gun in his cuffed hands, trained on Edward Hawk, who was curled on the floor, blood pouring from his nose. Hawk's moans of anguish weren't the only cries in the cabin. Jess and Wendy, both gagged and bound, sat in chairs beside the cabin's large table, rocking and murmuring as Frieda worked to free them. They seemed to be making a frantic effort to get her attention. Did they possibly think she wouldn't notice them?

She closed the few feet to the table in a fraction of a second, pulling the tape first from Jess's mouth and then from Wendy's.

"It's all right, now. You're safe," she said, but in spite of her desire to hug Jess, she turned to find a knife to help Frieda. "Abby, can you grab some water?"

Ward pulled a knife from the kitchen drawer and knelt before Wendy. For some reason, she wasn't ready to touch Jess yet. "Thanks," Wendy said to Abby when the water was placed to her lips. Her raspy voice told Ward she'd needed it.

Abby repeated the offering with Jess, and she drank but remained silent. Ward studied her as she carefully worked the ropes on Wendy's wrists. In spite of the fact that the cabin was cool, Jess was sweating profusely. Her pupils were dilated, and the hairs on her arms stood straight up. Tears poured in streams from both eyes, and even though she was tied to the chair, it was moving with the tremors wracking her body. Jess was in withdrawal.

While Frieda worked on Wendy, Ward started on Jess's ankles. "How are you? Are you hurt?"

Jess cleared her throat. "Every muscle in my body is cramped. He shot me with IM sux."

"Succinylcholine?" Ward asked to clarify.

"Yes. And let me tell you, it's as bad as they say."

With her binding free, Wendy stood and began stretching. "Oh, yes. It's that bad."

"You, too?" Ward asked.

"Yes, I'm afraid so."

Jess's feet were free and Ward stood, looking at Hawk on the floor. The posse had arrived, and they filed in to survey the situation. Several of the men pulled Hawk to a seated position and began to bind him with the same rope he'd used on his victims. Someone shoved a handful of paper towels into Hawk's face to staunch the bleeding.

"Don't suffocate him," Ward said.

"Why the hell not?" someone asked. "It'd save the taxpayers the cost of a trial."

"She's right. Go easy on him. He don't seem the type that can handle any rough treatment."

"Do I look like I give a shit? This scum don't deserve no special treatment."

Ward ignored their arguing and turned back to Jess. "You look like shit, Jess."

"In a good way?" she asked, her voice quaking but the humor unmistakable. The joke took Ward aback. That was the old Jess, the one she hadn't seen in years.

Ward leaned close enough to smell Jess's shampoo and sweat, and whispered in her ear. "Are you okay?"

Jess seemed to understand the deeper meaning in Ward's question. "No. I'm pretty shaky right now."

Ward saw it all so clearly now. The moods, Jess's desire to be alone, her disinterest in things she'd once loved, including Ward. She thought back to the day before. Jess had disappeared sometime around the time of her seven o'clock shift. Presuming she'd taken her last dose of the oxycodone at her bedside then, she was about thirteen hours out from her last dose. An addict on a regular schedule of this drug would start craving it after just a few hours and be in withdrawal at this point. The COWS, short for clinical opiate withdrawal score, would probably measure Jess in moderate withdrawal based on the severity of her symptoms. That was only going to get worse.

"Jess, why don't you walk around, see if you can get those muscles to loosen up a little. Do some stretching." Ward didn't mention that it might relieve some of the anxiety associated with opiate withdrawal as well.

Ward motioned to Zeke, who followed her onto the porch. "You still keep your medication in your truck?" she asked.

"Yes, I do. I always keep it with me, for emergencies."

Zeke's doctor had prescribed him oxycodone for the arthritis in his knees. "I want one of your pain pills. Jess is in agony, and it could be another twenty minutes before the ambulance arrives."

He reached into his pocket and pulled out his keys, then folded them into Jess's hand. "I'm sorry, Ward, for chasing you away. You're a good girl, and if it wasn't for you comin' in with the boys, me and those two would most likely be dead now."

Ward accepted the compliment with a shrug. "It's over, Zeke. No worries."

"Promise me you'll take care of Jess."

"I will," she said and nodded at him, then turned and nearly ran over Abby.

"Hi," she said.

Abby's expression told Ward she'd heard the conversation with Zeke, but Ward had no words for Abby right now. Her adrenaline was running out, and combined with the lack of sleep and the jumbled thoughts in her head, she wasn't sure she could form a coherent sentence.

"What's up?" she asked.

"I just needed to get out of there. Too much testosterone." Abby shrugged.

"They haven't killed him, have they?"

"Not yet."

"Give me a sec, Abby. I need to get some medications for Jess. She's really hurting."

Abby eyed her with concern, or perhaps suspicion, but Ward just winked at her before turning toward Zeke's truck. It was parked in the shadow of the hearse, and she was glad the multitude of men hovering about couldn't see her reach in and pull Zeke's medication pouch from the glove box. Fishing for the right bottle took a few tries, but then she pulled out the oxys and studied the label. They were five-milligram tabs, only half the strength of the tablets on Jess's bedside cabinet.

The problem Jess faced now was the acetaminophen dose. Each tablet of oxycodone, the medication Jess needed to fight her withdrawal symptoms, also contained acetaminophen, a common drug that wreaked havoc on the liver. Ward could give Jess only three of the tabs without risking trouble. Jess wouldn't die from the withdrawal. While narcotics leave misery in their wake, they only kill when they're used. Alcohol and benzodiazepine withdrawal, on the other hand, are fatal. Letting Jess sweat it out might have been a great way to teach her a lesson, but Ward feared that her reputation would suffer if someone figured out opiate withdrawal rather than succinylcholine toxicity had caused the constellation of symptoms Jess was exhibiting.

Ward wanted to just give her a modest dose of narcotics to bind in the empty receptors in her brain and ease her symptoms. After that, Jess was on her own.

She noticed Abby leaning against a railing at the far end of the porch and knew she should say something to her, and she would. Just as soon as she took care of Jess.

She found Jess in the kitchen, shakily lifting a glass of water to her pale lips. "I'll tell the medics to give you morphine, but this should take the edge off for now. How long do you think it'll take?"

Ward made it clear by her tone and the look she gave Jess that denial wasn't an option.

Jess answered without hesitation. "I should start feeling a little better in twenty minutes."

"Okay. Other than the sux, you don't have any injuries? He didn't punch you or anything?"

"No, just the sux. But believe me, that's enough."

"I'm going to give you IV fluids and some morphine, but I think you'll be fine. We'll check labs at the hospital. If you're feeling better this afternoon, you can probably go home."

Jess nodded but didn't add anything else, and the wail of the ambulance siren was suddenly audible in the silence. Faint, but getting closer by the second.

"So tell me what happened," Ward said.

"After I finished talking to you, I decided to get some work done. I turned on the computer and checked my e-mail. I had something from Wendy, an autopsy report on a young guy, a trauma victim with multiple broken ribs, a broken clavicle, facial trauma. I was suspecting cardiac tamponade or some other catastrophic injury. But he died from a venous air embolus."

"Shit."

"Yeah, that's what I said. As much as I didn't want to believe it, I figured I'd better check out the other deaths that happened under Hawk's watch. I walked over to the hospital a couple of hours before my shift, and he cornered me in my office with a syringe full of sux. I don't know how he knew I knew, but he did."

"I'd called the ER looking for you. Maybe it tipped him off."

"Maybe."

The ambulance crew pushed their way into the room and the crowd parted, leaving a clear path toward Ward and Jess.

"I'm sorry, Ward. For not trusting you." Jess's eyes brimmed with tears, and she reached a trembling hand to close the two-foot gap between them. She squeezed Ward's forearm, then raised her finger to gently brush Ward's cheek. "You didn't deserve to be treated the way I treated you. And even if I was going to push you away, I should have at least had the guts to tell you why. There's something else I have to tell you, too."

Ward turned to greet the medics, and her eyes met Abby's. Before she could even smile, the medics pushed their way closer, and Ward was trapped by the barrier the stretcher created.

"We'll talk later, Jess. Right now, let's get you taken care of."

The paramedics eased her onto their stretcher and began questioning her. One of them smiled at her in recognition. "Dr. Benson was given a large dose of succinylcholine, and the side effect is severe muscle pain. I want you to start an IV and give her a shot of morphine as soon you can. She's really uncomfortable."

As the medics set about their work, another siren sounded, and within a few minutes two state police officers walked into the cabin. One was a middle-aged man with hair graying at the temples, and the other was Ward's age and could have been the centerfold on the women-in-uniform calendar. She was blond and cute and fierce-looking. The officers were pointed in Zeke's direction. He'd taken a seat on the couch, and Ward suddenly realized he needed to go to the ER for an evaluation, as did Wendy. Both probably needed further testing to make sure Hawk's terror hadn't caused any serious injuries to their brains or their kidneys.

"Can I catch a ride with you?" Ward asked the medics. She knew it wasn't protocol, but this was Garden, and Jess was the medical director for the ambulance, so she figured they might bend the rules on this occasion. "You can call me your acting medical director. I'll fill in until Dr. Benson can return to her duties."

"No problem, Doc," the senior medic said to Ward. "Let's get her in the rig."

Ward took two steps toward Zeke and Wendy, who sat beside each other as they answered the officer's questions. "I'm going with Jess. But you both need to come to the ER and have some tests. Zeke, that head wound needs a stitch, and you need a CT scan. Wendy, you need some IV fluids. As soon as you're done with the officers, I want you there. Agreed?"

"I'll bring them myself, Doc," the cute, blond officer said as she winked at Ward.

Under other circumstances, Ward might have smiled, but she was too tired, too frazzled. She looked around for her friends. She'd abandoned them in order to care for Jess, and now she needed to let them know that she needed to stay until she was sure Jess and Zeke were okay. They were still her family, no matter what.

Abby was just climbing into the passenger seat of Frieda's truck when Ward found them. Frieda was behind the wheel. "Hey, wait up!" she called.

Abby offered her a weak smile. "Hey," she said.

"Where're you going?"

"Well, you've got your hands full, Doc. Frieda's going to take me home. Your car's still at her house, but we'll drop it off at the hospital on the way."

Ward was about to protest, but then she realized it was probably the best move. Her attention would be elsewhere for the next few hours, and truthfully, she needed to focus on Jess. Having Abby at the hospital would be a distraction.

"Okay. That's a good idea. I'll call you later." She wrapped her arms around Abby for a quick hug. Ward pulled her close, but Abby's arms seemed to hang limply. "You okay?" she asked.

"Fine. Just a little tired."

"Understandably. Go get some rest. And thank you."

She pulled away and looked around Abby to Frieda. "Frieda, thanks so much. You guys really helped save the day."

Frieda swatted away the compliment like a pesky fly buzzing around her face. "When are we golfing?"

Ward laughed. "I'll call you." Then she turned and followed the paramedics and Jess toward the ambulance.

CHAPTER THIRTY-ONE
SUTURES

During the ambulance ride to the hospital, Ward could see a visible transformation in Jess. Her complexion seemed less pale. The restlessness subsided. Sweat that seemed to pool on her forehead and lip had evaporated, and while her hair still looked a little damp, she no longer appeared to have just gotten out of the pool. She appeared uninjured. She really was going to be all right. Ward sat back and closed her eyes. For the first time in twelve hours, she relaxed.

Jess seemed to have a good handle on her addiction, Ward realized. It had taken about twenty minutes for the symptoms of opiate withdrawal to subside, just as she'd predicted.

Good, Ward thought. No one at the hospital was likely to suspect a thing. Jess still looked like she'd been kidnapped, tied up, and sleep deprived, with her hair in disarray and her clothes a wrinkled mess, but that was okay. It was expected. As far as what the ambulance crew knew—and they'd seen her at the worst of her symptoms—Ward was certain they'd been paying more attention to the excitement of the crime scene and the bloody killer tied to the chair than the subtle details of Jess's condition. Jess was fine, after all. The real action was still happening at the cabin, where the state police were taking statements and the local coroner and a bunch of ATV riders were going to make the news for helping bring down a serial killer.

A flurry of excitement greeted them in the ER, and while Ward was tempted to back off now that Jess was in capable hands, one look from Jess told her she needed to stay close by. Whether it was the psychological trauma of the kidnapping or the lingering anxiety from opiate withdrawal, Jess wanted Ward by her side.

For six months, that was all Ward had wanted. To be with Jess. For Jess to love her again, completely, the way she once had. For Jess to look at her with something other than contempt. And now, it seemed, all of her wishes had come true.

What had changed? Ward wondered. Had the near-death experience caused Jess to question the life she was living and the decisions she'd made? Was it dissatisfaction with the life she'd chosen to live in Garden? Or was it the relief that must have come with discovery that was allowing the real Jess to escape the biting shackles of secrecy that had held her prisoner for so long?

She squeezed Jess's hand. It was probably a bit of all of those reasons that had caused Jess to open her eyes. It didn't really matter. What mattered was she saw a glimpse of the real Jess in the eyes staring back at her, and she was happy.

"How do you feel?" the ER doc on duty asked Jess as he walked into her exam room. He nodded politely to Ward, and they both watched as the medics helped Jess onto the hospital stretcher and the nurses took over, attaching monitor leads and hanging the IV bag, adjusting the pillow and assessing their new patient.

"Achy all over, but much better since the fluids and the morphine." Jess smiled. "And a little groggy. I'd like to just close my eyes and take a snooze."

Ward was sure Jess had thrown in the last sentence as an after-thought, because the morphine was expected to cause drowsiness. Jess looked wide-awake to her.

"Probably the morphine. Just let me check you out and I'll let you rest while we're waiting for your lab results." He asked Jess a series of questions about her medical history and then about her ordeal and finally examined her carefully, checking each body system from head to toe. When he finished, he told Jess to close her eyes and rest, promising she could leave the hospital later in the day if her potassium level was okay and her pain was tolerable.

"Just what you said," Jess told Ward.

She shrugged at the compliment.

"Thank you for taking care of me, Ward."

Ward looked up into the eyes she knew so well, and they held. Jess's began to fill with tears, and hers soon followed. She retrieved tissues from a box on the counter and gave some to Jess before wiping her own eyes.

"How did this happen to you?" she asked after she regained control of her emotions.

Jess cleared her throat. "My broken wrist."

She was shocked. Jess had been knocked from her bike by a car, a relatively benign crash other than the damage to her left wrist. The fracture required a surgical repair, and Jess had spent two months in one sort of cast or another.

"God, Jess. That's been three years. You've been hooked on narcotics for that long and I never noticed? I'm such a jerk." She closed her eyes and shook her head in disgust.

"No, no. It's not your fault. Addicts are very good at hiding it."

"Still, I'm a doctor. I should have noticed."

"Well, you picked up the withdrawal crisis in a heartbeat."

Ward didn't tell Jess she'd broken into her house and found the large bottle of narcotics on her bedside table. That had certainly been a big clue. She wasn't going to mention it, either. Things were going well with Jess; she refused to give her a reason to be angry. Jess seemed to find them without any help from her.

"Again, I'm a doctor. But how did I live with you for those three years—well, two and a half—and not figure this out?" She closed her eyes and thought back to the accident and the months that followed. Jess had naturally been depressed. It was the summer, and instead of being able to enjoy the outdoors and the good weather by swimming and golfing and having fun, Jess had been stuck on the patio reading, because even walking jarred her arm and caused pain. A leave of absence from work had been necessary, and while her disability policy had covered her salary loss, Jess was isolated from her colleagues and friends and the intellectual stimulation she thrived on. Ward's schedule was even worse without Jess at the hospital, because she'd been one of the doctors called upon to help pick up the slack.

As she thought back to that time, she realized that's when the changes in Jess began. She'd enjoyed their time together before the accident, but afterward, she withdrew from Ward. She went to work and did the same good job as always, but it seemed to drain her. After work, she wanted to rest and be alone. She declined invitations to play golf or hike, and didn't want to travel. She cancelled a vacation to Italy they'd been planning. Even things like the theater, which had once entertained her, lost their appeal. When they moved to Garden, Jess had become even more distant. Ward had always thought Jess's grief had been the cause, but looking back, she knew it had been going on for much longer. Since her wrist injury. If she'd only known.

"Why didn't you tell me? I would have helped you."

"Please, Ward. You would have been the first one to report me to the state board."

Ward closed her eyes and rubbed her hand across them. Was that true? Yes, she would have been concerned about Jess's ability to function on such high doses of medication, but she wouldn't have just thrown her under the bus. Unless Jess was dangerous and refused to listen to reason. And then she realized Jess was correct. She would have turned her in.

Ward's silence seemed to confirm Jess's suspicion. "You would have been right, Ward. I shouldn't have been practicing medicine."

"You seemed okay to me, when you were at work."

"Work is what I lived for. I still had some control there."

"And now?"

"Now, I'm better. I take medication because I need it. For pain. I just also happen to need it because my body is used to it. But I'm not abusing it, Ward. I swear to you. I have a legitimate prescription from my doctor, and I'm only getting it from him."

Ward looked up, alarmed. "You mean…you weren't always getting it from a doctor?"

"Sit down," she said, and didn't speak again until Ward was seated. "I wasn't too bad at first, Ward. I really took the pain meds as prescribed. But when I was cleared to go back to work, the surgeon just sort of wiped his hands and said good-bye. I'd been taking four to six pain pills a day for almost two months, and then one day, he just told me to stop. And I wasn't taking them without cause. I really did have pain. So I tried some anti-inflammatory meds, and they relieved the pain to some degree, but within hours of my last narcotic, I was really shaky. I dug through the medicine cabinet and found a bottle of cough medicine with codeine. It took about half the bottle to calm me, but it worked. I was mortified. I knew exactly what was going on. I wrote a prescription in your name for thirty tablets. I vowed to wean myself off them, started taking half-tabs, less frequently. I couldn't do it."

Ward stared, speechless. Jess had gone from being an addict to breaking the law, abusing her medical license, and perhaps even jeopardizing Ward's career as well.

Jess closed her eyes, leaning back into the pillow. Apparently, she didn't have anything else to say. Ward did, though.

"So what did you do?" She could see that Jess was tired, and emotional, but she'd waited almost seven months to hear this story and wasn't going to let Jess off the hook that easily.

"The typical doctor shopping. I was careful not to see anyone from work, because I didn't want anyone to talk, but I saw my dentist for a toothache, a neurologist for migraines, my gynecologist for menstrual cramps, and the spinal specialist for low-back pain."

"What about me? Did you write me any more prescriptions?"

Jess looked into her eyes, and Ward knew her answer was honest. "No. That was too risky. If you'd gotten a call from the pharmacy or an insurance statement, it would have been a disaster."

"Oh, this is a disaster all right. But I can't believe all those guys just gave you narcotics."

Ward remembered Jess's sudden increase in medical issues a couple of years back. She hadn't suspected a thing.

"At first, yeah. But when I sensed they were becoming uncomfortable, I backed off. And I talked to Malcolm. He hooked me up."

"Malcolm Washington?" Ward was incredulous. Malcolm was a frequent-flyer in the ER, seen on a regular basis for pain related to sickle-cell anemia.

"Wow. That's pretty pathetic, Jess." Ward couldn't imagine such a state of desperation that would cause Jess to turn to a patient to help her buy drugs illegally.

Jess shrugged. "In some ways, it was easier. I could just stop pretending. I didn't have to sit in doctors' offices sweating it out, waiting to see if they were going to give me what I needed. I just gave Malcolm money and a prescription for extra narcotics, and he'd deliver them right to the ER. No hassles."

"How much did this cost you?"

"Oh, about three-fifty a week."

"Holy shit, Jess." She leaned back in her chair and studied the woman she'd loved for so long. How could you love someone, and live with them, and be so clueless? Was it some flaw in her, or was Jess just really that good at deception?

"Yeah," Jess said.

Ward wanted to ask what went wrong, but it had been wrong from the start. Jess had probably tried to keep up the charade for a while, but that was all their relationship was at that point, because she wasn't capable of anything more. And then she grew tired and just didn't have the strength to pretend any more, and that's when she'd cast Ward aside. At least that's what Ward was surmising. She wasn't sure how Jess would articulate it if she asked, and as she sat there, she realized she really didn't care. She knew now what was wrong, and that knowledge somehow erased some of the pain of having been cast aside by her lover for no reason at all. Jess had been right all along. She was the problem in their relationship, not Ward.

"Did you ever try rehab?" Ward asked.

Jess shook her head in vigorous denial. "What if I lose my license?"

"What if you lose your life?"

"I can't do it, Ward."

"What about out-patient therapy? Methadone or buprenorphine treatment?"

"I'd have to report it to the state."

"So, let me see if I understand this." She leaned forward and held onto the railing with both hands, her bedsheet-white knuckles betraying the anger she was trying to control. "You'd risk jail by buying pills on the street, but you won't risk getting treatment from a doctor? Can't you just lie about the med? Pay cash so no one knows. Shit, it has to be cheaper to pay cash for doctor visits and legal drugs than the fourteen hundred a month you were spending with Malcolm."

"I'm not doing that any more, Ward. I have a legitimate prescription, and I'm using the pills as directed."

Ward leaned back and folded her arms across her chest. "Oh, so you think you have this beat, just because you have a source for your meds? You're addicted to narcotics, Jess! You need to get help."

"Can we talk about this later? I'm really beat." Jess offered her a wan smile, and everything from her sagging shoulders to the tears in her eyes told Ward she really had had enough.

She stared off into the distance, thinking how typical this was of Jess. This Jess, anyway. She didn't want to discuss things, or face them; she was just shutting them off. She'd dealt with her addiction—was still dealing with it—in the same manner she'd managed her relationship with Ward. Ignore it. Avoid it. Deny it.

Ward wanted to say more, to shake Jess until she understood what she was doing, how harmful it was. Her path was heading someplace bad, but Jess didn't want to change course. The hard thing for Ward was accepting she had no power to change things, either. It was Jess's life, and she was no longer a part of it. Instead of saying anything else, she nodded. "Sure."

"There's something else, though, I want to talk to you about."

"What's that?"

"How'd you like to come back here? To work?"

Ward hadn't seen that one coming. Just a month ago, Jess had drained half their savings accounts and asked her to sell the house.

"Uh, I'm speechless."

"We don't have to rush into things, Ward. With us. This discovery has to be a shock, and maybe you don't want to get into a relationship with someone who needs to take narcotics every day, but I want you to think about it. I love you. When you looked at me this morning, and I saw the recognition on your face, I was so scared. Because through all of this, you were the one I didn't want to let down. I knew my parents would be disappointed in me, but I'd have dealt with that. You're just so good, and kind, and you would have tried to help me with this.

"But I didn't want your help. Quitting is hard, and I wasn't ready for it then, so I pushed you away. Now, though, maybe I am. When I looked in your eyes and knew you knew I was withdrawing, I saw only love there. Concern. Compassion. Not scorn or anger, even though there could have been. You're the kind of person I need, Ward. And if you're willing to give it a try, so am I. Will you come back to Garden? Back to me?"

CHAPTER THIRTY-TWO
VITAL SIGNS

Ward was whistling as she walked out of the ER in Garden nearly eight hours later. Zeke was fine, Wendy was fine, and best of all, Jess was fine, too. Or, at least, she would be. It would take some hard work to get her body through the struggles of detox, but she'd do it. And Ward had promised to help her every step of the way.

The state police had stopped by to get a statement from Jess and had talked at length to Ward as well. She gave them all the information she had—some names of patients she suspected Hawk might have murdered, the hospitals he'd worked in during his time in the mountains, and the names of the people working at those places who could help in the investigation. They'd need to talk to her again, and she might even be called to testify, but she doubted it. Everything she knew about Hawk was right there in the medical records of all the patients he'd killed in the past months. How many were there?

Ward doubted anyone would ever know. So many of his patients were elderly, and with medical issues, it would have been easy for him to push them over the edge of the cliff separating life and death. Easy, and without a single suspicion. In all likelihood, Edward Hawk was the only one who'd ever know the truth about how many people he'd killed. She was sure the state police would be looking into deaths at every hospital he'd ever worked in, and some concerned colleagues like Erin and Kathy Henderfield might help as well, but in the end, the secret was likely Hawk's to share.

The state police officers had asked her to stick around to answer any further questions that developed, and she'd promised them she would be around for a few weeks longer, but after that, who knew?

Jess's offer of a job and a reunion would have tempted her just a few weeks earlier, but not anymore. What did she want now?

She'd always thought she knew what she wanted, where her life was going. And then she'd gotten thrown on her ass, and her whole world was turned upside down. Nothing was right. But a funny thing had happened. After the dizziness cleared, when she looked around to see where she was, she liked the place.

She liked being with Abby.

Her heart belonged to Abby.

Being in Factoryville with Abby had taught her what a real relationship was about. The give and take. The working together. The laughter. The love. Even before Jess's injury, before the addiction that had been their downfall, their relationship had never been great. Good, yes. Satisfying, yes. Sensational? No. Inspirational? No. Easy? Never, ever.

But with Abby, everything was different. She sure as hell hoped Abby didn't really think she was the temporary, transitional woman. She was so much more than that.

She was in love with Abby, and although she'd felt obligated to stay with Jess through her ordeal today, as soon as Wendy had come to take Zeke and Jess home, Ward had headed in the opposite direction. Back to Abby.

As soon as she started the car, she instructed it to call Abby. "Damn," she said when Abby's cell went to voice mail. "Hi, I'm on my way and I'm hoping you're hungry because I didn't eat yet and I'm starving. Call me." A call to Abby's office also went unanswered.

It was nearly six in the evening when Ward pulled into Abby's driveway. The Porsche was parked in front of the open garage door, and the truck was parked inside. Abby was home.

The sun was making its way over the tops of the trees behind the house, and the deck would be bathed in a blanket of sun. She walked around the back, knowing Abby would be there, reading the paper and sorting through her mail.

"Anyone home?" she called as she approached, not wanting to startle Abby.

"I gave at the office."

"Well, I want more," she said as she climbed the stairs. She stopped at the top and smiled at the woman she loved. "Hello, gorgeous."

Abby's smile was reluctant, but she couldn't suppress it. "What are you doing here?"

Ward was confused. "What do you mean?"

"Why aren't you with Jess?"

"She's fine. Discharged and recovering at home. Did you eat?"

Abby shook her hair, then pushed her sunglasses up on top of her head. She studied Ward closely. "Ward. Why. Are. You. Here?"

Ward stared back. What was Abby talking about? Of course Ward would come to Abby's place. They'd been spending all their free time together, since that first day on the river. Then she replayed the events of the past day and understood Abby's concern. First the call to the locum tenens company saying Hawk was in Garden. Her frantic calls to Jess. Their trip to Garden and to Frieda's. The crazy rescue on the mountain. And then, Ward's day spent at Jess's bedside. Abby thought she was going back to Jess. Didn't she know how Ward felt? Hadn't they talked about August?

"I don't love her anymore, Abby. I told her that today. I'll try to help her in any way I can, and I hope you're okay with that, because I really want to be friends with her. But not if it bothers you. Because I'm in love with you."

"You came all the way here just to tell me that?" Abby asked, the smirk on her face so cocky Ward wanted to kiss it off.

"Well, yes. But I was also kind of hoping for dinner."

Abby stood and reached for Ward's hands, pulled her close. Their kiss was soft, unhurried. "I said I love you," Ward repeated as she pulled away.

"Ah, shit. I thought I was going to get away with it."

"With what?"

"Not answering."

Ward tickled her, pulled her tight. "Say it! Say it, even if you don't mean it!"

Abby giggled. "I love you, Ward."

"Do you mean it?"

"Yes!"

Ward didn't stop her assault with her fingers. "Say it again!"

"I still love you!" Abby giggled, then found her composure as Ward's hands stilled. "I love you."

"Then you should feed me."

Abby smiled and took Ward's hand in hers. "I have some power bars in the bedroom."

About the Author

Jaime Maddox grew up on the banks of the Susquehanna River in Northeastern Pennsylvania. As the baby in a family of many children, she was part adored and part ignored, forcing her to find creative ways to fill her time. Her childhood was idyllic, spent hiking, rafting, biking, climbing, and otherwise skinning knees and knuckles. Reading and writing became passions. Although she left home for a brief stint in the big cities of Philadelphia, PA, and Newark, NJ, as soon as she acquired the required paperwork—a medical degree and residency certificate—she came running back.

She fills her hours with a bustling medical practice, two precocious sons, a disobedient dog, and an extraordinary woman who helps her to keep it all together. In her abundant spare time, she reads, writes, twists her body into punishing yoga poses, and whacks golf balls deep into forests. She detests airplanes, snakes, and people who aren't nice. Her loves are the foods of the world, Broadway musicals, traveling, sandy beaches, massages and pedicures, and the Philadelphia Phillies.

Books Available from Bold Strokes Books

Deadly Medicine by Jaime Maddox. Dr. Ward Thrasher's life is in turmoil. Her partner Jess has left her, and her job puts her in the path of a murderous physician who has Jess in his sights. (978-1-62639-4-247)

New Beginnings by KC Richardson. Can the connection and attraction between Jordan Roberts and Kirsten Murphy be enough for Jordan to trust Kirsten with her heart? (978-1-62639-4-506)

Officer Down by Erin Dutton. Can two women who've made careers out of being there for others in crisis find the strength to need each other? (978-1-62639-4-230)

Reasonable Doubt by Carsen Taite. Just when Sarah and Ellery think they've left dangerous careers behind, a new case sets them—and their hearts—on a collision course. (978-1-62639-4-421)

Tarnished Gold by Ann Aptaker. Cantor Gold must outsmart the Law, outrun New York's dockside gangsters, outplay a shady art dealer, his lover, and a beautiful curator, and stay out of a killer's gun sights. (978-1-62639-4-261)

The Renegade by Amy Dunne. Post-apocalyptic survivors Alex and Evelyn secretly find love while held captive by a deranged cult, but when their relationship is discovered, they must fight for their freedom—or die trying. (978-1-62639-4-278)

Thrall by Barbara Ann Wright. Four women in a warrior society must work together to lift an insidious curse while caught between their own desires, the will of their peoples, and an ancient evil. (978-1-62639-4-377)

White Horse in Winter by Franci McMahon. Love between two women collides with the inner poison of a closeted horse trainer in the green hills of Vermont. (978-1-62639-4-292)

The Chameleon by Andrea Bramhall. Two old friends must work through a web of lies and deceit to find themselves again, but in the search they discover far more than they ever went looking for. (978-1-62639-363-9)

Side Effects by VK Powell. Detective Jordan Bishop and Dr. Neela Sahjani must decide if it's easier to trust someone with your heart or your life as they face threatening protestors, corrupt politicians, and their increasing attraction. (978-1-62639-364-6)

Autumn Spring by Shelley Thrasher. Can Bree and Linda, two women in the autumn of their lives, put their hearts first and find the love they've never dared seize? (978-1-62639-365-3)

Warm November by Kathleen Knowles. What do you do if the one woman you want is the only one you can't have? (978-1-62639-366-0)

In Every Cloud by Tina Michele. When she finally leaves her shattered life behind, is Bree strong enough to salvage the remaining pieces of her heart and find the place where it truly fits? (978-1-62639-413-1)

Rise of the Gorgon by Tanai Walker. When independent Internet journalist Elle Pharell goes to Kuwait to investigate a veteran's mysterious suicide, she hires Cassandra Hunt, an interpreter with a covert agenda. (978-1-62639-367-7)

Crossed by Meredith Doench. Agent Luce Hansen returns home to catch a killer and risks everything to revisit the unsolved murder of her first girlfriend and confront the demons of her youth. (978-1-62639-361-5)

Making a Comeback by Julie Blair. Music and love take center stage when jazz pianist Liz Randall tries to make a comeback with the help of her reclusive, blind neighbor, Jac Winters. (978-1-62639-357-8)

Soul Unique by Gun Brooke. Self-proclaimed cynic Greer Landon falls for Hayden Rowe's paintings and the young woman shortly after, but will Hayden, who lives with Asperger syndrome, trust her and reciprocate her feelings? (978-1-62639-358-5)

The Price of Honor by Radclyffe. Honor and duty are not always black and white—and when self-styled patriots take up arms against the government, the price of honor may be a life. (978-1-62639-359-2)

Mounting Evidence by Karis Walsh. Lieutenant Abigail Hargrove and her mounted police unit need to solve a murder and protect wetland biologist Kira Lovell during the Washington State Fair. (978-1-62639-343-1)

Threads of the Heart by Jeannie Levig. Maggie and Addison Rae-McInnis share a love and a life, but are the threads that bind them together strong enough to withstand Addison's restlessness and the seductive Victoria Fontaine? (978-1-62639-410-0)

Sheltered Love by MJ Williamz. Boone Fairway and Grey Dawson—two women touched by abuse—overcome their pasts to find happiness in each other. (978-1-62639-362-2)

Asher's Out by Elizabeth Wheeler. Asher Price's candid photographs capture the truth, but when his success requires exposing an enemy, Asher discovers his only shot at happiness involves revealing secrets of his own. (978-1-62639-411-7)

The Ground Beneath by Missouri Vaun. An improbable barter deal involving a hope chest and dinners for a month places lovely Jessica

Walker distractingly in the way of Sam Casey's bachelor lifestyle. (978-1-62639-606-7)

Hardwired by C.P. Rowlands. Award-winning teacher Clary Stone, and Leefe Ellis, manager of the homeless shelter for small children, stand together in a part of Clary's hometown that she never knew existed. (978-1-62639-351-6)

No Good Reason by Cari Hunter. A violent kidnapping in a Peak District village pushes Detective Sanne Jensen and lifelong friend Dr. Meg Fielding closer, just as it threatens to tear everything apart. (978-1-62639-352-3)

Romance by the Book by Jo Victor. If Cam didn't keep disrupting her life, maybe Alex could uncover the secret of a century-old love story, and solve the greatest mystery of all—her own heart. (978-1-62639-353-0)

Death's Doorway by Crin Claxton. Helping the dead can be deadly: Tony may be listening to the dead, but she needs to learn to listen to the living. (978-1-62639-354-7)

Searching for Celia by Elizabeth Ridley. As American spy novelist Dayle Salvesen investigates the mysterious disappearance of her ex-lover, Celia, in London, she begins questioning how well she knew Celia—and how well she knows herself. (978-1-62639-356-1)

The 45th Parallel by Lisa Girolami. Burying her mother isn't the worst thing that can happen to Val Montague when she returns to the woodsy but peculiar town of Hemlock, Oregon. (978-1-62639-342-4)

A Royal Romance by Jenny Frame. In a country where class still divides, can love topple the last social taboo and allow Queen Georgina and Beatrice Elliot, a working class girl, their happy ever after? (978-1-62639-360-8)

Bouncing by Jaime Maddox. Basketball Coach Alex Dalton has been bouncing from woman to woman, because no one ever held her interest, until she meets her new assistant, Britain Dodge. (978-1-62639-344-8)

Same Time Next Week by Emily Smith. A chance encounter between Alex Harris and the beautiful Michelle Masters leads to a whirlwind friendship, and causes Alex to question everything she's ever known—including her own marriage. (978-1-62639-345-5)

All Things Rise by Missouri Vaun. Cole rescues a striking pilot who crash-lands near her family's farm, setting in motion a chain of events that will forever alter the course of her life. (978-1-62639-346-2)

Riding Passion by D. Jackson Leigh. Mount up for the ride through a sizzling anthology of chance encounters, buried desires, romantic surprises, and blazing passion. (978-1-62639-349-3)

Love's Bounty by Yolanda Wallace. Lobster boat captain Jake Myers stopped living the day she cheated death, but meeting greenhorn Shy Silva stirs her back to life. (978-1-62639-334-9)

Just Three Words by Melissa Brayden. Sometimes the one you want is the one you least suspect. Accountant Samantha Ennis has her ordered life disrupted when heartbreaker Hunter Blair moves into her trendy Soho loft. (978-1-62639-335-6)

Lay Down the Law by Carsen Taite. Attorney Peyton Davis returns to her Texas roots to take on big oil and the Mexican Mafia, but will her investigation thwart her chance at true love? (978-1-62639-336-3)

Playing in Shadow by Lesley Davis. Survivor's guilt threatens to keep Bryce trapped in her nightmare world unless Scarlet's love can pull her out of the darkness back into the light. (978-1-62639-337-0)

Soul Selecta by Gill McKnight. Soul mates are hell to work with. (978-1-62639-338-7)

The Revelation of Beatrice Darby by Jean Copeland. Adolescence is complicated, but Beatrice Darby is about to discover how impossible it can seem to a lesbian coming of age in conservative 1950s New England. (978-1-62639-339-4)

Twice Lucky by Mardi Alexander. For firefighter Mackenzie James and Dr. Sarah Macarthur, there's suddenly a whole lot more in life to understand, to consider, to risk…someone will need to fight for her life. (978-1-62639-325-7)

Shadow Hunt by L.L. Raand. With young to raise and her Pack under attack, Sylvan, Alpha of the wolf Weres, takes on her greatest challenge when she determines to uncover the faceless enemies known as the Shadow Lords. A Midnight Hunters novel. (978-1-62639-326-4)

Heart of the Game by Rachel Spangler. A baseball writer falls for a single mom, but can she ever love anything as much as she loves the game? (978-1-62639-327-1)

Getting Lost by Michelle Grubb. Twenty-eight days, thirteen European countries, a tour manager fighting attraction, and an accused murderer: Stella and Phoebe's journey of a lifetime begins here. (978-1-62639-328-8)

Prayer of the Handmaiden by Merry Shannon. Celibate priestess Kadrian must defend the kingdom of Ithyria from a dangerous enemy and ultimately choose between her duty to the Goddess and the love of her childhood sweetheart, Erinda. (978-1-62639-329-5)

The Witch of Stalingrad by Justine Saracen. A Soviet "night witch" pilot and American journalist meet on the Eastern Front in WW II and struggle through carnage, conflicting politics, and the deadly Russian winter. (978-1-62639-330-1)

Pedal to the Metal by Jesse J. Thoma. When unreformed thief Dubs Williams is released from prison to help Max Winters bust a car theft ring, Max learns that to catch a thief, get in bed with one. (978-1-62639-239-7)

Dragon Horse War by D. Jackson Leigh. A priestess of peace and a fiery warrior must defeat a vicious uprising that entwines their destinies and ultimately their hearts. (978-1-62639-240-3)

For the Love of Cake by Erin Dutton. When everything is on the line, and one taste can break a heart, will pastry chefs Maya and Shannon take a chance on reality? (978-1-62639-241-0)

Betting on Love by Alyssa Linn Palmer. A quiet country-girl-at-heart and a live-life-to-the-fullest biker take a risk at offering each other their hearts. (978-1-62639-242-7)

The Deadening by Yvonne Heidt. The lines between good and evil, right and wrong, have always been blurry for Shade. When Raven's actions force her to choose, which side will she come out on? (978-1-62639-243-4)